For my mother, who loves Jane Austen as much as I do,
And my daughter, who I hope someday will.

DATE DUE

APR 1 3 2015			

DEMCO 38-296

For Darkness Shows the Stars

Also by Diana Peterfreund:
RAMPANT
ASCENDANT

For Darkness Shows the Stars

DIANA PETERFREUND

BALZER + BRAY
An Imprint of HarperCollins*Publishers*

Balzer + Bray is an imprint of HarperCollins Publishers.

For Darkness Shows the Stars
Copyright © 2012 by Diana Peterfreund
All rights reserved. Printed in the United States of America.
No part of this book may be used or reproduced in any manner whatsoever
without written permission except in the case of brief quotations embodied
in critical articles and reviews. For information address HarperCollins Children's
Books, a division of HarperCollins Publishers, 10 East 53rd Street,
New York, NY 10022.
www.epicreads.com

Library of Congress Cataloging-in-Publication Data
Peterfreund, Diana.
For darkness shows the stars / by Diana Peterfreund.
    p.   cm.
Summary: "Elliot North fights to save her family's land and her own heart in this
post-apocalyptic reimagining of Jane Austen's *Persuasion*"— Provided by publisher.
    ISBN 978-0-06-200614-1
    [1. Love—Fiction.   2. Social classes—Fiction.   3. Family problems—Fiction.
4. Science fiction.]   I. Title.
PZ7.P441545For   2012   2011042126
[Fic]—dc23   CIP
                                                                                 AC

Typography by Carla Weise
12 13 14 15 16 CG/RRDH 10 9 8 7 6 5 4 3 2
❖
First Edition

For Darkness Shows the Stars

Part I
The Unbroken Engine

There could have been no two hearts
so open, no tastes so similar, no feelings
so in unison, no countenances
so beloved. Now they were as strangers;
nay, worse than strangers, for they
could never become acquainted.
It was a perpetual estrangement.
—Jane Austen, *Persuasion*

Twelve Years Ago

Dear Kai,
My name is Elliot, and I am six years old and live in the big
house. Everyone says your smarter than me but I know I am the
smartest. I bet you can't even read this letter.
Your friend,
Elliot North

∿

Dear Elliot,
I can so read and write. I red your letter and your not so smart.
Your just ritch rich. You get tutors in the big house. My da teaches
me to read after we work for your da all day long. So I can read
and I can fix a tractor too. I bet you can't.
Your friend,
Kai

∿

Dear Kai,

You are very nice. Thank you for teaching me how to change the tractor tire today. It was realy fun, but my mother got mad about the mud on my dress. Don't wory I didn't tell her. I hope you like this book. It is one of my favorites.

Your friend (now I feel like I really mean it!),

Elliot

    ⤬

Dear Elliot,

Thank you for the book. Your right, it's really good. My favorite part was the story about Jason and his ~~adentures~~ *adventures on the ship. I would like to be an Argonaut. Or even Jason. Do you know they used to build ships like that right here?*

Your friend,

Kai

P.S. If you want to come back to the barn, I will show you more about the tractor.

    ⤬

Dear Kai,

Yes, I know about the ships. That was my granfather who did that, when he was younger. They call him the Boatwright, but his name is Elliot too, just like me, and my mother says he was the smartest man on the whole island. But he's been sick for a long time.

    I have bad news. My sister Tatiana told on me about the

tractor, and now my father says you can't come to the big house.
So from now on, if you want to rite write me a letter then fold it
up and put it in the knot in the board write next to the barn door.
I'll come by and get it.
Your friend,
Elliot

～

Dear Elliot,
That is nice about your grandfather. I don't know mine. My da
says he was Reduced. He says both his ma and da were Reduced,
and that they died a long time ago.
        I hope you like this letter. If you fold it up exactly like I had
it, it will fly on its own. It's an air glider. I can teach you how to
do it if you ever come see me again. I know your da said I can't
come to the big house, but he didn't say you can't come to the
barn.
Your friend,
Kai

～

Dear Kai,
I am sorry I couldn't come to see you. I hope you like my glider.
It's like yours but I think it flies even farther.
        I am also sorry to hear about your grandparents. Is it
strange to think you come from people who are Reduced?
        I would like to come back to the barn. My father goes to

5

Channel City every month and I think it's best if I come when he's gone. He usually takes Tatiana too, so she can't tell on me.

Your friend,

Elliot

One

ELLIOT NORTH RACED ACROSS the pasture, leaving a scar of green in the silver, dew-encrusted grass. Jef followed, tripping a bit as his feet slid inside his too-big shoes.

"You're sure your ma said the southwest field?" she called back to him.

"Yes, Miss," he huffed.

She picked up her pace, hoping there was still time to save some of the crop. But she could tell it was too late even before she saw the stricken look on her foreman Dee's face. "It's all gone," she said, meeting Elliot on the road. "I'm so sorry."

Elliot crumpled to the ground and rough road gravel scoured her palms. She scraped her fingernails against the dirt. All her work had come to nothing.

Jef came running up behind them and grabbed the edge of his mother's gray skirt. The woman swayed a bit, off-balance due to her rounded belly. At the end of the road, Elliot could just make out the figures of her father and

Tatiana standing at the edge of the field and watching the Reduced at work.

"He moved fifty laborers over first thing this morning," Dee was saying above her.

Of course he had. Ten or twenty would not have gotten the job done before Elliot had heard of it. If only she hadn't locked herself in the barn loft at first light. If only she'd attended the family breakfast. She might have been able to talk him out of this.

Elliot took a deep breath and straightened, unclenching her fists at her sides. She couldn't betray the extent of the damage to her family, but she needed answers.

Tatiana turned as Elliot approached, alerted by the sound of boots on gravel. Elliot's sister was in slippers, of course, and a day dress, and above her head she twirled a shell-pink parasol with deeper pink fringe, despite the fact that there wasn't even a hint of sunshine this morning. In all of Elliot's eighteen years, she'd never seen her older sister in work clothes. The closest Tatiana ever got was a riding habit.

"Hello, Elliot!" she warbled, though her expression remained sly. "Have you come to see the new racetrack?"

Elliot ignored her and faced their father. "What's going on here?"

Only now did her father turn, but his placid countenance betrayed nothing. "Ah, Elliot. Good to see you. You should have a talk with that COR foreman." He gestured vaguely toward Dee. "She was a full ten minutes moving over the laborers this morning. Is she too far along in her pregnancy to be of any use to us?"

Elliot watched as the last of the green-gold sheaves were trampled beneath the feet of the Reduced and their plows. Most of the workers were now raking up the remains of the carnage, and the field was returned to a dull, useless brown. The culmination of two years' work, destroyed.

"Father," Elliot said, fighting to keep her voice from shaking. She couldn't let him know. She had to treat it as if it was any other field. "What have you done? This field was almost ready for harvest."

"Really?" He arched a brow. "The stalks seemed terribly short. Of course, I don't have your way with wheat." He chuckled, as if the very concept were preposterous. "And besides, this field was the best choice for the racetrack. We're going to build the pavilion right over there, near the creek."

Elliot opened her mouth to respond, then shut it. What was the purpose? The crop was destroyed, and no amount of pointing out the folly of the move would induce her father to consider his actions before repeating them. She could tell him the percentage of his harvest he'd lost, and what that would mean in terms of money at market or Reduced that would go hungry this winter unless he imported some of his neighbors' grain. She could tell him how very near *they* were to going hungry given his lack of consideration to the farm. She could even tell him the truth; that the wheat he'd just plowed under was worth more grain than most in fields of this size. It was her special wheat.

It was important wheat.

Of course, that confession would come with even worse consequences.

So as always, she swallowed the scream building in her throat and kept her tone light. Helpful. Dutiful. "Are there any other of the planted fields you think you'll have need of *before* the harvest?"

"And if there are?" Tatiana sniffed.

"I'd like to make sure you don't suffer any more delays," said Elliot, mildly. "I can arrange for the laborers very quickly."

"So can Father, and so can I," said Tatiana. "Or do you think you have some special pull with the Reduced?"

Only because they would recognize her on sight, and not Tatiana. But Elliot would never say that. It would only serve to dig her hole deeper. "I'd like to make it more convenient for—"

"Fine," said Baron North. "This field will be sufficient for my needs. It was the only one I found"—he kicked at a stray stalk—"problematic."

He turned then to his eldest daughter and began pointing with his walking stick to illustrate the boundaries of his proposed racetrack. As he wandered off, Elliot did a quick calculation of how many laborers and how much money he'd no doubt require for that project. They'd have no extra grain to sell this fall, and hardly enough money to buy what they needed to make it through the winter. But her father wouldn't see it that way. He deserved a racetrack more than his Reduced laborers deserved bread.

Elliot slid between the crossbars of the split-rail fence and into the field. Moist, freshly turned earth crumbled beneath the heels of her boots, and here and there in the deadened dust she could see flecks of gold.

"I'm so sorry, Elliot," Dee said, joining her. "They were growing real nice, too."

"There was nothing you could have done." Elliot's voice was flat, but she spoke the truth. Any delay on the foreman's part would only have incited her father's anger—and his need for retribution.

"What did your da— What did Baron North say about me?" Dee's eyes were filled with concern. "I know he—"

"He's not going to send you to the birthing house." He'd probably already forgotten the Post's existence. Dee was nothing more to him than a tool, one he could use to direct the Reduced laborers . . . or punish Elliot.

"Because there'll be no one to care for Jef if—"

"Don't spend another moment worrying about it." Elliot cast a glance at the older woman's stomach. "You have more things on your mind."

"I only have to deal with two mouths to feed this winter," Dee replied. "I can see on your face that you're worried about a hundred."

"Not 'worried.' Disappointed that my project won't be tested for another year, but—" Her brittle smile cracked. Another year! Another year of rations, another year with no harvest festival, with watching the Reduced children grow thin and sickly when the weather got cold, with enduring the pointed stares of the few remaining Posts on the property as Elliot struggled to fairly allocate every sack of grain. This field could have saved them.

"Are things really so bad?" Dee's voice filled the space

Elliot had abandoned to silence.

"And what would you do if they were?" She knew what she'd do in the woman's place. Pack up Jef and depart for whatever points unknown Dee's common-law, Thom, had gone to two years previously, during the bad time when so many of the Posts had left the North estate.

Legally, the Post-Reductionists still held the lowly status of their Reduced forefathers. They were bound to the estate on which they were born. But lately, even that system had been breaking down. There was no way to police the movement of Posts who wished to leave the estates they were born to, and no incentive to try if you were a wealthy Luddite who attracted skilled Posts to your estate at the expense of your neighbors. Year after year, Elliot watched helplessly as the North estate emptied of its skilled labor force. But how could she begrudge them their chance to look for opportunities elsewhere, for possibilities her father would never allow? There were even whole communities where—Elliot had heard—Posts lived free. But up here in the north, the only *free* Posts Elliot had ever seen were beggars desperate for work or food.

She worried that was what had happened to Thom. She worried that was what had happened to . . . everyone who'd left.

"I would find a way to help you," Dee said. "Like you've always helped everyone here."

"Yes. I've been so good at helping them," Elliot said ruefully. She knew Dee must see Thom occasionally. Her pregnancy confirmed it. But the older woman had never told her where he spent most of his time. Dee didn't even trust her enough for that, though Elliot had long ago shared with Dee the shape of her own heartbreak.

Elliot couldn't afford any more Posts leaving the estate. She was already too much alone here.

Dee gestured to the field. "I know you wouldn't have done this if things weren't desperate, Elliot."

That went without saying. She was, after all, a Luddite, and while what she'd done was not strictly against the protocols, it was at the very least in the gray area. She looked out over the savaged field. Perhaps this was a divine warning—maybe her whole experiment was a mistake. After all, if her father suspected the truth, she was lucky that all he'd done was plow the wheat under.

It was always hard to tell with Zachariah North. What some men might do as an act of deliberate cruelty, her father was just as likely to do out of laziness and caprice. His comments had been just ambiguous enough to scare her— another talent at which the baron excelled.

"You'll figure it out," Dee said. "Don't be brought low by a setback. Not when your goal is so . . . high."

The Post's hesitation said it all. Elliot's goal was high indeed. It belonged to a realm that the Luddites had long ago abandoned. What she sought was nothing short of a miracle.

Eleven Years Ago

Dear Elliot,

Thank you for coming over yesterday, and for bringing the new books. I hope you liked lerning about the thresher. It was a good idea to come in those old ~~close~~ clothes, even though I almost didn't recognize you!

I talked to my da about the words we were fighting over. He says that your people call people like us CORs because it means Children of the Reduction. There is another word, but my da says we would be in trouble for using it in front of you. It's called Post-Reductionist. My da and his friends call themselfs Posts. Except you are my only friend. There are no other ~~Posts~~ CORs on the North estate who are my age—or even anywhere near seven years old, and none of the Reduced children can read.

I hope I don't get in trouble for telling you that word. Da says the Luddites don't like it because it means the Reduction is behind us.

Your friend,

Kai

Dear Kai,

Your new glider is the best ever! It even does loops!

    If your da's friends call him a Post, then I will call you that too. Because I want to be your friend. I have herd the word before, from the CORs that work in the big house, but they would never tell me what it ment. Now I know why. But it makes more sense to me than calling you a COR. After all, you are not a child of someone Reduced. Don't worry, I won't use it in front of my family.

    I was worried maybe you were mad at me for asking all those questions about the Reduced. It is just that you are the only ~~COR~~ Post who will talk to me. Did you know that you and I were born on the same day? That's how I knew who you were, because the CORs in the big house were always talking about us both. There is also a Reduced girl born on our birthday. Do you know who she is?

Your friend,

Elliot

Two

Ro LIVED ALONE IN a cottage at the far side of the Reduced block. She'd once shared it with two other Reduced girls, but they'd borne children and removed to barracks nearer the nursery. Ro appreciated the extra space, and filled the cottage with her precious pots. Elliot had given her even more on their eighteenth birthday a few months back. Her presents had grown a bit more indulgent in these past four years, since it was just the two of them celebrating now.

Ro had been on dairy duty that morning, and hadn't been one of the laborers to help destroy the wheat crop, so Elliot had come to Ro's for comfort. Tatiana and her father might prefer the darkness of the star-cavern sanctuary, but there were only two places on the North estate that Elliot considered a refuge, and the barn loft was too crowded with notes about her wheat to be a comfort today. Yet here, for a few precious minutes, she could be silent and fill her hands with soil and pretend that there were no worries that awaited her beyond the confines of this sun-drenched hut.

It was pointless to dwell, anyway. What good would it do?

Ro was already digging among her flowers when Elliot arrived. She dripped mud across the unfinished planks of the floor as she crossed the room to greet Elliot.

"Good day, Ro."

The girl's green eyes—so unusual, even among the Reduced—searched Elliot's face, and she frowned.

"Yes, I'm sad," Elliot admitted. She'd never successfully lied to Ro. Reduced her friend may be, but not insensitive. Elliot had been taught as a child that the Reduced could sense your emotions, like dogs. Over the years, she'd begun to wonder if their general lack of speech made it all the more important for them to read faces.

To some Luddites, the Reduced were children, fallen and helpless, but still human. To others, they were beasts of burden, mostly mute and incapable of rational thought. Elliot's mother had taught her that they were her duty, as they were the duty of all Luddites. Cut off as the population of these two islands had been since the Wars of the Lost, they might be the only people left on the planet. The Luddites, who had kept themselves pure of the taint of Reduction, therefore had the responsibility to be the caretakers not only of all of human history and culture but of humanity itself.

It had been generations since any Luddites had tried to rehabilitate the Reduced. Mere survival had taken precedence. But Ro was more than Elliot's duty. She'd become Elliot's friend, and sometimes Elliot even dared wonder what Ro could be—what any Reduced could be—if the Luddites had the resources to try.

Ro brightened and took Elliot's brown hand in her own reddened, muddy one. She pulled Elliot over to the pots, grinning, and Elliot allowed herself to be pulled. She knew what was coming. Ro's pots had been yielding the same profusion of blossoms for the last four years, but Ro still greeted every one with squeals of delighted surprise.

Ro led her to one particular group of pots set apart from all the others and Elliot's eyes widened in shock. These flowers were different from any she'd seen before—not red or yellow or purple or white, but a pale violet with streaks of scarlet running in veins along each petal from the depths of a deeply crimson heart.

"They're beautiful, Ro!" she blurted, while inwardly, she tried to work out the genetics. A simple cross-pollination perhaps, the purple flowers set too close to the red ones . . .

Ro bounced and clapped her hands. She pointed at the red and purple flowers planted nearby and then at Elliot herself. Elliot narrowed her eyes, remembering evenings Ro had spent by her side in the barn loft.

No, it was impossible. She was Reduced.

A few words, a few signs, and simple, repetitive tasks were the most the Reduced could handle. They were capable of being trained, but not for any skilled labor. And they required close observation. The young, the sick, the pregnant, and the elderly had an odd propensity for self-violence, which is why the Luddites were forced to confine them. The birthing house that Dee had feared was an unfortunate necessity for Reduced women, but torture for a Post like Dee.

But Ro was nodding eagerly, miming picking flowers then pressing her palms together. "Ro wheat," she said, in the awkward monosyllabic speech that was all the Reduced could manage.

Ro wheat. Ro's special wheat. It was impossible. A Reduced could never comprehend what Elliot had been working on in secret, could never re-create the grafts herself. Ro was Reduced. It was impossible.

But no repetition could truly banish Elliot's suspicion. "Ro," she said, "you mustn't show these flowers to anyone, do you hear?"

Ro frowned, her pretty, freckled face wrinkled with confusion.

"I love them, I do!" Elliot took the girl's hands in hers. "They are beautiful flowers and I'm proud of you. But it must be a secret, right?" She pressed a finger to her lips. "Shh."

"Shh," Ro agreed, muddying her mouth with her forefinger. Elliot wished she could be sure the girl was doing more than just parroting her. But this was the way it was, the way it had always been, ever since the Reduction. Each generation of Luddites would care for the Reduced and their offspring. They'd tend the land, obey the protocols, and keep humanity alive.

Then came the CORs.

Some reckoned there were four generations of them now, though others claimed only two. There were more every year, though, as if the human spirit itself had risen from the ashes of the Reduction. CORs—or Posts, as now almost everyone but holdouts like Elliot's father had taken to calling them—came from Reduced ancestry, but they were born and developed completely normally. Posts were as intelligent and capable as any Luddite. They'd been rare in the time of Elliot's grandfather, but now people said one in twenty babies born to a Reduced was a Post, and a Post parent never produced a Reduced child.

Posts quite naturally stepped into positions of power on the Luddite estates. By the time Elliot was born, it was a given that the Luddite farms, instead of being overseen by the actual Luddites as they had been for generations, would instead be manned by a staff of Post foremen, mechanics, chefs, and tailors. The Luddites themselves presided over all in a life of relative leisure.

When Elliot was younger, she'd asked her tutor why, if the CORs were as capable as the Luddites, did they still have the legal status of the Reduced? The conversation hadn't gone well. No one could deny the existence of the CORs, but it was still taboo to deviate from the Luddite way. No one had even studied the origin of the Posts, nor tested their genetics. It was not for Luddites to question the will of God or the nature of man. Such thoughts had led to the Reduction, and by their piety alone had Elliot's people been saved.

What, Elliot wondered, would her teacher think of her Luddite piety now? She knew her wheat was a sin, but what choice did she have? The North estate could not go hungry.

These flowers, though—they were something else. There was no reconciling it. She knew what everyone else would see. A creation of frivolous beauty, made by a Reduced who'd aped Elliot's crimes. It was insupportable. Unforgivable.

It was also pure Ro. She loved pretty things, which was why she grew flowers, and she loved Elliot, which was why she tried to do everything just like her. And she was Reduced, which meant she bore the punishment for the hubris of her ancestors. Ancestors who had held themselves higher than God, and had been brought lower than man.

If Elliot wasn't careful, Ro would suffer punishment for a sin of Elliot's making, too.

Ro began to shuffle the pots, burying the hybrid blossoms among the others. "Shh," she said. "Shhh, shhh." But she couldn't be trusted to keep the secret. Not like Dee or any of the other Posts.

Elliot plucked a single bloom and rubbed the petals between her fingers. They were so small and perfect, so alive and vibrant. How could such a thing, such a tiny, beautiful thing, be a sin against God? Surely a sinful flower would wither and die, but look how these prospered under the care of the most humble of creatures. Whatever else this meant, the existence of these flowers, on this day, told Elliot one thing: Let her father trample what wheat he may—Elliot would not give up.

ON SUMMER AFTERNOONS, BARON North and Tatiana made a big show of descending into the star-cavern sanctuary for Luddite services. Their piety waned in the winter months, however, when the ancient refuge was less a cool retreat from the sun and more the frigid, punishing darkness that their ancestors had endured only because the wars had driven them underground.

Elliot didn't begrudge them their activities, though. She used the time to have uninterrupted access to her father's study, so she could deal with his correspondence. Once, the job had been her mother's, and so by rights it should now be Tatiana's, but Elliot's sister showed the same interest and head for numbers as their father—which was to say, very little at all. Left to them, the desk would collapse beneath the weight of unanswered requests and unpaid bills—mostly the latter variety of late. Then again, people stopped asking for favors once they knew you owed money all over. Even if your name was North.

When her mother was alive, there'd been economy in their house. Economy and industry both, to balance out her father's worst tendencies. His older brother had been raised to manage the farm, not Zachariah North. Elliot's uncle had died before Elliot's parents were even married, leaving behind an infant son too young to take over and Zachariah, who hadn't been fit to lead but became the baron nonetheless. The North estate had never been the same. Elliot's father possessed the Luddite sense of superiority, but without its corresponding call to action. And ever since his wife died, he deeply resented anyone who made him remember it—by, say, suggesting that one's debts ought to be repaid.

Most days, that was Elliot. She had to be very careful with the bills now, or risk lectures from her father on the honor due to Baron North. They were not even ordinary

Luddites, the Norths, but one of the last great baronic families who had preserved the world in the wake of the Reduction. Their ancestors had led the remnants of humanity out of the caverns. They had held their land for generations.

Hard to remember all this family honor when Elliot spent every day staring into the eye of a cyclone of debts called due.

Her wheat could have saved them, kept the estate from needing to import food this winter. Even allowed them a surplus for the first time in Elliot's memory. But it was not to be this year. Her father would rather build a racetrack for horses he could barely afford.

One of the letters caught her eye. An unfamiliar correspondent, and a Post by the look of the address. Elliot opened it.

Most Admirable Baron Zachariah North,

Forgive me the trespass of writing this letter. I have never had the honor of being introduced to such a lofty person as you. Most likely, you do not know me, nor of my reputation amongst your illustrious fellows. I am an explorer in the service of my Luddite lords, and in the past ten years my activities have brought great distinction and wealth to my patrons, who include the honorable families of Right, Grace, Record, and Baroness Channel. For my references, you may apply to any of these families.

I have learned that you are currently in control of the shipyard belonging to Chancellor Elliot Boatwright. If the facility is not in use, I would be interested in renting it from you, as well as some residential properties and the use of some of your labor force while my shipwrights work. I seek to build a new ship, one much bigger than any of my current facilities can handle. I am told that Boatwright shipyard is the best in the islands, and I am sure we can come to an agreement that is profitable and advantageous to us both.

I remain your ever-humble servant,
Nicodemus Innovation, Admiral of the Cloud Fleet

Elliot had heard of the renowned Cloud Fleet. There weren't a lot of seaworthy vessels on the island—at least, not since her grandfather's shipyard had shut down before her birth. And since the wars had rendered magnetic compasses useless, very few braved the trip out of sight range of their shores. Was the Cloud Fleet, staffed entirely by free Posts, attempting an overseas journey? Elliot's heart raced at the very thought. It had been ages since she'd allowed herself to dream of that. Not since Kai had gone away.

Of course, she did her best not to think of him, either.

As far as anyone knew, there was nothing left of the world but these two islands, these quarter of a million square kilometers, these people and these mountains and these animals and this society. Admiral Innovation might change all that. His Fleet had first captured the population's notice when one of his exploratory trips to nearby islands had brought back a breed of horse not seen for generations. Sturdier, taller, and faster, the Innovation horse had quickly become the preferred means of transport on the trade routes. Another one of his expeditions had resulted in the rediscovery of a wild game hen that produced twice as many eggs as the standard estate chickens. Even Baron North had filled his henhouses with them. Most recently, Elliot had read of a Cloud Fleet expedition, one run by a Captain Wentforth, in which he'd found another island and a cargo hold full of salvaged, solar-powered vehicles in near-pristine condition.

This news, of course, had been greeted with mixed reactions from the Luddite community, who frowned upon any technology they hadn't already been using for centuries. But as many disapproved, there were other Luddites, not quite as fastidious, who had declared the machines nothing more than an innocuous, long-forgotten form of transport, and turned the sun-carts into a hot commodity. The Norths, of course, had not indulged. They couldn't afford to.

And now this Admiral Innovation wanted to build himself a new ship—and using the Boatwright facilities, too! This would be a tricky proposition to get by her father, but if she could manage it, it would certainly solve their financial woes. Innovation must be very wealthy to be able to rent the whole shipyard. Elliot wondered if the money would be enough to sway her father, or if he would view such matters as too tawdry for his taste.

Maybe she could find another incentive, though. Admiral Innovation had more than just money to offer, and her father did have that splendid new racetrack.

NINE YEARS AGO

Dear Kai,

I'm sorry I can't come see you today. In school last week, we had to write a paper about the Reduction. I don't know what I wrote that was so bad, but the tutor told me she had to give it to my parents, and now we're all four of us having a "conference." My mother said it's probably best if I stay away from the barn for a little while. It was hard enough getting this letter to you.

I'm really scared. Last year, when my cousin Benedict got sent home from boarding school, my father beat him. My father yells at me a lot, but he's never hit me before. I can't figure out what I put in the essay that was so wrong. Can you?
Your friend,
Elliot

WHY THE REDUCTION HAPPENED

By Elliot North

Before the Reduction, there were two kinds of people: people who trusted in God to create mankind in His own image, and people who thought they could do better than God. The first kind of people were my ancestors, the Luddites. The second kind of people, the Lost, did lots of experiments to make themselves better than God. They tried to create new kinds of plants and animals, the way God did. They gave themselves fake arms and legs and eyes that worked better than the ones God gave us, and they did experiments on unborn babies, too, so that they could make them different and supposedly better than their parents.

The Luddites were the only people who knew how evil this was. They refused to give themselves the fake body parts, or even the fake brains that were supposed to make them smarter than God. First they refused to eat genetically enhanced foods, and then they refused the ERV procedure to enhance their babies. They tried to warn the Lost, who believed Gavin and Carlotta and all had ERV, but the Lost didn't believe them.

Finally, God got angry at the Lost, and cursed them and all their children. From that point on, they would no longer be born in His own image. They were Reduced. After that, there were also two kinds of people: the Luddites and the Reduced.

The Luddites took pity on the Reduced, and helped them survive.

Except now there's a third kind of people, called the

Children of the Reduction, who are born just like Luddites,
which must mean that God has forgiven the Reduced. There
are many of those on the North estate.

∾

Dear Elliot,

I hope you are okay. I read your essay and it sounds like what
we learn too. I don't think there's anything wrong with it. I don't
know why you would be in trouble. The only thing I never heard
about before was the part where you said that the Posts were a
sign of forgiveness. They never say that to us at services. Do you
think that's true?

Your friend,

Kai

∾

Dear Kai,

I am grounded. I had to bribe Benedict with my dessert to send
you this letter. I hope it gets to you and he doesn't read it. My
mother says he's a very naughty boy and I shouldn't spend too
much time with him.

It was the part about the forgiveness that made my
teacher so worried. She and my parents explained to me that
we don't have the right to decide when God has forgiven you
and your ancestors, which I guess makes sense. But at the
same time, doesn't it seem like He must have? For so many
years, the Reduced only had Reduced children. But now there
are people like you and your father. If I were God, and I wanted

to show that I had forgiven the Lost and the Reduced, that's what I would do.

But when I told my father that, he got very angry and slapped my face. It's the first time he's ever hit me, and I hope it's the last. He said I also don't have the right to pretend I know what God would do and why. Although, if that's the case, then how is it that we know that the Reduction was a punishment from God? It's so confusing.

Since I'm grounded, I can't pick up letters in the knothole. If you write me back, try to get the letter to the housemaid Mags. She likes me ever since I gave her baby one of my old dolls. I trust her way more than Benedict.

Your friend,

Elliot

༄

Dear Elliot,

I hope your grounding ends soon. I miss you.

You're right, it's very confusing. I asked my da what he thought and he just stared at me for a really long time without saying anything, then told me to go clean out the stalls. I hate cleaning out the stalls. I'd far rather work on the machines than with the farm animals.

But what you wrote made a lot of sense to me. After all, God never tells us what he's thinking. At least, he never tells the Reduced or the Posts. I think that's supposed to be part of our punishment, right?

It's really unfair, I think, being punished for something

I didn't do. If I was going to have to be punished, I'd at least like to have the fun of being fast and never tired and having superhuman eyes and super smart brains and everything first.

  DON'T TELL ANYONE I WROTE THAT.

Your friend,

Kai

Dear Kai,

Your secret's safe with me. But I'm glad you sent this one through Mags and not through Benedict. Mother tells me I'll be done with my grounding next week. Please find something fun for us to do. I'm going crazy stuck here in the house.

Your friend,

Elliot

Three

ELLIOT BOATWRIGHT'S HOUSE WAS located on the border between the Boatwright lands on the tip of the island and the North estate. It was covered in flowers during the spring, but now dying russet vines crackled in the breeze as they crawled up the eaves and arched over the door. She'd hoped to make some improvements to the place before the Fleet's arrival, but time had been in short supply recently. Harvest was coming on, and even with the influx of money from the Fleet's rental of the Boatwright estate, it was vital that she produce as much grain as possible.

Perhaps the Innovations and their staff would consider these unruly vines pleasingly rustic after their years spent in the Post enclave down in Channel City. This was the home where Elliot's mother, Victoria, had grown up, and she always liked to remember the way her mother had cared for the garden, pruning the hedges and trimming the flowers twining over the railings of the porch.

The Boatwright had three nurses to tend to his needs.

They were all Reduced. A few years ago he'd had a Post housekeeper as well, but now they didn't have enough Posts to spare for the care of Elliot's grandfather. Once there had been fifty, but ever since the bad time, there were scarcely ten adult Posts to share between the two estates. Still, she knew her grandfather preferred this state of affairs to moving in with her father and Tatiana. Elliot liked to think that he wouldn't have minded so much if it was just her.

The Boatwright himself was seated on the porch now, and his good eye narrowed as she came up the path to greet him. "Good morning, Grandfather," she said. "This is the day, you know."

He grunted at her and seemed to sink down into his chair. Elliot sighed. So it was to be an obstinate morning.

"We talked about this, remember?"

The good side of his mouth frowned, and he did his best to look confused, but Elliot was not taken in. The strokes had destroyed his body and his speech, but not his memory.

"You know we've rented the house to those shipbuilders."

He stamped his good foot against the floorboards of the porch.

"Grandfather, you can't stay here. They need the room." And we need the money. She almost added it aloud.

But Elliot Boatwright was no fool. He made the sign the Reduced used for "father" and then the one for "mistake." She cringed. Luddites did not sign to each other—it was a mark of the Reduced. For her grandfather to use signs in reference to Baron North was as good as an epithet in the mouth of a man who could speak.

"My father did not rent out your house," Elliot said, even if he had made it necessary. "I did. If you want to be mad, be mad at me."

The good side of her grandfather's face smiled and he shook his head. No, he'd never be mad at her. She did what she ought, just as her mother had. Which was all well and good, but it still meant that her ailing, aged grandfather was losing the only home he'd ever known.

She brushed past him into the house, where, sure enough, she found his trunks waiting by the door, just as she had instructed the Reduced nursemaids to do several days before. The house had been cleaned and aired, and vases of fall flowers stood everywhere, ready to welcome the Cloud Fleet. Elliot took a quick tour of the house, checking to see that all the linens were laid out on the beds brought down from storage, that the larder was stocked with food quite as good as the kind they had at the big house. Her father had been insistent that the visitors would not think the North estate lacking in opulence, even as he loudly complained about sharing his supplies "with CORs." He'd even had ice delivered. Ice, this late in the fall, while Elliot was worried about how to keep the laborers in bread and coal this winter. She shook her head.

Her father had kept her tutors until she was sixteen, just as he had with Tatiana before her. They'd received the standard Luddite curriculum: history, music, literature, religion, and art, but as to what she'd need to know to keep the estate on its feet—that was trial and error. That was luck. That was whatever she could scrape together on the side.

Perhaps it would have been different had her father been raised to take over the estate, but it was her uncle who was supposed to be Baron North. Elliot's father had never liked anything but horses and the comfortable trappings of the Luddite lifestyle. The North estate had been paying for his disinterest ever since her uncle's death. Elliot's mother had done what she could when she was alive—raised a Boatwright, she had her father's work ethic—but she'd died four years earlier.

At the time, Tatiana had mourned the fact that her mother's death prevented them from traveling to Channel City for her debut, but Elliot feared worse than a deferred holiday. Her mother's death left two estates in peril: the one belonging to Elliot's invalid grandfather and the one her father had never bothered to maintain.

Elliot had been fourteen. She hadn't even been finished with school, but she had learned enough to know that only one thing mattered: the hundreds of people—Luddite, COR, and Reduced—who depended on the estates to survive.

Down on the porch, the Reduced were fighting to get the Boatwright loaded into the litter that was to take him to his new home, and he swatted at them with his cane. Elliot stood by the window and shook her head. She hated removing him, but this was the only house on the estate suitable for someone of the admiral's station. They could hardly put the Cloud Fleet in a Reduced cottage, and Elliot shuddered to think of the daily indignities they would be forced to suffer as guests of Baron North. Elliot's father would not care that these were free Posts, nor that they were paying him good money to rent his land and labor. Station was station to Zachariah North. He'd refused even to stay and greet the Fleet, but had instead left those duties to Tatiana and Elliot, while he rode out the "indignity" of being paid and saving his workers from starvation with a prolonged visit at the estate of one of his Luddite friends.

So much the better. Though Admiral Innovation's letter had been all that her father deemed proper, Elliot hoped to see the Fleet settled here before Baron North returned and was forced to deal with the reality of Posts over whom he did not have complete control.

Elliot placed her hand on the yellow plaster walls. This house needed people again. The admiral was bringing his wife and a large staff: shipwrights and metalworkers and captains of the Cloud Fleet. She hoped they would enjoy this house; enjoy the vines and the bright, sunny rooms; the shiny, worn wood floors and the creaking staircase. Elliot wondered what they were like, these free Posts who'd found success beyond the confines of the indentured estates.

For four years she'd waited for Kai to come back, too, but he never had. Nor had he ever sent word of his where-abouts. In her dreams, she liked to imagine he'd ended up like one of the admiral's men, content and employed. With his mechanical talent, he'd have made an excellent skilled laborer. But she'd heard too many stories of the things that happened to Post runaways. She'd heard of the dangers in

Post enclaves. The brothels and the workhouses, the organ trade and the people who sold their bodies for illegal experimentation.

Elliot let her hand drop and curl inward. She brushed her left fingers over the back of her right hand, touching each knuckle, tracing the path of each vein. She couldn't bear to think of Kai like that. She would stick to her fantasy of him being a safely employed mechanic somewhere—though that was a hope she kept to herself. She hadn't even shared it with Dee. After all, Thom was out there, too, and he was Dee's common-law and the father of the woman's babies. Kai was only a friend. Nothing more.

One of the Reduced nursemaids appeared at the door. The Boatwright was ready to go. Elliot nodded. Somehow she'd make it work. She always did—she managed the farm, she managed her family, and she managed her own heartbreak.

But perhaps . . . perhaps some of the Posts coming here were runaways who'd found a place of their own. Perhaps one of them had heard something of Kai and could tell her at last where he'd gone. Perhaps he was somewhere in the world, safe and happy, somewhere where a girl like her was straightening a picture frame or smoothing a bedcover in hopes of making the Post that slept there feel more at home.

Four

ELLIOT WALKED BESIDE THE litter that carried her grandfather back to the great house. Behind them, two Reduced pulled a cart holding all of the Boatwright's personal belongings. He'd attempted to argue with anyone who'd listen during the whole four-kay trip, but the Reduced were trained merely to nod, and Elliot pretended she couldn't understand his mumbled complaints. It signified nothing, at any rate; her grandfather must be moved from his house, and the Posts must be installed there, for the good of both estates. He might be ornery, but she knew he understood that.

As they reached the great house, Elliot quickened her pace. There were two horses on the lawn, giant, chestnut-colored things with glossy black manes and powerfully muscled legs. So these were the Innovation horses Elliot had negotiated for on top of the rent money in order to sweeten the deal for her father. Each horse was tethered to a strange, three-wheeled contraption the likes of which Elliot had never seen except in drawings. They must be the famous sun-carts, for each sported a pane of shiny, golden mirrors on the back. The Post housekeeper, Mags, was waiting on the porch, wringing her hands as the horses trampled the grass.

"Miss, they came early. They're already in the parlor."

"Thank you, Mags," said Elliot, bounding up the steps two at a time. "Take care of Mr. Boatwright, please. I have to go in to my guests—"

"Miss Elliot," said Mags, laying a hand on her arm as she passed. "Perhaps you'd like to go change first? Put on a nice dress?"

Elliot stopped and looked at the Post in confusion. Were these Cloud Fleet people so very fine? Were they out exploring the wilderness in lace?

"It's just that—" Mags looked pained. "In the parlor—"

But time had run out, for a man appeared in the doorway and filled the air with his booming voice. "Did you say Elliot? Is this Miss Elliot North?" He stepped into the light and Elliot resisted the urge to step back. Every bit as giant as his horses, the admiral was red all over, from his thinning, combed-over ginger hair to his ruddy complexion to his deep scarlet coat. Elliot had never seen such a color on a piece of fabric. It looked like the flowers in Ro's garden.

"I have been looking forward to meeting you, my dear girl. Nicodemus Innovation, at your service." He inclined his head in a move that was almost, but not quite, a bow.

"Admiral Innovation," she said, collecting herself. It wouldn't do for a North Luddite to be rendered speechless by a Post's jacket, no matter how red it was. "I'm sorry I wasn't here to greet you. I've been making the final preparations to your lodgings—"

He waved his hand. "Don't worry a bit. The sun-carts make great time when the weather's as clear as today's. Even my horses could hardly keep up. We haven't seen a flicker of your father yet, but your sister Tatiana's been, ah, entertaining us while we waited for you."

Elliot could only imagine. Well water perhaps, from tin cups? She wouldn't put it past her sister.

"Come in and meet the Fleet," he said, bustling her into her own house.

"The whole Cloud Fleet is in my parlor?" Elliot asked with a smile. "Very impressive, sir." In the hall, she could smell freshly baked cream biscuits and peach and chamomile tea. If this was Tatiana's doing, it was also very impressive. Perhaps she owed her sister an apology.

"Nah, not all of them," said the admiral. "Just the ones I like best, you know." He laughed and pushed open the door. "My wife, here—Felicia." The woman was as tiny as her husband was giant, with black and silver hair that curled around her freckled face. She nodded to Elliot and opened her mouth as if to speak, but the admiral was already steering her away. "And over there you've got the Phoenixes—captains both."

He gestured vaguely to two blond young people who were sitting near Tatiana with cups of tea in their hands. They looked over at her, and Elliot found her steps faltering under the intensity of the girl's gaze. The female Phoenix—Andromeda, the admiral was telling her—looked to be about Tatiana's age and had the most unusual eyes she'd ever seen, a light, glistening blue, like sunlight on seawater, and so clear it was as if Elliot could make out each speck in her iris despite the shade in the room. The male Phoenix—Donovan, according to the admiral—had eyes that matched, but he was younger, perhaps only in his mid-teens. Elliot was surprised that the famed "captains" of the Fleet could be so young. She was expecting grown-ups, not teenagers. The Phoenixes must be siblings, with their corresponding eyes and last name? Elliot wondered if they were born with the name, or if they'd grown up on an estate and adopted it later, as the Innovations had done. It had become fashionable these last few years for free Posts to change their names when they left their estates—to adopt new first names in the long, ornate style of Luddites and surnames of their own creation.

"And then—but we're missing someone." The admiral's heavy brows knit together. "I thought I brought three of you."

"You did," said Andromeda Phoenix. "Wentforth is out seeing to the horses."

"The horses?" Now the admiral appeared even more confused. "Wentforth?"

Andromeda gave Elliot a small, inscrutable smile. "Yes, very curious."

"Donovan," said the admiral with a sigh, "go drag him from his sudden fascination for animal husbandry and bring him in to meet Miss Elliot. I'm sure the horses will be very well looked after in the baron's stables without Wentforth's help." He turned to Elliot as Donovan snapped to do his admiral's bidding. "No introduction would be complete without my star pilot."

Andromeda helped herself to more tea and sat back in her chair, that same small smile playing about her lips. She was dressed in a most peculiar fashion, as were all the Posts. Fabrics like Elliot had never seen, soft and almost fuzzy, shimmered in the light from the window in dark, rich colors that stood out in the room like Ro's flowers hidden in a bed of fading autumn leaves. Andromeda and her brother were dressed like the admiral, in trousers, tall boots, and long, full jackets in purple and teal. Though Felicia Innovation looked slightly more traditional in a deep green dress, it featured none of the lace or embroidery on Tatiana's pink creation. Its only decoration was a pair of golden shoulder epaulets accented with braided tassels. The coats of the other Posts were similarly ornamented.

Elliot tugged the edge of her dirt-brown sweater down over the waist of her slate-gray trousers. Perhaps she should have taken the housekeeper's advice and changed, even if it was only into a dress. Luddites tended to wear only the faded, drab colors that could be derived from natural dyes. It had been their tradition long before the Reduction, and of course it had been necessary in the days of scarcity. Elliot supposed these new colors were common in the free Post enclaves.

Tatiana turned to Felicia. "Are you much involved in the operations of your common-law's business?" she asked mildly.

Felicia paused with her teacup halfway to her lips. "Nicodemus is my husband, Miss North. We are free Posts and do not subscribe to the restrictions the Luddites place on their servants." But she said this all without a hint of malice or defensiveness, and it took a moment for Tatiana to collect herself enough to look offended.

And Felicia did not allow the feeling to take root. "I am not involved in the operation of the Cloud Fleet, no," she said. "I am not much of an explorer of the beyond, I'm afraid. Not when there are still so many mysteries to solve here at home."

"Mysteries?" Tatiana asked with a raise of her eyebrows. Elliot marveled at the woman's behavior. Were all free Posts so open with heretical talk like this? Luddites held that nature's mysteries were meant to remain unsolved. Attempts to improve upon nature had led to the Reduction.

"Mrs. Innovation is a physician," Andromeda broke in. "She trained as a healer on the estate where she grew up and has been studying in the field for decades."

"My wife is brilliant," said the admiral. "She's saved dozens of lives."

"Really," said Tatiana. "Perhaps during your stay you can visit our COR healers and teach them a thing or two. We've been at very loose ends since our doctor passed away." Which he'd done before Elliot's birth, Elliot thought wryly.

"And maybe you would be so kind as to look in on my grandfather," Elliot said.

"The Boatwright?" asked the admiral, sitting up in his chair. "I was wondering, given the . . ."

Given the fact that Baron North controlled the shipyard.

"What is the nature of his infirmity?" Felicia asked quickly.

"A series of strokes, starting from when I was a very young girl," Elliot replied. "No one has been able to do much for him."

Felicia nodded gravely, and an uneasy silence hovered in the room. Once, much had been done for stroke victims, but the Reduction had changed all that. The mind of man was not meant to be rebuilt, even if broken.

"Oh, that would be lovely if you could find a way to help the old man," said Tatiana. "Provided you remain within the protocols, of course."

"Of course," said Felicia, exchanging a small glance with Andromeda, who merely sipped her tea.

Brazen, these Posts, with their flippant little glances. Elliot had never seen anything like it, even in the North Posts' most unguarded moments. The protocols had defined the Luddite way of life since the Reduction. It was simple: genetic enhancements had destroyed humanity. Advanced technology in the ensuing wars had nearly destroyed the world. The Luddites restricted both, and rebuilt. Elliot had long wondered if the Luddites' strict rules had managed to atone for humanity's sins all these years later. Was the rise of the Posts the result of their adherence to the protocols?

And if so, what had she done by experimenting with the wheat?

Tatiana's words had been a test, and Felicia's response neither as emphatic nor as automatic as Tatiana was used to seeing. It must come of the fact that these people owed nothing to the Luddite lords and therefore had nothing to fear from them, either. This behavior from one of their own servants would have sent Tatiana through the roof several minutes ago. But no, her sister seemed preoccupied with the weave of the tassels on Felicia's shoulder epaulets.

"Ah, here he is," said the admiral, bounding from his chair to the window. Two figures in free Post dress were coming up the steps of the porch. "Miss Elliot, I'm excited to introduce you to the pilot of the ship we'll be building here, to the captain of the *Argos*—"

But Elliot saw him clearly through the window. She needed no introduction.

No midnight blue jacket, no new, longer haircut, no strange, noble bearing—nothing would serve to disguise him to her eyes. She had only a moment to compose herself and then he walked into the room. Into her house, for the first time in years.

"Miss Elliot," said the admiral, as she staggered to her feet. Out shot her hand, reluctantly, mechanically, obeying a courtesy so ingrained as to be unconscious. He was taller now. Taller than her. And though he turned in her direction, his hand did not rise to meet hers, and his eyes remained fixed on the mantel beyond her head. "May I present Captain Malakai Wentforth."

"Hello." His voice was the same. It rang through Elliot's body like a thunderclap announcing a storm.

"Hello," said Elliot, for parroting him was all she could trust herself to say, there in her old, worn clothes, with her braids all mussed; there, in the same room with the same furniture and the same fire and her hand floating in the air between them, curling out into space like a misguided vine, yearning desperately for him to reach across the distance and touch her again.

Hello, Kai.

Four Years Ago

Dear Kai,

The sun is probably streaming in through the big barn windows now, which means you're awake. And if you're awake, it means you're wondering where I went.

I haven't run away from you, I promise. But I knew that today of all days, they'd need me in the house. Tatiana may be the head of our household now, but she's not the one the staff will look to in my mother's absence. And there is so much to do to prepare for the funeral. Also, I have to go tell my grandfather what has happened to his daughter. I don't want him to hear of her death from anyone but me.

Thank you for last night. I wish I could say I don't know why you are the one I ran to—you, Kai, not Tatiana or my father or even my grandfather. But I know why. And I have a confession to make.

After you let me cry, after you let me sob and shout and choke on all that pain—after you did all that, and didn't say a word—I didn't fall asleep like you thought. Not right away. I lay there, wadded up into a ball, and you curved your body behind mine. You were barely touching me—your thigh against the edge of my hip, your arm draped lightly across my waist, your fingers entwined with mine. How many times have our hands touched, when we were passing each other tools or helping each other in and out of machines? Hundreds of times. Thousands. But last night, it felt different. You cradled my hand in yours, palms up, our fingers curled in like a pair of fallen leaves. Fallen, maybe, but not dead. My hand never felt so alive. Every place you touched me sparked with energy. I couldn't sleep. Not like that.

And so I bent my head, just the slightest bit, until my mouth reached our hands. I smelled the oil you never quite get off your fingers. I breathed in the scent of your skin. And then, as if that was all I was doing, just breathing, I let my bottom lip brush against your knuckle.

Time stopped. I was sure you'd see through my ruse and pull away. I was sure you'd know that I was not asleep, that I was not just breathing. But you didn't move, so I did it again. And again. And on the third time, I let my top lip join my bottom.

I kissed your hand, Kai. I didn't do it to thank you for letting me cry. For letting me sleep in your arms. I thought you should know.
Yours,
Elliot

Dear Elliot,
I know. When will I see you again?
Yours,
Kai

Five

IT WAS OVER IN minutes.

Kai told the admiral about a problem with one of the sun-carts, recruited Donovan to assist him, and took his leave. He hadn't spoken more than those two syllables to Elliot, and she, for her part, allowed the admiral to do all the talking. As soon as he was gone, she looked at Tatiana, but could detect no sense of smugness or glee in her sister. It was as if Tatiana hadn't even recognized him.

Grubby little boy from the barn, why should she?

Especially since he wasn't that boy any longer. He wasn't even the skinny, half-grown adolescent she'd last seen. Four years had turned her old friend into something different entirely. He was taller, and with broader shoulders and longer hair and a jawline that belonged more to a man than a child.

But Tatiana might have seen all that and still failed to identify him, for the real change was that Kai no longer looked like a servant. He stood tall and proud with a haughtiness, a distance, that almost gave even Elliot pause.

Perhaps that explained her sister's strange behavior. Elliot had never seen her so respectful to Posts before, but then, the way these Posts acted, it was difficult to remember that that's indeed what they were. These weren't the obsequious or even quietly resentful bonded servants that her sister was used to. This was what Kai had run away to be a part of. And it seemed he'd succeeded beyond her wildest fantasies.

The shock wore off and Elliot attended halfheartedly to the Innovations' questions about the shipyard and the house. But all she wanted to do was chase after Kai. At last she knew what had become of him. He wasn't in danger, being exploited in some lawless Post enclave, or starving and wandering among the estates looking for work. He wasn't even employed as a simple mechanic. He was, in fact, one of the richest and most celebrated people on the islands.

And he was still angry with her.

Elliot longed for a moment alone to collect herself, but it was impossible. She had to settle her grandfather and direct the Reduced to take the Cloud Fleet's belongings to the Boatwright house. She had to answer questions for the admiral and his team that Tatiana, despite her status as head of the household, did not understand. She had to make excuses for her father's absence and assure them that everyone was quite pleased about the rental arrangements and the money and the horses, and that her father's last-minute trip had nothing whatsoever to do with the Posts' arrival—and she had to sound more convincing about it than

Tatiana. The process took the better part of the afternoon, and through all of it, she didn't catch another glimpse of Kai.

Where had he gone? Was he off visiting his old stomping grounds? Had he looked in on Ro? Had he, perhaps, gone to see his former living quarters in the barn? The Posts had seemed surprised that he'd show any interest in the horses, and now Elliot understood their shock. Kai had never cared much for livestock. He far preferred machines to animals, or even plants. But they were being kept in the barn . . .

Elliot stiffened in her seat as momentary panic gripped her. The door was padlocked. She had nothing to fear. She could afford to sit here quietly and occasionally volunteer answers on the many occasions that Tatiana— the acknowledged hostess—floundered when it came to knowledge of the Boatwright holdings.

Fortunately, Felicia Innovation's topics of conversation were far less taxing than her companions', and they were ones that Tatiana could elaborate on ad nauseum.

"I have heard tales," Felicia said to Elliot's sister, "that the Norths' star-cavern sanctuary is the most stunning natural formation on this whole island."

"Did you?" Tatiana asked, her tone coy. "I was not aware that any Posts had seen it."

"My report comes from Baroness Channel," Felicia replied without missing a beat. "Who visited, I believe, for your mother's funeral. She is an old friend of mine. The Channel sanctuary is quite lovely," she went on. "I wonder how they compare."

Tatiana blinked. Andromeda smirked. Elliot marveled.

She had spent the last four years trying to learn how to properly cajole her father and sister, and here this Post was playing Tatiana like an instrument after only a few minutes' acquaintance. She doubted her sister would be able to resist this challenge, and indeed, Tatiana could not.

"Perhaps I should take you on a tour," she suggested.

Elliot wondered if Tatiana would inform their father of the plans, and if so, what he'd think of lowly Posts tromping through his ancestral sanctuary.

"That's most kind," Felicia said. "I'm sure we'd love to see it."

You'd have to know Tatiana pretty well, Elliot thought, to recognize the look that flashed across her face at the word "we." It was too quick for the uninitiated to recognize. Still, Andromeda's eyebrows rose.

"The acoustics are legendary," Andromeda said. "Donovan would adore it."

"Your brother is a musician as well as an explorer?"

"My brother would prefer to be a musician, yes."

"How unusual for a Post."

"Certainly unusual in this area." It was a pointed statement, given what had happened on the North estate during the bad time. Elliot looked away, into the hearth, remembering the bonfires piled high with illicit pipes and string-boxes—some of those instruments engineered by her own hand.

And some by Kai's.

He must have heard of what had gone on here, Elliot realized. He must have been appalled.

She took a breath. The fire was dying, and the light outside was fading. She should add more wood. She rose to tend the embers as the conversation went on around her. She couldn't take this anymore. These subtle jabs, this sharp little dance of insults and put-downs. She couldn't even place the blame squarely on Tatiana. Her sister was trying. Perhaps there was no common ground between a Luddite and a free Post.

No wonder Kai wouldn't even look at her.

"Let me know when you wish to tour the star cavern, then," Tatiana was saying. "I'll invite our friends, the Groves, whose estate is southwest of here. Olivia Grove has a splendid voice. Very fine, and impeccably trained."

Even the window wasn't far enough away. Elliot made a beeline for the door.

The admiral followed, stopping her in the hall. "Miss Elliot."

She turned. "Excuse me, sir, I should really look in on my grandfather—"

"I wanted a chance to speak with you," he said, coming close and dropping his voice.

Elliot bobbed her head. Perhaps he had something to say about Kai . . .

"I know to whom I am really indebted to for this opportunity," he said instead. "Your father's was the signature on the bottom of the letter, but I'm not ignorant of the way things work on the North estate."

"Sir, I—" How did he know? If it was Kai who told him, then she was safe. But if rumors had spread beyond the boundary of the estate, if her father caught wind of them . . .

"Your father isn't even here to greet us. But you are."

"My father was called away . . ." But the lie faltered on her lips.

"I appreciate your advocacy," the admiral said quickly, as if he hadn't noticed. "Please. let me know if there's anything I can do to make sure things run as smoothly as possible."

Now Elliot met his eyes—blue and watery, with the start of cataracts from staring too long into the glittering sea. The admiral smiled at her.

"When I meet a Luddite like you, I have hope for our world."

Elliot blinked as his words stung someplace deep inside. A Luddite like her? Her father would argue she wasn't one at all.

Six

AT LAST SHE WAS alone, and of course she returned to the barn. The sky had turned the color of Post overcoats as the sun set, and now stars winked at the edge of the jagged black horizon. The barn was dark, and the familiar sound of lowing cattle had been replaced with the soft shuffling and snorts of the new horses. Elliot leaned her head against the door and sighed. The darkness was another relief. He hadn't come here.

Elliot lit a lantern. As always, her eyes went first to the knot of wood near the floor by the entrance. It was a habit she'd been unable to break in four years. And, just like every other time in the past four years, the knothole remained empty.

The dairy equipment had been stacked neatly in a corner to make room for the newcomers, and Dee and the dairymaids had been instructed on the new routines. With luck, there'd be no break in the milk production, despite the reduced working space. They couldn't afford that, even with the influx of money from the admiral's rental. Everything else in the barn remained the same. The giant shadows of their few remaining pieces of machinery loomed from every corner. Perhaps she could use some of the money to buy replacement parts for the pieces that were broken beyond Elliot's ability to repair them. After all, they'd been without a mechanic on the estate for four years.

There was a sound from above—the creaking of boards, an unmistakable footfall. Elliot lifted her lantern, but could see nothing on the stairs. She heard a small meow, but that step was far too heavy to have been made by Nero. Steeling herself, she ascended the stairs.

The passage above was similarly black, but as she shone the lantern down the hall, she saw him. He stood before the door to his old room, his back toward her, the old yellow barn cat Nero twining in figure eights round his feet.

"Hello," she said again.

"The door is locked," was his only reply. He didn't turn around. Nero was rubbing his whiskers against Kai's trouser leg. That cat hated every maid in the dairy. It was a wonder he'd lived as long as he had, that he hadn't drowned years ago in a pail of milk. But he'd been Kai's, and so he'd stayed.

Everything of his had stayed—his old pallet and blankets—though they hadn't smelled like him for years—a sweater she supposed was too holey for him to take, and, of course, her letters to him. He'd left them all behind, though she didn't know if it was because he'd been angry or because he had intended to leave them.

Thinking he'd have the real thing with him instead.

Elliot drew closer, then hesitated. Wouldn't he even face her? "Yes. I have . . . equipment in there."

"Unlock it," said the back of Kai's head.

"No."

Now he turned, but just as before in the drawing room, he wouldn't meet her eyes. "This is my old room." As if she didn't know. "I want to see it."

He wanted to see the room even more than he wanted to see her?

"I don't have the key with me." Elliot was glad now that he wouldn't look her in the face, or she was sure he'd see her lie. "It's just . . . storage."

That, at least, was the truth. It was where she stored things she didn't want anyone else to know about.

He cast one more glance at the padlock, then shoved away from the door. "Fine."

"Kai," she said, and he stopped. Enough of this silly, stilted conversation. They were alone now. Again, she stretched out her hand. "I can't believe it's you."

The corners of his mouth turned up, but no emotion supported the smile. Elliot realized her hand still hung there in space and snatched it back. She gripped the handle of the lantern until her fingernails bit into her palm.

"I look so different?" he asked.

Yes. "That's not what I mean. I didn't know *you* were Captain Wentforth. That all the things I've read, all the things he's done—I thought he was older."

"I guess my leaving didn't turn out to be the disaster

you'd thought." Still he stared past her, at the wall.

"No, Kai—"

"Don't call me that. That isn't my name any longer."

Elliot nodded and shifted a bit to the left, trying to see his face, which only made him avert his gaze even more. "I like your new name," she said softly. "Your father would have been so proud of you." When he failed to respond, she forged ahead. "What should I call you now? Wentforth, as the others do? Malakai?" She took a step toward him.

He faced her full on now, and she stopped dead. In the flickering lamplight, his black eyes seemed lit with stars, as cold and inhuman as the expression on his face. "I don't foresee that you'll have much reason to call me anything at all."

He brushed past her, his touch nothing more than a rasp of fabric against fabric, and disappeared down the stairs. Elliot heard the barn door open and close. He was gone. Just like that. She leaned hard against the wall, her heart pounding, her lungs screaming to cry out his forbidden name.

Kai. It bubbled to her lips, and she closed her mouth around it, felt it echo against her jaw and teeth and tongue. It wasn't his name any longer, and what was more, this man was no longer Kai. Not the Kai she'd known all her life. Not the Kai she'd held in her mind these past four years, the one she'd invented in the dark of the night, when she dared to imagine that things might be different. *That* Kai was clearly a fantasy. The man he'd become would probably deem it a nightmare.

Once her breath returned to normal, she straightened, reached into her pocket, and pulled out a key. She crossed to the lock and inserted it, but paused to shutter the lamp before she opened the door. She couldn't risk anyone seeing the light through the window. Not tonight. Not Kai.

Inside, the darkness rustled around her. She moved through the space from memory. The floorboards creaked beneath her feet, and slips of paper whispered upon her face and her hands. Her fingers reached her desk and then the window with its heavy shade. Beyond, the moon would be rising.

She lifted the shade and bathed the room in silver. Moonlight glinted off the glass and metal instruments on her desk and vanished into the eaves. Moonlight skimmed over the floorboards and made Nero's eyes a shimmering green. It wasn't enough to work by. It wasn't enough to read by. But who needed to read? She knew them by heart.

All around her, strung from the ceiling and wafting softly in the draft, Kai's paper gliders glowed in the moonlight like pale spring shoots bursting from the soil.

Five Years Ago

Dear Elliot,

Thank you for the textbooks. I put them right back where you told me. I can't believe my da doesn't know anything about the wars. Especially if they did all that stuff like your textbooks say. Can you imagine always knowing exactly where you are in the world, just with a machine? I can't help but be really mad at the people who screwed that up for us.

By the way, I'm putting all this in the letter because I don't think it's a good idea to talk about it in front of my da. He got very upset when I told him about the Reduced infantry in the Second War of the Reduction. I suppose that's why they only teach that stuff to Luddites.

Your friend,

Kai

ᕲᕲ

Dear Kai,

I know! I find it amazing, some of the things they could do before the Reduction. (Just don't tell anyone I said that.) My grandfather has one of those old compasses on the wall in his house. The wheel just goes round and round now. One day I'll sneak you in to see it.

What I learned in school is that the Lost were so desperate, knowing that all their offspring would be Reduced and in a generation their entire society would be gone, that it didn't matter to them what happened. They wanted to make sure that no one stole what they thought was theirs, even if all their descendants wound up Reduced and couldn't use it. They thought that if they couldn't have their technology, their land, their things, no one could. My Luddite ancestors survived, but there were whole countries that at the time were too poor to have the ERV procedure. The Lost bombed them into oblivion rather than let them inherit the Earth. The same thing would have happened to us if we hadn't hid away in the caverns.

I'll tell you a secret. Sometimes I wonder what it would have been like, to live before the Reduction. Can you imagine knowing what way you're going without using the stars? I read these stories in the books about England or Greece or Egypt or China and I wonder if they are still out there. Do you?

I'm sorry if I upset Mal, even inadvertently.
Your friend,
Elliot

Dear Elliot,
I know they are still out there. The wars couldn't have destroyed everything. They just can't find us, same as we can't find them. (Don't tell anyone I said that.)

And don't worry about my da. He's been cranky recently.
He keeps saying stuff like he's run out of things to teach
me. But about this I guess I understand. He can't help but
picture his parents or his brothers and sisters being used as
Reduced infantry to draw away the seeker bombs. That's really
upsetting.

 I'm glad we don't have wars anymore. The Reduced have it
bad enough without being used as living targets.
Your friend,
Kai

   ✺

Dear Kai,
I still don't understand. Obviously, no one in your ancestry was
ever in the Wars, or you wouldn't have been born. Your family was
protected by their Luddite lords. They would have been under the
care of the Norths, not someone who was Lost. So I don't see why
it bothers Mal.
Your friend,
Elliot

   ✺

Dear Kai,
Where were you today? You didn't write me a letter and you
weren't in the barn.
Your friend,
Elliot

   ✺

Dear Kai,

It's now been a week. I spoke to Mal today and he said he didn't know where you were. I know that's not true, and I know you got my last letter. If you're mad at me, I wish you'd tell me why.

Your friend (I hope!),

Elliot

Seven

ELLIOT SET OUT EARLY the next morning to see Ro. She should be told if Kai was back. After all, she'd probably been more outwardly upset than Elliot when he'd left the first time.

That morning, Ro's group was working in the easternmost field, and when Elliot arrived, the foreman, Gill, gave her a wry look. "Come to see what all the commotion is about?"

"What do you mean?" Elliot asked.

Gill nodded his head in the direction of the laborers. "It's not for me to say she shouldn't have it, Miss Elliot, but I can't guarantee there won't be a fight before the day's out. Favoritism and all that. My own common-law doesn't have anything half so pretty."

Elliot peered into the field, searching for Ro's bright hair, but saw no sign of it. Instead, she saw something else. "Ro!" she called, and waved the girl over.

Ro ran up to the boundary fence, her face split in two by a smile, her hair mostly hidden beneath a silky scarf the color of shaded summer leaves. It made her skin glow. It made her green eyes stand out from her face. Kai had not forgotten Ro. He even remembered the precise shade of her eyes.

Ro giggled and twirled, pointing to the scarf.

"It's beautiful, Ro," Elliot said, trying to keep the unexpected stiffness out of her voice. He'd brought *Ro* a present.

"I'd have already taken it off her," Gill added helpfully. "But I know you have a special fondness for this one."

She *should* take the scarf from Ro, Elliot thought, for all the reasons Gill had mentioned, and more besides. Ro was a very pretty girl, and not a child any longer, either. The vile sorts of things that happened on other estates were forbidden on the North estate—her father had his faults, but he was scrupulous when it came to the behavior of the people who lived on his lands. Her cousin Benedict had been sent away years ago for taking advantage of a Reduced girl. Still, there were dangers out there, as well as changes that she wasn't sure Ro herself was ready to make. Other Reduced her age were already mothers, but Ro had never shown much interest in children or the birthing house. All she cared about were her flowers.

Elliot beckoned Ro closer, then touched the edge of the scarf. It felt cool and silky beneath her fingertips and she wondered what it could be made of. Bamboo, perhaps? Not real silk, certainly. A silk scarf was worth a sizable percentage of the yearly income of the estate. Not even Malakai Wentforth could have that much to spend on a scarf.

How many sun-carts could he have possibly found?

"Kai!" Ro said with glee, tugging it off and handing it to Elliot.

She hadn't spoken his name since a few months after he'd gone. Sometimes Elliot wondered if Ro even remembered her old friend. But clearly, she hadn't forgotten him any more than he had her. This was such a very *Ro* gift— green and pretty and utterly decorative. It wouldn't keep her warm. It was far too slippery to hold back her hair. But Kai understood Ro as well as Elliot did. She loved beauty. And so that's what he'd brought her.

Elliot handed the scarf back. She wouldn't be the one to deprive Ro of that. "Be careful with it. It's very fine."

Ro nodded seriously, then pushed it back onto her head with muddy fingers.

As she returned to Gill, he clucked his tongue. "You spoil her."

"Do you have a complaint about the quality of her work?"

"Point taken." He gazed out over the fields. "Miss Elliot, I don't mean to pry, but there's talk . . ."

"Yes, Gill?"

"The Posts living up at the Boatwright house. The Cloud Fleet, they call themselves. There's someone we know up there, isn't there?"

"Yes." She toed the dust at the fence line before lifting her gaze back to the older man's. "Mal's son is back."

ELLIOT HAD DOUBTED THAT Tatiana's offer to show the Fleet the star-cavern sanctuary was a serious one, so she was surprised when her sister organized a tour the following day. Tatiana intercepted her as soon as Elliot returned to the house from the dairy.

"Take off those clothes and run a comb through your hair," her sister ordered. "We're taking our guests to the sanctuary."

Elliot's eyes widened. "Do you think Father would approve of that?"

"Do you think Father would approve of you appearing in front of our tenants looking like a Reduced servant girl?" Tatiana replied. "You might see them any moment."

Elliot wondered if Tatiana would be so concerned with Elliot's attire had the Fleet Posts not looked so very fashionable. But there was no arguing with her sister, so she went to her room and spent a good five minutes standing before her wardrobe in search of a suitable outfit.

Very little would do. Her nice clothes were old and ill-fitting. She had several of Tatiana's hand-me-downs, but no amount of seam letting-out and hem-dropping would disguise the fact that they had been made for someone smaller all around. And even the nicest of them featured the pale, drab Luddite colors. She finally settled on her darkest dress—the faded black mourning gown she'd worn four years ago at her mother's funeral. It didn't fit quite right, since she'd filled out a lot since she was fourteen, but it would have to do. She brushed her long black hair and pinned it up so it fell loose down her back, realizing even as she did that it hadn't been cut in four years, either. Her mother used to trim it for her. Lately, she just braided it to get it out of the way.

It was an all-too-common occurrence around here. Hasty repairs, because Elliot hadn't the means to really fix problems, stopgap deals struck with debtors who deserved repayment, pleas to the North Posts to be patient a little longer while Elliot tried to hold the estate together and bring in another harvest. Who had time to mess with clothes and hair?

By the time she met her sister at the front door, their neighbors Horatio and Olivia Grove had joined her. The Groves were another old Luddite family, though their estate was a fraction of the size of the Norths'. Horatio had inherited the estate three years ago as a young teen, and together with the help of his Posts, had managed to make their orchards and vineyards quite profitable by the time he was twenty. Elliot often wondered if she would have been capable of the same, had she been more talented at battling her father.

"A dress, Elliot?" Horatio asked wryly as she greeted him. "Not to be outdone by these fashionable Posts?"

"Oh, so you know what they wear?" she asked.

He chuckled and nodded at his little sister. Olivia Grove was clad in a scarlet gown Elliot had never seen before, and she was pretty sure the sour expression on her own sister's face was due to wondering if her icy blue dress looked tired and dingy beside it.

"Got it for her in Channel City this summer," Horatio said. "There are Posts all over there now, all of them dressed in the gaudiest outfits you've ever seen—" He cut himself off as a sun-cart pulled up outside the door, carrying Felicia

Innovation and Donovan Phoenix. "A bit like that, actually."

"I think you'll like them, Horatio, turquoise overcoats or not," she said.

"I know I will." He grinned. "They have sun-carts. They're my new best friends."

Elliot flashed her friend a quick smile, but it evaporated quickly as another sun-cart crested the drive. She felt more than saw Kai in the second cart, the way you can tell when the sun hits a patchy spot of cloud on an overcast day. The chill reached her before she even caught sight of his cold expression, of the way he was still steadfastly refusing to look in her direction. But she refused to give in to the temptation to smooth her skirt or her hair as the cart pulled up with Andromeda behind the wheel. She wondered if Kai thought she'd changed as much as she thought he had. If so, it could hardly be for the better.

Elliot's features, which had been harsh and solemn even when she was younger, hadn't softened with age. Her dark brows were thick slashes over the deep-set, almond-shaped eyes she'd inherited from the Boatwright side of the family. The round snub nose came courtesy of her grandfather as well, and the skin that turned brown in the sun, then sallow in the dark winter months. She'd also gotten his full lips, though, and her black hair took on ruddy highlights every summer. But Elliot was no beauty, and she knew it.

Her mind's eye was filled with the shade of Ro's new scarf, the deep verdant green that had suited her more than any of the tans and browns she'd worn her whole life. Elliot had never envied Ro—not her fair face nor her bright hair, nor the easy happiness with which she greeted every day. And she wouldn't start now. Nothing, not even presents from Kai, made up for the fact that Ro was Reduced.

"Hello!" Horatio called, waving at the Posts. "Pleasure to meet you! My name is Horatio Grove—I live on the estate next door. That one's my sister, Olivia."

"Good morning," said Andromeda, nodding. "I assume you are the Groves we have to thank for the bushels of apples sent to the Boatwright house." Andromeda's every word seemed to be carefully weighed before it was allowed to pass her lips, and even as she spoke, Elliot noticed her unusual eyes surveying the entire scene before her. She had little doubt that, were the light to suddenly vanish, Andromeda could re-create every particular of that morning, from the open, friendly expression on Horatio's face as he approached with Elliot to the way Kai had barely nodded at the introduction to the number of particles in the gravel drive at their feet. No wonder she was such an excellent explorer— nothing escaped her observation.

Elliot shuddered to think what the Post girl was noticing about her.

Olivia met them by the steps. "I'm Olivia Grove," she burst out. "I love your sun-carts. That's what these are, right? I've never seen one before. May I go for a ride in one? Are they very hard to operate?"

Now Kai did respond. "Yes; I'm not surprised; of course; and I can teach you if you'd like."

Olivia worked out which answer matched which of her

questions and Elliot became very concerned with the state of the dust beneath her feet. Perhaps he had not changed as much as she'd thought. His knack of remembering everything, of organizing it in his brain and acting as if everyone else did, too—it had grown only more pronounced over the years.

"My brother always teases me because I didn't learn to ride a bicycle until I was nine," Olivia said. "He says I'm marvelously uncoordinated. I bet you can teach me, though."

"I'll do my best," said Kai, and offered the girl his arm.

Elliot had always liked Olivia Grove. She was a sweet, unaffected girl who never had anything bad to say of anyone. She was kind to the workers on her estate, liked to sing and to walk in her orchards, and seemed equally comfortable discussing fruit with Elliot as she was ribbons with Tatiana. Had she been asked, Elliot would have denied the possibility of ever having a reason to hate the fourteen-year-old girl.

Had she been asked, she would deny a lot of things. That she ever doubted the Luddite ways she'd been taught to follow all her life. That she had broken a sacred trust in the locked room on the second floor of her family's barn. And most of all, that listening to Olivia pepper Kai with questions, hearing him explain the workings of the sun-carts to her in the same open, excited tones she'd once known so intimately—a voice very different than the stiff, stilted syllables he'd spared for her in the barn the previous evening—Elliot would go to her grave before she admitted that it made her heart hurt so much she could scarcely breathe.

FIVE YEARS AGO

Dear Kai,
I was sorry to learn what happened to your father today. These
pills are the medicine they gave to my grandfather after he had
his strokes. If you give two a day to Mal, it might help. I know
you're still mad over our argument about the Wars of the Lost,
but I hope you know I'm thinking of you. Please tell me if there's
anything else I can do.
Your friend,
Elliot

Dear Elliot,
Thank you for the medicine. I hope it can help my da. They've
taken him away to the healing house—I hate that name. They
never do any healing there. People just go there to die. It's hard to
see him. This is the man who taught me to read and write and
fix engines, and now he just stares at me like one of the Reduced.

He must hate that. He used to tell me how hard it was for
him growing up. It wasn't like now. He was one of the only Posts
on the whole estate. They didn't even have a name for what he
was growing up—they hadn't started calling us CORs yet. He

loved his family—his parents, his brothers and sisters who were Reduced, but he wasn't one of them. He spent his whole life proving that. And now he's trapped, he's mute, he's just like them.

And that made me think of the wars. If there was a war tomorrow, would your father send the Reduced out like they did in the old days? Would you send out my uncles and cousins? Would you send out my da, now that he can no longer speak or work for you?

I will tell you the truth. The truth is I was angry at you. The truth is that you're my closest friend, and I still felt like there was no way I could possibly make you understand what it's like to be me, what it's like to be my da. The truth is that my da is dying, and because he's a COR, he's shoved away to be forgotten in the healing house, while your grandfather gets medicine and nurses who wait on him hand and foot. The truth is, if there was a war tomorrow, everyone I know would be forced to do exactly what your father wants, just like they forced my father to go into the healing house, just like they will force me to go work as a foreman in the fields, because I'm not old enough or educated enough to keep being a mechanic if my da's not there to teach me.

The truth is that I'm scared to even write these things down and send them to a Luddite to read. Even if that Luddite is you.
Your friend,
Kai

Dear Kai,

*You are my closest friend too. And I promise I will do everything
I can to help you and Mal. I will talk to my mother. I will talk to
my father if I have to. You may not know everything you must to
be our mechanic, but you know enough to apprentice at it, and
my father will have to admit it would be a waste to track you into
a foreman job. My mother knows who you are, and she knows
what we owe you and Ro since your mothers died on the day we
were all born. I know she'll help us.*

*I wish the shipyard were still open. I think you'd have
liked it there, even if I'd've missed you. And my grandfather is
a good man. They say he even had a Post as his first mate, back
when he still traveled up and down the coast.*

*Is the medicine helping at all? I'm going to go sit with Mal
in the healing house, since I know you have to work.*
Your friend,
Elliot

Eight

THE STAR-CAVERN SANCTUARIES COULD be reached only through a tunnel in the North cellars, which helped the family restrict access to those they deemed worthy. A few Reduced housemaids were allowed down for cleaning purposes, but generally the space was reserved as a monument to the Luddites' great accomplishment: perseverance.

Elliot had always been in awe of her ancestors. They'd possessed the strength of mind to fight against the tide of their society. When everyone else was putting their faith in scientists like Gavin and Carlotta and getting the ERV procedure, the Luddites had their doubts, as they did about corporate foods whose very genetic codes killed competing vegetation, about computer chips designed to make your brain run faster, about living among people who'd filled the air and water with toxins. They'd saved the world by rejecting it all.

How could she abandon what they'd fought so hard to achieve?

The space was softly lit by sconces as they entered the sanctuary, and the predominant sound was Felicia's gasp of wonder. "It's even more spectacular than I'd thought."

The cavern's earthen walls sloped upward into vague shadows, and where the walls weren't marked by murals depicting the skylines of ruined cities and monuments that Elliot had only seen in antique books, they were blackened by the smoke from ancient fires. Here and there stood other artifacts from the Luddites' time underground. Elliot tried to imagine what it had been like for her ancestors, living their entire lives underground, kept from the turning of the seasons, from the feel of the sun on their faces or the smell of the fields.

Perhaps this was what she'd been missing. Perhaps her father was right, that she should spend more time in the sanctuary to reflect on the true weight of her heritage. Her forebears had spent untold years living in this darkness, subsisting on fish from underground streams, mushrooms, and stockpiled food, because of the horrors that genetic manipulation had visited upon their world. And now, because of a few lean years, she had chosen to tread down that same, dangerous path. Of course, her wheat grafts weren't ERV, but the idea was the same. Gavin and Carlotta had introduced Endogenous RetroViruses into the Lost in order to trick their God-given DNA into turning on only the best and most powerful expressions of their genes and delivering those same traits to their offspring. Elliot's grafting methods hadn't been nearly so intricate, but the result was the same: horizontal gene transfer and a transgenic wheat that produced thicker, heavier seed heads far sooner in the season.

She'd told herself it wasn't the same. She hadn't been mucking around with microscopes and DNA strands. It was safe, hardly any worse than the type of cross-pollination that occurred naturally when one plant sat too near another in the field. Of course, that was God's plan, same as when he'd cursed those with ERV and caused the virus to mutate within their genes and Reduce all their progeny. Elliot had manipulated this wheat herself. And she doubted her Luddite ancestors, who'd experienced much leaner times than this in their years spent huddled in the caverns, would accept her excuse that she'd been desperate to find a way to feed the people on her lands. She felt her cheeks burning in humiliation, and was glad for the dim lights that hid her shame.

Elliot braved a glance at Kai, wondering what he thought now that he saw the North star cavern for himself. He was staring straight up at the darkness in the ceiling, just like the Phoenixes, with an amused expression painted across his features. "So this is all of it."

"Fascinating," Andromeda said softly. "Well, at least I can say I have honestly never seen anything like it."

"You haven't seen anything yet," said Olivia Grove. "Shall we turn out the lights, Tatiana?" She leaned over and extinguished a nearby sconce when Tatiana nodded.

Elliot and the other Luddites began putting out the lights. As the cavern dipped into twilight, she looked back at Kai, waiting for the moment when the miracle overtook him, but his expression did not change.

"Our ancestors," Tatiana said, as the sanctuary was plunged into utter darkness, "were forced to take refuge during the Wars of the Lost. Some already lived on these islands. Some came as the reach of the wars grew ever wider. But all were forced eventually underground. When the Lost realized what they'd done, that they were the last generation of healthy people, they struck out with unthinkable rage against any and all who had avoided Reduction. They destroyed technologically backward countries that didn't have the money for the enhancements. They attacked each other, too, hoping to be the last ones, at least, left standing over a ruined world." She blew out the final light. Above them, the miracle flickered to life.

"For years—some say more than a generation—the Luddites lived in the darkness. And then . . ." Tatiana's voice fell silent, and they all stared up into the vertex of the cavern.

It was filled with stars. From every corner of the cavern, tiny, twinkling points of light glowed, a green so pale as to be nearly white.

Olivia began to sing, a soft Luddite hymn they'd all known since childhood. And as her voice grew, the stars glowed brighter, twinkling down on them with promise. As a child, Elliot had been amazed by this—that the stars in the cavern responded to human voices, when the ones in the sky did not. Now, even when she knew the truth, the effect was still quite beautiful.

"In the old stories," said Tatiana, "a man built his followers a boat to ride out the flooding of the world. And when the flood was over, God showed him a rainbow to tell him that the worst was over. And after the wars of the Reduction were over, God showed us the stars, and we knew we could come out of the caverns and take our rightful place on the surface of the world."

It was more complicated than that, though. When Elliot's ancestors emerged, it was into an unrecognizable world. A world where even some of the machines the Luddites were willing to use no longer worked. A world where there was no sign of life beyond the islands, where the needles of compasses spun uselessly, where there was no direction at all save the stars. All the Luddites knew was that they were alone, and that they alone bore responsibility for gathering up the shards of humanity.

"Amazing," whispered Felicia.

"Interesting," said Andromeda, her tone pedestrian.

"Ann," Donovan warned under his breath.

Elliot, standing close to the Phoenixes, heard the girl shift in the darkness. "Miss Grove," Andromeda said. "That's a very pretty song. You should hear my brother sing. It would no doubt blow you away."

"I would like that," Olivia replied. "He could sing now. The stars glow brighter with song."

"I wonder why that is," Kai said. "Do you think they suppose their food is closer and they hope to attract it into their webs?"

Tatiana made a choking sound. "How . . . do you know?"

Kai sounded bored. "That they're bugs? I thought it was common knowledge."

It wasn't. Elliot had told Kai herself, years ago, when she'd learned the truth about the glowworm "stars" her family venerated in the sanctuary. They *were* bugs—tiny, bioluminescent insects that crept into crevices in the rocks and attracted prey through their glowing lights.

"Really?" asked Olivia sadly. "I was so disappointed when I learned the truth. I was ten years old."

"I can imagine," Kai replied. But he didn't need to. Elliot had been disappointed back then as well, and so had Kai, though he'd never seen the stars for himself. Still, the knowledge of the truth behind the miracle didn't take away from the wonder of the sight, nor from the importance—even more so because it was natural and not manmade—that the appearance of the "stars" had held for Elliot's ancestors.

"I don't mean to belittle it," said Kai. "It's stunning. Not like the real thing, of course—nothing can compare to when you're out at sea, nothing around you but stars, shining above, reflected below." The Phoenixes murmured their agreement. Elliot gazed up at the sanctuary firmament and tried to imagine what it would look like. "These . . . well, they look like bugs."

"They look like stars!" Tatiana exclaimed.

"Not to my eyes," said Kai.

"Nor mine," Andromeda added. "Nor yours, right, Donovan?"

"I must admit they do not," Donovan said, his tone reluctant.

"I'm sorry for that," Felicia broke in. "If you cannot see

the wonder in this sanctuary, then your superior eyesight has done you no favors."

For a moment the three captains were silent, as if Felicia had scolded them like children. Finally, Andromeda spoke. "To be fair, the real stars don't even fascinate me as much as when I was . . . younger."

"I am sorry for that, as well." Felicia's voice was sad.

What did Felicia Innovation have to apologize for? It was hardly her fault that her young friends were unimpressed with the Norths' most sacred possession. Indeed, she suspected Kai's response was on purpose.

"It's especially disappointing," Felicia went on, "when you consider those who will never see this miracle with *any* eyes . . ."

Elliot heard Donovan's harsh intake of breath. Beside him, Andromeda mumbled an apology.

"It's quite all right," said Felicia, but her tone was so flat, Elliot felt sure that it was anything but. "Miss Norths, you must forgive these young captains. They have seen so many wonders beyond the shores of these islands, they forget the beauty of the wonders here at home."

"I would love to hear more of what you've seen," said Olivia. "I've long wondered what else is out there."

"Have you?" asked Kai. "That's an unusual desire for a Luddite. Even when I've heard them express it, they've never been sincere."

Elliot bit her lip and stared up at the stars until they blurred before her eyes.

Nine

"PERHAPS YOU'LL BE MORE keen on this," Olivia said, as if attempting to steer the conversation in a brighter direction. "Over here, there's a spot where if you whisper, you can hear it all over. Where is it . . . ?" Elliot could hear her stumbling about in the darkness.

"Let me help you," said Kai. "Give me your arm. There, that's better. This way?"

Their voices drifted away from the main group, and a moment later, Olivia's disembodied whisper echoed through the cavern. "Here it is," came her hushed syllables. "If you talk here, you can be heard everywhere. But over here—" Her voice cut out.

"Now that is interesting," said Donovan.

"There are directional whisper zones, too," Horatio said. "You can whisper in one place and be heard only in a very specific other. There are some markers that show how— whisper by the yellow rock, be heard by the other yellow rock, and vice versa. Let me put on a light so I can show you."

He relit a sconce so there was at least enough light that they wouldn't trip onto their faces, and within moments the group had dispersed over the interior of the cavern, each trying out a separate whisper zone. Tatiana alone remained aloof, and Elliot took a seat beside her sister.

"This is what I get, I suppose, for allowing a bunch of Posts into the sanctuary," Tatiana said with a long-suffering sigh.

"Now, Tatiana," Elliot said. "Don't pretend you never played with the whisper zones yourself. You used to make Benedict and me come down here and play Gavin and Carlotta with you."

"I was ten," Tatiana sniffed, but then her tone turned teasing. "How we scared you with that game! Is that why you hate coming down here? Are you still afraid of the dark?"

"No," Elliot insisted. It wasn't the ghosts of Gavin and Carlotta who scared her in these caverns. It was the ones of her ancestors and their Luddite expectations.

"You sure?" Tatiana leaned in and began to whisper the sing-songey rhyme. "*Gavin and Carlotta come, When their names three times are sung. Stand before a mirror clear, Let them whisper in your ear.*"

"Stop it!" Elliot shot out of her seat.

Tatiana laughed. "So you *are* still scared."

"No," Elliot said, and hoped it was true. "It's like you said. It's a children's game. And not a very nice one to play in front of the Posts."

Tatiana laughed again. "Why, because they come from Reduced stock? That's silly, Elliot. You're either born

Reduced or you're not. These people know what they are." She dropped her voice again. *"If your image doesn't give you fright, Then you are a true Luddite. But if the glass shows you a haze, Reduced you'll be for all your days—"*

"I said stop," Elliot hissed, and she swept off the bench and away from her sister, shivering a bit in the chill of the cavern. This dress wasn't warm enough for the sanctuary. She'd worn a sweater over it at her mother's memorial service four years ago, but that sweater had been long since relegated to the rag bin.

There was hardly enough light to see her way as she walked deeper into the star cavern. Horatio stood with one lantern and whispered near a stone painted yellow, while at a corresponding yellow stone across the way, Felicia and Donovan listened intently. The whisper zones were ancient, too. Her ancestors had to have something to entertain themselves with other than scary nursery rhymes during their years spent in the dark.

She walked around in a little circle, rubbing her arms and looking up at the stars in the roof. When she was younger, she'd dreamed about sneaking Kai in here to see them. Now he was here on her sister's invitation, and he was remarkably unimpressed.

"Miss Elliot," said a voice in the blackness, and out stepped Andromeda.

Elliot stopped short and pressed her hand to her chest in shock. "I didn't see you."

"I know. Luckily, I saw you." Andromeda's eyes looked even more odd in the distant, dim glow from the few lit sconces, their daytime glittering blue nearly swallowed completely by her dark pupils. "Are you going somewhere in particular?"

"Just wandering. What did Mrs. Innovation mean back there? Was she talking about the admiral? I'm sure if he wishes to see the sanctuary, my sister will oblige him—"

"No," said Andromeda stiffly. "She doesn't mean the admiral. She means her daughter."

The Innovations had a daughter? "Oh. Where is she?"

"Dead."

Elliot swallowed. "Oh, I'm sorry—"

"I think the Grove girl is down there with Wentforth," Andromeda said quickly, gesturing further into the sanctuary. "How old is she, by the way?"

"Fourteen," Elliot blurted.

"Fourteen." The Post nodded. "He's eighteen. Four years is a long time, don't you think, Miss Elliot? It makes for many changes."

"Please, call me Elliot." What was she getting at? At its surface, only the age difference between Olivia and Kai. But Elliot was quickly learning that nothing this Post girl said possessed only one meaning.

"Of course, Wentforth has always had a rather foolish preference for Luddites. I'd thought he'd grown past it. Excuse me, Miss Elliot." She brushed by and away.

Elliot stumbled forward into the darkness. So Andromeda, at least, knew of her former closeness to Kai. It was clear from the Post's attitude that she didn't think much of Elliot, either. Elliot wondered what Kai had told her.

"—stuck in the past." His voice stopped her dead on the path. For so many years, it had only existed like this—disembodied, solely the product of memory. It was hard to believe he was here again, even though he was more distant than ever.

"Not all Luddites are," Olivia's voice joined his, low enough to be a whisper.

Elliot put out her hands and turned around in the darkness, but she couldn't see them at all.

"My brother and I are very interested in the new Post technology. We have sun-lamps in our home, and Horatio wants a sun-cart, depending on how much we make from the harvest."

"I'm sure I could give you a discount," Kai replied with a chuckle that seemed to go straight through Elliot's soul. Since Captain Wentforth had discovered the cache of sun-carts, Kai owned every single one of them. Kai's voice sang through her nerves, making her hair stand on end and sending ribbons of heat over the gooseflesh on her arms.

"No, you're not like the Norths," he continued. "They're obsessed with their position, with the old ways. But there are too many Posts like me now, and more born every day. The world isn't the same place we grew up in, where the Luddites make the rules and we all have to abide by them. Look at their estate. It's falling apart. They'll be left behind."

"Tatiana can be a little snobby, yes," said Olivia. "But don't tar Elliot with that brush. You should see her and my brother talking about how they'd like to improve their farms. Fortunately, my brother has the means to actually implement the improvements."

"Your brother and Elliot are close?" Kai asked.

Now it was Olivia's turn to laugh. "Not like that. They're friends. We've been good friends with the Norths for the past three years, ever since we lost our father. Horatio and Elliot love to talk about their crops. Elliot's the only one of her family that seems very interested in the subject, in case you haven't noticed."

"I have noticed that the Norths do not seem as interested in their property as they might be."

"She tries her hardest," Olivia said defensively. "And if Horatio ever did take an interest in a woman, I wouldn't mind if it was Elliot North."

"Perhaps you don't know her as well as you think," said Kai.

Elliot caught her breath.

"I've known her for years," Olivia argued. "I doubt your opinion of a person can change after so many years."

There was a pause before Kai spoke again. "I envy you that innocence, Olivia. But people can be deceptive. I hope you never learn what that is like. I grew up on an estate, and I spent four years in a Post enclave, and the only people who have never lied to me are the Innovations. Even my father— though I don't blame him. He was trapped by the world he was born into."

Elliot bit her lip to hold back the sob that rose in her throat.

"How horrible," said Olivia. "Well, I'm not like that. I was born a Luddite, but I see a future that includes us all."

"You're unique among your caste then," Kai replied. "But do not trust the Norths. Any of them."

"Elliot?" Horatio came upon her so quickly, she almost jumped out of her skin. He held a lantern in his hand. "Have you seen my sister?"

She blinked in the sudden brightness of the lantern. Now she knew where she was—another whisper zone. This one was marked off by a blue stone.

"I think she's . . . just down here." She pointed ahead of her and Horatio widened the aperture on the lantern to shine ahead. Sure enough, about ten meters away, Olivia and Kai stood close together near another blue stone. Olivia was squinting into the light. But Kai stared back at them, his black eyes steady and focused on Elliot, his mouth drawn into a tight line. And, as she watched, he reached out his hand and placed it on the blue stone.

How he'd known she was standing there, Elliot couldn't guess. But he'd meant her to hear every word.

Four Years Ago

Dear Kai,
I can't come to the barn tonight. Tatiana is becoming suspicious. Ever since she took over the household duties, she's been acting like she can tell me what to do as well.
Yours,
Elliot

෨

Dear Elliot,
Of course she does. She knows your mother isn't here to protect you anymore. But you know what the solution is: stay out of her way.
> *Stay here.*
> *Stay with me.*
Yours,
Kai

෨

Dear Kai,
I only wish I could. But my mother isn't here to do quite a lot of

things anymore. So I'll have to settle for imagining I'm with you.

My father wants to tear down the apple grove. He says it obstructs his view to the sea. He wants us to buy all our apples in the future, but I doubt Mr. Grove will give us a good deal, given that my father hasn't spoken to him in years.

He's also been complaining about the Posts' string-boxes. You don't think he would make you give them up, do you?

Yours,

Elliot

&

Dear Elliot,

Tatiana isn't the only suspicious one. You know Case, who oversees the dairy? He saw us together in the loft last week. He says I'm the biggest fool who ever lived.

I don't think he's right.

But, just to be safe, I'll put out the lamp. We'll pretend we're the ancient explorers, and find our way by the stars.

Yours,

Kai

&

Dear Kai,

I don't need to see the trail to know you're at the end of it. My grandfather's compass may not work, but mine is still true.

Yours,

Elliot

&

E,

Your da made me move to the laborers' barracks. Find me there.

K

⟋⟍

Dear Kai,

I've sent this letter through the hands of Mags. I trust that it has come to you safely. Mags and Gill will offer you lodging in their cottage. You should take it. So far, however, I can do nothing about the work order. My father is being very unreasonable— there is no other Post on the estate as qualified as you to be his mechanic. I don't know what he's thinking!

You don't think Case said anything, do you?

Don't worry, I'm sure my father will come around. Eventually.

Yours,

Elliot

⟋⟍

Dear Elliot,

I miss you. And I miss the barn. It's not that fieldwork is hard, but it is so boring. Gill told me the tractor broke. He's sneaking me into the barn tonight to fix it.

Meet me there.

Yours,

Kai

⟋⟍

Dear Kai,

I have wonderful news. My father's record player broke tonight.
He needs someone to fix it. I wonder who that could be?

Yours,

Elliot

〜

Dear Elliot,

Another night in the barn . . . alone. There's nothing to fix.
There's nothing to build. And you can't come because your father
is at home. I thought the fields were bad, but I'm here with my
machines and I'm still bored out of my skull.

    Did you hear that Case has left for points unknown?

Yours,

Kai

Ten

ELLIOT HOPED TO BE free of further interactions with the Posts after Tatiana finished her tour of the sanctuary, but she wasn't granted the opportunity. As soon as Olivia was back on the surface, she started dropping heavy hints about taking a spin in the sun-carts, and before Elliot knew it, she'd been conscripted into a cart along with Tatiana and the Phoenixes. Kai drove the Groves and Felicia Innovation in the other cart.

The carts consisted of three-wheeled platforms, with a long bench seat in front and two tiny bucket seats in back, right before the panel of angled, golden mirrors that supplied the carts with their power. Metal frames arced over their heads for support and handholds, but the carts were open to the air. The control panels, to Elliot's eye, were no more complex than she might find on one of the estate's ancient tractors.

"If you're planning a long ride," said Elliot, climbing

into the shotgun seat, "perhaps you can drop me off at the barn? There are some things I need to see to yet today."

"Certainly," Andromeda replied. She signaled to Kai to take the road toward the barn. He frowned but complied, and they were off.

Tatiana gripped the handrails firmly. "I have things to see to this afternoon as well. My hostessing duties have, I'm afraid, forced me to fall behind on some pressing household matters."

Elliot wondered what those could possibly be. New flower arrangements for the table?

"Is that how you divide up your work on the estate?" Donovan asked. "You manage the household while Elliot takes care of the farm?"

Had their duties been a topic of conversation among all the members of the Fleet?

"My father, as head of our estate, manages the farm," said Tatiana. "He controls all the movement of the workers and the crop planning."

To their detriment, Elliot wanted to add.

"Elliot just likes to play at gardening. She's much like our mother in that way."

Elliot looked out over the fields and toward the sea. Contradicting her sister would only embarrass them all.

Up ahead, Kai had turned the controls of the sun-cart over to Olivia, and the machine noticeably slowed, moving in awkward jerks and jumps as the girl got a handle on its operation.

Donovan sucked a breath in through his teeth.

"Wentforth's got to be going crazy watching her ruin the transmission like that. She can't push the brakes at the same time as the accelerator."

"Perhaps," Andromeda replied as they swerved off the road to pass the other cart. "He probably has more patience with the sister than he would with the brother, though."

"Knowing him," said Donovan.

Elliot grimaced at the Post's words. *Knowing him.* When she had known him, he'd been nothing like that. Or had he? Did she just never notice because *she'd* been the recipient of his attentions?

Elliot looked away from the other cart. It was silly to make anything of it at all, no matter what Andromeda had said to her in the caves. She hadn't been jealous of Ro's scarf, and she wouldn't be jealous of a sun-cart lesson and a conversation, either. Still, Andromeda knew this new man that Kai had become. Perhaps she knew what it looked like when Kai was interested. Perhaps, now that he was a famous explorer, he was *interested* quite a lot.

Tatiana piped up. "Olivia is still a child. She has been given far too much liberty ever since the death of her parents. Horatio is a good man, of course, but he does not know how to raise a teenage girl. He was made the head of his household at seventeen, and she has been the lady of the house since she was eleven. They have some . . . strange ideas. Look at the way he allows her to dress."

Elliot was pretty sure that Andromeda steered them *into* the next puddle. Tatiana shrieked and drew back to avoid the splash of mud. Elliot barely managed to hide her smile. Tatiana had also been made the lady of the house as a young teen.

"There are those who've been holding their own since they were that young," said Donovan. "Like my sister. It's been eight years since she and I left our estate—she was only twelve, and I was eight. We made it all right."

Tatiana's eyes widened, but she remained blessedly quiet.

As they passed, Elliot got a quick glimpse into Kai's cart. His hands were covering Olivia's as he showed her how to work the controls. Elliot focused very hard on the horizon until the grinding noises coming from the other cart faded into the background. When driven properly, Elliot realized, the carts made almost no noise at all, just a soft whir as the wheels spun and a clank whenever the shocks moved over the bumpy dirt road. This was much better than the smelly roars of the tractor.

Andromeda spoke again. "Would you like to give it a try, Miss Elliot?"

Elliot looked down at the controls the Post was offering her, and then up into the other girl's strangely bright eyes. As usual, she could read nothing. Was Andromeda hoping to embarrass her, too, or was she trying, in some odd way, to even the score with Olivia? It had been a long time since Elliot had viewed the operation of machinery as anything more than a chore. She'd spent too many hours driving the thresher and tractor around in the heat of the midday sun.

And yet she found herself taking hold of the controls. The cart needed a light touch, she discovered quickly, as her first attempt to put pressure on the accelerator sent the machine careening over the next hill. In the backseat, Tatiana squealed and jounced into Donovan's lap. He gently pushed her off.

"Sorry," Elliot said, correcting the speed. The setup, she noted, was surprisingly similar to the tractor she'd grown up using. Because of this, she found her way around the controls with ease and was able to keep the cart going at a swift but steady clip until they arrived at the barn.

Elliot pulled the cart to the side, expertly parking in the shade of the barn. She handed the controls back to Andromeda. "Nice cart."

Andromeda smirked. "You aren't what I expected, Miss Elliot," and left Elliot to parse those words as she joined her brother on the grass.

Much to Elliot's chagrin, they decided to wait until Kai and the Groves had caught up to leave her alone in the barn. Tatiana took Elliot by the elbow and led her out of earshot. "Do you think . . . Were they insinuating that Captain Wentforth might have . . . designs on Olivia Grove?"

"They met less than an hour ago," Elliot replied firmly. It was the only true thing she could bring herself to say.

"Horatio would never allow it," Tatiana stated. "*Should* never allow it. A Post? It would do irreparable damage to their family's reputation."

"And if they did get together, it would do incomparable good for the estate's finances," Elliot couldn't help but point out. "I gather that all these Cloud Fleet Posts are extremely wealthy. Probably far more wealthy than the Groves." It would also do good to remind Tatiana that whatever fear she had for loss of reputation due to Post influence, the *Norths* had been the ones to accept their money—not the Groves.

"You don't think they'd *marry*!" Tatiana exclaimed in horror. "But they're Po—" And then she must have remembered what Mrs. Innovation had told her yesterday—that free Posts did marry. Nevertheless, the word seemed to curdle Elliot's blood, even if it was for a different reason than the one that so disturbed her sister. "Well," Tatiana continued, shaking road dust from her pale blue skirt. "She's only fourteen."

Elliot knew too well how little that meant.

The girl in question bumped and jostled her way up to the barn, cutting it quite close to the other machines. Horatio, in the backseat of the cart, was barely holding on to the rails and his breakfast, in that order. Kai's expression was one she knew well—carefully veiled frustration. Perhaps he wasn't as enamored of Olivia as everyone seemed to assume. And yet a moment later she watched him laugh and put his hands around Olivia's waist as he helped her down from the cart, and Elliot averted her eyes. He'd grown so much more graceful in the past four years. He moved now rather like one of the machines he used to fix—every motion swift, precise, and perfect.

Perfect. What words she was tossing around! She was pathetic.

As always upon entering the building, her gaze instinctively shot to the knothole, and then she ducked her head in embarrassment. Kai wasn't looking, but she wondered if he might have caught her doing so.

If he had, he gave no indication. Perhaps he'd forgotten their ritual entirely, or perhaps he preferred to triumph in secret over the fact that she hadn't. Elliot couldn't decide which option she preferred, for they both burned inside her.

Dee had already removed the dairy equipment, but Kai still found fault with the arrangement of the stalls, in the few bits of machinery still fastened to the walls, even in the stench. Tatiana's nose wrinkled as she gingerly picked her way across the hay-strewn floor.

"Yes, it stinks in here," Kai said. "Too bad for Innovation's horses—I mean, Baron North's horses. Can you imagine having to spend any length of time in here, especially in the summer?"

Tatiana shuddered. Elliot wished to sink through the earth. Had it really been so wretched? And if so, why had the thirteen-year-old Kai begged her to let him stay in the barn rather than go to live in the Reduced children's barracks or Mags and Gill's cottage? Had it only been the lesser of two evils?

"Elliot practically lives here," Tatiana said. "I don't understand it, personally."

Now Elliot wished her sister would sink through the floor alongside her. Kai was not looking at her, but what else could he be thinking of except that locked room above?

Olivia was busy recounting, in breathless detail, their adventures on the sun-cart. Andromeda and Donovan were listening, their wry expressions so similar that it left no doubt of their relation. Elliot watched them with a mixture of awe and jealousy. She had never once seen Tatiana's face mirror her own. What would it have been like to grow up with a sibling she liked? What if Tatiana had been a girl she could trust, could count on, could have turned to when their mother died and things got so confusing?

"Our ride with Elliot was much smoother," Donovan said at last.

"I don't doubt it!" Olivia's eyes were shining, her face flushed. "She has far more experience driving than I do. She can even drive this tractor." She kicked at the tires of the rusted-out bulk. Its chipped paint and curling metal edges looked all the more pathetic after the time they'd spent in the gleaming, lithe sun-carts. "Well, when it's working, that is."

"It doesn't work?" Every syllable of Kai's words buffeted her like swings from an ax.

"Rarely," Tatiana sniffed. "We haven't had a decent mechanic around in years."

Elliot nearly groaned at this. How could her sister be so blind?

"Let me take a look at it," Kai said, and heedless of his fine coat, he crawled beneath the axle, as he'd done countless times before. "This is a mess," he called from the shadow of the machine. A moment later he was out again, brushing the dust off his coat. "Who has been working on this?"

The Luddites looked at Elliot, who refused to confirm the answer only Elliot was aware Kai already knew. Why wouldn't they just go away and leave her alone?

"Can you fix it?" Olivia asked.

"Yes," he said, and Elliot was glad for once that he wouldn't meet her eyes. "But what good will that do? It'll fall to pieces again once I'm gone, with no one here who knows the first thing about upkeep."

Elliot balled her hands up inside the pockets of her skirt.

"They should really have a dedicated mechanic around here," Kai added.

Horatio kept glancing at her, but Elliot refused to speak. What could she possibly say to *Kai* on the subject that wouldn't sound ludicrous?

"The Norths have had some recent difficulty with staff," Horatio said at last, clearly trying to be careful. Elliot narrowly resisted tackling him to the ground to make him shut up. "They have lost several of their Posts in the past few years."

"Really?" Andromeda asked, in a tone that bore no real curiosity.

Tatiana gave a haughty shrug. "I can't imagine what is so attractive to them about the enclaves."

"I imagine, Miss North, that it's the opportunities for advancement they would not have here on your estate," Felicia said. "It's why I left my estate twenty years ago."

But Tatiana was never one to take a hint. "You are a special case, Mrs. Innovation. Surely you can't deny that the vast majority of these wandering Posts do not achieve the success that you and your husband enjoy."

"That is true," said Felicia. "But it does not change my mind."

Tatiana's eyes widened. "Really? But I have heard such terrible things. Too many Posts who leave the safety of their estates wind up as beggars, or worse. I for one would not be willing to take such a risk, were I in their shoes."

"How fortunate for you, then," said Andromeda in an icy tone, "that you were born a Luddite."

"Yes," said Tatiana, clueless. "I think so, too. I pity the Posts who have left this place."

For the merest flicker of an instant, Kai looked at Elliot, as if daring her to speak. The ax fell again, and this time it reached her heart.

Eight Years Ago

Dear Kai,

Happy tenth birthday! Like always, I'm going to save you some of my cake. What are you doing this afternoon? My parents are throwing a party, as usual, but there is some time after lunch and before the party. I thought we could take the cake and go get Ro and have a picnic down near the creek. Did you finish Ro's present? I know she's going to like it.

Your friend,

Elliot

Dear Elliot,

Happy birthday to you too! I like cake and picnics. I'm supposed to help my da this afternoon, though, so take Ro down to the creek and I'll meet you there.

Your friend,

Kai

Dear Kai,

I know this isn't one of our usual gliders, but father bought me this stationery specially for all my thank-you cards. Most people bought me dresses. My mother laughed, knowing how rarely I wear them. My father did not find it so funny.

Onto the thank-you card business. Thank you so much for thinking of me on my birthday. Your thoughtfulness is much appreciated. I love the wind-up kitty. I had no idea you were making me a toy also! You are really sneaky.
Your friend,
Elliot

Dear Elliot,
I had to. After you told me the Baron wouldn't let you have a real cat in the house, I knew exactly what you'd like.

I don't have fancy stationery, but thank you so much for the books. Your thoughtfulness is much appreciated too. I can't believe that these are mine to keep, that I don't ever have to give them back. I promise to keep them hidden, like you said, though.

My favorite so far is the one about the stars. Like I always knew about Alpha Centauri, because it was a Pointer, but I never knew it was part of a constellation that made a centaur. I guess I should have, given the name. I went and found it last night, but I don't think it looks much like a centaur.

Isn't it strange that we know about stars that we can't even see anymore? There are so many stars in the books that no one on the islands has ever seen. One day, maybe I can build a real glider and you and I can go see the rest of the stars, and the rest of the world, too.

Your friend,

Kai

ᕆᕐᐁᒍ

Dear Kai,

That sounds like fun. I have always wanted to see Ursa Major, for example. I wonder if it really looks like a bear. From the outlines in the star book, I think not, since Ursa apparently has a long tail, and bears are supposed to have short tails, I think. I have only ever seen bears in books, though, so how do you know?

Save room for me on that glider, and some day we'll go see the stars.

Your friend,

Elliot

Eleven

AS THE WEEKS PASSED and the Fleet settled into the Boatwright estate and their shipbuilding project, Elliot was relieved that there were few repeats of those first days. Tatiana seemed to have little desire to socialize with the Posts, though it left her pretty much alone, as from all reports the Groves were taking every opportunity to spend time with the Fleet.

Elliot busied herself with the harvest. It was sparse this year, thanks to her father's eleventh-hour meddling with her wheat fields, but with the influx of money from renting out the Boatwright estate, they'd make it through another winter, and even have a bit of a surplus. In her spare time, she tried to devise a way to repeat her experiment in a safer way. Perhaps next year she'd bury a plot of enhanced wheat in the center of a conventional field, surrounding it with stalks that wouldn't raise her father's suspicions at a glance. Maybe she'd mix her grain in with the normal seeds in order to hide it from everyone.

Maybe she'd give up on the idea altogether and be the

good little Luddite she was raised to be. After all, for all she'd tried to justify her actions, she knew they were illegal. She shouldn't have experimented on the wheat. This was where the evil began. What was the harm, the Lost used to say, in creating a wheat strain with a shorter growing time, one that would produce more grain per stalk? From there, things became slippery. What was the harm in devising a plant with such a complete array of nutrients that it would render growing anything else for food pointless? What about a plant that could subtly poison the ground so as to make it only capable of providing sustenance for that kind of plant? What about extrapolating all of that beyond the world of plants—to animals? To people?

Her ancestors twirled in their graves.

And as she wrestled with whether she would try it again, she avoided the barn and the lab she'd set up in Kai's old room. It was too hard to go in there now. The instinct she had to always look first at the knothole in the door was a constant reminder of his casual cruelty. His letters themselves were something worse. The words he'd spoken to her that first night, the ones he'd shared with Olivia in the star cavern, and the ones he'd said in front of everyone at the barn had left a tender place inside of her, a rotten spot that would burst if pressed. She'd prefer not to see him, and not to spend time in the room that had once meant so much to them both.

Elliot had kept herself so busy that she'd almost forgotten Felicia Innovation's offer to look at her grandfather and give her expert opinion. So when she saw the Post woman walking up to the house a few weeks after the Fleet's arrival, she was taken aback.

She met Felicia at the door. "Have you come to see my sister?" Elliot asked. "I'm afraid she's gone to the Groves' for dinner today." It was the first invitation she'd had from Olivia in quite some time.

"That's all right," the older woman said. "Your sister has invited me here to examine Chancellor Boatwright. Didn't she tell you? Apparently she wrote the baron and he consented."

Elliot shook her head. Why her grandfather needed the consent of Baron North to seek medical treatment was beyond her. "Better not mention that to the Boatwright," she said. "He's a little short-tempered when it comes to my father."

"That is often the case with fathers and sons-in-law, I think," said Felicia. "I'll follow your lead."

Elliot Boatwright was sleeping when they arrived in his chambers upstairs. He spent most of his time sleeping now, and when Elliot reported this fact to Felicia, the Post woman's mouth drew into a thin line.

"What does it mean?" Elliot asked.

"It means he's old, Elliot." But Elliot knew that wasn't all.

Once the Boatwright was awakened and had the chance to freshen up, Elliot introduced him to Felicia Innovation.

"It's quite an honor to meet you, sir. You once made excellent ships. Several of the boats my husband uses in his Fleet were originally built in your shipyard. You are spoken of everywhere as a great and gracious man."

The Boatwright nodded his thanks and grunted a few syllables in response. He shifted half toward Elliot, and the good side of his face was a mask of frustration. He made a quick gesture, but before Elliot had the chance to react, Felicia held up her hands.

"I know the Reduced signs, sir. I am a Post, remember? And though I'll understand if you don't wish to make them in front of me, I want you to understand that I see no shame in them, just as there is no shame in being carried in a litter if you cannot walk on your own feet."

The Boatwright's expression softened, and he directed his next gestures at Felicia. *You. Pain. Fix.*

"Yes, I am a healer."

The Boatwright began to make another sign, then sighed and shot a look at Elliot.

Felicia turned to her. "Perhaps, dear, you'd like to wait in the hall? I think it would be easier for your grandfather to speak to me without you present."

Elliot did as she was told. When Felicia emerged, several minutes later, Elliot jumped out of her seat and turned to her in anticipation. "Well?"

She smiled. "That man is very proud of you."

Elliot shook her head. "You can't get that from Reduced signs."

"You're right about that." The woman's salt-and-pepper curls were escaping from their braid and frizzing in a halo around her head. Her freckled face bore an expression of almost motherly concern. Elliot recoiled by instinct, and Felicia definitely noticed. She withdrew the arm she'd already been reaching in the girl's direction. "But he says you have his daughter's heart. I extrapolated."

"You were here to see about his health." Elliot didn't need this woman's pity.

"It's very bad, Elliot, but this is no surprise to you. He sleeps, I think, because he has strokes all day long, every day. Thousands of tiny strokes that snap the neurons in his head. He's dying."

Elliot nodded miserably.

"There are medicines we can give him that will ease his pain, stop the palsy, and maybe even slow the progression of his descent, but you cannot fix it. Not with the means we have at our disposal."

The rest was clear. The protocols were killing her grandfather, just as they were strangling the life out of this estate. No wonder the Lost had been so tempted! No wonder Elliot had been.

"Come. Don't be sad. Your grandfather is an old man, and he has lived a great life. If you are alone this evening, then you should come back to the Boatwright house with me."

"No, thank you," said Elliot, though she kept her tone mild. She had no desire to go to the Boatwright house. Not with Kai there. Yet she knew Felicia was only trying to be kind. The Boatwright's illness was not her fault, and as Felicia had said, Elliot's grandfather had lived a long life, unlike Felicia's own daughter.

"Then how about a tour?" Felicia asked. "Your sister showed me the house and the star cavern. Why don't you

show me the fields? We can take the Innovation horses. I've
missed riding, since we brought no horses of our own."

"I'm a poor rider."

"We'll go slow." Felicia was determined, and Elliot had
run out of excuses.

Twelve

ELLIOT SWAYED UNEASILY IN the saddle. This was not like Tatiana's pony, on which she'd learned to ride, nor like the chestnut mare her father had bought her sister after their mother had passed. Mounting the Innovation horse, even though it was a mare, felt more like climbing on the back of an elephant.

She understood now why the Innovation horses had made their masters such an enormous fortune. The Innovations had a monopoly on them; they only sold geldings and mares, and thus far, the attempts to breed the mares with normal horses had not yielded out-of-the-ordinary results.

Elliot's mare was named Pyrois, while Felicia rode on the back of the other mare, Aeos. "The horses of the sun," she said as they rode out past the fence that encircled the barn.

"Indeed," Felicia replied. "Unless your father sees fit to rename them."

Elliot laughed. "My father is not the most inventive

man, even when it comes to names. Tatiana was the name of my mother's mother, and Elliot my mother's father."

"Did you ever find it strange," said Felicia, "that they gave you the name of a son?"

"My mother knew she'd never have one," Elliot said. She led them into a fallow field to cut across to the woods. "There were . . . complications during my birth." But they were edging perilously close to ground Elliot feared to tread. She didn't want to talk to this woman, this healer, about how Elliot's mother had survived the day of Elliot's birth when Kai's and Ro's mothers had not.

"Did you name these horses?" she asked quickly. "I have long been a fan of Greek mythology."

"I did. I am fond of it as well." Felicia coaxed Aeos into a trot, then leaped over the split rail that bordered the field. Elliot gritted her teeth and followed, amazed that such a tall horse even needed to jump the barrier.

"I chose Andromeda's name, too," she added when Elliot caught up. "Do you think it suits her?"

"No," Elliot admitted. "The mythological Andromeda was a damsel in distress. Chained to a rock, forced to wait for Perseus to save her. But Andromeda Phoenix seems very little like that."

Felicia gave her a look as unreadable as any of Andromeda's. "I think she'd like to hear that from you."

Elliot was quite sure not. She'd gathered that Andromeda, perhaps alone among the Cloud Fleet, knew exactly what she had once been to Kai. "Perhaps she can say it's for the sky Andromeda, the galaxy you can see with the naked eye. I have read about it in the books, though I know you can't see it here. It's supposed to be very beautiful. Since Andromeda Phoenix is an explorer, it's a good name for her."

"You should definitely tell her that. We tried a few others, but nothing stuck, and this is closest to her old name, Ann. She's still adjusting to it, and to life as a free Post."

"I thought she ran away from her estate as a child," Elliot said.

"She did." Felicia looked out over the fields. "Not all Posts who run away from their estates wind up free."

Elliot led the way to a path that cut through the woods, but her mind whirled with questions. Where had Andromeda gone, if it was not to an enclave to be free? How had she found her way into the Fleet? How long had Kai been a member of the Fleet and how had he met the Innovations? But she knew those questions would just raise other ones in Felicia's mind, so she stuck to something simpler.

"Why do the free Posts change their names?"

"Why should we keep the names that mark us as secondary citizens?" Felicia asked. "I was born on a Luddite estate and given the name Lee. I was told who and what I was allowed to become. We give the Reduced one-syllable names because they can't handle anything more. But I am not Reduced. When I left that life, I left those limitations as well. I chose my own name." Felicia smiled at her. "If you were a Post, you would want that choice, too."

Elliot pretended to rearrange her grip on the reins, letting loose strands of hair fall into her face to cover her thoughts.

They broke through the other side of the woods, scattering fallen leaves in their wake. They'd reached the lower fields now, and the baron's racetrack. The shoddy state of many of the fences delineating the fields, as well as the unkempt gardens and crumbling, vacant Post cottages, seemed even more noticeable beside the neat lines of the racetrack and the shiny pavilion. Elliot could only imagine what Felicia thought.

"When your father is gone, will Tatiana be the new Baroness North?"

"No. My cousin will inherit. His father was my father's older brother. By some arguments, the land should be his now, since he's of age, but he left when he was very young."

Actually, he had been banished, but there was no need to air all the family's dirty laundry. Elliot spent a few minutes pointing out the sights and the boundary of the estate, then started up the road that led to the Boatwright estate and the sea. The path before them grew rocky, and Elliot slowed their pace as the horse whinnied and picked its way up the steep slope.

Pyrois's hooves slipped sideways on a patch of scree, and Elliot bit back a shriek as the horse raced to right herself. The mare took off, clambering up the hillside while Elliot clung to her neck for dear life. When they reached level ground, the horse stopped, snorting and tossing her head.

Felicia cantered up and reached out to soothe the animal. "There, there, Pyrois." She stroked Pyrois's ears and neck, and the horse leaned into the woman's touch, calming instantly and making Elliot even more embarrassed.

Elliot struggled to catch her breath. "I told you I wasn't good at riding."

"So, Tatiana is the horsewoman in the family," Felicia said with a smile clearly meant to put Elliot at ease.

Elliot forced a laugh. "Yes. She takes after my father. I take after my mother—I like plants more."

"With your name, I wonder you aren't a Boatwright like your grandfather."

"I might have been had my grandfather been able to keep the yard open long enough for me to learn. He became ill when I was still very young. My mechanical skills are— rudimentary at best."

They'd been taught to her by a boy who now delighted in detailing exactly how poor they were.

"Maybe we should return you to the shipyard now," Elliot said. "I'd love to see your work. After all, I've shown you mine."

Except she hadn't. Not really. Elliot wondered what the Post would think of her wheat—her desperate rebellion, her miniature heresy. Would she be appalled? Would she be proud?

And why did Elliot care so much what she thought?

"I am glad to see the shipyard in operation again," she added. "Especially for so worthwhile a project." And she'd been dying to get a glimpse at the Fleet's work. She'd only resisted because Kai had made it clear that, to him at least, she wasn't welcome.

"I'm glad you approve," said Felicia. "There are those

Luddites who have no desire to reestablish contact with the rest of the world."

"I have always wondered what else was out there." She and Kai had spent years fantasizing about it.

They rode along the cliff that bordered the sea, and as a salty wind wound its way through her hair and swept across her face, Elliot began to breathe easier. Off to the west, the shallows glittered golden in the sunlight and gave way to a darker blue in the deeps.

The shipyard was situated at the northernmost bay of the island. Beyond it, the land rose steadily upward like the prow of a boat jutting into the sea. No buildings graced this high plain, and it wasn't used for crops or pastures. Before the Reduction, the area had been reserved and off limits for development, and though the rest of the world had changed, this hadn't. Back when the Boatwright estate had been fully functional, they didn't need the land for their own food, and they derived all their extra income from shipbuilding. And now Elliot simply didn't have enough resources to devote to working this steep piece of land. It remained lonely and wild, and beautiful—a testament to a history that even the Reduction could not obliterate. It had been through this portal that Elliot's Boatwright ancestors had first come to these islands.

Whenever things got particularly bad on the estate, Elliot escaped to the cliffs to stand on the very edge, to stretch out her hands and feel the wind pulling at her, threatening to carry her away like she was nothing more than one of Kai's gliders.

Today, however, she was weighed down, by her own thoughts as much as by the giant horse she rode. As they steered their mounts toward the narrow path that cut through the cliff to the shipyard, Elliot gave one last, longing look at the promontory, at its rocky sides and the towers of broken rock that stood beyond. At the water that circled around it, turquoise on the side of the sea, blue on the side of the ocean. They were too low to see now where the waters mixed, where the constant upswell of warm and cool sent swirling, ghostlike ribbons of sediment up from the depths and as far as the eye could see. When she was young, her mother had told her stories of the old days, when the bridges to the rock towers remained intact and the Boatwright family had revered the cliffs and promontory as a sacred spot, the way that the Norths honored their ancestors through the underground sanctuary. But though the Norths never thought back farther than the Reduction, the Boatwright line was older, and they chose to remember that part of their heritage, too.

She hadn't been to the promontory in months. All summer, she'd been too busy with her experiment and trying to find a way to feed the estate. Then she'd been occupied with preparing for the Cloud Fleet's arrival and the harvest. And now, since they'd come—she'd avoided her grandfather's lands.

"Are you all right?" Felicia asked, as the horses picked their way down the narrow slice between the cliffs. "Should we have taken the supply route instead of the footpath?"

"I'm fine," Elliot replied through gritted teeth. She

should be a better horsewoman than this. Her father would find her an embarrassment. Felicia Innovation no doubt thought her pathetic.

"I hope I didn't make you uncomfortable back there," Felicia said. "I have spent so much of my life caring for young people like you. It's become a bit of a habit."

Even when the young person in question is a Luddite, and not a homeless runaway Post. Elliot could finish that thought on her own.

"I would like us to be friends, if possible, Elliot," Felicia said now, as the path ended on the shipyard beach. She stopped her horse and waited for Elliot to draw up beside her. "The Groves come to our house often for visits, but I've never seen you. I understand it might be difficult, to see a bunch of strangers have the run of your grandfather's house—"

"No," Elliot said. "That's not difficult. I'm glad to see it filled with people again. I think he would be, too." She'd been avoiding the Boatwright house because of Kai. But maybe it was time to stop. However much it hurt to be near him now, a stronger impulse prevailed.

Elliot wanted to hear Felicia's thoughts on treatments for her grandfather. She wanted to know where the admiral planned to take this wonderful new ship of his. She wanted to hear more about life in the Post enclave. She wanted to know what Donovan and Andromeda and even Kai had seen on their travels. It had been weeks since he'd walked back into her life. She should be over the worst of the pain by now. And if avoidance wasn't helping, then it was time to try a different method, before the Cloud Fleet finished their mission here and left, with Elliot none the wiser about their lives and their knowledge.

She still loved the man who called himself Malakai Wentforth. She knew that. But that didn't matter, just as it hadn't mattered four years ago. Then, she'd chosen to stay behind. But it didn't mean she wasn't curious. It didn't mean she didn't want to stand at the edge of the cliffs and stretch her face out toward the sea, toward a world she'd never be allowed to know.

Four Years Ago

Dear Kai,

Come back. Come back for me. I didn't mean it. I've changed my mind. I can't bear this, Kai. I can't bear this farm, this life, this world without you.

You've only been gone a month, but it feels like a year. Tatiana lives to torture me. She brings up the Posts' exodus from the Luddite estates at every possible juncture. And Ro misses you, too. She gives me a sad look whenever I go to see her, and I am alone. She doesn't understand where you've gone. I think she's afraid you have died.

I am afraid you have died. I hate not knowing where you are. If you're safe, if you're hungry, if you're alone, if you're afraid. I don't know what risks you'll take, or who you'll meet. I don't know if they'll love you as I do. If they'll protect you as I've failed to do. Tatiana revels in sharing with me horrible stories about what happens in the Post enclaves. I am sure they cannot all be as wicked as she says—after all, most of the runaway Posts just want better lives for themselves. But I spend my nights lying awake in my bed, praying that you do not let yourself be harmed.

I also pray that you still care for me. That one day you will understand why I made the choice I did. That one day, I will understand it better, too, for right now, I just hate myself for it. I know it's right, but I didn't know how hard it would be.

I wish there was a way to send you this letter, but I'm also glad there isn't. Because then I would be weak enough to go through with what I've written above, to follow you wherever you've gone, and if I did, what would happen to the North estate and all the people who depend upon it for survival? So instead, I just turn this letter into another little glider to add to my collection.

I miss you. May God keep and protect you, wherever you are in this world.

Yours,

Elliot

Thirteen

THE WAREHOUSE OF THE shipyard was closed up tight, and Elliot wondered how the builders had enough light to work by. And yet, she could hear the sounds of industry as she approached—strange whirrings and high-pitched whines and the clank of metal upon metal. The horses trotted up the beach, and Felicia waved to a knot of figures standing outside the building. Elliot shaded her eyes from the sun and tried to identify them. The admiral, Donovan, and Kai.

As they grew closer, she could see even more. They held long sticks in their hands and were scratching figures into the sand as they spoke. She watched as Donovan spun away from the group and began pantomiming whatever point he was trying to make by marching out the space on the sand. Kai threw back his head and laughed, then delineated his own version. They seemed to be arguing some element of design. Elliot marveled as she observed the same quick, precise movements she was beginning to realize all the Fleet captains shared. She supposed it was the result of their training, or the months they spent steering their ships. Perhaps they got used to perfect control, like the movements of a musician or a surgeon. Beside them, though, the old admiral seemed almost clumsy.

Elliot and Felicia were almost upon them, when from within the warehouse there was a deafening crash. The walls of the building shook and the ground shuddered beneath them. The horses reared and Elliot clung tight to Pyrois's neck, hoping to keep her seat. The horse bucked beneath her, and for a moment all was topsy-turvy and the air was rent with horsey screams. Elliot squeezed her eyes shut as her grip gave way, and she braced herself for the fall.

But it never came. She felt her hand sweep the sand, heard hooves hit the ground close to her head, and then two arms clamped around her waist and she was placed on her feet.

"You're all right." Kai's voice in her ear, very close.

He'd touched her. *He'd touched her.* Her skin buzzed like a wire, and her chest and face grew warm. She brushed her hair from her eyes, but he'd already let go, snapping away with that same unnerving precision, marking the space between them as if with a ruler. She took an unsteady step toward him, and his hand shot out again to bolster her by the elbow, and to halt her approach.

"Careful."

She blinked, willing herself not to reach for him like roots after water.

Beyond, the admiral had caught hold of Pyrois's reins and was soothing him, while Donovan was even now rushing into the building halfway across the beach. Everything must have happened in a second or two. But how? Surely Kai had been too far away to catch her in midair. He was always fast, but still . . .

Felicia remained on her horse, and watched Elliot and Kai with a concerned look on her face.

"Can you stand on your own?" Kai asked her now.

She nodded and he instantly left her side and headed into the shipyard warehouse. The admiral had somehow already tied up Pyrois and gone into the building. Felicia dismounted, led her horse over to the hitching post, and gestured to Elliot to join her on the bench.

"Please sit, Elliot. That was a nasty fall."

No, but it would have been had Kai not been there to catch her. How had he reached her in time? Had he been watching her much more closely than he'd let on?

"What happened inside?" she asked instead. "Is anyone hurt?"

As if on cue, Kai appeared at the doorway. "One of the hulls broke free from its suspension," he announced. "No one was injured, but we've lost several days' work."

Felicia shook her head. "What a shame."

"All things considered, the admiral thinks it best if we cancel our plans for the evening. We'll probably work through the night."

Through the night? "You must have a hundred sun-lamps!" Elliot exclaimed. Otherwise how in the world would they be able to work in that dark warehouse?

Neither Post replied at first. "Yes," said Felicia at last.

"And speaking of, I'll send someone to fetch a sun-cart to take Miss Elliot home. I doubt she wants to try the horses again so soon, especially if she's to lead the extra."

Elliot folded her hands in her lap as Felicia entered the building. She figured Kai would follow, but he remained still, standing over her like a guard. His shadow fell across her lap, and she traced its edges with her hands. The places he'd touched her—her torso, her chest, her elbow—still tingled. His words still echoed in her ears. He hadn't spoken to her directly since that night in the barn. She soaked up every syllable like it was rain on parched soil.

You're all right.

Careful.

Can you stand on your own?

They were as clear to her in her mind as the words he spoke now. "Are you recovered?"

She looked up, but his face remained turned toward the sea. "I'm better, thank you."

"If you are, then it's best you try walking home, rather than wasting someone from the Fleet's time by making them chauffeur you back."

These words broke something inside her. Perhaps it was his touch, perhaps it was the fact that they were alone again, perhaps it was the way Felicia Innovation had spoken to her, like she at least wanted to be friends, or maybe it was the weeks she'd wasted hiding from these Posts because she was afraid of this very moment. But whatever it was, Elliot could not prevent the burst of laughter that escaped her lips.

Kai whirled around and his face was shadowed by the

angle of the sun. Still, she knew his tone. Anger. "What's so funny? That our project has been set back several days? That we're stuck here longer? That you take a little spill from a horse and everyone wants to rearrange the world so you don't suffer a moment of inconvenience?"

"No," she said, and her voice was even. "That I would wait a month in agony just to hear you insult me. I'm a miserable girl indeed, don't you think?"

He glared at her in stony silence, which only spurred her on. No more of this waiting and worrying. She might not deserve much from Kai, despite all the time she'd spent loving him, but she deserved this.

"I have gathered that you don't want to reveal your origins to the Groves, or even to most of your friends, and that's your choice, but I have a question for you. Andromeda knows, doesn't she? She knows what happened?"

He said nothing.

"Please. I will tell you, and you will tell me, and then we can just go on ignoring each other afterward. Tatiana doesn't know who you are, which is ridiculous to me. She's as stupid as she's ever been. I wanted to die, that day in the barn. Our Posts, of course, talk of nothing else, but they have no occasion to tell your friends if you don't want it known on the Boatwright estate. They haven't even bothered correcting my sister, not that she talks to many Posts outside the house servants like Mags and her maid. And Ro . . ." Here Elliot faltered, but only for a moment. "Every time I see Ro, she wonders why we haven't come together."

She thought she saw him flinch, but it was hard to tell

in the light. She knew he visited Ro on his own. Did he get the same impression?

"Just tell me, so I can stop wondering if Andromeda's contempt is for all Luddites, or for me alone."

Kai was quiet, then said, "If you can stand on your own, it's better that you walk back rather than making someone from the Fleet take you."

Elliot rose, then swallowed the bile she tasted in her throat. "I have stood on my own for many years."

He didn't look away this time, and his eyes were like a stranger's. "You're not the only one."

PART II
Icarus Also Flew

*Anne did not wish for more
of such looks and speeches.
His cold politeness,
his ceremonious grace,
were worse than anything.*
—JANE AUSTEN, *PERSUASION*

ONE YEAR AGO

Dear Kai,

I wish I knew where to send this letter. I wish I knew where you were, or how you're doing. I am glad now that you're gone, that you didn't have to live through these past two years with me, that I didn't have to worry about you alongside everyone else.

So many of the Posts are gone now—gone who knows where. If they meet you, I hope they will write and tell me, but I don't expect it. After all, you have never written me. After leaving this place, I doubt many will have the slightest interest in sending back word, and most especially not to me.

I have failed them, Kai. I have failed them all. I cannot step into my mother's shoes. I cannot keep the farm running. I can't stop thinking of those first weeks after Mal died and we were trying to convince everyone you could follow in his footsteps as mechanic. I remember the all-nighters we pulled trying to keep all the machines in working order. Of course, that time we had each other.

Now I don't feel like I have anyone.

And that's why I'm sitting here, writing letters to nobody. You'll never see these words, but I can't keep this to myself anymore. You are the person I've always told these things to.

You've been gone for three years, and you're still the only one I can trust. I sit in this room, surrounded by your letters and by even bigger secrets than those . . .

I made something, Kai. Something new.

The other Luddites would kill me if they knew. My father wouldn't be able to protect me, but I doubt he'd want to. He believes in the protocols. Why don't I feel terrified tonight? I've been terrified for so long—of how I was going to make it through the bad times, of how I was going to keep the farm going now that so many of the Posts have left, if I had any way to control what happened to me and those I love—to this place I love, despite everything.

I've been terrified for a year that I wouldn't succeed. And now that I have . . . I'm not scared anymore. At least not tonight. I'm not scared that people will discover what I've done, because I know I did it for the right reasons. I'm not scared that we'll all starve next winter, because I hold in my hands the instrument of our salvation.

And most of all, I'm no longer scared that I made the wrong choice three years ago. Whatever it meant for us, I know that I was meant to stay here. For them. For this wheat. For the future.

Even if I never see you again, I remain,

Yours,

Elliot

Fourteen

As THE AUTUMN DREW to a close, bringing with it swifter sunsets and frigid days, Elliot was glad her duties kept her far, far away from the shipyard and Kai. He'd made his position clear at their last meeting. She saw no reason to try to speak to him again. But there was plenty of work to be done, especially since her father still hadn't returned from visiting his Luddite friends down south. She had to prepare the Reduced barracks and the Post cottages for winter, she had to throw a harvest feast for all the laborers on the estate, and she had to make all arrangements for the food they'd be importing to tide them over to spring. Elliot found that sometimes a whole afternoon would pass without her thinking of Kai—much as it had been before he'd returned.

But she dreaded the coming dark months. For the past two years, she'd spent the depth of winter reading or working on her experiments. Now that her experiment had succeeded, she wasn't sure what she'd have to occupy her time, other than thoughts of the boy staying on her grandfather's estate and internal debates about whether she should risk replanting the wheat she'd worked so hard to develop.

Late in the season there was a break in the weather, a mild spell, like autumn's last gasp of warmth before winter took charge. And in the midst of the mild days and nights, an invitation arrived on the North estate to a party. Both of the Miss Norths were invited, but when Tatiana heard that every Post on the North estate was invited as well, she declined. At that point, Elliot thought she had better go, lest the Innovations think her absence was due to the same reason.

"They say he may marry Olivia Grove," Dee told her as they walked through the woods on the way to the Boatwright house on the night of the party. They brought Jef and Ro with them, though the young Post boy was growing frustrated with Ro's regular detours off the path in search of remaining fall leaves. He'd complained twice to his mother, who'd just shrugged and smiled. He'd learn patience with the Reduced. He'd have to, to work on the estate.

"I believe you'll find that rumor originates with Tatiana's housemaids." Elliot's sister had grown obsessed with the notion, probably because of how much it terrified her. Elliot would allow no other possibility, not even as she noticed how Tatiana had begun incorporating stronger colors into her wardrobe and had even added a braided gold fringe to her fall jacket. That a Post would marry had been Tatiana's first shock; naturally it would give way to the fear that a Post would marry into a Luddite family.

"Oh, no," Dee said. "It's all the talk among the Posts at the Grove estate." Dee pulled her shawl tighter around her shoulders. She grew larger by the day, and Elliot wondered how long it would be before she was unable to perform her duties. Her father would surely force Dee to be confined in the birthing house then. "Apparently he and the other two Cloud Fleet captains are over there constantly. They say Miss Grove is in love with him."

"Since when does being in love with someone mean you get to marry them?" Elliot asked. "Olivia Grove is fourteen years old. She's not marrying anyone."

"You only say that because you're a Luddite," Dee replied. "I was fourteen when I met Thom, and we had Jef a year later. Things work differently for Posts."

Elliot brushed her fingers over the back of her hand, remembering being fourteen. Not so differently. Of course, things hadn't worked out so well. "What makes you think that a rich free Post could love a Luddite?"

Dee gave her a look. "I have heard of a poor bonded Post doing so."

"That's different. The poor Post"—this hypothetical poor Post who might have once, long ago, loved some hypothetical Luddite—"would have something to gain."

"I don't believe it," Dee insisted. "And there's something to gain even for free Posts. They'd bring money to the estates in return for a raise in stature and Luddite rights for their children. But with . . . him—" Dee had the same problem calling Kai by his new name as Elliot did. The words Malakai Wentforth felt wrong in her mouth, though it was probably because she couldn't connect the boy she knew to the person who now preferred that name.

"With him, he would have nothing to gain by returning here," Elliot finished. "And no interest in an estate."

Ro paused again on the trail. "Kai?" she asked hopefully.

"He's meeting us there," Elliot replied, wishing it were true. But it made Ro smile. She adjusted her scarf and took off, half skipping and half running. Dee gestured to Jef to keep an eye on her, and he groaned and ran to catch up.

Elliot was pleased to see that the Reduced had already switched to their winter clothes. A few years back, when they'd lost so many Posts, no one had been assigned to the duty, and as temperatures dropped, many of the laborers had fallen ill. One even lost a foot to frostbite after it was discovered she'd been wandering around all winter in her summer sandals. Elliot made sure it had never happened again.

She'd learned a lot in four years. The mistakes she'd made at fifteen that had led to the bad time would not be repeated. The mistake she'd made this summer of not doing a better job hiding the wheat—that would never happen again either. Four years ago, she'd never have been able to cajole her father into renting out the Boatwright estate to the Fleet. Things would get better.

They had to—otherwise, what had her sacrifice been worth?

Elliot was tired of hiding from Kai, of turning down invitations to the Boatwright house for fear of seeing him. Tonight's party would be large enough that she doubted they would be forced to cross paths. Elliot would stick close to Dee and the other North Posts, and leave Kai to spend time with the Fleet . . . or the Groves.

As they arrived, Elliot saw that the space above the lawn of the Boatwright house had been strung with paper lanterns, though the light burning inside was too white and steady for candle flame. Sun-lamps, then. How many did they have, if they were able to work by night in the shipyard and still have dozens to string up on the lawn? More lights bedecked the porch, and there were blankets and colorful cushions strewn about the lawn for seating. The arrangement brightened up the browning winter landscape and made even Elliot's careful decorations for the North estate's harvest feast look dim and old-fashioned. What were a few candelabras and some jugs of fall leaves to compare to a patchwork of blankets in Post-bright colors and brilliant, sun-lamp–bedecked ribbons crisscrossed against the sky?

The Groves' wagon was parked at the perimeter, and Elliot wondered if Tatiana would regret not coming along. Her sister had said that she'd already attended the harvest festival for the North laborers, and that she'd had quite enough for one season of picnics and peasant food.

"You go if you wish," she'd told Elliot. "I'll attend the next time the Innovations choose to throw a dinner party or something more civilized."

So much the better. She doubted the North Posts would be able to relax much if their mistress was present. And every North Post, from the housekeeper Mags to the youngest children, had turned out for the party. There were also more than a dozen Grove Posts milling about the cider kegs they'd brought in carts at the corners, and half a dozen more tending to a giant kettle of soup. It was a marvel to see so many Posts working in unison—it reminded her of the old days on the North estate.

Was this what it was like in the Post enclaves? Was this what it would be like everywhere in a few generations?

Felicia Innovation waved to Elliot from a cushion near the porch. She was surrounded by Olivia and Horatio Grove, both decked out in Post fashions, and Kai, who was reclining nearly in Olivia's lap. Elliot grabbed onto Ro's hand tightly as they approached.

"Elliot," Felicia said. "I'm so glad you could make our little party. Who is this you've brought?"

"This is Ro," Elliot said, as Ro buried her chin in her chest and drew back.

"Ro!" Felicia waved at the girl. "I am Lee. Nice to meet you." That was the Reduced name she was born with, the one she'd mentioned to Elliot on their horse ride. Elliot thought it suited her very well. She wondered if Felicia was as strict about using her new name as Kai was.

"What a pretty scarf you have." The woman gestured to Ro's hair.

Ro smiled. "Kai," she said, and pointed.

Felicia faced him. "Malakai? Do you know what she's talking about?"

Kai shrugged. "Her hair was in her face."

"Hmm," was all that Felicia said.

"I'm going to see if Donovan needs anything." Kai jumped to his feet and left.

"Oh good, now there's space for us all." Olivia scooted over. "Sit here, Elliot."

Elliot sank into the spot Kai had vacated. It was still warm with his body heat. She found herself staring at the swirling patterns on the thick hem of Olivia's red skirt. He'd touched that skirt. He'd been lying with his head on her knee.

All of Elliot's pretty words to Dee went straight out of her head. There was no point in denying it.

Kai was in love with Olivia Grove.

Fifteen

"Is Ro your handmaiden?" Felicia asked as Elliot caught her breath.

But she was spared from answering, as Horatio laughed. "More like her assistant. Elliot's always working with the plants, and Ro's a gardener herself. She's pretty good, too, for someone Reduced."

"Intriguing."

"Ro and I are precisely the same age," Elliot said, forcing herself to pay attention to the conversation instead of the massive sinkhole that had just opened in her heart. "I've always felt a certain degree of protectiveness over her for that reason. And yes, she is very good with flowers."

"But Captain Wentforth really gave her that scarf?" Olivia asked in disbelief. "It's silk—it must be." She held out her hand toward Ro. "Let me see your scarf, girl."

Ro put a hesitant hand to her head, and looked to Elliot for assistance.

"It's okay, Ro. She'll give it back."

Ro pulled the scarf from her hair and handed it over.

"Why would he do that?" Olivia asked. "Real silk? Just handing it to some laborer?"

"You forget he's a Post, Olivia," said Elliot, though not as unkindly as she wished to. It wasn't Olivia's fault. She was a sweet girl. Kai no longer loved Elliot. She'd known that for weeks. For years, if she was completely honest with herself. "You see some laborer. He sees someone who could be his sister."

For years, Ro had practically *been* his sister. Elliot had been something even more. But it was all over now.

"True," Olivia replied, letting the material slide through her fingers. "But still . . . silk. I don't own anything in silk." There was no need for her to say anything more. Captain Wentforth hadn't given *her* anything in silk. Elliot hated the small thrill of triumph she felt when she realized that.

And thinking this conversation had gone on long enough, she took back the scarf. "Come here, Ro. I'll braid your hair." Ro slid into place, and Elliot began the tedious process of finger-combing her tangled red locks.

Around them, the light began to fade, and Felicia asked Olivia if she intended to sing that evening.

Olivia blushed prettily. "I'd be quite outdone by Donovan."

"Yes. He has a beautiful voice," Felicia said softly.

"That's an understatement," Horatio said. "It's unearthly. I've never heard anything like it."

Felicia looked a bit uneasy. "It's something truly

special. I just wish he'd choose a different subject."

Olivia's expression turned grave to match her host's. "Perhaps you'd accompany me to the cider kegs, Mrs. Innovation? I think I might be persuaded to sing if I can get something to drink."

"Thank you, dear," said Felicia. "We both seem to have lost our escorts this evening."

"And what am I?" asked Horatio with a chuckle.

"My chaperone," Olivia said and stuck her tongue out at him. Elliot concentrated very hard on Ro's braid.

"Let us all go get some food and drink before the concert starts," said Felicia. "Perhaps I can even track down my husband. Elliot, can we bring you and Ro anything?"

"Cider for me, and cider and soup for Ro, please," Elliot said, and the Groves and Felicia departed toward the buffet tables.

Ro would love the idea of another special meal so soon. The Norths had never withheld food from their Reduced as some other Luddite lords did, but they only got special meals three times a year—midsummer, midwinter, and harvest. Elliot remembered their feast days as they'd been when her mother had been alive—they'd decorated and everyone had cooked for days. The Reduced had gorged themselves on sweets and pies and food they never saw the rest of the year. They'd burned lanterns and bonfires, and everyone had slept late and ignored their chores the following day.

Since the bad time, the feast days had turned into perfunctory affairs—the Reduced were given extra food, but with none of the pomp and circumstance that had come

before. Their most recent harvest feast had been more lavish than others, given the Fleet money, but Elliot still hadn't
had the courage to include more than extra food and a few
meager decorations. The bad time was too recent a memory
to risk it, even with her father out of town.

At least this party was thrown by the Cloud Fleet on
the Boatwright estate. It would be difficult for her father to
find fault with it here.

"There," she said to Ro, tying the scarf in a knot
around the end of her braid. "Done."

Ro tossed her head, admiring the part of the braid she
could see, then scampered off to show her new hair to some of
the North Posts who'd been gathering on the blankets nearby.
Elliot laughed, watching her descend upon Dee and Jef.

"Pretty girl," said a voice from above. Elliot looked up
to see Andromeda balancing some mugs and bowls. "Is she
your pet?"

"No," Elliot snapped. "She's not my pet, and she's not
my handmaiden, either. Ro is my friend."

"I find that difficult to believe," Andromeda said,
kneeling beside her and handing over her food. "I've been
sent by Felicia to bring you dinner."

If Andromeda hated her so much, why did she always
come around? At least Kai had the decency to avoid her. "I
don't care how difficult you find it to believe, Miss Phoenix.
It's the truth." She shut her mouth before everything else
she wanted to say came pouring out. That Kai could vouch
for Elliot, that Andromeda should not assume all Luddites
were the same—was she so unfair to the Groves?—and that

regardless of either, it was none of her business. Ro and Elliot's relationship belonged to no one but them.

Andromeda regarded her for a long moment, staring until Elliot was forced to turn away from the penetrating look in the Post's crystal blue eyes. "Do you think it's dangerous for us to give a concert on your lands, Miss Elliot? I know what your family likes to do to musical instruments."

Another line of attack, because she wasn't getting so far with her first? "You rent this land," Elliot said. "You may do as you wish." She turned her attention to her cider. If Andromeda Phoenix was determined to be rude, she would steal a card from Kai's playbook and ignore her presence.

But Andromeda made no move to leave, and the others did not return to the cushions. As the night turned cold and violet around them, the musicians began to play a slow, mournful melody underscored by a drum that sounded like a beating heart.

"Oh no," Andromeda said softly. She looked about the crowd. "Do you see Felicia anywhere?"

Elliot shook her head.

"There's no talking to him," Andromeda went on. "He insists on singing it, even when she's here to listen . . ."

"Who?" But Elliot needn't have asked, as Donovan climbed the porch steps and began to sing.

My eyes open to the sun
The brightness of a brand new world
The wave of our tomorrow breaks

Beneath our ships, our sails unfurled.
And yet a streak of darkness
Swirls throughout this cloudless dawn
And even my eyes cannot see
Into the place where you have gone.

So I don't want to see anything now
Not the sun or the sky or the distant shore
I don't want to see anything new
Because I can't see you anymore.

Your sightless eyes could always see
To distances I could not reach
Without you I am truly blind
You've fled to shores I cannot breach.

You were the lantern in my heart
You were the first star in my sky
As far as I could ever roam
You were the light that showed me home.

And I don't want to see anything now
I am lost inside our yesterday
I don't want to see anything new
Now that you are gone away.

Sixteen

A HUSH FELL OVER the crowd as Donovan's deep, clear voice faded into the gathering darkness. Elliot surveyed the lawn. Even Ro, still engaged with a few of the North Posts, looked subdued. She'd never heard a voice like that in her life. His lyrics might break your heart, but it was the pain evident in every note he sang that would grind all the shards into irredeemable dust.

Elliot turned to Andromeda in shock and understanding. Now she knew why Donovan had been so cowed by Felicia's lecture in the sanctuary. "He's singing about Felicia's daughter, isn't he?"

Andromeda sighed. "Yes. Sophia Innovation died six months ago. She was sixteen. It has been hard on the admiral and on Felicia, but most of all on my brother."

That much was clear to every person in attendance. Donovan walked off the porch steps, and nearby Elliot caught sight of Horatio wildly gesturing to his sister, who looked near tears. Eventually Olivia took the stage and began to sing an old folk tune. The spell over the attendees broke at the more familiar sound, and a few even began to clap along.

"I am so sorry for their loss," Elliot said to Andromeda.

"All our loss. Sophia was . . . special. I don't expect you can imagine it."

No, Elliot was sure Andromeda wouldn't expect that.

"She was the first free Post I'd ever met," said Andromeda.

"You must have known her a long time."

"Three years," Andromeda said, shrugging. "When the Fleet was formed. She was the embodiment of everything we all wanted. She was the future. We all knew it. We all loved her."

"I *can* imagine that," Elliot said.

But Andromeda did not, for once, rise to the bait. "If you want to know why Felicia is always so motherly, now you do. She can't turn it off for anyone—not even—"

"Not even me?" Elliot finished, unable to keep her tone from turning snide. She could no longer bear the older girl's casual cruelty. Though her primary objective when visiting the Boatwright estate was avoiding Kai, she was going to have to start steering clear of Andromeda as well.

"Not even you," Andromeda said. "Motherless you, poor little rich girl you, the Luddite who gets her hands dirty in the mud, who plays at farming while she allows her family to let the farm burn—"

"Miss Phoenix," said Elliot, "I think you are done assuming you understand anything about my life, no matter what you may have been told." If she was done putting up with abuse from Kai, there was no way she'd accept it from Andromeda. "In return, I will not assume that I can guess what it is you have against me."

"You know one at least."

"That I'm a Luddite?"

"No. That you betrayed him when he needed you most."

Elliot lifted her chin. No one, least of all this girl, would know what it had cost her. "Yes, I did. It was either him, or everyone else I knew."

Andromeda opened her mouth, then shut it again and stared very intently at Elliot. Even in the gloom of twilight, her eyes seemed more intense, as if she could see through Elliot's skin and divine the inner workings of her brain.

But Elliot had had enough. "If you can't be civil to me, Miss Phoenix, I wish you'd leave me in peace. I have never done anything to you, and if you seek to punish me for past misdeeds, there is nothing you can devise that I haven't already suffered." Four years of worrying about Kai, followed by all these weeks of having him back here, but hating her. Was that not punishment enough?

"You baffle me, Miss Elliot," Andromeda replied in the same high-wrought tone. "I can't reconcile the young woman I see before me with the reports I have had."

What lies had Kai been spreading abroad? "I'm sorry to hear that, but it's none of my concern. I am the same person I've always been." She turned her face away from Andromeda, away from the crowd and from Kai. "Maybe you should ask yourself why, if I am the person you've been led to believe, someone would put their faith in me at all?"

"People are foolish when it comes to love."

Elliot hadn't been. She'd been rational, logical, reasonable, prudent. She'd been cold and cruel and disloyal and distant.

She hadn't been foolish.

She'd been the most foolish girl on the island.

Olivia's song ended and behind her, on the porch, Donovan reemerged, carrying his fiddle. He started playing a familiar song, and the other musicians took up the tune on their pipes and string-boxes. Olivia kept singing, but Donovan easily outshone her voice, and everyone else's playing, too. Elliot had never heard music like that. The finesse and precision she'd witnessed in these Cloud Fleet explorers came across in his musical abilities. His rhythms were complex but perfectly controlled, and he somehow managed to weave in any misstep of the other players. It was a good thing Tatiana wasn't here to listen or she'd be green as grass.

"He's amazing," Elliot said, mostly to herself.

"Yes." Andromeda shrugged. "He's got a special talent. And he's been funneling everything into his music, lately. It's the only thing left that gives him any peace."

"Was Sophia sick for a long time?"

"Always," Andromeda replied. "She was born blind, and she had a weak heart. Had she not been born a free Post, she probably would not have survived at all. The Innovations were able to properly provide for her. Whatever medical attention she needed, Felicia would find it. If it didn't exist, Felicia would create it."

"Create it?" Elliot asked. That wasn't a word she heard often.

For a split second, Andromeda appeared discomposed. "Does that word frighten you, Luddite?"

Elliot bristled. "Create" might not frighten her, but the way these Fleet Posts used "Luddite" as an epithet was beginning to. If only Andromeda knew what a bad Luddite Elliot was. "No."

"But you believe in the protocols."

"Of course I do." Spoken like any good Luddite who didn't have notes in the barn detailing the steps she'd taken to create some rather troubling wheat. She'd say nothing else—and certainly not to Andromeda Phoenix. Instead, she recited the lines given by every teacher she'd ever had. "They are there for our protection. Without them, humans would risk trying to become gods."

"And what if breaking them would have saved Sophia's life? What if they'd save your grandfather's?"

At that moment, Elliot hated Andromeda. She hated being forced to play devil's advocate for, of all things, the Luddite protocols! "Is there an answer here that wouldn't bolster what you've already decided about me?"

"Which is?" asked Andromeda with an evil glint in her odd eyes.

Elliot wasn't going to spell it out.

Olivia's song ended, but Donovan merely turned his music into something wilder, a more obvious dancing tune. A cheer went up from the assembled crowd. Several couples even rose from their picnic blankets to dance beneath the glowing lanterns. Kai gave his hand to Olivia to help her down from the porch steps. She tugged him toward the dancers, and after a moment, he joined her. Elliot stared down at her lap.

"Aren't they a lovely couple?" Andromeda said.

"Please go away."

"As you pointed out, Miss Elliot, we rent these lands. We may do as we please."

Yet Elliot was not forced to remain, and she highly doubted that Felicia had invited her to the party that evening merely to receive sarcastic remarks from Andromeda. The older Post might imagine they could be friends, but Elliot knew better. She'd had a lifetime of experience learning how few people she could count on to be her friend.

She rose and went over to the blankets occupied by Ro and the North Posts. Judging by the number of empty plates and mugs strewn about, they were enjoying the party immensely.

Here, at least, were some true friends. "May I join you?"

"Certainly!" Dee was sitting cross-legged, cradling her belly in her lap and keeping her eye on Jef, who was twirling with a few of the young Grove Posts several yards away. She lowered her voice and leaned in to Elliot. "I caught a few words of your talk with that Fleet girl. She's not very fond of you, is she?"

"Not that I can tell."

Dee chuckled. "Do I need to have words with her?"

"She'd probably think I beat you into it."

Dee put a hand to her heart in mock shock. "You beat your CORs, Elliot North?"

"Haven't you heard?" Beside them, Ro clapped along to the music, watching the dancers with delight. Elliot wondered if she should have brought the girl a string-box from the stash she still kept safely stowed away in the barn. But then, Ro's clumsy plucking might mess with the music, and Ro didn't seem to mind.

"Well, someone ought to enlighten her, and that's a fact."

"I don't care what Andromeda Phoenix thinks of me, Dee."

"And what of *Captain Wentforth*?"

Elliot hesitated. "What he thinks isn't likely to be changed, is it?"

"You did the right thing, Elliot. We all think so, and I've no qualms telling him as much, either."

"Please, Dee," Elliot begged. "Don't. We're long past all that now."

"Not if he's badmouthing you to the Fleet Posts."

"I don't need to be friends with Andromeda Phoenix." Elliot threw her hands in the air. "I don't need to be friends with Kai. I don't even need to be friends with the Innovations."

"But you want to be," said Dee.

"No, I don't," Elliot insisted. Whatever it took to keep her people fed, that's what she wanted. And for that, it wasn't necessary to make friends with these people. In fact, it was preferable not to socialize with them. Less danger, then, that she'd miss them when they were gone. "I want to take their money and let them build their ship and get them off my land. That's all I want."

"Good to know," said a voice above her head.

Elliot and Dee looked up, and there, shadowed against the light from the swinging sun-lamps, stood Kai.

Four Years Ago

Dear Elliot,

Last night I went with some other Posts to the Grove estate to hear a traveling musician. It was fantastic. I'd always thought that music was something that you or your mother or Tatiana played on your instruments, but at the Grove estate, several of the Posts have string-boxes or pipes, and they all play together.

I wish you could have been there. The Grove Posts talk a lot about the free Post settlements. Apparently they're allowed to visit family and such that have left for there. They don't make it sound half so scary as the beggars who've come to the North estate do.

They say other things I believe even less. They say Baroness North used to visit the Grove estate quite often. I thought none of the Norths spoke to the Groves.

Your friend,
Kai

Dear Kai,

I'm so jealous! Were the Luddites there, too? I have never met the Grove children. I believe there are two—a boy several years older than us, and a little girl.

I don't know the precise nature of my father's argument with Mr. Grove but I think it's gone on longer than Tatiana and I have been alive. I think it must have something to do with a land dispute of some sort. It is too bad, really. If they were on speaking terms, it's likely Tatiana and I would have had the children as playmates. As it is, she hasn't had a true friend since Benedict left the estate.

But I don't need to travel to another estate to find a friend. I have our gliders, I have our barn-wall knot. I have you.

Did anyone show you how to make a string-box? I think we should make one and play it for Ro.
Your friend,
Elliot

∾

Dear Elliot,
I've included the list of Posts who have ordered string-boxes. I can't believe how many people want one now. I'm not sure we'll have to paint them all the way we did for Ro. It will slow the process a lot, and besides, people might want to paint them themselves.
Your friend,
Kai

∾

Dear Kai,

I managed to make three over the weekend and put them in the usual place. But I'm out of the silk fiber we were using for the strings. I stole it from the hem of one of my mother's old shirts. I don't know what else we can use.

Your friend,

Elliot

      ∽

Dear Elliot,

I believe these wires will work well. It changes the tone of the instrument, but not in a bad way. Thank you for doing this. I hope your mother doesn't miss her hems. I know how hard you've been working to make sure the boxes are properly tuned . . . so I know you won't resent it when you see this newest list of requests?

      Come on. For me?

Yours,

Kai

      ∽

Dear Kai,

Your wish is my command. I mended my mother's shirt with hemp thread and she didn't even notice. By the way, the wire works beautifully. The new sound is very different, but you're right, it will just add to the richness of our little orchestra. I can't wait to hear them!

Yours,

Elliot

Dear Elliot,

I've never been tempted to show our letters to anyone until now. But "your wish is my command"? Those are some dangerous words for a Luddite to write to a Post.

Yours,

Kai

Dear Kai,

Are you planning on telling on me?

Yours,

Elliot

P.S. Made five more.

Dear Elliot,

It depends. Will you make boxes for this new list?

Yours,

Kai

Seventeen

"YOU LOOK RADIANT, DEE," Kai said. "I'm so glad you could make it tonight."

He looked radiant, too. Smack in his element, decked out in an oxblood jacket that soaked up the light from the lanterns and set off the darkness of his black hair. In these colors, he stood out from all the other partygoers, but then again, Elliot might have thought he stood out anyway. She drew her knees up to her chest. She wore her old black dress with a lavender sweater over it. It didn't hold a candle to the Post clothes, but it was the brightest color she owned. Now, she didn't know what she'd been thinking. Trying to emulate the Post style of dress did nothing to make her fit in. It only served to highlight her shortcomings.

"I'm happy to see you, too, Malakai," said Dee, stressing the last syllable. "I have heard some disturbing things. Perhaps you wish to clarify for us—"

"I'd be happy to, later," said Kai. "Right now, I need to dance with Ro. She'll think I'm snubbing her." Ro looked up at the sound of her name. "Dance with me, Ro?"

The girl hopped up and right into his arms. Kai laughed and spun her away. Elliot tugged at the fraying cuffs of her sweater and tried to forget how well she knew that laugh.

"Try as I might," Dee said, "I can't hate him completely, Elliot. He hasn't forgotten where he came from."

"I wouldn't want you to, Dee. You'd be no better than Andromeda if you did." The jig went on and on, and Donovan's music became more frantic and frenetic by the moment. As mournful as his last piece had been, it was utterly eclipsed by the melodies reeling off his fiddle now, as if he could exorcise his pain if only he could find the proper chord progression. The music was overwhelming in its intensity. Donovan must be some sort of prodigy— even Luddites with a lifetime of training didn't possess such talent.

Dee still watched Kai. "But his behavior now is inexcusable."

"He doesn't want to be my friend. It's his choice."

"What choice did he give the Fleet girl, or did he simply poison her mind against you?"

"Drop it, Dee. This is the way it is. Like so many other things." Elliot took a breath. "The way it is."

Dee shook her head. "I refuse to believe that. Look at us, here. Together, listening to music on a Luddite estate. It's like the old days, Elliot. And look at Kai, who went away and made something of himself. I want that for Jef. I want it for this baby, whoever he or she is. They have been born into a thrilling time. It's even like that song Donovan sang—the world isn't a certain way. We reinvent it, every day, something new. It's changing around us, as fast as a weed taking root."

And yet, Thom was still in exile. And her father had plowed under her wheat. And her grandfather lay dying in his room back at the house because treatments that could help him were illegal under the Luddite laws. This winter they had money and food, thanks to the Cloud Fleet. But what would become of the people on the North estate in the years to come? What else could they rent? How could they make do?

If things were changing, it wasn't nearly fast enough to suit Elliot.

She watched Kai and Ro dance. Long after the song ended and another began, they remained out there. Kai danced with Olivia again, and Ro with anyone—Grove Posts, Jef, all by herself beneath the swinging lanterns. Part of Elliot wished to join her, but then she caught sight of Kai whirling very close, Olivia Grove held tightly in his arms, and her legs remained glued to the blanket. She could not dance on the same ground as him.

She shouldn't have come tonight. She'd thought she could enjoy the company of friendly faces and ignore the ones who weren't, but she couldn't. Not until she could teach herself to stop looking for Kai at every chance.

The dancers whirled on inside their island of light. Above the bobbing lanterns, Elliot could see a few stars flickering in the sky—the Cross; the pointers; Scorpius, its tail slashed across the sky; and Antares glimmering like the red heart of one of Ro's flowers. Most of the smaller stars weren't visible in the glow of the sun-lamps. Elliot wondered if this is what the skies had looked like once upon a time, when there was so much light in the air that no one could see the stars.

"Are you here to keep the pregnant woman company?" Dee asked.

"I'm tired myself," Elliot said, and hoped she sounded convincing. "It's been a long week, and I still haven't figured out what's wrong with the tractor."

"Don't beat yourself up too hard, Miss," said Gill, looking up from his third mug of cider. "We won't need it again for another few months."

"We could always have a visiting mechanic take a look," Dee suggested, a mischievous smile on her face.

"Don't you dare," Elliot said. If it were spring, she'd consider swallowing her pride enough to ask Kai for help. But she had a few more months yet. The crops weren't in any danger. She still had time to fix it without risking Kai illustrating her incompetence.

By now, many of the Posts not dancing had taken out their instruments and were adding to the din. There was still an undercurrent of melody, if you listened hard enough, but with dozens of string-boxes and pipes, with the drums and the fiddle and the voices and the hand clapping, it was difficult to identify exactly what the song was.

It was also growing harder and harder to hear the flow of conversation. Over here, a bunch of Grove Posts were talking about the likelihood of getting jobs and leaving with the Fleet. Over there, a knot of North Posts was discussing a drainage problem on the new racetrack.

Ro came rushing up to her and broke her from her reverie. The girl was breathing hard, her face flushed, her scarf askew. She held tight to Kai's hand, but he was a few steps behind her, their arms outstretched to their limits. Dee regarded him coldly, and Elliot did her best to keep her eyes averted.

"Dance!" cried Ro. She held out her other hand for Elliot.

"No, I'm fine right here," said Elliot. As Ro captured her hand, she squeezed back to reassure her, but refused to let the Reduced girl pull her to her feet.

Ro shook her head with gusto. "No! Dance!" She yanked on Kai's arm to bring him forward, then tried to place his hand in Elliot's.

For a moment their knuckles brushed, then they each pulled back.

"Ro, please don't do that," said Elliot. "I don't want to dance."

"And certainly not with me."

Elliot's gaze shot to Kai, but as usual, his face was unreadable. At least tonight he was looking at her, though she found herself fighting the urge to squirm beneath his gaze. His eyes had become so cold, so alien, in the past four years.

"Certainly not," repeated Dee. "Not with the way you've been treating her ever since you showed up here."

"Dee!" Elliot cried.

"Oh," said Kai. "Have I been somehow remiss in my duties as a North Post? How rude of me. Guess it's good I'm not a North Post anymore."

Elliot closed her lips over a gasp.

"None of that, boy!" said Gill. "You're not too old for me to turn you over my knee. Your da would expect me to if he heard you talking that way about Miss Elliot."

"My father would be glad to know I'm no longer forced to pretend I'm happy with a slave's lot in life."

Her breath became choked in her throat. That couldn't be true. He couldn't have been her friend all those years simply because she was the master's daughter. Not all those letters. Not all those hours in the barn. Not what they'd shared.

"If you are . . . ," Kai said, and let his words hang in place.

"Kai!" Elliot cried, and stood. It was a lie. It was a lie because he was still angry at her. It had to be. "Stop it. Stop it right now. You can be as cruel as you want to me, and I'll bear it with no complaint. But do not take your anger out on these people who have never done anything to you." Andromeda might hate her because of how the Post girl thought she'd betrayed Kai, but it was Kai who'd left Elliot and the others alone on the estate. They had a right to anger as well.

"Protecting your CORs, how *noble*," he replied. "And how effective it is—at least when your father's not around."

Elliot blinked, then blinked again, as her eyes began to burn. Ro started to whimper.

"Any Post who remains on this estate is a slave, and they know it. And if they are afraid to leave, that makes them cowards as well."

"That's it," said Gill, standing and brushing crumbs of pie from his pants. "I've had enough lip from you—"

"You have no right to belittle the choices made by me and mine, Malakai Wentforth, or whatever you're calling yourself these days," said Dee, still seated. Her voice was calm, but then again, she'd been defending her choice to stay after Thom left for years. "Not when you're off flirting with Olivia Grove all night. She's a Luddite, too, don't forget."

"Olivia has no love for the estate way of life. She knows we're the future and embraces it."

"Easy for her to do, when she's grown up in the Luddite lap of luxury," Dee pointed out, her voice textured with the patience of a decade spent dealing with children.

The same could not be said for Gill. "You're upsetting a pregnant woman, boy, and you're disrespecting all the people who helped you get raised—including Miss Elliot here. And you'll stop it right now or I'll fight you and I don't care if I've got twenty years on you . . ."

"Stop it," said Elliot, holding out her hands between Kai and Gill. Nearby, Ro was openly weeping. These were her *friends*. Her true friends, not nice to her because she was a North, not nice because she might be able to help them. Kai could hate her now, he could even claim he hadn't loved her at all, but he couldn't speak for the rest of them. "There will be no fighting at the Innovations' party."

"Oh, yes, Miss," Kai drawled in a mocking appropriation of Gill's voice. "Whatever you say."

"That's it," said Gill, and stepped forward. Elliot moved in between them.

"I said *stop it!*"

Kai grabbed her by the wrists. "You'll fight . . . for her?" he asked them.

Elliot tried to move away, but his grip was too tight. Ever since the day on the beach, she'd wanted him to touch her again. But not like this.

"You'll do anything . . . for her?" He shook their hands as Elliot struggled to get free. "And you don't sit here and wonder why none of you have string-boxes anymore, why none of you have listened to a lick of music in three years?"

"Let go," Elliot said. The folks on other blankets had begun to look over, despite the music and the revelry. Ro was tugging in vain at Kai's sleeve. Gill's face had turned crimson with anger. "Let go. Please, let go."

"You don't miss the people she's responsible for driving away? Dee? *You* don't?"

"I put the blame where it belongs, Kai," was all Dee said. "Now stop making a scene. This is no example for my son."

"Neither is living here," Kai growled. "You're idiots, all of you. Believe me. I thought that way once." He drew her in and stared into her eyes. Elliot flinched. His gaze was dark, so dark. His eyes seemed filled with more stars than the sky above. Now she could see it was more than just a trick of the light. His eyes *had* changed in the last four years. She didn't know such a thing was possible.

"I thought she could protect me, too. I thought she cared. But it's all a lie." He released her and she stumbled back, holding tight to her wrists and her tears. This was Kai.

The Kai she'd loved from the moment she knew what that meant.

But she didn't know him at all.

"Ma!" Jef came running up. "Ma—"

"Not now, Jef," said Dee, standing and putting her arms around the boy. "It's all right."

"But Ma," said Jef, as the music died. "It's not all right. The baron's here."

Eighteen

BARON NORTH WAS NOTHING if not civil to his tenants, but declined to stay more than a few moments at the party on the Boatwright lands. He paid his respects to Felicia Innovation and made arrangements for a more thorough meeting with the admiral the following day. Then he crooked his finger at Elliot, who'd trailed forward a few steps from the near-melee going on at the North Posts' blanket. Had he seen what had transpired among his servants? Had he recognized Kai? Elliot got the distinct impression that she was very close to making a bad situation much worse.

"You will meet me in my office in half an hour," said Baron North, in a voice barely audible over the few instruments still in use.

Elliot nodded. "Yes, sir." But her father had already climbed back into his carriage. Elliot caught a glimpse of another male figure inside as it drove away. He hadn't even offered her a ride back to the house. She should leave quickly, if she hoped to make herself presentable before she was required to meet with him.

"I'll take care of Ro," said Dee, coming up to her. "You should hurry."

Gill and Kai were still glaring at each other as if they'd come to blows the moment she turned her back.

"I won't let them fight," Dee said. "Gill wouldn't risk it now, anyway."

No one knew what the baron might do, least of all Elliot. He couldn't hold the concert against them, could he? They were merely listening to the music provided by the Fleet, Olivia, and the Grove Posts.

Elliot quickly took her leave of her hosts and turned toward the path leading home. If she ran, she'd have more time to prepare herself, but then again, she might be in worse shape.

What was certain, however, was that she had no time to think about Kai. She rubbed her hands over her wrists, which still tingled where he'd touched her. His grip hadn't been hard enough to hurt, but it had hardly been tender, either. And his words . . . she'd known he was angry, but now she wondered if he hated her. If he'd always hated her.

Had he hated her the day her mother died? Had he hated her the day after?

No. She refused to believe it. Hating her now was bad enough, but she could survive it. She'd been doing well these past four years, like a fallen tree that clung to the ground and continued to grow, despite all odds. Elliot's roots were buried deep, and nothing Kai could say would convince her that the soil was any less solid.

The temperature had plummeted in the hours since the sun had set. They'd have a frost tonight. Above her head, branches waved in the autumn wind, sending dry, crackling leaves into the air, and swirling them into eddies and tiny tornadoes at her feet. She couldn't see them well in the darkness, but she heard their crunch and whisper, and caught glimpses of their movement. They were lucky in the islands, she had always learned. Lucky to be free of wolves and bears and giant, fanged-toothed cats. There were rabbits, and possums, and egg-eating stoats, but nothing that could hurt a person. She'd read stories, growing up, where children were attacked by lions or eaten by wolves, but she'd never feared the darkness or the forest. The Luddites ruled the world.

Elliot was barely one hundred meters down the road when she heard the crunch of gravel beneath wheels. She turned, and saw a sun-cart gaining on her, its headlights unlit, even in the darkness. The cart pulled up beside her. Andromeda and Ro sat inside.

"Get in," said Andromeda. "I'll take you back."

Absolutely not. "This isn't necessary—"

"Of course it is," the older girl said. "You're terrible at protecting them, but you're all they've got."

Elliot climbed into the car. "I am doing this because the cart will get me back to my house more quickly."

"I am doing this," the Post girl said, her tone world-weary, "because I don't think I've been entirely fair to you."

That was putting it mildly. In the privacy of the darkness, Elliot thought it safe to roll her eyes.

"Yes," Andromeda said, as if in agreement. "I don't

have too much pride to admit that." She took off. Within moments, the sun-cart seemed to have reached full speed—or at least as fast as it went on reserve power. They whizzed past the shadowy silhouettes of trees and bounced hard over tree roots and dips in the trail. Elliot couldn't even see the path in front of the wheels, but it didn't seem to slow Andromeda down. At least she could be certain of reaching home in time. She might even catch up to her father.

"Besides," Andromeda went on, "there must be some reason you can collect all these Post admirers. And I hear Ro here has excellent taste."

In the darkness, Elliot squeezed Ro's hand. How much of their conversation could the Reduced girl pick up? "I thought the prevailing opinion would be that someone Reduced doesn't know any better."

"My mother was Reduced," said Andromeda. "Still had more sense than most people I know."

She steered them around a corner at a speed Elliot found imprudent, given the darkness. She couldn't see a thing ahead of her. "Don't you want the headlights on?"

Andromeda grunted and flicked a switch. Elliot and Ro flinched in the sudden glare, but Andromeda didn't slow down at all.

"Care to tell me what your father has against music?" Andromeda asked abruptly.

"It's not music," Elliot replied. "It's control." It was always control.

Three years ago, Baron Zachariah North had caught wind of the unofficial orchestra operating on the North estate. Where some of the estate lords would have taken advantage of the spontaneous resource—as if they'd come across a patch of natural gas or a seam of coal—Baron North had been displeased. He'd not authorized any such endeavor, and he wouldn't have approved of it at any rate. Music was a distraction from his laborers' duties, much like school or books or more than the allotted number of feasts. Things were bad enough on the estate already, and they'd been getting steadily worse since the death of the baroness a year earlier. Baron North had had far too many duties to take over and concerns to keep himself occupied with. If someone was going to get more leisure time, it would be him, not his servants.

He'd forbidden the concerts and practice sessions and confiscated the instruments from all the Reduced on the estate. Elliot could still see the bonfires—the flames that had once been a hallmark of harvest celebrations turned into pyres for the laborers' only joy.

Yet the restrictions had had little effect. More pipes and string-boxes had appeared, seemingly out of nowhere, and the practice sessions had gone on in secret. When the baron discovered that his own daughter was helping his people in their treason, he'd finally had an object toward which to aim his wrath.

The first and only time Elliot had been glad that Kai had left was when the bad time came. Her father had come first for the Posts she'd liked best. Kai's position on the farm had already been too precarious to have survived.

"You hear some pretty scary things about the North

estate down in the Post enclaves."

Elliot squeezed her hands together in her lap. "From him?"

"From everyone."

Elliot grimaced. She could well imagine the stories that followed the affair. Reduced who disobeyed the baron's orders were shown no mercy and no quarter. He extended the restrictions to the CORs, and when he learned that they were hiding their instruments, he dissolved the COR family housing units that had been in place as long as Elliot had been alive, and relegated all the CORs to single-sex, age-organized barracks alongside the Reduced. Children were taken from their mothers, common-laws were separated, and that's when the real trouble started.

And Elliot couldn't protect any of them. Not then, not alone. She'd messed up badly, and the estate was still paying for it. It wouldn't happen again.

"Of course," Andromeda said, "bad as you are, the estate where I was born was far worse."

"You left when you were quite young, I understand."

"Had to," she replied. "Where I'm from, the lady of the estate believed all Posts were the product of . . . *relations* between the Luddites and the Reduced. We were made to bear the punishment for her husband's sins."

"That's horrible!" Elliot cried. And of course, since her mother had been Reduced, she could hardly have protected them—not like Dee could protect Jef. "Was your father Reduced, too?"

Andromeda hesitated. "My father *was* the master,

Elliot. Our lady wasn't wrong about everything."

Elliot was glad for the darkness, glad Andromeda couldn't see her mouth hanging open. Such things did not happen on the North estate. Hadn't happened since she was young and Benedict had been sent away. Her father wouldn't have it.

"But even my father could not account for all the Posts that started crowding his estate. And you know Luddites. They wouldn't do genetic testing to prove their theory one way or the other. My lady's belief was that her God would never allow anything other than Luddite, Reduced, and the abominable combination of the two. To her, we were as abhorrent as a hybrid plant."

Elliot stiffened. Why, of all comparisons, had the Post chosen that one?

"Here we are," said Andromeda as she pulled up in front of the big house.

Elliot looked over at the Post girl, but now that they were bathed in the light from the house window, Andromeda had once again fallen silent.

"I am very sorry for what you were made to endure," Elliot said at last.

"Don't be sorry for me," said Andromeda. "Be sorry for those who still live there." She stared down at the controls in her hands. "I hate the estates, but you are no monster. As long as there are people under your care, I hope you will care for them."

Elliot's jaw tightened at her words. She didn't need the blessing of this Post, no matter what Andromeda had been through. She'd known her duties since she could pronounce the word "Luddite."

"Be strong, Elliot."

Elliot didn't respond, and instead turned to Ro. "Good night, Ro. I hope you enjoyed the music."

Ro nodded and leaned over the edge of the cart to give Elliot a hug.

"She'll show you where she lives," Elliot said to Andromeda.

"I'm serious," said Andromeda. "Everything . . . else aside, I am aware that you are all that stands between your Posts and your father."

She was wrong. Elliot knew that now. The Posts themselves stood there. Dee stood, without her common-law. Gill stood, a forty-year-old laborer willing to fight a teenager for saying Elliot was useless. Or worse than useless—complicit. Thom and so many others had stood, willing to walk away from the farm rather than let Baron North continue with his reign of terror. She may have made those instruments, but it was the Posts who wanted to play them. It was the Posts who were willing to hide them, the Posts willing to defy her father as his punishments grew ever harsher.

No, she couldn't protect them then. Not then, at fifteen, still reeling from the loss of her mother and Kai and trying to figure out how the baroness had managed her father with such finesse all those years. She couldn't stop her father from putting Gill's eleven-year-old daughter in the women's barracks, from slapping Dee in stocks for two days after she was discovered sneaking instruments out to the Grove estate, or from beating Thom for trying to break Dee out of those stocks.

And perhaps she couldn't protect them now either, but she'd learned something important back there at the concert. She might do her best to protect them—and fail—but she hadn't realized until now they were also protecting her.

Dee chose to sneak those instruments. Thom chose to rescue the woman he loved. And then, when so many of the Posts left the estate, Dee and Gill and Mags and the others chose to stay behind. Maybe they chose like Elliot had one year earlier. They chose to save the estate, to protect the Reduced that had even less agency than they did.

Maybe they chose to protect Elliot herself.

She'd always told herself that the reason Dee wouldn't reveal where Thom had gone was because she didn't fully trust Elliot. But maybe Dee didn't tell her about Thom so it wasn't possible for Elliot to get in trouble for keeping it a secret. Elliot was a Luddite and their superior on the estate, yes, but it was Dee and Gill and Thom who were the grown-ups.

Elliot turned away from Andromeda without another word and marched into the house. She didn't change her clothes or redo her hair but went straight up to the door of her father's office and knocked. If he sought to punish her, she wouldn't hide. If he hoped to punish the others, she would fight.

EIGHT YEARS AGO

Dear Elliot,
Where have you been? You haven't come to the barn in days. Tell
me when you are coming back.
Your friend,
Kai

Dear Kai,
I guess by now you have heard the news. Benedict has been
sent away from the North Estate. I don't know what it is he did.
Mother won't tell me, and all I've been able to find out is that it
was very bad and has something to do with the Reduced. What is
the word among the CORs?
Your friend,
Elliot

Dear Elliot,

I haven't heard anything at all here. My da never listens to gossip. Where did he go? Another estate?

Your friend,

Kai

∽

Dear Kai,

I don't know. No one tells me anything. Tatiana said he was turned out into the cold, but I don't think that's true. She always makes up stories. Like she tells me all the Posts that run away end up in butcher shops. I didn't eat meat for a month, and then my mother found out what Tatiana had said.

I can't think of what Benedict might have done. Beat a Reduced?

Your friend,

Elliot

∽

Dear Elliot,

If I know your father, it was probably because Benedict didn't beat the Reduced enough. You know where that butcher shop story comes from, don't you? Long ago, before there were CORs, before the Estates could manage to feed themselves, there were Luddites who ate Reduced. At least, that's what the legends say. The older Posts tell that story on feast nights to scare the rest of us.

So, when can you come back to the barn? I have something to show you!
Your friend,
Kai

Dear Kai,
I'm not coming to see you until you take that back. Luddites never ate people!
Your friend,
Elliot

Dear Elliot,
Did so.
Your friend,
Kai

Dear Kai,
TAKE THAT BACK NOW.
NOT your friend,
Elliot

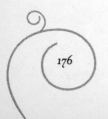

Dear Elliot,
I know why Benedict was sent away. I will tell you if you come
see me.
Your friend,
Kai

Dear Elliot,
Come on. I know you want to know.
Your friend,
Kai

Dear Elliot,
Fine. Be that way. I never want to see you again. Though you are
really missing out.
Not your friend, either,
Kai
PS: If you think the Luddites eating the Reduced is bad, you
should hear what Benedict did.

Nineteen

"COME IN." HER FATHER was standing by his desk. There was a fire in the grate, and every lantern was lit. Elliot squinted in the sudden brightness, so different from the cool forest night.

"Ah, Elliot, you're early. Good." He lifted his hand as if in presentation. "My younger daughter. You may remember her."

A man stood up from the chair near the fire. He was dressed in a plum-colored velvet coat that wouldn't be out of place on any member of the Fleet. "I remember her, but I never would have recognized her. You've turned into a beautiful young woman, cousin."

"Benedict?" Elliot asked in bafflement, too shocked by his presence to even offer a lame note of gratitude in response to his flattery. She hadn't seen him in more than eight years. He'd been younger than she was now when her father had banished him from the estate. As her eyes adjusted to the light, she was able to make out his features.

The sharp, high cheekbones, the incongruous dark eyes in his pale face that still held the unmistakable stamp of North blood. His hair, once a sandy-brown mop of curls, was now cut close to his head, revealing an angular skull and a sculpted neck. *He* was beautiful, she realized. Far more than she, with her face still flushed from her fight with Kai, with her hair all mussed from her wild ride through the forest. Far more than any of the Norths. Perhaps, with his fine clothes and keen expression, more beautiful even than Ro.

But what had she expected? A monster, just because what he'd done was monstrous?

Elliot looked at her father to gauge his mood. Why had the prodigal nephew returned? How did her father feel about it?

"We were surprised that you weren't here to greet us, daughter," Baron North said. "Tatiana explained that you'd gone to our tenants' little picnic."

"I thought it was proper to have one member of the family there," Elliot responded carefully. Was it possible he hadn't called her here to berate her about the concert? "And it saved Tatiana from going—"

Baron North snorted. "What did I tell you, Benedict? She is obsessed with anything having to do with these CORs."

Benedict smiled. "A rare quality, sir. It's little wonder you find it so shocking."

Elliot shot him a look, but if her father understood the alternate take on Benedict's words, he took no notice of it.

"I'm glad you agree with me, young man. I feared that

living so long amongst them might have given you strange ideas—"

"There are many good people among the Posts, Uncle," said Benedict, "but the best are those who remember what they owe to us. I suspect, from what you've told me, that these Innovations are exactly the type I mean."

"Is that so, Elliot?" her father asked. "Have they been showing us all the proper respect since their arrival?"

"What did Tatiana say?" Elliot asked, still careful.

Her father smiled at her as if to offer indulgence, but she knew better. "I am interested to hear your take."

Elliot hesitated. If Tatiana had shared the truth, she had nothing to fear. The Innovations themselves had been nothing but proper, even if Andromeda and Kai had taken pleasure in pushing Tatiana's buttons—and her own. Indeed, the only thing Tatiana could possibly have complained about was Kai's ongoing flirtation with Olivia Grove, and if anything, her father would probably gloat to hear about a Grove acting in a way he'd consider inappropriate. Though he'd buried his grudge against the family after Horatio's father died and Horatio took over the farm, Baron North was not above making digs at the Grove's supposed inferiority.

But the question remained: Had Tatiana shared those stories, or was her father merely looking for a way to trip her up? Could he not find a way to blame her for a concert on his tenants' lands, and so sought to introduce his punishment for another cause?

"They have been very respectful, Father," Elliot replied at last, "which is why I thought it would be proper of me to accept their invitation this evening. I'm sure it was an honor for them to have a North attend their party."

"More than just *a* North attended, though, did they not, Elliot?" her father asked. "I saw our CORs there."

"They were invited by the Innovations," Elliot said. "Their behavior, as well, was beyond reproach."

"No doubt because Elliot was there to oversee them," Benedict pointed out. "It was good that she attended, to remind your servants of their place, Uncle Zachariah."

Elliot gave her cousin another look of surprise. Why was he coming to her defense?

"Indeed." Her father's expression remained shrewd. Abruptly he straightened. "Well, Elliot, as you can see, Benedict has come home at last. He needs a room made up for him for tonight, and then tomorrow we can see about having his old rooms redecorated for him."

"His old rooms are currently housing Grandfather," Elliot said.

"You don't say!" Her father shook his head in disbelief. "But he's bedridden. He can't possibly need an entire suite."

Her grandfather was used to having an entire home, and was forced to give that up so the Norths could save their estate in the wake of the baron's mismanagement. Elliot checked her frown before her father noticed.

Where had he expected her to put the Boatwright? In the cellar?

"I'm sure there's no cause to uproot an old man twice in such quick succession," said Benedict. "And I'm not used to large quarters anymore, anyway. Please, Elliot,

Uncle Zachariah—don't worry on my behalf. Now, where has Tatiana gone? Shall I go fetch her? I'd love to spend the evening reminiscing."

Her father's face softened at once, though Elliot wondered what it was these two men would have to reminisce about. Benedict's rebellious teen years? The way her father had devalued the estate since Benedict's father had died? The disgusting infraction that had gotten her cousin banished seven years ago?

"I'll go look for Tatiana," Benedict said. "It would be a shame to waste all this lovely light." He tapped the edge of a lantern. "Uncle, you should truly consider replacing some of these with Post sun-lamps. There is an initial investment cost, but sunlight is always free, and you get so much more of it in the north." He smiled and departed.

Elliot looked at her father, but he appeared neither red nor sputtering, as one would expect following a recommendation to use a Post product. Then again, he was also in possession of Post horses, and he hadn't been too proud for those.

What was Benedict doing here? Why had her father chosen now, at long last, to retrieve the missing heir? Or had it been Benedict who'd finally come home to his estate, and was her father's apparent welcome an effort to heal the breach should her cousin attempt to take the estate from him at once?

She didn't know what to make of the man, either. The rumors she'd heard all her life made him out to be little better than the master of Andromeda's old estate. But it seemed obvious he embraced Post fashions and technology. And his subtle jabs at her father hinted at something else: a mind-set more like her own.

Her father turned to the desk. "Do you have the numbers for the harvest?"

"Yes, Father." She pointed to a piece of paper on the desk.

He glanced at it. "I see the loss of your precious field for my racetrack didn't affect the bottom line as much as you feared."

"No, Father." The loss of a normal field of wheat would not have. However, had it been left standing, its contribution to their stockpile would have been significant. Perhaps so significant that she couldn't have hidden it from him if the grain had been brought to harvest. In all of her careful planning, she hadn't thought of that. She'd been too eager to make sure there was enough food, enough money, to keep the estate afloat. Perhaps the next time she tried her experiment, she wouldn't do a whole field. Half a field would more easily hide the additional grain, and she could steadily increase the percentage each year so that . . .

"Oh, Elliot," her father said, not looking up from the paperwork. "I noticed that COR foreman of ours at the picnic this evening. You know, the one with the child?"

Elliot's blood ran cold. "Dee."

"That's the one. She's quite far into her pregnancy to still be walking about, isn't she? Move her into the birthing house tomorrow."

"But father," Elliot said, "she lives in a Post cottage.

She has a son to care for. And her condition has not affected her work at all—"

He raised his eyes from the papers to meet hers and Elliot promptly snapped her mouth shut. "Tomorrow," he repeated.

Twenty

"YOU SHOULD LEAVE."

Dee blew some hair out of her eyes and exchanged the full bucket of milk for an empty one before leaning back under the cow. "And leave Jef behind? Your father wouldn't like it either way, I'd wager. Nor me running off with one of his new Posts hiding in my belly."

Elliot had come to the new, makeshift dairy first thing that morning hoping to catch Dee before the shifts changed. Around them, the Reduced dairymaids were hard at work, but there were no other Posts within earshot when Elliot delivered her father's decree. "My father hardly cares if Jef's a Post, nor you, nor your baby. He wouldn't be confining you to the birthing house if he did." Elliot crouched down beside Dee. "You can't stay there, Dee. You have a home . . . a family."

"But it's okay for Reduced women to stay there for a year, confined to their beds like animals in a cage?" Dee didn't look up from her milking. "The birthing house is torture for everyone, Elliot, not just Posts. You know that, too, or you wouldn't have so carefully protected Ro all these years."

Elliot flinched. "You think I'm being cruel to the Reduced?"

"I think the world is cruel to them," Dee said. "Because the world is a cruel place. This estate is a cruel place, but there are other places far more cruel."

Like Andromeda's old estate. Like the dangerous areas of the Post enclaves. Yes, there were places worse than the North estate, but many of the North Posts were willing to risk it, anyway. Why wasn't Dee?

Dee leaned back and puffed out a misty breath. The frost had come, late last night, blanketing the lawns and roofs of the estate in silver. The day promised to be gorgeous, but it was still too early for the sun to break through the mist. "Speaking of cruelty to the Reduced, what's this I hear about Benedict North?"

"He's come back," Elliot replied. "And father brought him."

"Will wonders never cease." Dee's eyes narrowed. "What do you think it means? Is your father planning on handing over his inheritance?"

Elliot gave her friend a skeptical look. They both knew Baron North too well for that. But Benedict was aware of what he was owed. "Too early to tell what my father has planned."

Dee considered this for a moment. "Elliot, what if

I did as he said? Go there for a bit, wait until his attention is elsewhere, come back? If we're agreed that your father is only doing this because of the concert or because of our relationship . . . well, he'll find something else to occupy his thoughts soon enough. It's happened before. And if he's concerned about Benedict, I don't want my defiance to become a scapegoat for his frustration."

"Or we could tell him you went in, and really you could go . . . elsewhere."

"Else . . . where?"

"The Grove estate. Or wherever it is Thom has gone."

"Elliot . . . ," Dee said in warning.

"Or what about asking the Innovations?" Elliot suggested. "We could talk to Felicia. I know she would help us."

Dee looked skeptical.

"They aren't all like . . . him."

"Oh, don't you worry about Captain Malakai Wentforth," said Dee. "He's been all apologies this morning. Dropped by my cottage at dawn, and he's been helping Gill with some of his mechanical difficulties for the past few hours."

"He's been *what*?" Elliot asked in disbelief.

"Amazingly contrite. I think he knows he was over the line last night. Maybe he'd had too much cider."

"The Groves' cider isn't that strong."

"Well then, maybe he just realized it's a good deal harder to defend his behavior in front of people who actually know you than it was to make up lies for that Phoenix girl.

Either way, I expect he'll be coming by to apologize to you any time now."

Elliot rubbed her wrists where Kai had grabbed her at the concert. "I think not." He may have insulted the North Posts last night, but he had nothing against Gill or Dee personally. He was angry at Elliot.

And he'd spent years with Andromeda Phoenix, who had a much more concrete reason to hate Luddites. Their friendship had fanned his anger into hatred.

"As for throwing myself at the Innovations," Dee continued, "that's a nonstarter. We shouldn't risk their relationship with your father."

"He wouldn't have to know where you were." But as soon as the words were out of her mouth, Elliot understood. This was just like with Thom. No one could know. Certainly not Elliot. "Dee—"

The older woman wiped her hands off on her skirt and stood. "This conversation is over, Elliot. I'm under your father's authority, not yours. My choices are to follow his rules or leave."

"You know that's not true. We've been breaking his rules for years, you and I."

But Dee ignored that. "If I leave, I endanger Jef."

"If you stay in the birthing house, how can you protect him?"

"If you disobey your father's direct orders, *you* can't protect him if something goes wrong." Dee sighed, and when she spoke again, her voice had a hitch in it. "And I need you to be able to do that, Elliot. Can't you understand?"

"I'm not a child anymore," Elliot cried. "I can protect you both."

"We're done talking about this. I've made up my mind." Dee smacked the cow on the rump and it moved back into its stall.

"So you make up your mind and that's it? It's done?" Elliot lifted her chin.

"Don't you give me that look, Elliot North. That haughty, Luddite look of yours. Kai wasn't wrong about everything, you know. I know I can leave if I want. I knew that three years ago. I chose not to then, and I make the same choice now."

Elliot swallowed until her eyes stopped burning. "But *why*?"

"I just gave you half a dozen reasons." Dee sighed again. "Fine. I'm willing to compromise. If this doesn't blow over by the time I have this baby, you are free to break me out of the birthing house. I'll leave, and I'll take my family, and you won't have to worry about us anymore."

That wasn't true. She'd worried about Kai for four years. And with more Posts leaving the estate, she'd worry about the fate of the farm as well. But it was all she would get from Dee.

"Enough of this," Dee said. "Shift change is coming. Let's go see if Gill and the young captain have made any progress on that tractor. I want to be there when he apologizes to you."

"Don't hold your breath," Elliot replied. "It's not good for the baby."

KAI AND GILL WERE finished by the time Dee and Elliot arrived, and judging from their moods, they'd completely forgotten their argument the previous evening. Gill was laughing and slapping Kai on the back as the tractor hummed and sputtered away. Kai wore his sleeves pulled up and a grin Elliot hadn't seen in four years. It stopped her in her tracks. She feared coming closer, dreaded being the reason for the smile to vanish from his face.

Despite the previous night's frost, the morning had turned unseasonably warm for winter, helped along somewhat by the bright sun and the deep blue of the cloudless sky. Much of the barnyard had turned to mud as the heat softened the frost, but Kai looked as if he'd escaped the worst of it, even if he had been on the ground beneath the machine.

"Ladies!" Gill called. "The mechanic's triumphant return!" He affected a flourished bow worthy of any Luddite lord, and Dee laughed and clapped. Kai still grinned, though once again he was not looking at Elliot.

"Thank you," she said to him nevertheless. "I'm afraid I never had the skill you did with this old hunk of junk."

He turned to grab his velvet jacket off a hook. "Yes, well. It was the least I could do."

"After . . . ?" Dee prompted, as Elliot wondered anew why there was no convenient sinkhole in the barnyard she could vanish into.

"After my rudeness last night," said Kai, doing up the

buttons on his jacket. His hair covered his eyes as he spoke. "I never should have interrupted the festivities in that way."

"Really?" Dee crossed her arms. "That's all you're sorry about?"

"Dee—" Elliot murmured.

"Not all." Kai lifted his head and looked at Elliot at last.

Twenty-one

HIS EYES SEEMED TO bore right through her again, and Elliot had to ball her hands into fists to keep them from trembling. Had she been wrong last night, at the party? Had they always been like this? In her myriad memories of Kai, why could she not recall the strangeness in his clear black eyes? Was it the stark comparison between the handsome captain he was now and the grimy mechanic she'd once loved? Or was it that now she feared meeting his eyes and seeing his hatred and disdain of her reflected in their depths?

"I'm sorry I implied that Elliot doesn't care about the Posts on her property."

As apologies went, his was pretty pale, yet her name on his tongue warmed her more than the morning sun. Where everything had changed, this at least was the same. Three syllables, and three thousand memories.

But Kai wasn't done. "It was wrong of me to say that, and it's untrue. I think she cares about them very much."

For a moment, she thought he'd say more and braced

herself for the inevitable put-down. But it never came, as he turned toward the sound of sun-carts approaching. A moment later, Andromeda and Donovan crested the hill with Olivia and Horatio in the passenger seats.

"We're going to the dunes," Olivia announced when they arrived. "I'd like to take advantage of the weather before it gets cold again."

"You mean you'd like to take advantage of the Fleet's sun-carts on the dunes," Horatio corrected.

Olivia blushed, very prettily, but recovered herself quickly. "Malakai, you must come along. And Elliot, too."

"I have work," Elliot said automatically. She could happily live out the rest of her days without serving as witness to Olivia and Kai's courtship.

"We all have work," said Horatio. "Except for my sister, lady of leisure that she is. She's a bad influence."

Olivia laughed, and Elliot reminded herself again that the girl was not to blame for the pain in her heart.

"Come have a picnic with us," Horatio said. "You left our party so quickly yesterday that I didn't even get the chance to dance with you."

"You expect to dance on the dunes?"

Horatio chuckled. "I'm going instead of tending to my farm. If you don't come, you'll make me look bad."

His farm was not in such desperate shape. He had no broken tractors, and he had plenty of Posts to fill in when he wanted a day off. But Elliot would never say that aloud. She was still a North, and had too much pride for that.

"Go," said Dee. "The dairy is running smoothly, and

I can't think of anything else that needs your hand this afternoon."

Elliot narrowed her eyes. "You're trying to get rid of me so I can't protest your move." She had half a mind to appeal to Kai on the issue—she knew he hated the birthing house as much as she did. But when she turned to him, he'd already draped his hands on the overhead rails of the suncart that carried Olivia and leaned down to listen to her. His attention was not on Elliot or Dee, or the concerns of the North estate. She couldn't expect him as her ally.

"Should we invite Tatiana?" Olivia asked.

"Tatiana's busy this morning," Elliot said. "She's entertaining my cousin, who came to the estate with my father last night."

Kai stiffened. "Benedict North has returned to the estate?"

"Do you know him?" asked Horatio. "We've never met, but I hear he's been living in a Post enclave."

Kai's forehead furrowed, and his glance in Elliot's direction was so quick she almost missed it. "I haven't seen him in years."

"We don't have enough room in the carts," Andromeda said firmly. "Come on, let's go."

Perhaps Andromeda wasn't so bad, Elliot thought. She was saving her from having to spend the day with her sister.

In a few minutes it was all decided, and they set off for the dunes. Donovan was letting Horatio drive his cart, and Elliot joined their party, while Andromeda climbed in the back of her cart to let Kai take the driver's seat next to Olivia. It was only once they were on the road that Elliot realized there were two extra seats. No doubt Andromeda didn't want to be outnumbered by Luddites.

The dunes lay to the north even of the Boatwright estate, where the island grew thin and pointed like an arrow into the vast expanse of the sea. There was nothing but beach out here—no houses, no fields, no sign of civilization at all. In ancient times, this beach had been preserved as a religious artifact. The original settlers of the island had deemed it a home for the spirits, but no one believed that anymore. Indeed, wild places were the only ones truly free of spirits. All the real ghosts lived farther south, in the shells of the burned-out cities that had once belonged to the Lost. The Boatwright house and the shipyard was the closest anyone had gotten to building out here. The Boatwright family kept the cliffs mostly pristine in reverence of an ancestry that stretched back long before the Reduction.

"What beautiful country," Donovan said. "It reminds me very much of some of the wild islands we discovered on our explorations."

"That makes sense," said Elliot. "Once upon a time, these lands were home to herds of wild horses. Was this what it looked like on the island where you found the Innovation horses?"

Donovan looked at his hands. "I was not on that particular voyage. It was from . . . before I joined the Fleet."

"Still, you must have seen many spectacular sights. Things no one else has witnessed in hundreds of years."

"Yes," Donovan replied, his tone stiff, and too late,

Elliot remembered his song from the concert. He had seen them, and he now regretted every moment he'd spent away from Sophia.

"That was a very beautiful song you gave us last night," she said. "I am told that . . . I am very sorry for your loss."

"Thank you," said Donovan. "There are days that go by now where I'm fine. Where I believe that everything is better, and I can go through my day without thinking of her every second. But it's almost worse after that. For then, when the memories do return, they bring with them remorse for having ever forgotten her."

"You haven't forgotten her," Elliot said, "just because a few minutes or days or eventually weeks go by without having your grief in the forefront of your thoughts. She wouldn't like it if you dwelled only on your sadness."

"You say this from experience in loss?" Donovan replied.

"Yes. I lost my mother four years ago." And she'd also lost Kai. Neither person had been far from her thoughts in the ensuing years. But Kai had lingered more, because she knew he was out there somewhere. Her mother only lived in her heart. "And I try to honor her memory by doing what I know she would have done had she survived. But if I ever forget her, momentarily, I don't berate myself when I am reminded. She can't be the only thing I ever think of, or I'd be catatonic, as unable to cope as I was the day I lost her."

"Ah, there you have it. I *am* unable to cope. I am not a credit to the Cloud Fleet at present. I write sad songs, but I haven't been working much on our ship."

"You will move past this," she said.

He gave her a pitiful smile. "I don't think so. Your mother, I am sure, was taken before her time, but she was a grown woman. She had made a life, she had grown children in you and your sister. Sophia died so young—all of her potential was wasted."

"And would she be happy to see you wasting yours?" Elliot asked. "I didn't know her, but I have heard she was a great fan of the future. She wouldn't like you to think only of the past."

Donovan laughed mirthlessly. "Elliot, you sound nothing at all like a Luddite when you say things like that."

"Perhaps I do not have a very Luddite outlook," she said. "But I am serious. You must continue to live your life, and remember her with fondness, not with guilt. You were not meant to think always and only of the person you have lost. That is not the way the human mind was meant to operate."

Donovan looked up at the flawless expanse of sky above their heads. "Perhaps I do not have a very human mind."

SEVEN YEARS AGO

Dear Elliot,
By the time you read this, I'll be gone. I don't want to stay here
anymore. I've been here for my whole life—all eleven years—and
I've had it. I don't want to live and die on this farm like I'm one of
the Reduced. I don't want to work on your father's stupid tractors.
I want to read more books. I want to see more places. I am going
away and I'm going to see the world. I heard there are places
where there are Posts like me—Posts that don't live on Estates and
work for Luddites. I want to be one of those.

> *I know I will miss my da, and I know I will miss you. Don't*
miss me too much. Take care of Ro. Maybe someday I'll come
back and visit, and we can go see the stars like you said.
Your friend,
Kai

∽

Dear Kai,
Please don't be mad. I had to tell someone. It's not safe for you
to wander off the Estate. Ever since Benedict left, all I hear
are horrible stories about the things that happen in those Post

enclaves. Bad things. I can't imagine them happening to you. And I can't bear the thought of you leaving, either. I can't be without you, and neither can Ro.

Your father promised me he wouldn't punish you. I only told him, you know. It's not like I told mine! Please don't be mad at me. Pretty please. I couldn't bear it.
Your friend (I hope!),
Elliot

ༀ

Dear Elliot,
It doesn't matter anyway. Apparently I'm too stupid to even realize which way is north and which is south. The problem is you can't see the stars in the daytime. I accidentally went north, and the land ran out. There's nothing but cliffs up there and towers of rock sticking out of the sea. It looks like there used to be bridges that connected the towers to the mainland, but they're all gone now.

Do you know anything about them? Since I'm not running away anymore, do you want to go see them with me? I'll think about forgiving you if you do.
Your friend (maybe),
Kai

ༀ

Dear Kai,
Sure I'll go with you. I know the towers you mean. They were formed when the sea ate away at the cliffs. It apparently

happened long ago, before even the Reduction. But the towers have been getting longer ever since, as the sea eats more and more of the land.

My mother says the bridges fell when she was still a young girl, and my grandfather decided it was too dangerous to try to rebuild them. I don't know who built them the first time. Perhaps it was a Luddite who was desperate to catch a glimpse of the rest of the world.

Your friend,

Elliot

❧

Dear Elliot,

Maybe it wasn't a Luddite. Maybe it was a Post who built the bridges so he could escape to the North, to his own piece of land, untouched by the Luddite lords.

Your friend,

Kai

❧

Dear Kai,

I have hidden your last letter. Be careful what you write to me!

Your friend,

Elliot

Twenty-two

THE SUN-CARTS CHUGGED ALONG now as they ascended the promontory at the northernmost tip of the island. The beaches on either side dwindled into nothingness against the sides of rocky cliffs. Ahead of them lay the point and the end of Elliot's whole world—the end of the world entirely, as far as anyone knew.

And yet, one day soon, Kai would be sailing off into that nothingness. Elliot shivered suddenly. She'd worried about him for four years. How much more worry was in store for her now that she knew how far he planned to go? On the other hand, she reminded herself, what difference did it make? He'd been beyond the reach of her influence and ability to help him from the moment he'd left the North estate. He was gone for good either way.

They parked the carts near the very edge and spilled out onto the remaining tufts of dry winter grass. The sun was even stronger now, and Elliot unwound her scarf as the boys doffed their jackets and Olivia shed her heavy coat and began setting up the picnic. She'd brought a lot of leftovers from the party, Elliot noticed—fruit pies and meat pies and jars filled with hot apple cider.

"Let me help you," Elliot said, and knelt next to her on the blanket. Olivia was unpacking with one eye on the boys, who were peering over the edge of the cliff face and pointing at the waves that crashed against the rocks and sent spray hurtling a hundred meters in the air.

Beyond the edge stood spindly spires of rock, a line of towers the wind and sea had left behind after carving out the more porous earth that had once formed a jagged spear out into the sea. In her grandfather's time, there had been a bridge—a man-made one that stretched from tower to tower and formed a path out into the beyond. But it had long ago rotted away. Connections still existed between some of the spires, and others had tumbled into the sea. There was nothing at all that connected the mainland to the first stone tower, which stood about seven meters out in the abyss.

When she was younger, she and Kai had played a game, standing at the edge of the cliff and throwing their arms out to the breeze, letting it lift and buffet them until they grew timid and backed away. Elliot always lost. Even then, Kai had been fearless and she had been cautious—Luddite to the core.

A blast of salt-tinged wind shot up the cliff face and blew the boys backward. Horatio tripped and took a knee. Andromeda laughed.

"They should be careful," said Elliot.

"They're amazing!" Olivia exclaimed. "Not like anyone

I've ever known. The whole Fleet—it seems somehow as if their lives are bigger, their spirits greater."

Elliot chuckled in spite of herself. She supposed the Fleet could come across as superior, but wasn't it warranted? A group of estate-born Posts with fortunes that made every Luddite she knew drool with envy? They *were* important. It was a refreshing change to get that impression from a Post, rather than her sister.

"And what they're doing," Olivia went on. "To go out as they do—to risk their lives to see if there's anything at all left beyond these shores. That is the most worthy goal, isn't it?"

"More worthy than feeding people?"

Olivia blushed. "No. Perhaps not. I know what our duty is. But I wish I wasn't a Luddite, Elliot. I wish I could be an explorer, like them."

Elliot refused to be mean to the younger girl. It wasn't Olivia's fault that she was in love with Kai. It wasn't her fault that she was fourteen, and carefree, and still fantasized about a world where she could run away from her estate and go exploring with the bravest boy she'd ever met. Once, Elliot had done the same. Once, she'd believed she could, that one day she and Kai would sail away and find the world that everyone else had lost.

So now, she couldn't resist asking Olivia, "What is stopping you?"

"My brother, I suppose." She shrugged. "I don't think Horatio would let me go live in a Post enclave, at least not for another few years."

"Then do it in a few years," Elliot replied, her tone

growing short. She would *not* be cruel to Olivia. The girl was not to blame for Elliot's situation, for her choices, for her heartbreak. Kai would hate Elliot even if Olivia Grove had never been born. "You're free. Why shouldn't you follow your heart's desire?" Even if that desire included Kai.

"A few years," Olivia mused. "That seems too long to wait for—" She stopped herself, then looked at Elliot. "You must think I'm very foolish. A little girl with a crush."

Elliot weighed her words. "I think . . . I think if you mean what you say about wanting to be an explorer, that your wishes are valid. I think if you mean it, you should pursue it regardless of the actions of Captain Wentforth." There. That was fair. And it was the most she could trust herself to say.

"Thank you," Olivia gushed. "Tatiana was telling me the other day what a fool I was being, and that everything I want is only because of him. And it is—but not in the way she supposes. Rather, being with him—or even near him—has taught me so much. It's a new world out there. I can't hide away on the estate. I can't forget about it now that I've had a taste."

Elliot busied herself with setting out the last of the food. Part of her wanted to strangle Olivia, or jump off the cliff, or even just cry. But she couldn't allow herself to do so, no more than she could allow herself any of the indulgences she was encouraging Olivia to take. Elliot would never forget Kai, nor the world of possibilities they'd once dreamed of. But she could never have it for herself, either.

Kai was now busy teaching the Phoenixes their old game of cliffside chicken. He teetered on the very edge, arms outstretched, face upturned toward the sun. Something desperate and devilish woke inside Elliot. Now they had nothing, but once they'd had this. Once she'd given in every time. But she was older now. She'd taken bigger risks. Elliot stood, brushed off her knees, and joined him at the cliff's edge. He could hate her now, he could resent her, he could never forgive her, but he *would* know what she'd become. She positioned her toes just a bit farther out than his and threw her arms out to the side.

"Have you spent these four years practicing to beat me?" he whispered. She glanced at him out of the corner of her eye, but could not read the expression on his face. Was he joking? Teasing? Seeking to wound her again? He'd apologized today in front of the Posts. She'd thought it was to bury the hatchet with Gill and Dee. Was it to make amends with her as well?

In the end, she kept her response neutral. "How do you know I didn't used to let you win?"

Kai wiggled his toes a bit farther out. Elliot copied him.

"Enough is enough, you two," said Andromeda, back on the blanket.

Elliot felt wobbly, but she steeled herself and looked straight ahead at the horizon. Of course, it proved nothing. Her ability to stand on a cliff edge did not make her better than Kai. It did not make up for his words the previous evening, or his treatment of her for the past few weeks. It certainly didn't make up for all the smiles he shared with Olivia, or all the rumors going around about them.

But my, it felt good.

"Wentforth," Andromeda warned. Elliot didn't dare turn around, or even look over at Kai. She couldn't afford to lose her balance. Out of the corner of her eye, she saw a figure step up next to him. Olivia.

"This isn't so bad," the younger girl said. She leaned a bit from side to side, trying to find her balance as the wind tugged at her full skirts.

Kai moved even farther out.

"Malakai, quit it." Andromeda's tone had turned commanding. Elliot bit her lip. She could feel the abyss beneath her toes. She was already out as far as she dared. The wind picked up again, buffeting them all back, then pulling them forward. Olivia wavered. Kai remained firm. Elliot locked her knees and circled her arms to keep her balance.

"Olivia," said Horatio. "A step or two back, please."

Kai dropped his arms. He took a few steps back.

Elliot sighed in relief.

And then he leaped.

Somewhere, Olivia was screaming. Somewhere, the wind still blew. Somewhere, the earth remained firm beneath her feet, but she might as well have been standing on smoke, for all she saw was Kai, bicycling his legs, arcing high, silhouetted against the sea and the sky, dark clothes, dark hair. . . . And as he fell, Elliot felt everything inside of her plummet, too.

Then he landed, two feet firm on the rocky surface of the first tower.

Again, Elliot could breathe. She reeled back from the edge.

Olivia was sitting on the grass, gasping. Horatio had dropped his meat pie. Andromeda stood with her arms crossed over her chest and shook her head. "Show-off," she cried to Kai across the water.

"How did he do that?" Horatio asked. "He could have been killed."

Andromeda rolled her eyes. "There's an updraft of air in between the towers, every so often. He just took advantage of it."

"Impossible," Elliot said. Her ancestors had lived on this land for generations. No one had ever leaped across before.

"Not really, Miss Elliot," Donovan said quickly. "You just . . . learn to read these things, if you're pilots like we are. We read the shape of the wind on the surface of the sea. Watch."

He, too, leaped. Over on the tower, Kai shouted in approval as Donovan landed beside him.

Andromeda sighed. "Prideful, reckless show-offs. They'll be the death of us, I swear."

"The death of themselves," Horatio corrected.

Elliot stared at the boys standing on the nearest tower. Kai met her eyes, then whirled around and took off for the next. Again, her heart dropped into her stomach, but a moment later she saw him land, hard, scrabbling against the scree that sat on the top of the tower of rock.

There he was, on the land beyond the islands. There he was, the lord of his own four meters of rock.

"Enough!" Andromeda shouted, as her brother

followed Kai. "Don! Stop!" She stamped her foot in frustration. "Do you have any idea how *dangerous* this is?"

Olivia clapped her hands with delight. "Oh, I must learn how to do it! To think that these towers were accessible all this time. We could have rebuilt the bridges long ago."

"They aren't," said Andromeda, frowning. "Not really. I mean—the conditions of the wind have to be just right, and you need really skilled pilots, like my brother and Wentforth to . . . read the currents. They'll get stuck out there if they aren't careful. They are being so foolish."

"Teach me!" Olivia insisted. She grabbed for Andromeda's hands.

Andromeda forced a laugh. "Not likely. Your brother would kill me." She shook her head at the figures bouncing around out there. "This is ridiculously dangerous. Felicia will have their heads when she finds out."

Andromeda glared daggers at the boys out on the towers. She didn't look worried about them. She looked angry.

Kai had now jumped back to the closest tower, and stood with his face turned up into the blue.

Elliot watched him, and Donovan. She watched them time their leaps. Were there really updrafts of wind helping to propel them? And if so, how in the world could they see them? The same wind that blew the waves a hundred meters down could not lift their bodies. She'd seen the power of wind back when her mother had used it to run the turbines in the Boatwright orchards. She'd used it herself to fly kites or sail Kai's paper gliders. He'd been good at reading the winds, yes, but not able to fly himself.

Andromeda was still explaining the complexities of the calculations involved in determining when one might jump, the subtleties of the observations, the amount of training that her brother and Kai had undergone to be able to do both in an instant, to gauge the distance, to leap . . .

And all the while she was doing it, she was wringing her hands behind her back and casting nervous glances at the boys with her strange, crystalline eyes. The eyes she shared with her brother Donovan. The eyes, Elliot realized, that looked like blue-green versions of the ones Kai had finally let her see.

All three of the Cloud Fleet captains had those eyes. Those strange, *superior* eyes that let Andromeda drive through the woods in the dark, that let Kai wander around the barn at night without a lantern, that let all three of them stand in the sanctuary and see insects instead of stars. Kai had known, even in the blackness, that she'd been standing in the whisper zone. And he wouldn't look at her. Kai, who had once been able to communicate so much with a mere glance—he would never let her see into his eyes. She thought it was because he was angry, but it was much worse. He was afraid she'd see it. And now she had.

That wasn't all. The jumps they were making—they weren't merely improbable—they were impossible. As impossible as Donovan's virtuoso performance on the fiddle. As impossible as Kai catching her when she fell off the horse on the beach, even though he'd been fifty meters away.

Andromeda wasn't scared that the boys would fall. She was scared that the Luddites on the cliff would see something they shouldn't. Something that shouldn't be possible at all. Something that had been impossible for generations, for the safety of the world.

No.

Kai.

No, not her Kai.

Elliot stared at Kai in horror. He was still dancing around on the ledge but he noticed her and froze. His arms dropped to his sides. Even across the gulf of years and distance, he could read her. His smile faded. His mouth opened.

"I think I get it," said Olivia. So did Elliot. "You mean like this?"

Andromeda tried to grab at her, but even with her reflexes—her swift, inhuman, abhorrent reflexes—she was too late.

Olivia jumped.

Olivia fell.

Twenty-three

THE WIND HAD PICKED up, but the most it did was catch the edges of Olivia's russet skirts, twisting them around her like a current in a bloody river. She slammed against the stone and bounced hard, once, twice, before her body caught on a ledge of the nearest tower, a few stories below the cliff's edge.

"Dear God," Horatio shouted. "Olivia! Olivia!" He rushed to the edge of the cliff and looked down.

Elliot ran to his side and drew him back. Olivia lay crumpled there, a flower crushed beneath a boot. "Careful," she whispered. "Let the Fleet captains go." After all, they could.

Already, Kai was climbing down the side of the spire, feeling out handholds in the cracks. Already, Andromeda was rummaging through the boot of the sun-cart for a piece of rope. Up on the tower ledge, Donovan was shouting directions down to Kai, easily spotting then notifying him about footholds and loose stones.

"She's not moving!" Horatio cried. "She's not moving!"

Elliot wrapped her arms around her friend. "Shh. Don't look." She squeezed her eyes shut, her previous outrage all but forgotten in the moment. *Please, Olivia, please. Don't be dead.*

When she opened her eyes again, Kai had reached the girl. He held her head in his hands, and even from here, Elliot's merely human eyes could see the red that stained his skin and the rocks beneath Olivia's body. Andromeda returned to the cliff edge with her rope and tossed it, easily, to Donovan, who caught it just as easily. Their movements were the same as always—graceful as a cat's, precise as a machine's.

It was horrifying.

Below, Kai bent his face close to Olivia's. "She's breathing," he shouted, and the words reverberated across the chasm. Horatio shuddered in relief. Donovan lowered the rope, which Kai tied to Olivia. With Donovan's help, he climbed with her to the top of the tower.

"Can you make it across while carrying her?" Andromeda called.

Kai looked at Elliot as he answered. His tone was flat. "Yes."

Of course he could. He was a superhuman.

"Don't look," Elliot said softly to Horatio. "Don't watch this part." She wished that she, too, could avoid it, but even if she didn't watch, there was no denying that it was done. Kai jumped across to the cliff again, and this time he did it with a full-grown person in his arms. It was impossible. It should have been impossible.

Oh, Kai, how could you?

But there was no time, no time to even contemplate what had happened to the Cloud Fleet Posts. No time to do anything but offer a quick prayer that Horatio was too overcome by worry for his sister to think about the abomination before his eyes. Donovan leaped back to the mainland and they laid Olivia out on the grass. Andromeda wrapped bandages around her bleeding head. She was unconscious, but breathing. And every moment, she was losing more blood. Elliot felt her limbs for broken bones. Her leg was bent at a funny angle, and there was clearly something wrong with her collarbone, but the biggest damage by far was to her head. Elliot pressed cloths against the wound, hoping to slow the flow of blood.

"We have to get her home," Horatio said.

"No," said Elliot. "Take her to the Boatwright house. It's closer, and Felicia Innovation can help her." Indeed, Felicia might be the only one in two hundred kay who could. She'd known about their eyes that day in the cavern. What's more, she'd *apologized* for taking away the wonder of the sanctuary's stars. Felicia had been the one to do this to them. She'd doomed them all.

Elliot looked up at Kai, who was standing over them, breathing hard. His glittery, inhuman eyes were wide with fear, but they widened even more at her words.

"Felicia," she repeated. There'd be time later to give in to her shock. "Perhaps it would be best to send one of the carts down there as quickly as possible. You can explain the situation and she can get ready. We'll have to drive slowly with Olivia so as not to jostle her too much."

"Great idea," Andromeda said. She turned to her brother. "Take Horatio and Wentforth and go. Elliot and I will take Olivia."

"I can't leave my sister," said Horatio.

"The ride will be smoother with less weight," said Andromeda. "I can drive it, and Elliot seems to have a handle on what Olivia needs, medically."

"I'll drive Olivia and Elliot," Kai blurted. Elliot cringed at the sound of her name in his mouth.

"No." Andromeda's tone was firm. "You drive quickly. *I* drive carefully. Now go. Every second we waste might be her last."

Horatio seemed appeased by this, and they helped load the unconscious girl into the cart. Then the boys all piled into the second cart and took off. As Andromeda steered carefully down the path toward level ground, Elliot cradled Olivia's head from the worst of the bumps.

"That was smart," said Elliot. "Sending Kai down first." He'd bristled with energy he needed to race off.

"Well, I'm smart," Andromeda answered simply. After a moment, she spoke again. "Though you wouldn't be able to tell it from my behavior today."

She didn't, Elliot noticed, correct her about using Kai's old name.

The ride seemed to go on forever. Soon they lost sight of the boys' cart, though Andromeda was still driving as fast as she dared. Now that Elliot knew the appalling truth, she marveled that she'd never noticed it before. She'd never suspected how Andromeda could have driven like a maniac through the woods the previous evening. She'd never wondered how it was that she could so skillfully steer around every dip in the path. Or if she had, she'd simply chalked it up to the Fleet's skill as pilots.

Elliot felt sick to her stomach. She wanted to scream, to leap out of the cart, but what good would that do? She could act like a model Luddite if she wanted, run away, denounce Andromeda then and there, and it wouldn't help save Olivia's life. Like it or not, she must not show anyone what she knew until the younger girl was safe. No matter how wrong it was, right now she needed these people to keep Olivia alive.

After an age, they finally arrived at the Boatwright house. Felicia Innovation ran out to greet them. "Bring her inside, quickly," she cried. "I have to see to her head. Are there any broken bones? Has she stirred at all?"

Elliot answered the questions she could as Felicia got Olivia situated on a bed and began tending to her wounds. The Posts gathered around, their faces ashen. Horatio stood like a statue at the door.

"Olivia," he moaned. "Wake up, please. Please wake up."

Elliot went over to him and squeezed his hands. "She'll be all right. Felicia will help her." After all, the woman could work miracles.

Dangerous ones.

AT LAST THE BLOOD stopped seeping from Olivia's head. At last Felicia set the final broken bone. At last the young girl's breathing stabilized, and Felicia emerged from the sickroom and told Horatio that nothing more could be done, that they would have to wait to see if Olivia would wake up.

The *if* seemed to break him all over again, and he buried his head in his hands.

Both Elliot and Andromeda helped him to a chair. Donovan stoked the fire, and Kai stood, frozen, like he'd been ever since they'd arrived at the Boatwright house.

"I can't lose her," Horatio said. "She's the only family I have."

"Don't say things like that." Elliot stroked his arm. "She's only asleep. We don't know anything yet."

"I'm so sorry," said Andromeda. "I should have warned her. I shouldn't have let her think she could make the jump."

"It's my fault," said Kai. "I shouldn't have jumped at all. She never would have been tempted to try if she didn't see me out there."

Horatio raised his head and forced a smile in Kai's direction. "Look at us. You look like death, my friend, and I'm sure I do, too. We'll never stop blaming ourselves. I guess that's the price of love?"

Kai's abnormal eyes widened and Elliot nearly cried aloud. "I should go," she blurted. "I'm of no use to anyone here." She touched Horatio on the shoulder. "As long as you can spare me?"

Horatio nodded. "I think I'll be fine. The Innovations have offered me a room here so I can stay close to my sister tonight. Thank you, Elliot, for all your help today. Your quick thinking in bringing her here probably saved her life."

Elliot shook her head. "It was nothing at all." She longed to be gone from this house, away from the Posts, whose odd eyes and precise movements now made her skin crawl. She needed to get her thoughts together. She needed to figure out what she was going to do next.

"I'll drive you back to the North estate," said Kai.

"No."

"I insist." He stared at her, and this time Elliot was the one to turn away.

"No. I'm fine. I need to walk. To clear my head."

"Elliot—" Kai's voice curdled the tones of her name. She could not bear it from him now.

"Leave her alone," Andromeda snapped. Kai glared at the older girl. Andromeda glared back. Elliot noticed the lights refracting in their eyes and felt bile rise in her throat.

She needed to run, or she would scream their secrets for all the world to hear.

FIVE YEARS AGO

Dear Elliot,
There was a reason I didn't wait for you yesterday. There was a
reason I didn't want you to come with me to visit my da at the
healing house. Do you think you can butt in wherever you like
just because you're a North?
Kai

∽

Dear Kai,
I'm sorry! I didn't realize you wanted to be alone with him. I
have gone to visit him other times—you know that. Why should
yesterday have been any different?
Your friend,
Elliot

∽

Dear Elliot,
It just is. When I go with you, it's not about me and my da. It's
about everyone staring at you because you're a Luddite. We can't
help but look at my da, at all the people in the healing house,
and think that when your family is sick, you don't go there. Your

grandfather gets round the clock nursing. Your grandfather gets medicine my da doesn't.

For what it's worth, my da doesn't want your medicine anymore. It won't fix him. It just prolongs his suffering.
Your friend,
Kai

∽

Dear Kai,
I just want to help. You don't have to be mean. If I had medicine for everyone in the healing house, I'd give it to them. It's not my fault that all I can do is sneak you things meant for my grandfather. I'd fix everyone if I could.
Your friend,
Elliot

∽

Dear Elliot,
Would you? Would you really?

I get so angry sometimes, Elliot, thinking about all the people stuck in there. Reduced sent there to die because their hands or legs don't work. Something as simple as that. There are Reduced who have been in the "healing house" for thirteen years. That's as long as I've been alive. If they were the tractor, I could change their tires, but because of the protocols, we can't fix them. We're not allowed. How does that make sense?
Your friend,
Kai

∽

Dear Kai,

It doesn't always make sense to me, either. Is that what you want me to say? But it must be true. Everyone believes it. The protocols are there for our protection. We broke them once, and we got the Reduction. Isn't it better that a few people die, as God wills it, than we risk destroying humanity all over again?

Humans tried to play God once, and we failed. We tried to make over humanity in our own image. It's forbidden. We have to accept that.

Your friend,

Elliot

∾

Dear Elliot,

Not everyone believes it. That's all.

Your friend,

Kai

∾

Dear Kai,

I heard about your father. I'm sorry. Please let me come see you tonight.

Your friend,

Elliot

∾

Dear Elliot,

I've thought it over, and I've decided I don't care how much trouble I get in. Not now. My father is dead, and the rest of the people in the healing house are going to die, and they are going to die even though we know how to fix them. We know how to save them. And we don't?

No, not we. You. Luddites.

I <u>don't</u> believe in the protocols! It's not right to let people die for them. You can use technology without risking another Reduction. There has to be a happy medium. And if we never challenge the protocols, we'll never know if we even need them anymore! It's like I said years ago—I'm a Post. How do you know I'm not immune to the Reduction? How does anyone know that every Post in the islands wasn't born immune?

Here's what I think: The Luddites use the restrictions to make sure the Reduced stay that way. If it weren't for the protocols, humanity might have found a cure, long before the Posts ever came. That's human nature—to make our lives better. But the Luddites would rather let people die than risk giving up their control of the world. They'd rather let my father die.

You say that the protocols are to keep us from playing God. But I think you have it backward. When we have the ability to save someone's life, and we decide they aren't worthy of being saved—isn't that playing God as well?
Your friend,
Kai

∾

Dear Kai,
I have tried and failed to write this letter four times now. Your father was a good man, and everyone here cared for him. He raised you, and that makes him a great man in my eyes.

I know things are bad right now. I have heard from the servants at the house that all the Posts on the estate are getting together to hold a memorial service. I would like to attend, if no one thinks that is odd. My mother has given me permission.

I am so sorry for your loss,
Your friend,
Elliot

∾

Dear Elliot,
Honestly, Elliot? I'd rather you didn't come. Everyone will stare. But after it's over, I would like it very much if you came and visited the pyre with me. We can bring Ro as well.

Is there any news about where I'll go?
Your friend,
Kai

∾

Dear Kai,
I understand. My mother told me that you will stay in the barn. We all want you to take your father's place as a mechanic. My mother knows you are young, but you were your father's apprentice, and you're the closest thing we've got right now.

I am so sorry, Kai. I'm so sorry about everything.
Your friend,
Elliot

Twenty-four

As soon as she could, Elliot escaped to the barn. She could not avoid discussing the accident with Tatiana, nor Benedict, nor her father. In her version, Olivia had accidentally slipped and fallen down the cliff face, though she doubted her ruse would last more than an evening or two, as the story spread.

And when it did spread, how long would it be before people started to wonder how the Posts had done it?

As she entered, Elliot's gaze slid to the knothole in the door and she reprimanded herself. Would the ritual never die? For four years she looked, though she knew Kai was gone. And now she looked, even though he was home and he hated her. The habit had been imprinted on her brain for all of her life—she was doomed to stare at empty knotholes for eternity.

Elliot went to the loft and sat before her work desk, but couldn't push away the thoughts in her mind. Those two years she'd spent developing her strain of wheat, she'd deluded herself into thinking it was all right. It was safe.

That what she'd created was not as bad as the abominations of the Lost. Tonight, she reread all of her notes on the wheat— each indefensible, aberrant, heretical page. In every line, she read hubris; in every word, she read defiance. She'd convinced herself she was only defying her father. But that wasn't true. She was defying nature itself. She was doing exactly what Kai and the other Fleet Posts had done.

She was courting death.

What had she been thinking? It wasn't worth it. It wasn't worth it, even to save a single life. The protocols were in place for a reason. Yes, it could make lives easier. Yes, it could save people when nothing else could. But it wasn't worth it. Humans were not meant to play God. They couldn't play God, or they'd wind up as something less than what humans were meant to be. They'd be Reduced.

Her father had been right to trample her wheat if he suspected what she'd done. She was surprised he hadn't gone further. He could have turned her in to the Luddite tribunal for reprimands or worse. After all, she was eighteen. Granted, it was just wheat, but even that—who knew what it would become inside the humans who ate it? Who knew if it would never grow back, or if it would infect the other crops with a plague, or if it would turn to poison? Before the Reduction, the Lost had enhanced crops to use them as weapons. They could make enemies sick or destroy countries' entire ecosystems.

And not always on purpose, either. Long before the Reduction, people had killed off entire species of food by attempting to improve it, just like Elliot had done. The ways of the Lost had brought only death and destruction. Elliot knew that. She was a Luddite, charged with protecting the survivors of the Reduction—human, animal, and vegetable—from the horrors that lurked in the heart of their own twisted DNA.

Only God could make a tree.

And only God could make a man. Only God had the right to decide how far a man might leap, or how well a man might see. If these Posts had done what she suspected . . .

Never mind all that. She knew they'd done it. She'd looked into Kai's eyes—eyes she'd once known as well as her own—and she'd seen the truth.

And he knew it, too.

At last, she left the room. She locked the door behind her. She walked back down the hall and descended the stairs, and she wasn't the slightest bit surprised to see Kai waiting for her at the bottom.

He stood in darkness and didn't even squint when the lantern hit his eyes. Now that she finally saw the truth, it was all she *could* see. His pupils didn't contract in the glare of the lantern, and strange lights danced in his irises. His face was utterly flat.

"I need to know," he said. There was no *Elliot* this time. And why should there be? He hadn't come to apologize.

"How is Olivia?" Elliot asked instead. "Has she woken up yet?"

But Kai didn't answer her question either. "The knowledge I suspect you possess can be very dangerous."

"I suspect the thing you bear is more dangerous still."

"So you do know."

"Only that the things I saw today were actions that could not be performed by the boy I knew." But the man who stood before her was not the boy she'd known. Wasn't that what he was always saying to her? "Or by any natural human."

"I am a human. I am a *most* human of humans."

A dozen generations of her ancestors recoiled at the thought. "I know what you are. I know what you did." Her voice was very soft, her tone very grave. It was the sound of the Luddite speaking to the liege, but she couldn't help what slipped out next, Elliot to Kai. "How could you?"

He seemed to grow several centimeters. Was it a trick of the light, or some other kind of trick, some monstrosity she'd not yet discovered? "I will not stand here and be judged by a Luddite who knows nothing of my life."

There was no point in continuing the conversation. Yes, she was a Luddite. There had been times she'd doubted it, but the proof lay in every churn of her stomach as she thought of what he'd become. For weeks now, Elliot had told herself there was no way Kai could hurt her anymore.

Every day, she was shown to be wrong again. He hurt her when he looked her way, and when he did not. He hurt her when he spoke to her with derision, and when he ignored her.

But now . . . now, surely, it was over. For this man—this Malakai Wentforth—he'd killed her Kai. Overwrote his very DNA.

It was ERV. She'd never seen it, but she knew the

signs. They'd been the stuff of nightmares since she'd first learned them in her nursery. The insidiousness of ERV lay in its very simplicity. You didn't need to replace your body with computerized parts. You didn't need to insert tiger or jellyfish or hawk genes into your spinal fluid. ERV simply reached into your DNA and flipped a few switches. Anyone could do it, and once, long ago, nearly everyone had.

He was Kai, and yet not Kai. More than Kai, better than Kai, *different* than Kai. All this time, she'd thought it had been his years of living free that had brought him back to her so strong, so swift, so fine. But it was more than that: he'd mucked around with the body God had given him. Didn't he care about the risk? Didn't he care what he might have done to his descendants?

"You don't know what it's like, down in the enclaves."

Elliot shook her head. "I surely don't, you're correct about that."

"It's not just stories the Luddites tell to scare their Posts into submission. There are desperate people there. They do desperate things."

"And that's what you did?" she asked him. "Something desperate?" Her voice broke on the words, shards of hope bursting through the skin of her anger.

Was this how frail her entire upbringing was? There was no excuse. None!

"I would have been desperate if I hadn't taken this risk," was what Kai said. "There are people who've done things far worse than this. When you're hungry, when you're cold, when you're *alone*—I consider myself lucky that this was what came along and not something worse."

"There's nothing worse," Elliot insisted.

"There is. You know people who could tell you about it." Kai's face was cold, his jaw set. "There are bad people in the enclaves. There's opportunity, yes, but a lot of danger. People whose slavery is worse than that on any estate. I learned to start measuring risk on a different scale. You can't judge me. You weren't there."

Her skin burned. No, she hadn't been there. Was this her fault? Could she have stopped him, if she had been there? Or would she have been just as desperate? Would she have been willing to risk her values, her future children, her life?

"So I did it. Me, and Andromeda, and Donovan. We were all part of an experiment, and it succeeded. We have faster reflexes, stronger stamina, keener vision. It's what makes us such extraordinary pilots."

"And what makes you still Kai?"

"I told you not to call me that." His face might have been made of marble, it showed so little feeling. "You must know by now that I am not that person anymore."

"Oh yes, I know." Everything she was raised to believe had taught her that what he'd turned himself into was an abomination. A dangerous one, that if allowed to live, to thrive, would bring about another disaster, a second Reduction.

She knew it, and still she didn't care. Elliot hated herself for that, but she couldn't deny it. He could have come to her in a tin body with glass eyes and a metal heart, and she'd still know him for Kai. Always always always Kai.

"Will you betray us?" he asked.

"You know me better than that."

"I know you are a Luddite," he said. "And that what I have become must disgust you."

Then he didn't know her at all. For she was something less than Luddite, and she felt so much more than simple disgust. "I don't know how you could do it," she said instead, staring into eyes that were so much like the ones she knew, and yet so different. "How you could take that risk. You say your experiment was successful. Were there others that were not? Other subjects who wound up Reduced? Dead?"

He was silent for a long time, and Elliot began to think she didn't want to know that answer.

"How could this be worth it?" she asked. "To what? See in the dark? Sail your ship with a little more finesse?"

"Is there a reason you'd find acceptable?" he asked. "Can you not imagine what could drive a person to break the protocols?"

Her jaw grew tight. "Not to become a better pilot," was all she trusted herself to say.

"What about to save a life?"

Twenty-five

SHE CLOSED HER EYES, but she doubted it hid her response from him. He knew her too well, and now he saw too much. "Whose life?" she asked. "Whose life was worth risking a dozen generations of your children?"

"Sophia Innovation," said Kai, and she opened her eyes. "Her mother was looking for a cure for her condition. She needed controls—other young Posts, especially second generation like me. I was looking for a chance. We each had what the other needed."

"But Felicia didn't find a cure," said Elliot.

"No." Kai shook his head. "Unfortunately not."

Sophia had died, and Kai—her Kai—had the seeds of Reduction sown within him. For nothing. For nothing!

"They used you," Elliot hissed. "They ruined you."

"They employed me," he replied coldly. "They saved me. Do I look like nothing more than a test subject to you, Elliot? Felicia's experiments failed with Sophia, but they didn't fail with me. And the Innovations are my friends.

We've turned the project into something so much greater, something that means all our work, all our risk, was not in vain. I'm a captain of the Cloud Fleet. I'm building a ship that can travel across the ocean. I have everything I've ever wanted in my life. Power, freedom. Who was I here? A mechanic? Living in a barn? You think about that and then tell me who it was that used me."

Elliot squeezed her jaw shut to keep the sob from escaping. She had no response. But it wasn't fair. The Cloud Fleet had had options. What could she have done for Kai? Nothing. He was a North estate Post, and she was a North. She couldn't change it. They'd known it back then. He'd had to leave, and to be together, she'd have had to go, too. Once, she'd told him she was willing to give up everything for him. And if it was only Elliot that would have been sacrificed, she might have gone through with it, too.

But she hadn't, and now everything was destroyed. Did he even care? Did he even *want* children someday?

He spoke again, and his tone was soft for once. "What choice do we have, Elliot North? What is the purpose of escaping Reduction if we are still forced to live within its limits?"

In his face dwelled a sadness she knew well, and a perception she could not comprehend. He was not her Kai. He could not be, for his DNA had been changed. He was an alien, an abomination, a ticking bomb that could set fire to everything her ancestors had managed to salvage of the world.

He was not her Kai.

He was not her Kai.

He was not her Kai.

But it was no use. She could burn the words into her skin and she would still not believe them. She breathed in the scent of hay and wet wood. Of manure and spoiled milk, of oil and leather, of lanterns and the night wind. The scents she'd known all her life. The ones that said barn, and freedom, and him. She took two steps toward Kai and laid her hand on his chest.

His heart pounded beneath his shirt, but he did not move. The deep thrum sounded so normal, so familiar. This, at least, they had not changed.

Elliot raised her face to his, recognizing in every plane and line the boy who lived inside her heart. He was breathing hard, matching the pace of his pulse. She was sure she was in the same state. For four years she'd subsisted on memories of this—his voice, his face, the sound of his breath and his heartbeat. She felt him like a leaf feels the sun, like a magnet feels metal.

"Elliot . . ."

She listed toward him, unwilling to reply with his name and risk breaking the spell. For four years, she'd been looking for direction, spinning as uselessly as the compass on her grandfather's wall. She'd tried her hardest, but without Kai she was lost.

"Please . . ."

His voice sounded like all the Kais in her memory. The ones who'd asked for books, for string-boxes, for company on his adventures. He sounded now like the Kai she'd once loved, like the Kai she still loved more than she loved the life she'd been born to lead.

"I'll give you whatever you want. Whatever it takes for you to keep our secret. A sun-cart? Or money? I have plenty. How much will it take?"

She blinked, as the dream smashed around her. So this is what it had come to. Kai didn't trust her. He'd never trust her. If he did, he wouldn't think he'd have to buy her silence. Because now it was Elliot, the Luddite lord's daughter, who was the beggar, the desperate one, who'd compromise the principles she'd had drummed into her since birth . . . for *money*. He thought she was a hypocrite, a traitor to her people, and he might be right. But not the way he thought. She'd do it for him. Not for money. Not for a *sun-cart*.

He loved the people who'd stolen his humanity, but he'd never loved her.

She stepped back. Stumbled, really. And sputtered. "Get out."

It was Kai's turn to blink in surprise.

She waved the lantern at him. He was fortunate she didn't throw it at his head. How could he know her so well and so little at once? "Get out of my barn. Now."

He stepped away from her, his hands held out to brace himself should she choose to swing. "I'm serious."

"So am I." She advanced, and he retreated toward the door. "I don't want anything from you." Not his money, not his pity, and most especially not his false kindness. "Don't you ever speak to me again, *Malakai Wentforth*. I hate you. I hate you. And I'm not sorry anymore."

"What?"

"I'm not sorry I didn't go with you. Because I hate the man that you've become."

He had passed the threshold now, and she slammed the door shut in his face. For a moment, Elliot let that door support her. She panted against the wood, giant, gulping breaths that did nothing to soothe her or stop the tears that sprang to her eyes.

The Kai she'd known could never have made her that offer. He would have asked a favor from a friend. She'd been wrong about him all along. He must have been telling the truth the night of the Innovations' party. He'd never cared for her at all. Perhaps he'd always only seen her as the rich girl in the big house, the one who could help him, who could give him things, who could protect him from punishment, who could get him out of trouble. Why shouldn't it work the same in reverse, now that he was the rich one? He'd never loved her. Maybe he'd never even *liked* her.

She slid to her knees on the packed dirt floor. She rested her forehead against the ground. She raked her hands through her skirt and her hair, and she wept.

Many minutes later, she heard his voice, soft and low, on the other side of the door. He was centimeters away. "You were *sorry*? You were sorry you didn't go with me?"

Hadn't he spent every moment since his return making sure she was? Hadn't it been the unspoken meaning behind every cruel comment? "I said go away!"

"No, you said 'get out.' I'm out."

"*Now* go away."

Silence. And then, "No."

For a second, they were both fourteen again, bickering. Bantering. For another second, Elliot wished it could stay that way. But too many things had changed. "I mean it," she tried, though she was terrified she didn't.

"I need to know—" she heard him growl under his breath. "I need to know your mind."

She jumped to her feet and threw open the door. He was kneeling on the other side, and when he looked up at her in surprise, he nearly took her breath away. But her anger prevailed.

"Get out of my sight this instant or I'll scream," she ordered him. "I will scream to the world what you are, Kai. Believe me, I will."

He regarded her for a long moment, and then he, too, stood. "I have been unfair to you," he said at last. "I know you wouldn't tell. You never have."

Ten minutes ago, those words might have meant the world to her, but it was too late. Not after what he'd said. "Good. You have the answer you wanted. You and your abominable friends are safe. Now go away."

"Elliot—"

She shuddered. If she heard him speak her name again she might vomit. "Don't you understand? *You disgust me.* Go. Away."

His expression turned hard, and then he left. Elliot breathed a sigh of relief.

It was true. He did disgust her. But not for the reasons he should.

Part III
True North

I can listen no longer in silence.
I must speak to you by such means
as are within my reach.
You pierce my soul.
—Jane Austen, *Persuasion*

Four Years Ago

Dear Kai,

Please do not hate me. I couldn't bear it if you hated me.

But I cannot go with you.

I thought I could. Last night, I thought everything was possible. I thought you were right, that there was nothing for me here, either. Mother's dead, Grandfather's locked in his own head, and you're leaving. Why in the world should I stay? It was a beautiful dream. But outside your room, outside the barn, in the cold light of morning, I realized that was all it was. A dream. There is nothing for me here, but that doesn't mean I am nothing to the North estate.

Today, when I was supposed to be packing, I wandered the estate. I watched the Posts in their little cottages, I watched the Reduced in the fields, and I thought about our lots in life.

We can't escape who we are born to be, Kai. The Reduced are Reduced. They will always be Reduced. And I will always be a Luddite. I was born this way. I will die this way. I can't turn my back on that. Luddites were handed a sacred trust—we are the caretakers of humanity. Without us, the world would have burned, and all mankind would have been destroyed. I cannot ignore that. I cannot forget who I am.

But you are not a Luddite.

That's why I cannot go with you. And also why I can't ask you to stay.

God be with you.

Yours,
Elliot

Twenty-six

ELLIOT HAD ALWAYS HATED the birthing house. Of all the indignities the Reduced were forced to endure on the North estate, this was the worst. Left to their own devices, too many Reduced women harmed themselves or their unborn babies during the final stages of pregnancy. Many, following some sort of primal, animal instinct, wandered off the estate and hid when they went into labor. Without assistance, they didn't survive the birth. Afterward, it was no easier—both Reduced mother and baby needed special care. Long ago, it had been deemed necessary to literally confine mothers for the months before and after birth, which came with its own troubles, especially when there weren't enough caretakers on the estate.

Eighteen years ago, the mothers of Ro and Kai had died in the birthing house when the estate's healers had been called to Victoria North's bedside to deliver Elliot. They'd died helpless and alone, and it was a miracle that they hadn't taken their newborn infants with them.

And now Dee was trapped here, with a single Post nurse to watch over her and all the pregnant Reduced women and their babies. Elliot could hardly contain her dismay when she saw her friend among the cots, surrounded by bawling infants and their exhausted, hollow-eyed mothers. The windows had been shut to keep out the cold, and the smell of sour milk and soiled baby clothes hung in the stale air.

"Don't feel bad for me, Elliot," Dee said, her tone more cheerful than it had any right to be. She was knitting despite the gloom. It was winter, so there weren't even any fresh flowers Elliot could have brought in to relieve the drab daub walls and everyone's plain gowns. She needed to recruit Ro and her house-grown blooms. "I'm experienced at this now. And I have the opportunity to help these women get the hang of things."

Around them, the Reduced women in the other beds lolled, staring dumbly at the ceilings and occasionally moaning with discomfort. The ones in the latest stages of their pregnancy were even secured to their beds to keep them from wandering off. Elliot abhorred the practice, but there was little choice in the matter—there weren't enough people to watch over them. Several of the women in the beds nearest Dee were Elliot's age, or even younger. Elliot balled her hands in her lap. Ro would wither here. These other Reduced girls must be miserable.

"How's Jef?" Dee asked, her bright tone not fooling Elliot at all.

"Staying with Gill and Mags," said Elliot. "He's helping Gill in the dairy today, but he said he'd be by this afternoon."

"I'm glad there are still Posts on this land to take care of him in my absence," said Dee. "He's not old enough to be on his own, as Kai was when Mal passed."

"I don't know if Kai was old enough to be on his own, either. Maybe he wouldn't have run away if he was placed with a Post family instead of left alone in the barn."

"And then where would he be?" asked Dee. "Things seemed to have worked out for the best."

He'd still be human, for one thing, thought Elliot. It had been a week since the disaster on the cliff, a week since she'd fought with Kai in the barn, and she hadn't seen him since. Olivia still hadn't woken up, either, and reports placed her devastated brother and equally devastated admirer, Captain Malakai Wentforth, at her bedside night and day.

Elliot had been too scared to visit Olivia and risk running into Kai, but she reasoned that if the girl was still in a coma, she wouldn't notice Elliot's absence. And while she waited, she couldn't stop thinking about her argument with Kai in the barn. She'd been foolish, she'd been hasty, and, most of all, she'd been too unguarded with her feelings.

"Dee?" she asked. "Would it be wrong to accept money for something you were planning on doing anyway?"

Dee narrowed her eyes. "You're asking the wrong person. I've never gotten money for anything in all of my life. I don't know much how it works. But isn't that exactly what the point of money is? It's much better than accepting money for something you don't want to do."

"I mean—if it's something that someone shouldn't have to pay you for. Something they'd think less of you for if they paid you for it."

Now the Post's eyes went wide. "What kind of thing are we talking about, Elliot North?"

Elliot shook her head. "Nothing like that." On a purely practical basis, if Kai was willing to give her money for silence, then she should take it. She could be calm and rational about that now, despite her response in the barn. The estate could certainly benefit from such an arrangement. But she didn't know if she could bring herself to broach the topic with him. She didn't know how she'd ever speak to him again after the things she'd said to him in the barn.

Time for a change in subject. "Things have been going well in the dairy. You know that old churner I haven't been able to get working for six months? Turns out there was just a screw loose."

"Really!" Dee said. "I thought you'd been over every piece of that machine half a dozen times."

"I know." Elliot shrugged. "Guess I was just distracted with my work on the wheat before. Thank goodness for winter boredom."

"I'm sure the dairymaids thank you. Things have got to be much easier with the mechanical churner running again."

"They are, but we're still shorthanded. We didn't have enough Posts on duty even before you came here."

"Give it ten years." Dee nodded her head in the direction of a nearby cot, where a Reduced woman dozed with a big-eyed newborn in her arms. "That one's a Post, you know."

Elliot examined the baby. "You can't tell already."

Common opinion held that Post children started showing their colors around six months.

"Oh yes I can," Dee insisted. "I raised my own, didn't I? Jef was just like her at that age. Watch her looking around. She's already figuring out the world. She already wants to see what else is out there."

What else *was* out there? The infant, if a Post, was still bonded to the North estate. And if she remained here, one day she'd be back inside these four walls, confined, just like Dee. The alternative was to take the path Kai had chosen.

And all the dangers that came with it. Posts like Dee thought the Reduction was ending, that soon every new baby would be a Post. But what if Kai and his friends had started the nightmare all over again?

Elliot was just finishing her duties in the barn several days later when Benedict found her.

"Hello," he called over the top of one of the dairy stalls. Elliot was inspecting the cows while Ro and two other Reduced girls cleaned out the rest of the stalls. "I've come to see if you've heard anything more about that poor Grove girl."

Elliot brushed hay off her tan skirt. "I haven't had a chance to." It wasn't a lie. With Dee moved into the birthing house, Elliot had her hands full with extra duties. But even if she'd been as free as Tatiana, nothing would induce her to return to the Boatwright house.

Benedict was dressed in the same Post-style plum jacket he'd worn when he arrived. Apparently the Norths were missing out on a major fashion trend. Elliot had spent the morning listening to her sister hounding the baron for a new riding habit made with Post fabrics. A few months ago, Tatiana would have sneered at the thought.

"Are you planning to visit her? I'd love to come with you."

"I wasn't, no." If she never saw Kai again, it would be too soon.

"Would you?" Benedict's tone was insistent. "I barely got a look at the Boatwright estate the day we arrived, but I've been all over the North estate with your sister."

Elliot was taken aback by his words. The Boatwright estate was not Benedict's, nor would it ever be. It belonged to Elliot's grandfather. "Is there a special reason you wish to see it?"

"I'm curious about their project, of course!" Benedict exclaimed. "It's all anyone will speak of in Channel City. I want to see what they're up to, but I haven't been introduced to anyone over there. I feel awkward going by myself."

She glanced up at him. He felt awkward? The heir presumptive of the entire North estate, the man who'd seen as much of the world as the Fleet Posts and far more than she, felt awkward going alone to say hello? Elliot sighed. "I'm a little short staffed this morning, I'm afraid."

"It's because of that pregnant foreman, isn't it? Tatiana mentioned she'd been taken off her duties—perhaps a bit earlier than she needed to be."

Elliot raised her eyebrows. "Tatiana knows that? I'm shocked."

Benedict smiled. "Your sister follows more than you think she does, Elliot. It makes it easier for her to justify not getting her hands dirty herself."

Less than two weeks here and already he knew the lay of the land pretty well. Elliot regarded Benedict carefully. She didn't know what had brought him back to the North estate, or why her father had chosen now of all times to reconcile with his nephew. Eight years ago, Benedict had been sent away from the only home he'd ever known, and yet he appeared not bitter or angry about it at all. It was a mystery.

The Reduced girls had by now lined up outside the stalls for Elliot to inspect their work. Benedict looked them over, too, and Elliot stiffened, remembering the old rumors. If Benedict did take over, would the North lands become like the estate where the Phoenixes had grown up?

"Very good," she said to the laborers, gesturing in signs they'd be sure to understand. "You're free to go." Two of them ran off, while Ro lingered, clearly wanting to spend more time with Elliot, but nervous about Benedict's presence.

"Pretty girl," said Benedict. "And that's a lovely scarf. It's nice that you let them have their own possessions. Did she do anything special to earn it?"

Elliot frowned. "Ro," she said. "I would like you to go visit with Dee in the birthing house today. Can you do that?"

Ro nodded and took off.

Benedict turned back to Elliot. "So you are free now."

"Not really." She cast about for a way to broach the

topic. "Benedict, I am glad you and my father have reconciled. While you're here, I think it's important that you know the things that happen on other estates do not occur on North lands—"

His eyes lit up with amusement. "You don't put credence in that old story, do you, cousin?"

"I don't know what you're talking about." Yes, she did. Everyone knew why Benedict had been sent away.

"Yes, you do," he replied. "And frankly, I'm surprised."

Elliot folded her arms. "That I could think it of you?"

"That you haven't figured out that it was all a lie," Benedict said, practically scoffing. "Your father manufactured a reason to send me away. I was a threat to him as I came of age, because I'm the rightful heir to the estate."

Elliot considered this for a minute. It made a lot of sense. Of course her father would feel threatened as the boy he'd fed and housed and clothed grew old enough to take over his birthright. After all, Elliot herself had been de facto running the estate since her early teens. Could not Benedict have run it as he'd been supposed to? She wondered what would have happened if he'd been allowed to take over. Would the North estate have been in better hands? Would it be now?

Seeing her reaction, he smiled. "Come now, Elliot. I'm not here to start a fight. I have made peace with your father. I've learned much more these past years traveling the islands—seeing the estates and the enclaves—than I ever could have trapped up here in the north. Uncle Zachariah's so-called punishment has made me a rich man on my own terms."

"How fortunate for you." And if that was the case, that he neither needed the estate nor wanted it, then why did he bother to return?

"I am fortunate, and your father knows it. The past is . . . an embarrassment to him, and I have promised not to call him out for it."

Why? Elliot didn't know if she'd be so gracious, and unlike Kai, she doubted her father had the money to pay Benedict off. She wondered if Benedict was receiving something else—a promise to give up rights to the estate sometime soon?

"But I do not want you laboring under a false assumption. I have no interest in the Reduced women on this farm. I never did." He leaned forward. "In other words, you do not need to chase away that little redhead."

Benedict stepped back, satisfied. "And now that we've cleared the air, I'll ask again—would you do me the honor of accompanying me to the Boatwright house so that I may meet the neighbors?"

Not *my* neighbors, Elliot noted. *Was* he here to take back the estate? Regardless, she shook her head. "I can't. I have too much work to do."

"What do you have to do?" Benedict asked. "I'll help. And when we finish in half the time, you'll take me to the Boatwright house."

Her eyes widened, but her cousin was completely serious.

"Do not let it be said I'm shirking my duties here."

Elliot examined his fine coat and his city-softened hands. He wanted to know what it took to manage the North estate? Fine. She'd show him, and he'd be far too tired to drag her back to the Fleet.

Twenty-seven

BENEDICT TOOK ELLIOT BY surprise. He hauled feed bags and curried horses and helped her check on the supply of food and other goods at the Reduced barracks. He made the rounds with her as she visited each of the remaining Posts, and smiled and chatted with all of them, even those who were suspicious and openly hostile.

"It's funny," he said to her as they traveled from cottage to cottage. "There does not seem to be much love for your father among the CORs on the estate, but they are still willing to believe his story."

"We tend to call them Posts now, as they desire," Elliot said.

"I'm glad to hear it." Benedict's expression was jovial. "COR sounds so artificial in my mouth, but it's the terminology your father uses. Not much of a surprise."

Elliot was silent, as every minute a new theory bloomed in her mind. Did he hope to win the North Posts to his side in a potential battle over his inheritance? Did he hope to win her over, too? One thing was clear, her cousin was no fool. It had taken him no time at all to assess how things worked on the estate. Of course, Admiral Innovation had told her when he first arrived that it was well known throughout the islands that Elliot was the only person to get things done here. Perhaps Benedict had known it long before he arrived.

Perhaps he thought the workers' lack of loyalty to Baron North would be an easy way to reclaim what was his.

"When I was younger," he said, "I didn't realize why they preferred to be called Posts. Living in the enclave down in Channel City taught me the difference. A 'Child of the Reduction' is just that—an offshoot of the Reduced, a juvenile, and still inextricably linked to his ancestor's limitations. There is also the theory very popular on a few of the estates in the south that CORs are nothing more than the product of illicit Luddite liaisons with the Reduced. That they never overcame the Reduction on their own at all. You can imagine how the term might be offensive to the Posts."

She didn't have to imagine. She'd met Andromeda.

"But a *Post-Reductionist* . . ." Benedict raised his eyebrows in appreciation. "That's something else entirely. A Post has moved past his humble beginnings. A Post is looking at the future, and not the past." He regarded Elliot. "I assume these Cloud Fleet Posts are filled with the same sort of boundless optimism?"

"They are focused on the future, yes," Elliot replied safely, as they walked on.

"Little wonder," said Benedict. "There isn't much in the past that they'd find appealing. But even I, born a Luddite, prefer the potential of the future. Don't you, cousin?"

Elliot was so taken aback by his bluntness that she nodded before she could stop herself.

"I knew we'd see eye to eye. You think like me. You know, watching the enclaves grow these last ten years from tiny shantytowns filled with beggars and thieves to prosperous neighborhoods, seeing the success of Posts like your Fleet, it isn't hard to read the writing on the wall."

"Oh really?" Elliot asked. She ignored his use of "your Fleet." It was not hers. Certainly not.

"The Post-Reductionists are right." Benedict nodded with certainty. "The Reduction is coming to a close."

Elliot was rendered speechless. She'd never heard anyone talk such heresy. And certainly not a Luddite.

"For now," Benedict continued, "Posts who are dissatisfied with their estates have merely run away, but mark my words, revolution is coming. Perhaps not here, but on other estates. Estates where the Luddite lords' mistreatment veers into cruelty. Or maybe just when there are so many free Posts that the Luddites can no longer maintain control. Do you know where you want to be when that happens, Elliot?"

"Here," said Elliot immediately. "If there's an uprising, then the Reduced on the estate are in danger."

Benedict blinked several times, as if surprised by her response.

"The Reduced haven't died off yet," she added. And, even by the most generous estimates, only one in twenty children born to a Reduced was a Post. It would be many generations, if ever, before the Reduction could truly be over.

But Benedict still wore an odd expression, and sheepishly Elliot realized what he'd meant by his question. He'd been asking which side she'd choose, not who she'd choose to protect. She ducked her head in embarrassment.

"Perhaps we should go to the Boatwright estate now," he said, smirking, and Elliot was too flustered to protest.

"I'm glad to see that the Norths have mended their breach with the Groves," Benedict was saying as they took the path through the forest. "I saw Horatio Grove down in Channel City last year, and I wasn't sure if I should approach him or not."

"Relations have been good between us ever since Horatio and Olivia's father died," said Elliot. "I always gathered that my father's argument was with him, personally, but neither the Grove children nor my sister and I ever knew what it was about, so it seemed foolish to continue holding grudges from the last generation."

Benedict grinned. "You really don't know? Well, I guess I'm here to reveal the truth behind all the family secrets, then."

Elliot stopped on the path. "What do you mean?"

He chuckled. "Elliot. You're serious?" When she made no response, he continued. "It never occurred to you to wonder why your mother, who was as capable a woman as anyone ever knew, would marry a man like your father?"

Of course it had. "Are you saying that my mother was in love with old Mr. Grove?"

"I'm saying your mother was engaged to marry him."
Benedict nodded as Elliot's mouth gaped open. "Oh, yes. I
remember going to their betrothal party when I was very,
very young."

"Then why didn't they get married?"

"Because my father died."

Elliot stared at him in disbelief, but there was no
deception in his words or face.

"The North estate is the largest one on this side of the
island."

"You're saying my mother left Mr. Grove for my father
because he was richer?" Little wonder Kai had offered to pay
her off. She came from a long line of women for whom love
was nothing in the face of money.

"No!" Benedict burst out laughing. "Because they
all thought that marriage to her would help keep Uncle
Zachariah in line. The Boatwrights and the Groves—they
needed the North estate to survive. If it were to fail, then not
only would the people living on the North lands starve, but
everyone else would suffer as well. You know that. You're just
like your mother."

No, Benedict was surely not stupid. He knew precisely
what to say. She used to lie awake nights, hoping her mother
would have approved of the choice she'd made four years
ago. Now she knew it for certain. She and her mother were
the same—she'd given up the person she loved for the good
of the North estate. And her father had never associated with
his neighbor because of Mr. Grove's history with his wife.

"I can't believe you didn't know this. I thought it was

the reason you're still here."

Elliot swallowed. "What do you mean?" Had he heard, down in the enclaves, that she'd once promised Kai she'd run away? Did he know every secret her family had ever held?

"If you didn't think you needed to remain here and work, wouldn't you want to marry Horatio and get out from under your father's thumb?"

Now it was Elliot's turn to laugh. He must have been talking to Tatiana. "Horatio Grove?" she joked. "You think he'd marry me?"

Benedict's voice was soft when he replied, "Anyone would marry you, Elliot."

Elliot was saved from responding by the sound of a horse's hooves pounding down the path. A moment later, one of the giant Innovation horses came galloping toward them. Tatiana sat in the saddle. She pulled the beast up short before it mowed them down.

"Watch it!" she cried, scowling. Her sharp, pretty face looked pale. "What are you doing wandering around in the woods with Benedict?"

"We were going to the Boatwright house."

"Me, too," she said, flipping the reins in her hands. "We need Felicia back here at once. I hope she's not so busy with Olivia that she can't spare time for Grandfather."

"What happened?" Elliot asked. "Tatiana, what happened?"

Tatiana gave an aggravated snort. "He had a stroke this morning, Elliot. Maybe if you'd been home instead of out socializing, you'd know that."

Ten Years Ago

Dear Kai,

I'm sorry I can't come see you today. My dad overheard me calling you and your dad Posts instead of CORs. He thinks I spend more time than is good for me with you and Ro. I don't really understand it, personally. I mean, if we're supposed to own the lands and take care of everyone who lives on it, doesn't it make sense to be involved? To make sure we know every bit of the land and the people who work it as well as possible? My teachers are always going on and on about Luddite ~~stuwart~~ stewardship of the Earth—if that's true, then shouldn't we actually make sure that the Earth is being properly stewed?

I don't think that's the right word.
Your friend,
Elliot

∽

Dear Elliot,
No, it's not.

I'm bored here today. Whenever the harvest is in, there's nothing much to do and there aren't any good books in the COR

257

library right now. There never are.

Not that that's a hint or anything.
Your friend,
Kai

∞

Dear Kai,
Here are some books. I think you'll like the ones about the old
inventors. I got them from our library. My dad must not know
they are here. I'm sure he'd burn them if he did.
Your friend,
Elliot

∞

Dear Elliot,
These are amazing! I love these stories. I love the one about Tesla
and Edison. And Marconi, and the Curies, and Einstein, and
Watson and Crick, and Gavin and Carlotta. The world must
have been such a fascinating place before the Reduction. Can you
imagine being allowed to make anything you wanted? I wonder
if there's anyplace on Earth where they still can.
Your friend,
Kai

∞

Dear Kai,
I hope not! Can you imagine how dangerous that would be?
Didn't you read the part where Marie Curie died because of
all the experiments she did with radiation? And Einstein was

sorry he helped make the atomic bomb. Some experiments are okay, I guess, but there are too many that are way too dangerous.
Your friend,
Elliot

༄

Dear Elliot,
But you don't know they are too dangerous until later. Like Watson and Crick and Gavin and Carlotta—they were just trying to help people. They had no idea it would cause the Reduction.
Your friend,
Kai

༄

Dear Kai,
My teachers say that's why it's best if you just don't do anything that hasn't been done before. That way you always know it's safe.

Although now that I think about it, that's kind of stupid. Nothing can ever be exactly the same. We plant wheat every year, year after year, but it's always a bit different. Like a different tempratchure, or the amount of rain. And now we have CORs. When my grandfather was young, there weren't any CORs. They were totally new, but we didn't get rid of them.

And I'm really glad of that!
Your friend,
Elliot

༄

Dear Elliot,

Me too! I would like it if things changed. Not being able to do experiments seems very dull to me. I've been hearing stories about places where Posts live all by themselves without any Luddites telling them what to do. They get married, they go wherever they want without permission, they have their own businesses, they have solar-powered lights, and they all wear clothes in ~~brite~~ bright colors. I wonder if they do experiments too?

One day I want to go live there.

Your friend,

Kai

ॐ

Dear Kai,

Don't go live in a Post enclave. I'd miss you if you went away.

We can do experiements here. We just have to keep them a secret from my father—or anyone that would tell on us. Like Tatiana.

Stay with me, Kai. I promise we can do whatever you want.

Your friend,

Elliot

Twenty-eight

ELLIOT SAT IN A stiff-backed chair in the hallway outside her grandfather's bedroom. The light coming through the window turned from white to yellow to orange, the Reduced servants came around with candles, and still, Felicia Innovation remained sequestered with the Boatwright.

She'd barely been able to meet the woman's eyes when she arrived at the house. This woman, who was responsible for creating abominations with human faces. This woman, who had risked the life of the person she cared for most in the world. This woman, who broke the protocols and placed them all in danger of another Reduction. Felicia had been kind to Elliot, and Ro, and her grandfather. She clearly cared for the Cloud Fleet captains, despite what she'd done to them. And, if Kai was to be believed, she'd only done it to save her beloved daughter's life.

But there was still no excuse. It was an atrocity. Love didn't matter. Neither did life or death. It didn't.

It didn't.

Elliot squeezed her hands together and pressed them hard into her lap, digging the ridges of her knuckles into her thighs. Every moment, she made herself a new promise.

If Tatiana comes down the hall, I'll stop her and make her kick Felicia out.

If Felicia tells me we can save my grandfather by breaking the protocols, I'll let her.

If my father asks after my grandfather's health, I'll confess everything to him.

If the Cloud Fleet offers to help us, I'll keep their secret forever.

No one came. Not her sister or her father, not Benedict or the Fleet Posts or even Admiral Innovation. No one appeared in the hall all afternoon but the mute, shuffling figures of the Reduced housemaids as they went about their chores. Time passed, and Elliot sat in the chair, waiting for the verdict from Felicia.

How much of her life had she spent waiting? Waiting for a plant to sprout? Waiting for her father's judgment? Waiting for another letter to appear in the knothole from Kai? Waiting for years after Kai left to feel at peace with her decision? She fed the Reduced, she did her chores, she avoided her father and her sister, and she waited. She did the duties she'd been taught as a Luddite, and she lied with every breath.

Her grandfather, the man she was named for, the last person who could remind her of her mother—he couldn't die. He couldn't die before the Fleet was finished and he had one more chance to see a ship—Kai's ship—launched from the Boatwright docks. He couldn't die here, in the North's back guest room instead of his own bed. He couldn't die and leave her alone with her father and Tatiana and two estates counting on her, only her.

And then, as the sun dipped low over the horizon, the door to the Boatwright's chamber opened, and Felicia Innovation emerged.

Elliot rose to her feet and steeled herself for the news—whatever it may be.

But Felicia's expression was grim. "The most I can do is make sure he's comfortable for his final days."

"Really? Even you?" The words spilled out before Elliot could stop them.

Felicia gave a little shake of her head. "Your grandfather is very old, Elliot. He's had many strokes. The damage to his brain—"

Elliot sighed in sudden relief. Felicia wasn't even going to try, then. Good. She nodded brusquely. "I understand. Thank you for coming to see him."

Felicia appeared taken aback, and gave her a curious look. "You take disappointment too much in stride for someone so young, Elliot."

Elliot wasn't sure how to respond. Was she expecting an argument? A confrontation? "I— didn't have much hope. He's been sick my whole life. I barely remember what it was like before. I didn't think there was much you could do. Not with the protocols in place."

It was bait worthy of Tatiana, and Felicia blinked—a move that on any other woman would have been a flinch. "You should hope for more," she replied at last.

As she put on her coat, Elliot noticed that she didn't move like the others. And earlier, she'd seen the admiral's cataracts. So they, at least, had not been enhanced. And yet the young Posts had. Why was that? Were the enhancements too dangerous for Felicia to be willing to attempt on herself or her husband? Kai had mentioned something about second-generation Posts, like himself and Sophia. But the Phoenixes weren't second-generation. Not if they had a Reduced mother and a Luddite father. She longed to ask, and was ashamed by it.

"You live in a wonderful time, Elliot—though perhaps you haven't been taught to think of it as wonderful."

"I have not. But neither am I blind."

Now Felicia did flinch, and too late, Elliot remembered Sophia and her blindness. Her two halves warred within her. The Luddite she'd been raised to be wanted to hate this Post and the things she'd done to Kai and the others.

But the girl with the cross-bred wheat and the sick grandfather wanted only to understand. Felicia must have been just as desperate as Elliot. She shouldn't be condemned for that.

But what if she'd killed them? What if she'd killed Kai with her experiments? What if they were dead already, their cells mutated with Reduction?

"I mean," Elliot said, "that I'm aware that things are changing. Maybe too fast."

Felicia gave a tiny laugh. "You are the only person your age I know who would say that. Most think it's happening too slowly."

Most people Felicia knew were not Luddites.

"I should go see my grandfather," Elliot said quickly, but Felicia stepped in front of the door.

"You should let him rest." She regarded Elliot carefully. "You know, dear, he is an old man. He's lived a long life. Most men would not choose to go on forever, even if they could. It is not in our nature."

"'If they could,'" Elliot repeated coldly. Once they could, and did, and almost destroyed the world. "Where do you draw the line?"

"*I* don't," said Felicia, and there was an edge of devil-may-care in her tone. Would she speak so freely in front of Tatiana? Was she trying to learn if Elliot planned to keep her promise to Kai? "Every person must draw his own line. How can I decide for another person what risks he's willing to take? How can I be the one to decide if he should live or die?"

"The Lost decided for their children," Elliot said. "They made decisions that condemned their offspring to Reduction."

"They didn't know. Don't you think they would never have done it if they'd known?"

"Is that how you would work?" The words burst from Elliot's lips. "Would you always know exactly what effect your therapies will have on the people you treat? What effect it will have on their descendants for hundreds of years? Would you be sure they knew the risks before they signed their children and their children's children's children up?"

Felicia stared at her for a long moment and Elliot was afraid she'd gone too far.

"If we are speaking in hypotheticals, I will say that it's a wonder the protocols are not relaxed for those past childbearing age, like your grandfather. There is no risk to anyone, then."

If Felicia believed that, why didn't she perform ERV on herself or her husband?

"I would say—but not to everyone, Elliot—that many Posts believe they're born with the power to overcome Reduction. Their genes manifested a workaround from birth, and so the protocols don't apply to them. They are safe."

"Safe!" Elliot scoffed.

"But we are not speaking in hypotheticals, are we?"

Elliot North stood straight as a rod and faced Felicia, her mouth a thin line. She would not speak. She couldn't, even now. And maybe that's why Felicia didn't seem to be afraid. If Elliot had planned to betray her secret, surely she'd accuse her of it out loud, right? Instead, the youngest of the Norths simply stood in her ancestral home and made cowardly insinuations, because what she wanted to say was too unbearable to form into words.

Yes. The protocols should be relaxed. They should be broken for my grandfather.

Felicia looked at her sadly. "My husband would have me be circumspect. He's not as radical as I am. And neither of us are as radical as the younger generation. Your generation."

"You mean your Fleet Posts," said Elliot. "I don't think my sister is a radical."

"And what about you?"

Elliot said nothing.

"Oh, my dear girl. There is so much we could talk about."

Elliot said nothing.

"I trust you. I wish you would trust me."

Elliot said nothing.

Finally, Felicia sighed. "All right. I am leaving now. But I want you to know you can speak to me whenever you want, about anything you want." She gestured to the closed door behind her. "I know what the Boatwright is to you. I know what you've lost, and what you're about to lose. I am a mother, not just a Post." She headed off down the hall, her Post-bright cloak making even the polished North floorboards look dingy and old. At the top of the stairs, she paused.

"Elliot?"

Elliot dragged her eyes up to the woman's face, half terrified Felicia would see the tears clinging to her lashes.

"You should know that you're exactly the person you think you are."

Elliot turned away as the tears escaped. That's what she was afraid of.

Twenty-nine

ELLIOT BOATWRIGHT WAS RESTING peacefully now. His breathing was even, if shallow, and he made no noise of pain in his sleep. His dark skin seemed paper-thin, his scalp like leaves of old parchment beneath his sparse white hair. With both sides of his face relaxed like this in repose, Elliot could almost imagine what he'd looked like before his first stroke had damaged the nerves in his face.

Had Benedict been telling the truth? Had this man forced her mother to marry her father? Elliot tried to remember a time when her mother had displayed any bitterness toward the Boatwright. From a young age, she'd known her mother wasn't happy in her marriage—known it almost from the time she'd become aware of the type of man her father was. But it was the only life she knew, so she hadn't examined it all that closely. Her mother managed the estate, smoothing over the worst of Baron North's extravagances and cruelties. Elliot had learned enough from her to try to do the same after her mother's death.

What would her life have been like had she been born a Grove? She's never known Horatio and Olivia's father, but judging from them, she imagined he was a more progressive, hardworking man. The Groves had some Post technology in their house. They were open to new ideas. They were friendly with the Fleet. Perhaps, if she'd been Olivia Grove, she could have asked Felicia to do the unthinkable. Perhaps Kai would love her now.

But if she'd been Olivia Grove, would Kai have ever known her at all?

She pressed a kiss to her grandfather's forehead and departed. Her family would expect her to come to dinner. Appearances had to be maintained, no matter what was going on upstairs . . . or inside.

By the time she arrived in the parlor, there was a lively debate occurring between Tatiana and Benedict as to who was the better rider.

"When I saw you today, on the back of that Innovation horse," Benedict was saying, "it seemed perfectly clear that you have great talent."

Tatiana blushed prettily. She seemed to have taken extra care with her clothes and hair this evening, utilizing some of the Post-style fabrics she'd purchased after the Fleet moved in. Tonight, she wore red, and the color set off her olive skin and dark hair. Elliot still hadn't changed from the trousers she'd been wearing in the dairy. Her father's eyebrows had nearly hit the ceiling when she'd entered.

"Surely you've seen better horsewomen in Channel City."

Benedict smiled indulgently. "I think you would impress everyone in Channel City. Innovation horses are spirited mounts, and you have taken to yours quite well. Besides, they are rare—it's not many that even have the opportunity to ride them."

This was precisely the kind of response Tatiana had been fishing for.

Elliot folded her hands in her lap, hoping to still the nervous energy that coursed through her system. How could she bear a whole evening of this, while her grandfather lay dying above and the Posts and their secrets waited, a few kay away?

"It's a shame you haven't done very much travel, as I have," Benedict said to Tatiana. "You—and your sister—would be such an asset to society in Channel City."

"Father says the city has been overrun by Posts," Elliot blurted. Three faces turned in her direction.

"I most certainly did not," her father huffed.

Elliot's jaw tightened. That was a lie. He'd been using it as an excuse not to take them for years.

"It's true," he continued, "that there are many free Posts there these days . . . but it's hardly overrun. Indeed, most of the Posts there are quite genteel and remarkably stylish—for what they are. Not unlike these Cloud Fleet Posts renting our lands."

"Of course," Benedict said quickly. "There are many very fine Posts."

"It's surprising to me to hear you say such a thing, Elliot," said Tatiana. "You always seem so generous toward our own Posts. Remember back when you were a child, you had that little Post friend. You know, the son of that mechanic . . ." she trailed off, and her mouth gaped. She stared at Elliot with an expression of astonished accusation.

Elliot forced herself not to smile. Finally, her sister had put it together. A few months too late, perhaps, and even more embarrassing, given Tatiana's obsession with Kai and Olivia Grove.

Tatiana's face turned just as red as her new dress. Part of Elliot wanted to gloat over her sister's cluelessness, but the other part worried about how she'd punish her maid for not telling her, or worse, if she'd look at Kai more closely now, and compare him to the boy she remembered. It could prove dangerous.

It could prove deadly.

But Tatiana composed herself quickly and steered the subject away from Elliot and back to herself. "I would love to travel more," she admitted, "but I have had the responsibility of caring for the estate for so long. When my mother died, I was left the head of this household. I don't know how I'd manage it from so far away."

"Of course," Benedict said, though his eyes were on Elliot as he spoke.

Elliot turned away, toward the window. She'd long ago grown bored by Tatiana's complaints about the imaginary version of her life. That Benedict still found it a source of amusement was of little interest to her. Not when her grandfather lay dying upstairs. Not when Felicia and Kai and the other Posts were holding such remarkable secrets just out of reach. Not when the temptation to learn more about those secrets was making her doubt everything she'd ever been taught. How could she care about some petty, decade-old battle with her sister?

Thanks to the light from the fire, the window reflected the room rather than revealing the fields and the stars. Felicia must be back at the Boatwright house now, driven safely through the darkness thanks to the unnatural vision of her Fleet Posts. She wondered if Felicia had spoken to any of them about her conversation with Elliot. She wondered if she'd spoken to Kai.

He'd probably tell her how useless it was to discuss anything with Elliot North. The Luddite. The coward. The passive, put-upon daughter of the laziest lord in the islands.

Elliot closed her eyes, and only opened them when Benedict spoke again.

"That won't do," he said. "You've been isolated here for long enough. And your father, with his beautiful new race-track to enjoy, and his extraordinary new horses to race on it—you should have a house party. It can be an opportunity for some of your friends and neighbors to see the improvements."

Elliot looked at him in surprise. "Now? This isn't the time—not with my grandfather so sick, and the Boatwright house filled with the Fleet—"

"Actually," Benedict said, "it's the perfect time. I understand you have a surplus cash flow due to the rent the Fleet is paying, and should the worst come to pass for your grandfather, I know there are many who would like to come pay their respects."

"Good point, Benedict." Baron North turned to Elliot. "We would do your grandfather a great disservice if we kept him isolated to the end of his days, now that we have the means to properly entertain here."

Would her father be so concerned about her comatose grandfather's social schedule if he didn't have horses and a new racetrack to show off?

"And of course," Benedict said, "you can invite the Cloud Fleet to the festivities as well."

"Of course," Tatiana said. "It would be rude not to, although they aren't Luddites."

Benedict nodded in agreement. "No, they aren't. But they are staying on your land. And, after all, the horses are Innovation horses."

"Yes." The baron cleared his throat. "I am not concerned by all Post products, you see."

Benedict directed another sly smile at Elliot, trying again to get her to share in his jokes at her father's expense.

She didn't begrudge Benedict his right to make these little jabs, and was impressed by his ability to do so in a way that left both Baron North and Tatiana completely ignorant of his true meaning, but Benedict North had nothing to lose—he'd already lived life outside the baron's good graces and seemed to have survived it quite well. She didn't have such luxury. Her father could still hurt Elliot if he wanted to—and if she started teasing him, she was sure he'd want to very much.

The others soon fixed on a date for their proposed house party and horse race, and their plans left Elliot doing mental calculations as to how much the event would eat into their savings, and into money she was hoping to make last several years. Her father and Tatiana might be optimistic, but one couldn't expect someone to rent the Boatwright facilities every year.

"You see, Elliot," the baron said at last, "this is a much better use of the field than a few extra stalks of wheat."

Safe at the window, Elliot rolled her eyes, but if her cousin saw it, she neither knew nor cared. It had taken her years, but now, at last, she realized the truth. Her father would never stop goading her. If she responded, he could punish her, but he didn't need her reaction to press on. Her very existence was provocation, was failure, was outrage enough for him. She could remain silent forever, never build another string-box, never graft another plant, and still he could see the lie that bloomed in her heart.

As SOON AS SHE could, as always, she slipped away to the barn. As always, her eyes went immediately to the knothole—their knothole. And as always, for the last four years, it was dark and empty.

Well, at least Kai was complying with her request not to speak to her. She ascended the stairs and drew her key, but there, at the door to her workroom, she paused. She could not go in there tonight. She could not work on her illegal wheat. She could not stand there surrounded by a hundred gliders that all said the same thing:

She was not a Luddite.

She might not have asked Felicia to break the law with

her grandfather, but she had wanted to. She'd made the wheat and she'd taught Ro how. And then there was Kai. She should hate him. She should fear him.

She did neither.

Elliot returned to the ground floor and swept the stalls. She fed and watered the horses, and then she gritted her teeth and curried them, even Pyrois. And when that failed to exhaust her, she turned to the machinery.

She'd been useless with her grandfather today. Perhaps she could fix something tonight to make up for it. Her recent success with the churner had galvanized her to tackle some more of the projects that remained. The estate didn't need to suffer because she wasn't a properly trained mechanic. Stupid Kai, fixing the tractor just to spite her. He'd been raised to fix machines. She'd just picked up what she could from watching him and Mal. But she wasn't completely helpless.

She turned to the thresher. It had been smoking for the latter half of the season. She changed the oil, and tightened a few bolts. She'd thought Gill had mentioned something about a worn belt, but he must have fixed it, because everything appeared in working order.

This wasn't as challenging as she'd thought. No wonder the Posts had pitied the state of the North machinery, if the repairs were so easy, after all. Finally, she turned her attention to the plow with its faulty gearbox. It needed new parts—she'd write to a craftsman in Channel City. She could afford to fix her machines now. The Fleet had been good for something.

Surely Gill would find it a relief if she managed to get

that up and running again before spring. Elliot hauled it out of its corner and prepared to brush away the cobwebs . . .

Only to discover none.

And that wasn't all. There were three new hoses and two new bolts attached, and when she turned on the engine, the machine hummed happily. Elliot stared at the gearbox in bafflement. It wasn't *brand* new. Perhaps Gill had found an extra somewhere, fixed it, and neglected to tell her.

Except she knew there was no extra. Not on the North or Boatwright estates, and not on the Grove estate either—she'd asked Horatio a few months ago. Either Gill had fixed this plow today and hadn't had a chance to tell her because she'd been busy with her grandfather, or there was something else at work. And the idea that he'd fixed the thresher, too? Come to think of it, the oil in the thresher had looked remarkably clear.

She turned slowly in the barn, looking for once beyond the empty knothole. Each machine stood silent and still, but Elliot could see a flash of new metal here and there. Lots of things had been fixed, apparently. There was only one possibility, and it wasn't that her father had finally determined to take a more hands-on approach to his farm.

High above her, Nero the cat perched on a beam and watched her, purring. Elliot fisted her hands at her sides. She probably wouldn't have looked at these things until spring, when it was time to start the planting and the Fleet was scheduled to depart.

She never would have known.

How dare he?

Six Years Ago

Dear Kai,

I waited for you in the barn tonight, but you never came. It was dark and scary in there alone. Where were you? How can you stand it in there, with all the machines and the creaking? Do you believe in ghosts?

Your friend,

Elliot

∽

Dear Elliot,

I want to believe in ghosts. It would be nice to think that we stay around after we die. I also like what the ancients thought about our spirits traveling up the island and into the sea. But, honestly? I don't know if I do.

When I was younger, the older Posts used to try to scare me with the old Gavin and Carlotta stories. I used to have horrible nightmares, before my dad told me that none of them are true. But that was ages ago. I'm twelve years old. I'm not scared anymore.

Your friend,

Kai

∽

Dear Kai,

The Gavin and Carlotta stories scare me too. Tatiana makes me play that game with her in the star-cavern sanctuary sometimes. But they don't need to be ghosts to haunt us. They were real, and what they did haunts all of us, every day, forever.

Your friend,

Elliot

ᘒ

Dear Elliot,

Well, I guess it's your job to be scared of Gavin and Carlotta, right? I mean, you're a Luddite. If Luddites weren't scared of the technology, they would have done it themselves, and then everyone would be Reduced.

Though that makes me wonder. If I'm a Post, it means my genes overcame Gavin and Carlotta. Overcame the Reduction. I wonder if it means that I'm immune now? Maybe I could stand in the mirror chanting a thousand times and Gavin and Carlotta couldn't do anything to me. Maybe I could resist Reduction if I had ERV.

Your friend,

Kai

ᘒ

Dear Kai,

I'm going to burn your letter. Do you have any idea how much trouble we could both get in if anyone read this?

Your friend,

Elliot

Dear Elliot,

*Then burn this one too. Sometimes I wonder about Gavin and
Carlotta. What if they weren't monsters like everyone says?
They didn't think they did anything wrong because it was
all so natural, so simple. It didn't take surgery, or billions of
stem cells or whatever the Lost used to use. The blueprint was
already inside of us. They just reached in and turned it on.
They made us the best versions of ourselves—more human than
human.*

*I know what happened, and I still think I would have
chosen to get ERV. But I guess that's why I'm not a Luddite.
Because I just sit here wondering what kind of machine breaks
just because you try to use it to its full potential?*
Your friend,
Kai

༄

Dear Kai,

*I don't pretend to know as much about machines as you, but I
know the answer to that question. Machines are designed to run
a certain way. If you remove their safety constraints, if you put
them in permanent overdrive or run them faster or harder than
intended, they will break. That's what Gavin and Carlotta's
enhancements did. They tried to make humans into Gods. They
tried to make us work better than what God intended.*

And we broke.
Your friend,
Elliot

༄

Dear Elliot,
I'm not broken.
Your friend,
Kai

Thirty

THE SOFT LIGHT ILLUMINATING Ro's window was not the flicker of a candle, but the steady white glow of a sun-lamp. Even there, Elliot had been trumped. No doubt Ro could garden all night now that she had help from Kai.

Except who'd been taking care of Ro for the last four years while Kai ran off and made his fortune? They didn't need his largesse. They didn't need his pity. They most certainly didn't need him sneaking around her barn, fixing her machines behind her back. She stomped up to Ro's door and knocked. There was a quick shuffle inside.

"Ro?" Elliot knocked again. "It's okay. It's just me."

But again there was no answer.

"Ro!" Elliot pushed open the door, annoyed, but stopped dead on the threshold. Kai and Ro sat on the floor, their hands in mud up to their elbows, while an array of pots, half covered with a tarp, lay between them.

"Oh." Elliot began to back up, but Ro cried out, and she hesitated. What was he doing there so late at night? She hadn't seen his sun-cart outside. Had he walked here? Had he run on swifter-than-they-should-be enhanced feet?

Kai also seemed to be weighing the situation. He glanced down at the half-covered pots, then up at Elliot, his inhuman eyes blinking in confusion. "How is your grandfather?"

Four words. Four words after days of silence, and yet they were the ones she expected least. It wasn't about the past. It wasn't about his secrets. It wasn't even about his surreptitious and unwelcome repair work. He asked about the Boatwright, like he was just anyone. Like he was a friend. She balled her fists in her skirt and didn't answer him.

Ro looked back and forth between them and frowned. She was wearing her scarf like a turban tonight, with all her bright hair tucked up underneath its twists and weaves.

Kai pushed himself to his feet. "I'll go."

"No!" Ro grabbed for his arm with her muddy hands.

He looked down at her. "I'm sorry, Ro. Elliot doesn't want me here."

Ro shook her head. "Me." She gestured to the room. *Her room.* Where what Elliot wanted didn't really matter. Kai sank to his knees again, though Ro didn't let go of his arm. Instead, she looked at Elliot until she, too, came inside and closed the door behind her.

Then Ro smiled and went back to her pots. She pushed one toward Elliot, and Elliot stared in awe at the striped beauty it held. Ro had certainly been busy with her experiments, unless this was some Post varietal that Kai had sneaked to her. She wouldn't put it past him.

"It's very beautiful, Ro," she said. "Is it a gift, like your scarf?"

Ro made snipping motions with her hands, and Elliot cringed.

Kai's voice came from above. "She's quite the geneticist, isn't she?"

"Shut up," Elliot grumbled. Ro threw a clod of dirt at her.

"How long have you known this was going on?" Kai asked.

Elliot said nothing. She pressed her hands into the dirt, packing the soil around the cuttings as Ro instructed.

"I can't figure out how she knew what to do," Kai said. "There must be Posts on this land experimenting behind your back."

She bit back a laugh that was more like a scream. Of course he'd think that. Of course he'd give credit to anyone else. She flew through the pots Ro handed her. Some were sickly, withering in the winter chill, or perhaps without sufficient light, or maybe because they were varietals that were never meant to survive—little flower versions of the Lost. And yet others were astounding—full and rich and beautiful, and despite the darkness of the winter, despite the gloom of Ro's cabin, they were as bright as the colors on the Posts' coats.

"Elliot?" He reached over, stilling her muddy fingers with his own, and she froze. She stared unblinking down at their hands. Once, she had taken his touch for granted. Now, it meant everything, and she wished it did not. "You *know* there are Posts here doing experiments? Who?"

"I want you to stay out of my barn," she mumbled without looking up.

"I know," he replied. "You were quite clear a few weeks ago."

She had also been clear that he should never speak to her again. Didn't seem to have stopped him. "You have no right to mess with my machines."

"Ah." He sat back on his heels, and his hand slipped off hers. Elliot swallowed, but whether it was in relief or disappointment, she dared not guess. "So you see a few new gears and because you know that you have no one on your estate competent enough to fix them, you assumed it must have been me."

Elliot met his eyes. "Wasn't it?"

"Answer me, first." Kai leaned in. "Who are the Posts on your estate doing agricultural experiments?"

She took a deep breath. "There are no Posts on the North estate doing experiments."

"You lie." He sounded more hurt than accusing.

She shook her head.

"You mean you don't know, and you don't have the heart to try to root them out."

"I'll thank you not to make such assumptions."

Ro looked at the array of unfinished pots she'd pushed over to Elliot and whined. Elliot started work again.

"Elliot—"

"I answered your question!" she snapped at him. "And I don't need you to answer mine. *You* fixed those machines.

You did it to show me up. Good on you. Aren't you the expert! I am properly humbled."

"I didn't do it to show you up. I did it so the workers on the estate would have an easier time."

She snorted. "Very magnanimous." She lowered her head and mumbled beneath her breath, "And a good deal more practical than a silk scarf."

Kai chuckled. "Along with my other abominations, I have extremely keen hearing."

"And yet you're wretched at comprehension. I thought I made it clear to you that I don't want to talk to you, that I don't want to see you." She could lie well enough to convince him.

"Which is why I never let you know when I came to the barn."

"Sneaking around behind my back is not obeying the spirit of my request!"

"So I'm banished from the North estate, is that what you're saying?" Kai asked. "Never mind about the people living on your lands who want to have me here—you're the lord, so what you say goes?"

Yes! Elliot bit her tongue to keep from screaming it. He was right. If Ro wanted him here, if Gill wanted him to fix the machines, there was little Elliot could do to stop it. And it would be petty of her to try. Her argument was not theirs. Unlike Kai, she didn't require that all her friends hate him on her behalf. After all, she couldn't even muster up hatred for him herself. She pushed herself to her feet. "Ro, I'll come back another time."

Ro's face crumpled. "No . . . El . . ."

Kai was also standing. On a normal man, it might have been a scramble, but with him, it just happened. He went from sitting on the floor to blocking her path to the door in a blink. "Don't leave. You're upsetting her."

She'd upset Ro if she burst into tears, too.

"Please," said Kai. "I didn't mean to hurt you."

She gave a rueful laugh. "That's new."

"It is." The words brought her up short, and he pressed his advantage. "You know what is happening in this cottage, don't you? On this estate? Why keep it a secret from me?"

She stiffened. "I can't believe you're asking that question after your behavior to me since you returned. I do not trust you, as you have told me time and again that you do not trust me."

"I trust you now. I'm trusting you with my life. With the lives of everyone I love."

"Oh, please!" Elliot exclaimed, fighting to keep her voice steady. *Everyone he loves . . . Everyone* was the Fleet. No one else. No one here, and yet he wanted to know all her most dangerous secrets. Her family took advantage of her. She was unlikely to give Malakai Wentforth the same leverage. "You say that as if you willingly took me into your confidence, and now I owe you the same exchange. We both know that's not the case."

Ro now stood between them, wringing her hands.

When Kai spoke again, his voice was kind. It had to be for Ro's benefit. "What would I have to gain by ruining whatever they are doing here?"

"Supremacy over the North estate when you become a

Grove?" Elliot suggested.

His eyes narrowed. "I have no wish to—to live on the Grove estate." He sighed in exasperation. "And I certainly have no wish to triumph at the expense of the Posts I grew up with."

Not like he wished to triumph over her. She stood there, almost shaking her head in pity at what had become of them. Once she'd thought there were no two people in the world who had more to talk about. They could say anything to each other—they *had*—and their affection had only grown stronger. But it had all come to nothing.

If only she could speak to him as she once had. If only he had been willing to be honest with her from the start. It didn't need to be the same between them for it to be worthwhile. For it to be something.

Elliot took a deep, shuddering breath. She closed her eyes, and when she opened them, all she saw was Kai. "There are no Posts on the North estate doing experiments," she repeated.

And this time, he understood.

Thirty-one

Just then, Elliot heard the sound of sun-cart wheels on the gravel outside. With one last, incredulous look at her, Kai left the cottage. Elliot followed him, remaining behind the door. "What is it?" she heard Kai ask in a low voice.

"Olivia." It was Donovan's voice. "She's awake."

"Just now? This is wonderful news!" Kai sounded ecstatic. Elliot wanted to be just as happy for the poor girl, but a small part of her wondered if Kai would sound as excited if the news was about her.

"That's Elliot in there with Ro?"

"Who else?"

Elliot's eyes widened for a moment. How? Had he heard her breathing? Were the enhancements that good?

She opened the door and Ro crowded behind her. "Hello, Donovan."

The Post waved. "I'm sorry to interrupt you, but Horatio thought Wentforth would want to know right away."

"Of course he did," said Kai with a brusque nod.

He looked back at Elliot. She thought she saw something familiar in his expression. He appeared as torn as she felt.

Then he got in the cart with Donovan and departed, leaving Ro to her muddy pots and Elliot to her even muddier thoughts. He'd admitted he'd been trying to hurt her since he'd arrived, and as good as admitted he didn't want to anymore. And the repairs he'd done to the equipment—he'd claimed they were for the workers on the estate, but it had been Elliot who'd been parading around these last few days feeling like she'd finally fixed the machines all by herself.

Why was Kai being nice to her? Why now?

FOR WEEKS ELLIOT DIDN'T see him. She was baffled. He must have understood her, but then he'd just walked away. Was Olivia keeping him so very busy? Did he just not care? That night, at Ro's, she'd almost thought he'd wanted to stay. She almost wondered if they'd all been wrong about him loving Olivia. But he must, if he didn't care enough to return and listen to the rest of her secret.

Though it wasn't as if Elliot didn't have plenty to occupy her time, despite the frigid winter weather. Day by day, her grandfather drifted a little further away, the tether holding him to this life grown thin and brittle with age. Day by day, Dee lay in the birthing house, getting fatter and more frustrated with her sedentary state. Elliot visited as often as possible, bringing Jef and news of the estate's preparations for the horse race and house party, which were planned to coincide with the first thaw.

"I think I'm glad I'm not working," Dee said, stretching

a bit in her bed. "Bet Mags and Gill are being run ragged, though. A horse race in the depths of winter! What will your father think of next?"

"The problem is that he built a racecourse out here in the wilds of the north," Elliot replied. "Winter is the only time he'd be able to get people to visit for a house party, since the weather's so much warmer here than in the south, and during the growing season, most of the Luddites are busy with their farms."

"Your father knows something of that, then?" Dee asked.

Elliot dared to laugh, but immediately sobered. Nearby, the Reduced woman with the infant Dee suspected of being a Post slumbered peacefully in her cot. "I'm doing my best to curb his more lavish ideas, but party planning is Tatiana's area of interest, not mine." Across the room, another Reduced woman was crying into her pillow while the Post nurse, Bev, rocked her whining baby. Elliot cringed. "Can nothing be done for her?" she asked Dee softly.

The Post shrugged. "It passes eventually. It's worse in the winter—when it's even darker in here than usual, when no one can bring flowers—well, except Ro, of course."

"I hate this place."

"It's not that bad, honestly."

"Don't bother, Dee. I don't like seeing Reduced women here. There's no way I'll accept it when it comes to someone capable of taking care of herself."

Dee chuckled. "You sound like Thom. He—" She stopped herself.

Elliot sighed. Her troubles with Kai seemed foolish in the face of Dee's situation. "Dee, I'm not sure what you think you're protecting me from at this point. Obviously I know you're in contact with him. I see the evidence here before me."

Dee smiled. "Oh, Elliot, if it was up to me, I would. But Thom—he doesn't know you like I do. He doesn't know how things are now. He only remembers the bad time, and he's very . . . wary." She shrugged. "Besides, what would you do with the knowledge if you had it?"

"Get him to come back here and steal you away? I've had no luck convincing you to leave yet."

"And could anyone convince *you* to?"

"I don't have a child to think of, Dee. You do. You'll soon have two." She remembered what Kai had said to her in the barn, and took a deep breath. "Do you really want them to grow up on this estate?"

Dee threw her hands in the air. "There are a hundred children on this estate who need mothers. Grown children who don't have anyone to look after them. Little children with hungry bellies who need to know that food is going to come, winter after winter." She cast a glance at Elliot. "Rich children who think they are going it alone."

"I'm not a child," said Elliot. "And if you think I am and stay, you're as bad as Thom thinking I am and leaving. Neither of you can trust me to handle things on my own."

"If trusting you requires abandoning you," Dee said harshly, "then I'm happy to say that no, I don't."

And when Elliot wasn't sitting at bedsides where

she could do nothing to help the occupants, she worked. She rearranged the dairy, utilizing the freshly fixed machines to make the laborers' jobs easier. She finished the maintenance on the remaining machines, surveyed the fields, and planned for the spring thaw and planting season. And, night after night, she debated with herself over whether she'd try again with her illegal wheat. They were not in as desperate straits as they'd been the previous year. They could live without her heresy. And yet, it would be a safety measure—a stopgap. Plant this wheat, and they'd have food enough for the year without having to buy from more productive neighbors. Plant it, and they might even have enough to sell.

Plant it, and admit once and for all that she held no respect for the sacrifices of her Luddite ancestors. Things had progressed far beyond a field of wheat meant to keep her people from starving. Now she was keeping deadly secrets. Now she was unable to stop herself from thinking about a boy who—even now—could be one of the Lost. Every night, she visited the barn and her gaze went, unbidden, to the knothole where they'd left their letters. She sat in the locked room, pretending to work but really reading over and over the words he'd once sent her on paper gliders.

In every letter, in every line, she saw him. He hadn't changed—he'd only grown into the man he'd been meant to be. An explorer willing to cross the sea. A mechanic who would someday build himself the best ship on the islands. A rebel who'd always been willing to question the wisdom of the protocols. As different as he looked, Kai was still the same person. It was Elliot who'd grown unrecognizable.

The old poems said that lovers were made for each other. But that wasn't true for Kai and Elliot. They hadn't been made for each other at all—quite the opposite. But they'd grown together, the two of them, until they were like two trees from a single trunk, stronger together than either could have been alone.

And ever since he'd left, she'd been feeling his loss. He'd thrived without her, but Elliot—she'd just withered.

No wonder he preferred the company of Olivia, who'd never let him down. Maybe he even thought she was lying about her experiments—actually, he must. He thought she was a Luddite to the core. He'd never expect that she'd engineer a strain of wheat.

One evening, the Innovations came to dinner on an invitation from her father that Elliot thought was several months late. Nevertheless, she was glad to see them after so many weeks spent solely in the company of her family. From the beginning of the evening, the talk centered on a single topic—the horse race—and Elliot realized why her father had finally deigned to play host to the Posts. If he wanted to get the best performance possible out of his Innovation horses, he must ask the Innovations.

Admiral Innovation was more than happy to oblige Baron North, and they spent the evening chattering away about how to get the most out of the horses, and who should be the North that rode in the race. The baron had been quite the rider in his day, Tatiana was younger and skilled in the saddle herself, and Benedict possessed a great desire to celebrate his homecoming by representing the family on the course.

"Symbolically taking the reins," he said. Baron North laughed. Tatiana tittered. Elliot sipped her tea.

"You have no desire to throw your hat in the ring, I take it, Elliot?" Felicia asked.

"Not a bit," said Elliot. "One ride on an Innovation horse is more than enough for me."

"I think I remember that ride more fondly than you do," she said.

"I'm still disappointed that I didn't get a tour of the ship that day," said Elliot. "You must promise to show it to me before you leave. How has construction been going?" There. It was the closest she'd dared come to asking after Kai.

Admiral Innovation snorted. "It would be coming along much more quickly if we still had our chief engineer. We lost Wentforth three weeks ago when an order for suncarts came in. Had to send him down to Channel City to retrieve them."

Elliot gripped the handle of her mug. Kai was gone? Had been gone? For weeks? All this time, she thought he'd been tending to Olivia. All this time, she thought he'd been avoiding her, uninterested in hearing about her experiments, uninterested in exploring the fragile truce they'd come to back in Ro's cottage. But he hadn't been here at all.

In spite of the darkness, in spite of the cold, in spite of the hostile ground where she sat, hope bloomed in Elliot's heart.

Thirty-two

"How aggravating," Benedict was saying. "Wasn't there anyone down in Channel City who could deliver the carts for you?"

Felicia broke in. "Malakai restores each of the carts by hand before delivering them to the purchaser. They were found in good condition, but we don't want to risk anything but the best for our Luddite clientele."

"Naturally," said Baron North.

"But you're right, young man," said Admiral Innovation. "Very aggravating for the project. Wentforth's the only one who knows every piece of the ship."

"What wonderful mechanical training he must have had," Tatiana drawled. "And what a great loss to his estate." She rolled her eyes in Elliot's direction.

But Elliot paid her no mind. Kai hadn't been avoiding her. He wasn't on the estate. Who cared about Tatiana's potshots?

"The ship, you see," said the admiral, becoming more animated now than he had for all the hours of tedious discussions on horseflesh, "it runs on the same principle as the carts."

"Wentforth was lucky to find them," Felicia said quickly, "and he studied them carefully to extrapolate the technology." She shot her husband a glance of warning, but it was too late.

The baron sniffed disapprovingly. "I wasn't aware that you were building a new kind of ship on my lands. Or rather, my father-in-law's. Are you sure you've cleared this with the tribunal?"

"Oh, it's not new," said Felicia, smiling. "We've merely extrapolated the design of the sun-carts for something larger and ocean going. It's no different than if Miss North here," she nodded in Tatiana's direction, "were to get one of her dress patterns made out of new material. Nothing wrong with that."

Benedict grinned while Tatiana, clad in Post velvets she'd had shipped all the way from Channel City, straightened her skirts and looked away.

"At any rate," said the admiral, clearly wishing to change the subject, "Wentforth's been gone, and it was a hardship. Of course, he went reluctantly enough." He chuckled.

Reluctantly! Elliot squeezed her mug in suppressed glee.

"With his sweetheart awake, it took some real convincing on my part to tear him from her bedside."

"Did it?" Elliot blurted. "I mean—how lovely for Olivia." She yearned for him to say something useful, maybe estimate a time for Kai's return.

"Yes," said the admiral. "He's been quite glued to her side ever since he returned yesterday."

Her hopes withered on the vine. He was back, and he still hadn't come. Elliot dipped her head forward, praying no one could see the disappointment etched onto her features.

The admiral nodded. "It's wonderful to see such devotion in a teenager to a sick young woman. My captains seem particularly steadfast in this regard. I'm sure you've heard of my dear daughter. My Captain Phoenix—he cared for her very much, and did not let her sickliness sway him at any point." Felicia laid her hand on his, and they exchanged a soft, sad smile. "I love him for how much he loved my Sophia. I love him as the son-in-law he never got the chance to be."

Elliot blinked hard. They loved him because he'd risked his life to help their daughter. Of course, the risk wasn't without its rewards. She wondered how much of Donovan's musical talent the ERV procedure had been responsible for. Kai's voice hadn't changed, so perhaps Donovan's beautiful singing was natural talent. Surely, however, his violin skills were helped along significantly by the muscular grace and finesse his enhancement conferred.

"It seems as if Malakai Wentforth has the same love for the Grove girl."

Elliot had to agree. To fantasize otherwise would be foolish. She'd seen it with her own eyes, and it had been confirmed by everyone else she knew. Kai loved Olivia. As he should.

"Indeed," said Tatiana, raising her eyebrows. She'd lost any pretense of respect for Kai's relationship with Olivia now that she knew who he was. A rich Post originating from anyplace else was one thing, but a runaway North Post, parading about on these lands like a lord—that was something else entirely. "I imagine that's a bit premature."

It was, perhaps, the most supportive thing Elliot's sister had ever said. Even if it was by accident. But if Tatiana was her only ally, Elliot doubted there was any possibility of mistake.

"I wonder that Horatio Grove allows it," Tatiana added.

"Pardon?" the admiral asked.

"Captain Wentforth must be at least eighteen," Tatiana replied smoothly, though she knew his exact birthday. "Olivia is still a child. It's disgraceful."

"Not by Post standards," Felicia piped up. "But, I suppose, to each his own. For instance, the Posts are not so keen on close family relations. But it's common enough among Luddites." Her smile said it all. She knew Tatiana's complaint was not with Olivia's age, but rather with her admirer's identity.

Later, after the Innovations had left, Tatiana let herself fume. "That Post woman forgets herself sometimes, I think."

"What is it to you," Elliot asked, "if she approves of a relationship between two people so unconnected to you?"

"It's the principle of the thing!" Tatiana exclaimed. "Olivia is a Luddite. No matter how rich these Posts are, they do not have the right bloodlines."

"And yet Mrs. Innovation implies otherwise," Benedict said. "You heard her disparaging the Luddite practice of family intermarriage." There was a cunning little smile playing about his lips as he addressed his two cousins. "She's quite bold."

"That's the problem with Posts," said Tatiana. "They think they're invincible because they overcame the Reduction. It lives inside of them. There is no escaping that." She gave a little sniff.

But what if there was? It was heresy to say it out loud, but the look on Benedict's face reflected the thoughts that were threatening to burst out of her. The Posts had come to believe that they had escaped it—that they had overcome the genetic taint of Reduction. They believed it so thoroughly that they would even risk ERV.

"Perhaps if they didn't think themselves so mighty," Tatiana continued, "Olivia would never have been injured."

She glared at Elliot, as if somehow she was responsible for anything Kai had done in the last four years.

At that moment Mags appeared in the doorway, her face pale and somber. "Miss Elliot," she said softly, and then remembered who it was she should be addressing. "Miss North."

Tatiana rolled her eyes. "What is it, Mags?"

"The Boatwright, miss. He's passed."

IT WAS VERY LATE when Elliot was finally left to her own devices. She hadn't had a chance to do more than look upon the sheet-wrapped body of the Boatwright in the presence of her father and sister. She hadn't had a chance to go into her own room and cry. Tatiana had squeezed out a few ladylike tears in the parlor, but Elliot was not the type to quietly weep and dab at her face with a handkerchief while the baron and Benedict looked on. She couldn't let herself go in front of them. Just like with her mother's death, when she did cry, it would be volcanic.

And she had to do it alone. But she never got the chance to excuse herself and go to her room. Her father didn't seem to see why it was necessary. There were so many preparations to be made—the body needed to be moved and dressed, and adjustments had to be made for the party plans to accommodate a funeral. Elliot would have preferred to cancel, but her father wouldn't hear of it.

"People will want to come and pay their respects to the Boatwright," he argued. "Why not combine the events?"

He made the same argument, it seemed, whether Elliot's grandfather was alive or dead.

At last she knew that to get any real peace, she'd have to leave the house entirely. There was only one place to go. Elliot had long ago made peace with herself over the fact that, every time things in her house became too unbearable, she needed the barn. It was no great mystery. In the barn is where she'd known almost every moment of peace, happiness, and triumph in her life. It was her secret joy, her refuge . . . and her shame. She couldn't pass through the doors without her eyes going immediately to that little knothole as if, magically, a letter from Kai would be waiting as they used to be so many years ago. She couldn't enter without cursing her own body's memory.

One day she was going to get a new door put on the barn. No more knothole. No more ritual. No more pain, every time she passed through and remembered all she'd lost. But for now she just wanted to escape to the little room in the loft and rest. Rest for a moment. Forget about everything that had changed and everything that hadn't. Lie down on the pallet that still sat on the floor, though all trace and scent of Kai had long ago been leached out of it. Look at the gliders that fluttered down from the beams—her final gift from Kai, though for all she knew, he'd left her their letters out of spite. Close her eyes and remember a time when her grandfather and her mother were here to temper things for them all. Just spend a few minutes not thinking about the estate, not being a North, not worrying about anything.

She made her way in silence across the floor of the dairy, past the machines Kai had repaired, past the stalls where the Innovation horses dozed, and headed toward the stairs that led to the loft.

Nero was waiting for her on the landing.

So was Kai.

He startled her, sitting there in the darkness, silent and unmoving even when she almost jumped out of her skin. The cat sat on his knees and he was scratching the animal's neck. Were it not for those tiny flicks of his fingers against the fur, Kai could have been a statue. She turned up the lantern, but he didn't blink in the sudden brightness.

Elliot composed herself, as much in response to his uncanny presence as to her raw reaction to seeing him again. "How's Olivia?" she forced herself to ask, though her voice broke on the words.

"I don't want to talk about Olivia right now." He studied her. "I heard about your grandfather, Elliot. I'm so sorry."

"Thank you." She stood still. His body blocked the stairs. She couldn't push past him. She didn't *want* to push past him. If she inadvertently touched him, she might dissolve. For weeks she'd waited for him. He hadn't sent word that he'd left the estate; he hadn't come to visit when he'd returned. And now, of all times, he came to her?

"I thought, maybe . . ."

"What?"

He waited. Took a breath. "I thought maybe you . . . needed to talk to someone."

"You mean like when my mother died?" The words fell like stones into the space between them. That night. That wonderful, terrible night when her mother died and her whole world had been destroyed, when she realized she loved Kai and her whole world had been created anew. Now he wanted to take that night away from her, too? Her throat began to burn, and a vise squeezed at her heart. "I think you'll find, Malakai, that I'm a different person than I was then. I don't need anyone. The last four years are proof of that."

"So now when you come to the barn, it's to be alone?"

She stiffened. "Yes."

Kai stood and moved to the side of the stairwell so she could pass, but still she did not. He looked at the locked door to the loft, and back at Elliot. "Go ahead."

She didn't move. Damn him. He knew what she hid in there. He had to know. Or at least suspect. "I thought I told you to stay out of here."

"Go ahead, Elliot. Open the door."

She shook her head. No. If he saw she'd kept the letters, he'd know how much she still cared. She couldn't bear for him to see, not tonight, when she'd already lost so much.

"Why?"

"I don't owe you an answer." Did his unnatural eyes give him X-ray vision? Could he see through the boards of the door and tell what she was hiding inside? Had Felicia given him the power of flight? Had he levitated up to the window and peered inside?

Or did he just know her so well that he could guess?

"You told me you did experiments, Elliot." So he did believe her. "You must trust me. I came tonight because I knew you'd be here. Please, will you unlock the door now?"

It was too late for that. He might not hate her anymore, but that didn't mean she was ready to give up all her secrets. "Go back to Olivia," she said flatly. "She needs you more than I do."

Six Years Ago

Dear Kai,
After giving it a lot of thought, I've decided that this will be my
last little note to you. I've grown tired of playing with a boy who
lives in a barn and only owns one pair of pants. I can't possibly
imagine what you find so fascinating about bunches of rusted
metal. It was a fun game while it lasted. But I'm bored now.
Please don't ever talk to me again.
Not your friend,
Elliot

Dear Elliot,
I really wish you'd stop coming and bothering me. I have lots of
chores to do, because I'm a servant. I would much rather do the
work I'm supposed to than waste everyone's time by playing with
you. I'm twelve years old now, and that means I have to work my
allotted twelve hours a day on the farm, and if I don't, I won't get
fed. I'm sure you don't want me to starve. So leave me alone.
Not your friend,
Kai

Dear Kai,

That was Tatiana. Don't worry. Mother has punished her.

Your friend,

Elliot

    ∾

Dear Elliot,

No kidding.

Your friend,

Kai

PS: Would you really let me starve?

    ∾

Dear Kai,

That was the craziest part of her letter. I had no idea you worked twelve hours a day. How do you have time to see me at all? How do you have time to read?

Your friend,

Elliot

    ∾

Dear Elliot,

What do you mean? There are twenty four hours in a day. I only have to work for twelve.

Your friend,

Kai

Thirty-three

"YOU'RE COMING TO THE race and that's final. The Reduced laborers can prepare grandfather's body without your supervision." Tatiana stood at the door of Elliot's room and slapped her riding crop impatiently against her thigh. Her dark hair was swept up in an elaborate system of braids that must have taken her maid hours to achieve, and her new riding habit was a deep, rich green velvet, complete with fringe, tassels, and gold buttons. Elliot supposed if she was going to ride a Post horse, she might as well dress up in a Post costume.

The irony was lost on her sister though. Today she was hosting a party for her fellow Luddite lords, but every detail, including the money used to pay for the extravaganza, was Post. This funeral was already an embarrassment. A horse race, to honor the Boatwright? It was ludicrous. Even a boat race would be preferable, but Tatiana and her father wouldn't triumph there, and there was a real danger that the Cloud Fleet captains would.

"If there is no need to supervise the Reduced, then why do we?" Elliot asked. "Why do we imprison them when they are pregnant? Why do we control their movements? Why do we keep them like slaves?"

Tatiana rolled her eyes. "Don't be dramatic, little sister. You know what I mean. We have set them a task and they can accomplish it quite well without your help. You are a daughter of Baron North and my sister, and you should be there to see me win this race. If you aren't there, everyone will wonder why."

"Or maybe they will think that I am in proper mourning for our grandfather." Unlike Tatiana, who insisted on riding in the race, despite Elliot's misgivings. After much more debate than Elliot would have thought possible, they'd come up with a solution that pleased three of the four of them: Benedict would ride one of the Innovation horses for the Norths, and Tatiana would ride the other in honor of her Boatwright heritage.

"The Fleet Posts are coming," Tatiana said, ignoring Elliot's remark. "You like them so much, I'm certain you'll want to see them. And Horatio is bringing Olivia. That means *Captain Wentforth* will be there." Her voice dripped with disdain over Kai's Post moniker. "Don't you want to see them?"

See them together? Tatiana was truly making a case for herself. "I know you'd prefer not to," Elliot said.

"If I were you," Tatiana replied, "I'd attach myself to Horatio as quickly as possible, lest Olivia and her Post friend try to take over the Grove estate."

Elliot was sick of this argument. Almost as sick as she was of imagining a future where Kai remained here permanently—with Olivia Grove. "The last thing Captain Wentforth needs is an estate. And the last thing we need is any more arranged marriages."

Tatiana raised her eyebrows in confusion. "What do you mean? Who has arranged a marriage around here?"

So Benedict hadn't told Tatiana of their mother's history.

"Elliot?" Tatiana repeated. "Has Father said anything to you?"

Elliot almost laughed at the idea of her father telling her anything. But her father's renewed closeness to his nephew finally made sense. There was nothing he could do to change Benedict's claim to the estate. Benedict had been invited home with open arms for Tatiana's benefit. Her father knew his best chance of keeping the estate for his eldest daughter lay in marrying her off to the Norths' rightful heir.

But she doubted Benedict would be so easily swayed. No matter what he'd said to her when he first arrived, his snide remarks made it clear he hadn't forgiven his uncle for the banishment, and he would be unlikely to do anything to oblige him—like following the Luddite tradition of an arranged marriage . . . to his cousin.

"I'm not going to the race," was all Elliot would say. "I'm going to stay with Grandfather until the funeral. We've put it off long enough."

Tatiana pursed her lips, slapped her riding crop

against her leg a few more times, and glared at Elliot. Elliot glared back. Then Tatiana opened her mouth and called out, "Father!"

Elliot sighed.

Her father appeared in the doorway. "Get dressed, Elliot. And not in black, either. Your grandfather would not have wanted you to look so dismal. Remember, this is a celebration of his life."

"She says she's not going," Tatiana whined.

"She most certainly is."

"But, Father—"

"You're going to the race," he stated. "Or I shall bar *all* visitors from the birthing house."

Elliot stared at him in bewilderment. If she didn't attend a party, he would punish an innocent servant and her son. It made no sense whatsoever. None of it had. Putting Dee in the birthing house was a nonsense rule as well. It was nothing but a display of his power over the Posts on the estate. And this—this was nothing more than a display of his power over her. It couldn't be important to him to see her present at the race. It would only reflect poorly on Tatiana and him if it was revealed that Elliot had chosen not to go.

It was Elliot who held power over *him*. She couldn't help the bark of laughter that bubbled up in her throat, couldn't prevent the escape of words that seemed to have been awaiting their freedom for years.

"Really, Father?" she asked. "And how exactly do you intend on implementing that? Will you be guarding it yourself, or do you expect one of the Post foremen to obey your orders in order to break the heart of a mother and son he has known all his life?"

The second the words were out, she regretted them. Her father's face turned deadly serious. "You are going to the race, or I will move that Reduced girl out of her private cottage and into the adult barracks. It's high time she found a man."

Elliot caught her breath. No. No, she took it all back. This is what came of spending time with the Posts. She thought she could change the world.

The baron smiled mirthlessly. "Not so haughty now, are you? Think I don't have control over my own estate? I do, and I can do much more besides. I can cancel the laborers' funeral feast. I can change the locks on that room in the barn you're so very fond of. You think I don't know what happens on my own lands, Elliot? You think you're in charge here? I am sick of your disobedience. You are going to the race because I said so." He turned to go, then paused. "Oh, and Elliot, these penalties shall apply to any further infractions. Consider it a standing order."

And then he was gone, leaving Elliot to sink weakly into her chair and Tatiana's smile to broaden considerably.

"That will teach you."

"Go away, Tatiana." Elliot shook her head. What had she been thinking? She was supposed to be too smart for this. She had been too smart—for three years, ever since the bad time, she'd been oh-so-careful to work around her father. But he still knew just how to hit her. He always did.

Tatiana frowned. "Elliot, you think we don't care about

the Reduced. We do. We're Luddites. We were born to care. But all the little luxuries you provide them—do they make them work any harder? You were once so kind to that Post boy, and how did he repay you? He ran away and left us all without a mechanic. And how has he repaid you now that he's so rich? Hasn't that taught you anything? Our job is not to raise them up. It's to keep them alive and working and *here*, for the good of us all."

Elliot raised her eyes to her sister. "How is the common good served by going to a horse race, Tatiana? When you can explain that, then maybe I will see things your way."

Thirty-four

THE LUDDITES WHO'D COME to the horse race were a varied lot. It had been so long since the Norths had thrown a house party, Elliot hardly knew what to expect—but the assembled group surprised her. Down in the Channel, things must be changing as quickly as Benedict and the Fleet Posts had hinted at. It was interesting to note which of the visiting Luddites embraced the Post styles and which resisted, more interesting still to see the reactions of the more conservative when Baron North and Tatiana came out in their new, bright velvet clothes. Eyes widened, eyebrows raised, and there were definite whispers among the assembled crowd.

"This is what comes of taking Post money," was one comment that Elliot managed to make out.

"I'd never have thought it of the Norths, but desperate times, I suppose," was another.

And, "Harbinger of the end times, if you ask me. Knew it as soon as I saw the invite. Innovation horses, indeed!" rounded out the bunch.

Her family didn't seem to notice. "One positive of your little outburst this morning," Tatiana hissed in Elliot's ear as they walked through the crowd, "is it allowed us to be fashionably late to our own party."

Elliot tugged on the sleeves of her dress and said nothing. Her hair, too, was arranged in braids and looped up over her head. Her dress was old—it had been her mother's—and a pale orchid color. She caught the approving nods of some of the harsher critics and inwardly cringed. Little did they know, beneath the Luddite dress, she was more of a radical than anyone in her family.

The Fleet had also arrived, and had concocted a marvelous system of heated pavilions attached to the sun-carts. The Innovations and Groves sat inside, watching the festivities and staying toasty warm. Perhaps the only good thing to come of this spectacle was Olivia's first appearance in public since her accident. Elliot hadn't been able to bring herself to visit her yet, for fear of running into Kai, but Tatiana had gone on several occasions. Her sister had reported back that Olivia was as pretty as ever, but had grown "a bit odd." She was quieter than she used to be and preferred to stay close to her brother.

"Give my regards to the tenants, Elliot," Baron North said—or rather ordered. "And invite Horatio Grove to sit in our pavilion."

"Yes, father." She doubted he would leave his sister's side, though, nor that he'd prefer the smoky smudge pots in the Luddites' pavilion to the clear air in the Fleet's.

As Elliot approached the Post pavilion, she saw that

several Luddites sat there, too. Elliot supposed they were former patrons of the admiral's.

"Good morning, Elliot," said Felicia. She was dressed in magenta today, and sat on a giant marigold cushion she shared with her husband. Kai stood behind her. "You look lovely in that dress. Its color suits you so well. But I am surprised to see you here today. I thought you might be staying with your grandfather."

Elliot swallowed and kept her eyes averted from Kai's face, though he wasn't doing the same for hers. Indeed, she worried she might melt under the directness of his too-bright gaze. He'd stayed away from her since the night of her grandfather's death. She wished she could say she was grateful.

"I seem to have warring duties, ma'am. My father sends his regards. You know he has high hopes for your horses." How many weeks had she longed for him to look her way? Now she dreaded the sensation. His dark eyes seemed to bore right through her and it was all she could do to pay attention to the adults.

"As well the baron might," said the Luddite woman sitting nearest the admiral. "I am Baroness Channel, Miss Elliot. I don't believe I've ever had the pleasure of meeting Baron North's youngest daughter before."

Elliot shook the woman's hand. She was dressed in shell-pink velvet, marrying the best in Post fashion with Luddite sensibilities. Her matching hat had a shimmering half-veil that shielded the woman's eyes from the sun. Elliot remembered her name from Nicodemus's letter of introduction. "Nice to meet you."

At the racetrack, the riders were being announced, and each stepped forward, leading their horses by the reins. Elliot heard her sister's name called, and then Benedict's.

"I was so sorry to hear about your recent loss. Chancellor Boatwright was a great man. I used to do lots of business with him, before he shuttered his business and the admiral here approached me about starting his Fleet. I am happy that I could be here to celebrate his life."

"Thank you," said Elliot.

Felicia lifted a small set of binoculars to her eyes to observe the horses as they paraded them around the track. Many of the other attendees had similar devices. "Three Innovation horses in this race. I see the Record family has brought Zeus."

The baroness turned to the admiral. "I remember I was a bit skeptical when you first approached me. A Post, wanting to build a fleet of ships to explore with? But by that time, you had already become quite well known for the horses. They were the first fruits of your exploration, were they not, Nicodemus?"

Felicia laid her hand on top of the admiral's, and he smiled at her as he said, "Ah, yes. Our first expedition. And what luck we had, didn't we, dear?"

"The island didn't have a name," said Felicia. "I don't think it was ever inhabited. Just wild horses, everywhere. We brought back a pair to start the breeding program."

"And the money we made was enough to begin to finance the Fleet," the admiral finished. "That was so many years ago now. Our late daughter—she was little more than a child at the time."

Elliot nodded once more to the Innovations and the baroness and, hoping to escape Kai's steady gaze, she moved toward the cushions where the Groves sat with the Phoenixes. Even if he followed her here, she was sure Olivia would distract him. The girl sat propped up on cushions near her brother and Donovan and Kai didn't move from his place near Felicia. Elliot supposed they couldn't spend every waking moment together.

He didn't stop watching her, either.

"Elliot," said Donovan. "What a pleasure to see you in our humble tent." A string-box sat in his lap and he plucked idly at it as he spoke. Olivia wore a dreamy half smile at the sound of the music.

"She's jumpier than she used to be," Horatio explained in a low voice. "Too many people, too much noise. She'd been refusing to come at all until Donovan offered to bring an instrument. The music soothes her somehow."

"Only when Donovan plays," said Olivia, with a slur in her voice Elliot had never heard before. "He's so good at it."

"You're doing so well," Elliot managed to tell the younger girl. "It is so good to see you again." She'd been too hasty, casting aspersions on Kai for visiting Olivia first. The poor girl had been through so much. Who knew if she'd ever really recover? And of course Kai would blame himself—this wouldn't have happened if he and Donovan weren't playing on the cliffs.

This wouldn't have happened if he and Donovan didn't

have abilities no human should possess. Even at the time, Andromeda had tried to stop them, tried to warn them.

Now, Andromeda wouldn't even look her way. Elliot wanted to groan aloud. What had she done to offend the older girl this time? She sat stiff as a rod on her cushion, her crystalline eyes staring, unfocused, on the blanket before her, her lips pursed into a thin line. A set of binoculars lay forgotten near her feet. Elliot supposed they must be for show, anyway. With her eyes, Andromeda would never need them. Elliot was tempted to ask if the Post girl was all right, but Andromeda would likely only snap at her, as always.

As she exchanged pleasantries with the others, Elliot listened with half an ear to the conversation going on at her back. Baroness Channel was still curious about the Innovation horses.

"But with the horses being so rare and valuable, I have often wondered why you never returned to retrieve more."

The admiral chuckled. "Can't flood the market, can we? The Innovation Horse remains our biggest moneymaker, in part because they are so rare."

Felicia laughed, too. "In truth, Baroness, we did. But something must have gone wrong one winter on the island. The horses were gone. Died out. It's a mystery."

Something in her tone rang false to Elliot's ears. Was it truly a mystery? Had they killed off the other horses to make sure they had the only supply? She cast a glance back at the older guests on their cushions. That didn't seem like either of the Innovations—to wipe out an island of horses. They were explorers, not destroyers. They were the only explorers, too, so it was unlikely anyone else would go get the horses instead.

"Indeed!" the baroness exclaimed. Beneath the shade of her veil, her mouth formed a perfect O. "How lucky, then, that you were able to preserve the breed."

"Yes," said Felicia. "We were very lucky."

Lucky . . . and convenient. That Felicia with her prodigious medical knowledge could take advantage of such a fortunate find. That Kai and his mechanical training had happened upon sun-carts that only he was capable of readying for buyers.

Elliot's blood ran cold as the truth cut through her like a scythe on a blade of wheat. She turned to stare at the Innovations in shock.

Felicia winked at the admiral. "To get the only two horses like that in all of existence."

Of course they were the only two. The Innovations had never discovered any horses—any enormous, incredibly fast, impossibly beautiful, amazingly strong horses.

They'd made them.

Thirty-five

"OH LOOK," SAID THE baroness. "The race is about to start." Most of the people in the pavilion turned their attention to the track, but Elliot was too distracted. She looked full on at Felicia, unable to hide the expression of shock on her face.

But of course. Why should she be surprised? They were willing to experiment on human beings. Why not horses? And then, to pass them off as an undiscovered breed, as a product of their totally legal explorations . . .

She pressed a hand to her cheeks. Her flesh burned, and once again she felt the need to run. Here, surrounded by a large contingent of Luddite society, they were about to witness the triumph of abominations. They were about to cheer them on. Did no one else suspect? Or did they just not care? Like her family, so many of these Luddites had taken Post money and wore Post clothes. They drove Post sun-carts and accepted Post hospitality. Was the hypocrisy of the Luddites so embedded that they didn't mind who broke the protocols as long as there was money and amusement in it?

If they knew what the Fleet Posts had done, would the Luddites condemn them, or feel tempted to follow in their footsteps?

Elliot was a hypocrite, too. She liked Felicia. She liked the admiral. She'd sympathized with their desire to cure their daughter, and no matter what they did, she didn't want to see them hanged for their actions. She hated to admit it, but she believed in their goals too much.

She shuddered as new realizations swept through her. If she was a false Luddite, was she not alone? Was there anything keeping their way of life afloat aside from lies and a lust for power?

Everyone's eyes were on the race as Elliot stumbled blindly from the pavilion. She forgot her father's instructions. She just needed to get away. She was two steps past the back of the sun-carts when she broke into a run, and halfway across the nearest wheat field when she collapsed in a heap. The ends of her skirts twisted around her ankles when she tried to stand, so she just pounded the dirt in frustration.

"Elliot," said Kai. "Don't say anything. Please."

She spun to see him standing over her. Of course he'd come after her. He'd been staring at her since she entered the tent. Was it his duty to see what deception of the Fleet's she'd uncover next? Had Felicia given him mind-reading abilities to help him along, or was Elliot simply that easy for him to read?

"Is any of it true?" she asked as he knelt in the dust at her side. Around them, hay bales still stood. They were shielded from the sights and sounds of the race. "Any of it at all? Are you really a Fleet? Are you really explorers? Did you really go forth at all, *Captain Wentforth*, or do you all just invent things and then claim you found them? Are you just a roving band of science experiments and liars?"

He looked at her with his too-bright eyes. "Are you a Luddite, or did you invent a breed of high-yield wheat?"

"Who told you?" she cried.

"I can figure things out on my own, too," he replied. "When you wouldn't talk to me the other night, I decided to do just that." He shook his head. "I don't know whether to be shocked or proud."

"I'll take shock."

"You don't get to choose." His face was kind, and Elliot wanted to smack it. He hesitated for a second, and when he spoke again, he sounded almost nervous. "Are you proud of me? I have to admit, I wondered when I saw you driving the sun-cart, all those months ago."

She felt like a fool. The Fleet had made fools of them all. Naturally, there were no island lots filled with abandoned sun-carts. They were the invention of her oldest friend. The controls looked like the tractor controls because that's what Kai had been used to. He wasn't restoring them for buyers; he was building them.

"Even then, I was glad you liked it. I wondered what you'd think if you knew I'd made it."

She gritted her teeth. She'd been proud enough when she'd thought he'd merely *found* them. But how could she countenance this? "Don't change the subject."

He lifted his shoulder. "Fine. What happened to your wheat?"

"That wasn't what I meant."

But Kai wouldn't let up. "What happened?"

She gestured back at the pavilions. "The racetrack."

He nodded. She didn't need to say anything more. He knew what the baron was like. "What were you thinking, Elliot? I'd never have expected it from a Luddite. Even you."

"We needed to survive," Elliot said, ignoring his "even you." How did this become about her? A field of crossbred wheat paled in comparison to illegal inventions and abominable animals. "Now you explain. This isn't about Sophia this time."

"No, it's bigger than that. It's about every Post on the islands. Yes, the Innovations lied. And your kind ate it up with a spoon. Look at the Luddites—beholden to their high-minded ideals, yet so desperate for something new, something better, that they don't even ask basic questions."

"Our naiveté is no justification for your deception," said Elliot. "Are they all lies? Everything?"

Kai hesitated, then sighed. "We do go to nearby uninhabited islands. But they aren't filled with miraculous inventions and highly convenient livestock, just off the coast. Or rather, they are, but it's because we make them there."

Elliot's breath broke on a sob. "So if it's all lies, what have you been building in my grandfather's shipyard?" What had she been a party to?

"A ship!" Kai responded. "A real, ocean-going ship.

It's the truth this time. That's why we've done all of this. For the money. For the support. The ships we have won't take us beyond the islands. We need to make a new one—one that can harness the power of the sun to travel faster than sails. And a few other vehicles to help us on our journey. Everything we've done has been in preparation for this." He leaned forward. "You know me, Elliot. I've always wanted to get away."

"And go where?"

"Anywhere other than here." He stood. "We don't know what's out there, beyond these islands. Are there people? Are there other people who have overcome the Reduction? Are there people who have cured it? I want to find out."

"You sound like we did when we were children."

"When we were children," Kai said, "we were right."

Elliot looked down into the dirt.

"You think we should, too, Elliot. I know you do. But the Luddites would never let us if they knew. So we bring them back little presents, make them think there's treasure out there to find if only they help us. And there is—but it's not the kind of treasure that will ever help them."

She shook her head in defeat. He was right. She hated it, but more than that, she hated the bone-deep ache of envy that threatened to crush her at the thought of Kai's mission.

Kai was silent for a few moments. "What bothers you most?"

She looked up at him and laughed mirthlessly. Like she'd ever admit it. "What bothers me most about the abominations you've created? About the laws you've broken?

About the way you've made fools of us all?"

"Ah," he said, nodding in triumph. "What bothers you most is that you didn't sniff us out sooner."

"No, I—"

"No, you're a Luddite?" he asked. "No, you don't think the Reduced should be cured? No, you hate the idea of new experiments? No, you would never lie to a Luddite lord to give everyone—including the Luddites—something they needed? I know you weren't going to say anything like that."

Elliot pressed her lips together. The wind tugged at her hair and cooled her cheeks.

His tone was insistent. "We rented the shipyard to build a ship, just as we said. A ship worthy of taking us across the ocean. We needed your facilities to do that—they are the only ones on the island that would have worked." He shrugged. "If there was anywhere else I could have gone, don't you think I would have? I would never have come back here by choice."

Elliot buried her hands in her lap, hoping the folds of her skirt would hide the way they trembled. Would she have been better off if he'd never come back? If she could have just remembered him as he was instead of realizing that he'd achieved everything he'd ever wanted—and that he'd done it without her? No, more than simply without her. He'd done it *because* he'd left her behind. "I suppose then, you wouldn't want to stay." He would take Olivia away with him. That, at least, would be a relief.

"What?"

"Here. With Olivia."

"Of course not! I told you—" He rubbed at his forehead in frustration. "This is all a nightmare."

A nightmare. Of course. It was also her home. Elliot stood and turned away from him, looking back at the brightness of the pavilions. Her eyes narrowed. There, behind the sun-carts, hidden from the others by a flap of the tents, stood Andromeda Phoenix. Elliot did not have superhuman eyes. She could not see like Kai; she could not hear like Donovan. But it was impossible to mistake.

Andromeda was sobbing.

Eight Years Ago

Dear Kai,
My mother and I are going to my grandfather's house today. They
are going to turn on the windcatcher. If you don't have work to
do, would you like to come and see it?
Your friend,
Elliot

∾

Dear Elliot,
I have to work with my da, but I'm jealous. I've heard about the
windcatcher. Is it true that's all the Boatwright uses to power his
tractor? I imagine it smells a lot better than ours.

Though I guess that depends on the type of wind.
Your friend,
Kai

∾

Dear Kai,
Very funny.

The windcatcher was amazing. I asked my mother why we
don't use one on the North estate, and she told me it was because

it only works near the cliffs. But there is shoreline on the North estate.

After we watched it for a little while, we visited my grandfather. He is sick, but he's still a lot of fun. He let me play with his big old compass. I can't believe people used to use it to find their way. You know you can fool it with nothing but a magnet? He showed me how to make the arrow point in any direction I want with a magnet. It's so easy to make it wrong, it's a wonder people ever trusted it.

Your friend,

Elliot

෧෭

Dear Elliot,

You saw the windcatcher and played with a compass? Now I'm really jealous.

I think your mother is right. I have heard the windcatchers don't work everywhere. But there are other things that work. I have heard in the south, when it's sunny all day long in the summer, they have lamps that capture the sunlight and glow all night. I would love to have one. It would mean I didn't have to hoard candle stubs and I could read my books whenever I wanted.

And don't worry about the compass. That's not all they used. They also used the stars, and no magnet makes them move.

Your friend,

Kai

Thirty-six

KAI FOLLOWED HER GAZE and he frowned.

"What's wrong with her?" Elliot asked. She recalled Andromeda's frozen expression earlier and remembered the reason she'd left her home estate. She'd never heard the name of the place, though. Had the Norths invited Andromeda's old lord and lady to their party?

"I don't know." Kai looked at her. "I should go and check on her."

"Yes." Elliot figured she should stay back—the Post girl had never liked her, and she doubted Andromeda wanted her company when she looked so . . . vulnerable.

Vulnerable had never before been a word Elliot would have used to describe Andromeda, but she also couldn't imagine her crying, either. Even if the Post girl's Luddite father was here, Elliot couldn't imagine Andromeda crying. Using her superhuman aim to lob a drink at him from across the pavilion, maybe. But nothing like this.

"But I don't want to walk away from you without

finishing our conversation. There are things I need to make you understand."

What more was there to say? His whole life was a monument of mockery to Luddite society, and Elliot couldn't even hold it against him. He hated being here and couldn't wait to get away, and she couldn't blame him for that, either. She didn't need to listen to him detail his plans for a future with Olivia once the younger girl's brain was put right. She didn't need to hear him gloat about how all his dreams—the ones they'd once created together—were about to come true. Envy hurt exponentially more than heartbreak because your soul was torn in two, half soaring with happiness for another person, half mired in a well of self-pity and pain.

If she spent any more time with Kai, he'd see it written all over her. He'd perceived everything else about her. She couldn't let him know this. "Don't worry," she said. "I have no intention of spilling your secrets. Any of them." And she wouldn't spill her own, either.

Kai held her gaze for a long moment and Elliot thought he was going to speak, but at last he went after Andromeda.

A cheer shot up from the pavilions and Elliot heard the announcement.

"The winner is Tatiana North, on her Innovation mount, Pyrois!"

She hadn't expected anything less.

BECAUSE OF THE PRESENCE of the Luddites at the house party, it was easy to expedite the reading of the Boatwright's will. The heads of most of the great families convened in the parlor of Elliot's house, waiting somewhat impatiently. The reading of a will was always such a dull affair compared to the fireworks and excitement of a funeral, especially a Boatwright funeral.

Since time immemorial, that side of Elliot's family had bucked tradition. Instead of being laid to rest in the star cavern, they were sent out to sea on a pyre, like their ancestors had been doing long before the Reduction. When her mother died, there had been quite the debate about what to do with her body. Eventually, she was buried in the sanctuary, as a North, but Elliot always thought she'd been robbed. And though Elliot was born a North, she wondered if there was any way she could be treated like a Boatwright upon her own death. She vastly preferred the idea of sending her body out to sea to being permanently trapped in the earth beneath the North estate.

The Norths were all there for the reading of the will, of course. Tatiana was still glowing with delight over her showing at the horse race the previous day, and Elliot was pretty sure the blue gown she wore today was merely an excuse to accessorize with her winning ribbon. The Innovation horses had been the big winners at the race, taking first, second, and third place several strides before any other finisher. Hardly surprising. They'd been genetically engineered to do just that.

"It's odd, is it not, that your father is not the executor of the Boatwright's will?" Benedict asked from his seat at her side. He seemed to accept his second place standing in the race with good humor. And why shouldn't he? Tatiana might have won the day, but he'd still get the estate. "After all, Uncle Zachariah was his son-in-law."

"I don't think my father and my grandfather were particularly close," was all Elliot trusted herself to say. She also doubted her grandfather could trust her father to give away any little trinkets or even larger items—like some of the Boatwright's personal ships—if he was made executor.

Instead, Baroness Channel was acting as executor, and for that Elliot was glad, if only because it meant that any of the more troublesome chores in the will would not fall into Elliot's own lap as extra work.

The baroness was even now getting the attention of the group. Today she dressed in dove gray, with a matching veil attached to her hair with the assistance of a pair of bright peacock feathers. "We gather here today to read the Last Will and Testament of Chancellor Elliot Boatwright, of the Boatwright Estate, North Island." The baroness cleared her throat and smoothed out the paper.

I, Elliot Boatwright, being of sound mind and body, do set forth this will, to be executed only upon my death by my appointed representative, the Baroness Lucinda Channel.

I hereby partition out the following items from among my worldly goods to my Luddite brethren:

To the Baroness Channel, I leave my schooner, Morning Dew.

To the honorable family of Grove, I leave the fishing vessel Charybdis, *as well as their choice of any of my three dinghies.*

To the Baron Record and his family, I leave the catamaran

Rhodes, *with the stipulation that they extend the offer of the same terms of employment to the COR crew as they currently enjoy.*

To my granddaughter Tatiana North, I leave my carriage, as well as my two horses, Thetis and Amphitrite, in hopes that she will become an ever-finer horsewoman.

To my granddaughter Elliot North, I leave my compass, in hope that she will someday make it work again.

A lump rose in Elliot's throat. He'd known she was always obsessed with his compass. He must have also known how she'd longed to use it to run away.

To my son-in-law, the Baron Zachariah North, I leave my dining room table, as he has always admired it.

In addition to these listed items, I leave the following to my faithful servants:

To the COR known as Sal, who worked in my kitchen, I leave my collection of copper molds, as well as three ounces of gold. She is free to remain on the Estate until the end of her days or leave to seek her fortune elsewhere.

Elliot sneaked a glance at her father as the baroness continued reading about the bequests to individual Boatwright Posts. She wondered if the baroness would be forced to track them down, as some had left during the bad time. And of the ones who remained, the will granted them their freedom and enough money for them to get a good start in a Post enclave, if that was what they desired. Would her father be angry to lose so many servants? Was he angry that other Luddites got boats, while he got a table? But her father's face was serene. She supposed there was little to get angry about. After all, the entire Boatwright estate would soon be his in fact, as it had been in theory for so long.

Finally, the baroness reached the end.

The remainder of my worldly goods, and the house, outbuildings, shipyard, and lands of the Boatwright Estate, as well as the title of Chancellor, I hereby bequeath to my only daughter and heir, Victoria North, wife of the Baron Zachariah North, for the term of her life.

The baron nodded at this. So, Elliot noticed, did Benedict. But the baroness wasn't done. "There is an addendum from four years ago."

Four years . . . when her mother had died? Elliot saw her father straighten in his seat.

Upon her death, the estate and all of its belongings shall not become part of the North Estate, but will instead pass directly and undivided into the possession of my granddaughter and namesake, Elliot North.

Elliot gasped. She wasn't the only one.

Should this occur before Elliot reaches the age of majority, the estate shall be held in trust for her jointly by the Baron Zachariah North and the Baroness Lucinda Channel, with the

provision that it become wholly and completely Elliot's upon her
eighteenth birthday. This is the full and complete rendering of
all my directives, and I have made these bequests of my own free
will and in accordance with the laws of my Luddite brethren.
Signed,
Chancellor Elliot Boatwright

Witness: Baroness Lucinda Channel
Witness: Honorable Jeremiah Grove

The baroness raised her head from the paper. "And that is that."

Elliot snapped her mouth shut. Half the people in the room were staring at her. The other half were staring at her father. His face was unreadable.

The same could not be said for either of his daughters. "Wait." Tatiana held up her hand. "You're saying that the Boatwright estate is . . . Elliot's? The whole thing?"

The baroness nodded. "That's what the will says, yes."

Tatiana shook her head. "But that's not fair! I'm the oldest granddaughter. He can't leave me a carriage and Elliot the entire estate!"

"Perhaps," offered the wife of Baron Record, "he thought you would inherit the North estate. After all, no one knew if Benedict would return to claim his birthright." The woman's husband shot her a warning look, and she ducked her head and fell silent.

Elliot blinked several times. The estate was hers. The farm, the gardens, the shipyard . . . *hers?*

She cast her eyes about the room, searching for a friendly face, and she found Benedict's. He was smiling at her. "Congratulations, Elliot," he whispered. "I think this will solve some of your problems."

Her father had still said nothing. Instead he merely stood and straightened his jacket. "Well, that should be easy enough to execute. Those of you who have received articles belonging to the Boatwright should make arrangements to transport them as soon as possible. Except for the larger boats, I imagine many of you can take the items with you."

"There's no hurry, Father," Elliot said.

He turned to her then, and the look in his eyes made her shiver. "Elliot. I'd like to speak to you in my study."

Thirty-seven

ELLIOT CALMED HERSELF WITH long, deep breaths as she followed her father into the darkly paneled room. He sat down behind his desk, steepled his hands before him, and looked at Elliot with a deeply disturbing smile.

"Quite an inheritance your grandfather provided you with, daughter."

"Yes." Elliot's tone was cautious, born from a habit of years. It seemed like a dream. Possession of the Boatwright estate hovered before her, bright as a star and almost as distant. Did she dare to reach out and grab it? She bore no illusion that her father had invited her in here to congratulate her.

And she was right.

"It's ridiculous, of course. I understand that the old fool didn't want his estate subsumed by the Norths, but if he left it to anyone, it should be by rights his oldest blood relation. That's Tatiana."

Was that the same rule that supposedly gave Benedict

the North estate? And yet, who was Baron North now? It was on the tip of Elliot's tongue to say so when her father went on.

"I'm sure you agree. Your grandfather should have given the estate to Tatiana, namesake or no." He shrugged. "We could fight the terms of the will, of course, at the Luddite tribunals. And we'd win, eventually. Not only was this supposed 'addendum' put in after the old man had his strokes, but Baroness Channel is the only living witness, and as the largest landholder on the island, she has good cause to want to see the two estates split up again. It's very fishy."

He couldn't honestly believe that was an arguable stance. There was no guarantee the estates would be kept together if Tatiana were to inherit. She might not end up with the North estate at all. Or was he imagining her marriage to Benedict as a foregone conclusion?

"But I'm sure you don't want to go through all that trouble. So you can just sign the estate over to your sister."

For years, Elliot had dreaded her father's wrath. For years, she had acquiesced to all manner of unreasonable demands and wasteful plans. For years, if she disobeyed him, she did it in secret. She might have been a Luddite, but until today, he'd been her lord and master.

She was done.

"No."

His unpleasantly pleasant smile grew even wider. "Yes."

He'd bullied her this morning. *He never would again.*

"You can't threaten me anymore, Father. You've nothing to threaten me with." The words burst forth with each new realization, impossible vistas of opportunity that spread wide as the sea. "I've my own lands. If you mistreat any of your Reduced or Post laborers, I'll invite them to the Boatwright estate. Our holdings aren't as large as yours, but we can survive. The Luddite tribunal will support me."

"I'll tell them about the wheat." There it was. Out in the open. He knew exactly what he'd plowed under last summer.

This gave her pause but only for a moment. For Elliot had learned things since then, too. About what people thought elsewhere in the islands. About what they thought of *her*.

"Tell them." Tell a host of Luddite lords who welcomed Post clothes and Post horses and Posts themselves. "Tell them how on your farm, which you *supposedly* control, your daughter planted a crop of illegal wheat. Who would be in trouble for that?"

Her hands were shaking, so she clenched them together under the desk. She could do this. She had to. "Tell them and see if they put me in prison, or if they come to me to buy my grain."

The smile faded, replaced by a tight-lipped line. "Do you really wish to challenge me on this, Elliot?"

Elliot would not blink. He was just trying to scare her. But if the Boatwright estate was hers, hers to do with as she wished, then all her troubles were over. With the additional productivity of her wheat, they'd manage despite the smaller size of the Boatwright farm. She could liberate Dee from the birthing house and bring her and Jef somewhere safe. She could plant whatever she wanted. She could let Ro graft as many flowers as she chose. She could make a sea of string-boxes.

Her lands. Hers. All she had to do was stand up to her father right now.

"Then you leave me no choice," the baron said. "I hereby ban you from my lands. You want the Boatwright estate? It's all you'll have, at least until I challenge the will and gain it back for Tatiana. And then, my dear child, you'll have nothing."

"Father!" she cried. The Boatwright's funeral was this evening. There was no way he would provoke a public family squabble before they laid her grandfather to rest. "You don't want to do this!" But of course he did. It was how he'd responded to the threat of Benedict taking land he thought belonged to him. Why wouldn't it be the same for Elliot?

"I don't want to lay eyes on you again," he replied. "You are a grasping, ungrateful daughter. An embarrassment to this family. To all Luddites."

Elliot took a deep breath. He was trying to scare her. She would not give in. "You won't get the estate back, no matter what you tell the tribunal."

"It's a pity you're so sure of yourself," he replied. "You're like that silly compass the Boatwright gave you—eternally heading down the wrong path."

A YOUNGER ELLIOT MIGHT have spent time mourning for the loss of the only home she'd ever known. A more inexperienced

Elliot might have been conciliatory, squandering valuable minutes trying to get her father to see reason.

This Elliot wasted no time at all.

She had no leisure for second thoughts. Her father had backed her into a corner and forced her to make a sudden decision. And what good were second thoughts? Once, she'd listened to them, and then spent four years regretting it.

She had no time to seek out advice, either from friends like Horatio Grove or impartial but well-meaning strangers like Baroness Channel. Or from Kai, who was neither friend nor stranger, but something more than both. And yet what would any of them have told her that she didn't already know? Baroness Channel was her grandfather's executor—naturally she agreed with the bequest. And Horatio would support her as well.

As for Kai . . . Yesterday, he'd admitted he'd hoped she approved of his sun-carts, and told her he was proud of her for defying her father over the wheat. If she knew him at all, she was already well aware of what he'd say.

For four years she'd contented herself with scraps of a life, convinced herself not to fight, not to even want to fight. For four years she'd resigned herself to a reality in which she could not decide her own fate, let alone the destiny of those she loved.

Kai had been right. It was no life at all. And though she'd never have him, by God she would take whatever else she could get.

Within twenty minutes she'd packed her clothes, the few books she knew were hers, and the portion of her mother's jewelry that Tatiana hadn't claimed. On the way out of the house, she stopped Mags and asked her to send Jef to her in the barn. She didn't tell her why. Mags and Gill would be fine for the time being, and she wanted to make this as smooth a transition as possible.

Jef, Dee, and Ro. The rest would come in time.

It was insane. It was radical. The very idea would have seemed ludicrous to her a few days ago. But Luddites were luring skilled Posts to other estates all the time now, and no one was preventing them. She would make the Boatwright estate the most attractive one on the island, and there was enough precedent that she was certain there was no way for her father to stop her.

Elliot made short work of packing up her materials and the bundles of notes she'd taken on the wheat. The gliders, however, gave her pause. If she were smart, she'd burn them. She couldn't leave them here, in the barn. But the only place she had to go was the Boatwright house. Her house.

Where Kai lived.

She should burn them. They were nothing but old letters, and besides, she'd memorized their contents ages ago. She should burn them, lest they fall into the wrong hands—which could be her father's or Kai's, as far as she was concerned. She should burn them, because she knew they were a part of something long gone. She should burn them, and be brave.

But she'd already used up all her reserves of bravery. She stuffed the gliders into the bottom of her bag, crushing their papery wings beneath her sweater. They'd likely never fly again, just like Elliot. But that didn't matter. The memories remained intact.

There was a knock at the door. At last, Jef. She shot across the room to pull it open.

"Hello, cousin," said Benedict. "So this is where you hide."

Thirty-eight

BENEDICT'S GAZE ROVED THE room—from the hooks in the ceilings that once held the gliders to the beakers and shears on the desk. "I always wondered where you went all the time." He stepped into the room and continued his survey, hands in his pockets. Elliot backed up until she stood before her bag, shielding it from his prying eyes with the edge of her black mourning skirt. "Your sister thinks you're working whenever you're gone from the house—either that or in the cottage of that Reduced girl. But I knew that wasn't the case."

"How?" Elliot couldn't help but ask.

"I looked for you there, of course." He circled back around to face her. "So."

"So?"

"This changes things significantly. Your inheritance, I mean."

"Yes," she said. "It does."

He whistled through his teeth. "I don't think I under-stood the reality of the arrangement that the Boatwright had with your father. I thought the land was his already."

"And therefore yours," Elliot volunteered.

"Exactly." Benedict gave a sheepish shrug. "Though of course, this makes more sense. Why would the Boatwright let Uncle Zachariah have it, knowing that it wouldn't stay in his family?"

Benedict tapped his foot on the floor. Elliot watched him warily, as one might a spider in the corner. But what could Benedict do to her that her own father hadn't already threatened? Did he even know of her father's banishment? Perhaps he'd sympathize, having been through something similar.

"You looked pretty shocked at the reading, cousin. I take it you didn't know the terms of your grandfather's will."

"You'd be correct." This was not the time to chat with Benedict. Where was Jef? He'd better not be dawdling. She wasn't leaving this property until she had all three servants with her, just in case her father decided to take her defection out on his laborers.

"And what are your plans now?" He cocked his head at her. "Are you going to leave the North estate? Go live at the Boatwright house?"

She hesitated. So her father hadn't said anything. "Why do you want to know?"

"Self-interest." His tone was even, open. "I have good reason to suspect that if you leave, many of the people here would follow. All my land isn't going to be much good to me unless I have a workforce to run it."

"I see."

"I don't think they have any particular loyalty to your father, but I know they do to you. Which is why I am here."

"What?"

He took a few steps closer to her. "I like the Boatwright estate. I like it more, even, than the North one. Farming is dead. The Cloud Fleet knows where the future lies. Shipbuilding. They are going to get off this island, and soon other Posts with money will want to, too. Your estate is the one with the future, Elliot."

She raised her eyebrows. "You're saying you want to switch?"

"No, I'm saying I want to join. I have every right to the North estate, and I'm going to take it." The anger in his tone left Elliot with no doubt that his primary motivation in doing so would be to revenge himself on her father. "And the Boatwright lands, according to the terms of your grandfather's will, should be yours. But we both know your family will fight those terms. They have to. Right now, neither your father nor your sister has anything. They are backed into a corner. That's why Uncle Zachariah has brought me home. He's hoping that if he makes nice now, I won't turn him out the second the land is mine. He's hoping to throw Tatiana at me. But I don't want her."

"No?"

Benedict took another step, until they were face to face. "I want *you*."

When she tried to move back, he caught her by the arms. "Benedict, I—"

"I know," he said. "You're filled with newfangled Post

sensibilities. You aren't interested in your cousin. Perhaps you even find it creepy. That doesn't bother me."

Her eyes widened.

"You're not the first woman in your family to marry for something other than love, Elliot. You're not the first Boatwright heiress to marry a North for the good of both estates, either."

She moved back another step, but she hit the wall. He pressed even closer. "You can't be serious," she said.

"I find you very . . . pleasant," he offered halfheartedly. "I think we would do well together. And consider how it could help both of us. As Baron North, I would help you advocate for your inheritance against your father. He would have much less leverage to stop you once he's stripped of his land, title, money . . ."

And her father would have similarly little leverage or credibility if he tried to bring charges against her for the wheat. She hated to admit it, but Benedict was right. If she married him, he could protect her.

But . . . marry? Benedict? Some other Elliot might have laughed at the idea, but today she just wanted to put an end to the conversation and find Ro.

"And you could help me. You could help me bring the North estate back to what it could be. If you were my baroness, the workers would stay here. There's less and less holding Posts to their ancestral lands every year. But they would stay, for you."

Would they? Dee insisted on staying even when Elliot

tried to shove her out the door. But Kai had left, despite everything they shared. Benedict was wrong. It wasn't for her. It was for the same reasons she herself had stayed four years earlier: the benefit of those on the estate who had no choice.

"They would accept me," he went on. "And together we could turn your grandfather's shipyard into something truly spectacular."

She stared at him, mouth gaping. Ever since his return, she'd wondered why Benedict had chosen now to come home. It wasn't that he needed the money—whatever job he'd had in the Post enclave had made him wealthy. He didn't seem to care at all for Luddite prestige. And despite appearances, he had no interest in reconciling with his uncle.

Now she knew. It was the reopening of the shipyard. Benedict had come for that. He'd pressed her to take a tour of the Boatwright estate the day of her grandfather's stroke, and now that it was clear the Boatwright estate was not automatically his, he'd come to stake a claim to it— through her.

"Marry me, Elliot." He leaned in to kiss her.

"Stop!" she shouted, raising her hands to block him.

"Not on my account, surely," said a voice by the door. They turned to find Tatiana standing on the landing, her face a mask of disgust. She was still clad in her blue dress, but her ribbons had drooped significantly. "You have to have everything, don't you, Elliot?"

"Tatiana," Elliot said, pushing Benedict aside. She'd deal with him later. "Did Father tell you? He's making me leave the estate."

"If you don't give your inheritance to me, yes." Tatiana nodded, and shot a withering glare at Benedict. "I think it's rather silly, myself. Did he really expect you to take that offer? What do you care if you leave here, if you have an estate of your own? You're better off."

Elliot was surprised by Tatiana's frank assessment. She said it with no malice. It was a simple statement of fact. Benedict had moved away from her and was standing by the desk, glancing back and forth between the two sisters.

"And you'll certainly be happy there now with your Post friends," Tatiana added. She looked out the window. "You should be leaving now, I think?"

"I'm waiting," Elliot said.

"For what?"

"Nothing."

Tatiana smiled. "For your little Reduced friend? Or that pregnant foreman and her son? Or both?"

Elliot took a breath. What was the point in lying? "All of them, yes."

Tatiana gave her a pitying smile. "That's not going to happen, Elliot."

"What do you mean?"

"Don't you know our father at all?" Tatiana asked. "They're leverage." She pointed out the window.

Elliot rushed over. Outside on the lawn, Baron North stood by the gate. In one hand, he held a pistol. In the other hand, he held tight to Ro's arm. "No," she whispered. "What is he doing?"

It was a foolish question. She knew the answer.

A few moments later, she was out on the lawn. She didn't see Jef anywhere, but wasn't sure if it meant that the baron didn't have him, or if he'd just chosen Ro to make an example of. "Let her go."

"Oh, I don't think so," said her father. "I have provided for this laborer her entire life. I have provided for all of them. Too many have walked off my lands with no repercussions. It ends here. Today."

With Ro. Elliot shook with a rage she hadn't known she'd possessed. Ro was Reduced, but she was a *person*, not a pawn. "Let go of her, Father."

"Happily. She's so dusty. Simply sign over the Boatwright lands to your sister."

He'd always controlled Elliot by threatening the Reduced and the Posts. If she gave in this time, she'd never be able to help them again. "No."

The baron shrugged. "You will not take her with you. You will never see her again. I will establish myself on the border of our lands and shoot any servant who tries to cross."

Elliot's heart constricted. He wouldn't. Would he? Ro wasn't even squirming in his grip. Just standing dejected, limp, flinching a bit every time he spoke. Her face was turned to the ground. Elliot longed to call her name, but she was afraid it would give her hope.

Tatiana and Benedict emerged from the barn and

met them by the gate. Tatiana carried Elliot's bag. "Are you taking this, Sister?"

"Tatiana," said Elliot, gesturing at Ro. "You know this is wrong."

Tatiana held out the bag. Her face was impassive. "That we don't want you to steal the workforce keeping our estate alive? The one we've protected and cared for, for generations? No, Elliot, I must say that I don't."

"Last chance, Elliot," said the baron.

Elliot looked at Ro. The girl still wouldn't look up, but tears dripped off the edge of her nose. On some level she understood. She must. "Ro, it's going to be all right," she said, as if she could convince them both.

And then she walked away.

Four Years Ago

Dear Kai,

Father is being unbearable tonight. He wants me to comb through all our ledgers. But I can be here till dawn and he won't find anything extra. I only know a little about how the farm works from watching my mother, but even I know what the problem is. The harvest numbers aren't good. Father didn't listen to his foreman about the crop rotation, and since he pulled down the orchards for a better view of the sea, he isn't going to get any help there, either. If it weren't for the stockpiles on my grandfather's estate, we'd be in real trouble this winter.

I know I should be more understanding—after all, it can't have been any easier on him to lose Mother than it was for us. I want to believe they loved each other, and sometimes, when we're down in the star-cavern sanctuary and all the lamps are off and he thinks we won't know, I've even seen him shed a tear.

But on nights like tonight, I think he doesn't miss her. He misses all the work she used to do for him.

Yours,

Elliot

∽∾

Dear Elliot,

I have heard rumblings that there might be food shortages this winter. All the Posts are scared. A few of us were visiting the Grove estate recently, and there was talk of trading with them, even over your father's objections. But the situation there isn't great, either. Have you heard Mr. Grove is ill now too?

Things are falling apart all over, it seems. It makes me wonder about the future. About whether being tied to an estate is a good idea at all.

Yours,

Kai

∽

Dear Kai,

I am worried for the future, too. Sometimes, I wish these gliders were big enough to carry us both away.

Yours,

Elliot

∽

Dear Elliot,

I can't build you a glider, but that doesn't mean we can't leave. Come to me tonight. I have a plan.

Yours,

Kai

Thirty-nine

"HE BANISHED YOU?"

Elliot North stood on the steps of the Boatwright house—her house—with all her worldly possessions in her hands, and asked its residents for admittance. Both Innovations stood above her on the porch, their mouths slack.

"It is his favorite remedy for dealing with a threat to his property, it seems," she said, keeping her voice as light as possible. "He did the same thing to my cousin Benedict when it looked as if he'd claim his inheritance. It seems my inheritance is this estate."

Felicia blinked. "The Boatwright estate is . . . yours?"

"Mine in fact, as it's been for so long in practice," Elliot said. Perhaps this was how she'd survive. Act gracious and formal and pretend that her heart had not just been ripped out of her chest. "And yet my first act as owner is to beg you for a place to sleep."

"Of course!" said the admiral, beckoning to her. "We've

bunked in far tighter quarters than your grandfather's house—your house, I should say. And we should get used to it, too. Soon enough we'll all be crowded together on the ship. We can find a place for you."

He led her up the steps of the porch. "After you, Miss Elliot—I mean Chancellor Boatwright."

Her new title echoed in her ears and reverberated in her heart, and Elliot gripped the handle of her bag even more tightly as the weight of what she'd done settled like a mantle on her shoulders. There was no other choice. Not just for her sake and the sake of the laborers, not just to make her friends proud, but for the memory of her mother and her grandfather and every Boatwright who'd ever held these lands. She couldn't let them down.

Elliot dipped her head in thanks and entered her new home.

"If you give us a few hours, we can move out of the master bedroom," Felicia said.

Elliot shook her head. "That won't be necessary. If I find I want a bigger space to sleep, I can wait until you've left for good."

Her tone remained even, but inwardly, Elliot quaked at the thought. *Left for good.* As hard as it was now, surrounded by Fleet Posts she could count on as friends and with the countryside full of Luddites she knew were on her side, how hard would it be when everyone left? When the nearest ally she had were the Groves a whole estate away and she was forced to face the consequences of her choice alone, completely cut off from the rest of the islands by her father's land.

But she couldn't back down now. She'd been alone before, and she'd managed. She'd do so again. Here, at least, she had a chance. If she gave in to her father, she'd have nothing. Not even the chance—distasteful as it was—that Benedict had offered her.

Even if she was forced to entertain that possibility— to save Ro and the others—she wouldn't consider it until the Fleet left. She couldn't bear for Kai to know. Not even now.

No sooner than she'd dropped her bag in a small back bedroom did she turn around and head out. There was so much to do. Though she longed to find Kai and get his take on things, other matters took precedence. She needed to make sure that all the Boatwright workers were informed as soon as possible, in case her father tried to expand his edict to those who belonged to her estate and trap them on the wrong side of the border. She needed to get in contact with Horatio Grove at once and let him know of the feud and the danger now posed by a North estate put entirely in the hands of Baron North. This needed to be resolved before the planting season started. It was already afternoon, so Horatio would likely be preparing for her grandfather's funeral . . .

Elliot stopped short. Wait. The Boatwright's body was on the North estate, but in order to send his pyre out to sea, they had to travel to her lands. The baron wouldn't ignore her grandfather's last wishes, would he? She hurried back to the porch to ask Felicia for use of one of the sun-carts to visit the Groves, but stopped when she saw an unfamiliar sun-cart parked on the lawn with a Post driver getting out from behind the wheel.

"I've a message for the baroness from Tatiana North," said the man, handing a note to Felicia.

The baroness was here, in the house? That made things simpler for Elliot.

"Thank you, Tev," said Felicia. "You may wait here this time. I imagine she'll want to return soon."

The Post nodded and looked pointedly at Elliot. "There might be a riot on the North estate tonight, ma'am. Word has spread about what your father did. Have you spoken to my mistress yet?"

Elliot's hands flew to her cheeks. "A riot? No, there mustn't be." Not with all the Luddites there. They had pistols, and they'd be obliged to go to her father's aid. Things could get messy, very fast. With a flash of horror, she remembered Benedict's prediction of revolution beginning at a bad estate. Would it be the North lands? And would Benedict be on the side of the Luddites? "Please, talk to the Posts on my behalf. Tell them to be patient . . ."

And what? She'd fix everything? She couldn't promise them that. She hung her head.

And then she felt a hand on her shoulder; warm, firm fingers that comforted as well as a hug. "There will be no riot." Felicia's voice floated above her. "I'll go speak to the North Posts if you want, Elliot. We can avert several acts of violence today."

"What do you mean?" Elliot looked at her in confusion. The driver Tev had returned to his sun-cart and was out of earshot.

Felicia hesitated. "I should not have spoken. You have already dealt with too much today."

Elliot laughed mirthlessly. "Yes. Inheritance, banishment, a marriage proposal . . ."

Felicia raised her eyebrows.

"From Benedict," Elliot clarified. "As soon as he heard my grandfather's will. Apparently, it was never the North estate he wanted." She sighed. "And the funny thing is—"

"Do you want to marry Benedict?" Felicia asked, her tone a little hard.

"No." Firm. Definite. She didn't want to, but it might be the best way to help the people on the North estate. Still . . . "I don't love him. And I don't think I can trust him."

"You're right not to trust him," said Felicia. "May I tell you something in confidence? Something I would only tell you in the interest of helping you right now?"

"You may tell me anything if it will help me." Elliot was desperate. And in return, somehow she'd find the words to tell Felicia everything, too. Weeks ago, she hadn't been brave enough to share confidences with Felicia. But now, with the fate of everyone on the North estate in question, she'd have to cobble together enough confidence to listen to the older woman. Through Kai, Elliot had learned so many of Felicia's secrets, and she'd been able to accept them all. It wasn't too much to hope that Felicia would do the same.

Felicia took a deep breath. "Baroness Channel is here

to talk to the Phoenixes. I begged them to give this method a chance before taking out their grievances in a way that could get them hurt—or endanger our mission."

"Their grievances? Against Benedict?"

"You are aware, I suppose, of some of the more . . . unsavory things that happen in the Post enclaves."

"More unsavory than human experimentation?" Elliot asked, her tone pointed.

Felicia's response was utterly serious. "Much more. Not all the stories about the Post enclaves are propaganda designed to keep estate Posts from running away. Some of them, unfortunately, are true. There are bad people there. People who take advantage of those who have no one to turn to. Benedict North is one of those people."

Something soured in the pit of Elliot's stomach. And when Felicia went on, she found that she felt no surprise.

Felicia led her over to the chairs set up against one wall of the porch. Nearby, a small table held a pot of tea on a sun-warmer, and Felicia poured them two cups. "I told you once that Andromeda Phoenix was not used to life as a Free Post." When Elliot nodded, the older woman went on. "That's because despite leaving her estate as a young child, she hasn't been a Free Post for very long."

Elliot's eyes narrowed. "I don't understand. What does this have to do with Benedict?" Benedict, who'd proposed to her not an hour ago, who'd told her he wanted to support the Posts, who might be her only chance of rescuing the people she cared for most in the world.

"The Phoenixes—they were Ann and Don then—they

were children. They had nothing. They had no one. It was nearly impossible for Ann to find someone who would hire her. I've seen so many of these children, Elliot. They've made me desperate offers."

"You've accepted some of them!" Elliot couldn't help but say. Felicia had experimented on Kai and the Phoenixes, and who knew how many other young Posts.

Felicia nodded gravely. "Yes, I have. Everyone who came to me knew the risks of what we were doing, and the benefits if we were successful. It's a dangerous job, but it's not an exploitive one."

But she couldn't be sure of that. None of them could. She might have doomed them all, unless they never married, never had children . . . Tatiana was right there. The Fleet Posts thought they were invincible. Posts always had Post children. But that was thanks to the protocols.

And maybe Tatiana hadn't been the only member of her family who was right. Perhaps her father had been right, too, so many years ago. The sourness in her stomach grew, like a bit of rot that could infest an entire bushel of fruit. "What was Benedict's offer?" she asked Felicia, though she could already guess.

"You must understand," said Felicia, "Ann was very desperate. And her brother—he was so young—and he was starving."

She'd been so quick to believe Benedict when he'd said her father had made up everything about his banishment. It made sense. It was something she could easily imagine her father doing.

But that didn't mean it was true.

"There is a house in Channel City," Felicia was saying. "It is filled with young women. Little girls. Posts, mostly, but there are Reduced as well. Benedict worked there. It was his job to find new recruits."

Elliot shuddered.

"He was perfect for the position. He was young, and handsome, and charming, and he pretended to be a Post, just like them. Called himself Ben."

"Stop," Elliot whispered. "I don't need to hear anymore." Of course he needed her help getting the North workforce to stay. An eight-year-old rumor was bad enough. But news of this business?

"Their work contracts, however, merely bonded the runaways into service to a new Luddite. And unlike the lords of the estates, these masters did not tolerate runaways," Felicia finished, her face drawn. "Andromeda has never trusted a Luddite since."

"Though I seem to be alone in that," came a voice from behind them. Elliot turned to see Andromeda in the doorway, her face pale and drawn, her glittering blue eyes red and swollen with tears. "First you send me off to tell my sob story to the dragon lady, and then you spill everything to the princess."

"Andromeda, I'm so sorry . . . ," Elliot began.

She snorted. "Pity from you? Save it. You've been harboring him a few kay away for a month."

"I didn't know . . ."

"No one knew," said Donovan, appearing behind his

sister. "Until the race, no one had any idea that 'Ben' was Benedict North. Only Andromeda had ever seen him."

So that's why she'd been crying at the race. Elliot could imagine the shock the Post must have had to realize how close she'd been to her old tormentor. To realize that he was the heir to the North estate.

Baroness Channel and the admiral came out onto the porch, followed by Kai. His face was drawn, and there was murder in his dark eyes.

"My dear," the baroness said to Elliot, her veil shaking in indignation, "I just heard from Nicodemus what your father did. Are you all right?"

"I will be," said Elliot, "as soon as I can be assured that the people on the North estate are in good hands." It was even more important than before. Whatever faults her father had, he was not exploiting his workers. Once Benedict took over, there was no telling what he'd do.

Felicia called the baroness to deliver Tatiana's note, and Elliot looked at Kai. He stood apart from the others, leaning against the wall of the house and staring unabashedly at Elliot. His hands were clenched at his sides. Elliot caught her breath as she realized his anger was not on Andromeda's behalf. It was on hers.

"Where is Ro?" he asked her softly, as if they were the only two people on the porch.

"There." Elliot strangled the sob that rose in her throat. "My father made her watch me leave."

"I'll go get her."

"No," Elliot said. "He's promised to shoot any of the

North workers who cross the border between our estates."

"I'll go fast."

"It's too dangerous."

"*Very* fast," Kai insisted.

"No, you won't," said Felicia, cutting in on their tête-à-tête. "Luddites have guns, don't you remember? We aren't going to risk either of you getting shot just to make a point. Even if you are successful, it will only incite the baron to be more unreasonable."

Kai shoved away from the wall. "He's always at a maximum level of unreasonable."

Felicia went on. "Ro isn't in any danger tonight."

"Oh really?" Andromeda drawled. "Even with Ben there?"

"Ann!" said Felicia sharply. "Stop it. You're just trying to scare Elliot now."

But Elliot wasn't scared. Not of Benedict and Ro. For he still wanted to marry Elliot and get his hands on the shipyard, a situation he was smart enough to realize would never happen if he did anything to hurt her Reduced friend. Still, she had no desire to leave Ro alone on the North estate in the long term.

"Fine, Felicia," she said. "What will we risk? We can't take my friends off the North estate by force, and even if we could, the rest of the estate would suffer."

"One crisis at a time, Miss Elliot," came the baroness's voice from across the porch. "And unfortunately for your little Reduced friend, this one takes precedence." She held out Tatiana's note.

Dear Baroness Channel,

Due to unforeseen circumstances, the funeral for Chancellor Elliot Boatwright will not be able to proceed as planned. We are unable to gain access to the beach where the Boatwright's pyre is, and must therefore lay him in the North family tomb inside our star-cavern sanctuary. We hope to see you at the ceremony at sunset.

Sincerely,

Tatiana North

Forty

ELLIOT WAS TOLD THAT the Boatwright's funeral was very sparsely attended, most of the Luddites having vacated the North estate as soon as the story of Elliot's banishment and the baron's change of funeral locale got around. Idly, Elliot wondered which more offended their neighbors: the fact that the baron had disowned his by-all-accounts capable and hardworking daughter for daring to accept the bequest of her grandfather, or the way he dishonored his father-in-law's funeral rights. No one could remember a Boatwright whose body had not been sent out to sea.

He'd done it to spite her—of that Elliot was sure. If her grandfather was not put on the pyre and sent off to sea from the Boatwright estate, then Elliot would not be able to witness it. She'd kept Tatiana's note to the baroness, reading it over and over for some hint of her sister's state of mind when she wrote it. But it had been carefully crafted to contain nothing but a simple conveyance of information and common courtesy.

That's what made it so curious. Elliot had rarely seen Tatiana without an opinion or a sarcastic remark. She'd lived with her sister's cruelty and self-importance all her life. Where was the judgment on Elliot in this note? Where was the frustration?

Even her words to Elliot in the barn loft that day had been suspiciously void of emotion. With Tatiana, that was almost as good as approval.

The baroness had been one of the few to attend the Boatwright's funeral. "He deserved more honor than that," she explained to Elliot, as they sat in the parlor of the Boatwright house and enjoyed the lemony light of the winter morning. On the wall, the rubbed bronze of her grandfather's compass glowed dimly in the glare, its wheel, as always, spinning gently.

"But I chose not to add insult to injury by ignoring him. A shoddy piece of work. The North star cavern is beautiful, of course, but it's not the Boatwright way."

Elliot had closed her eyes to keep from weeping. At least, she thought, her grandfather had been laid to rest beside her mother.

"Also," the baroness went on, "I went to keep my relationship with your family strong. I hope to invite the North heir to visit me in the Channel. I think it would be a most productive trip for all of us."

Elliot nodded in understanding. In Channel City, the baroness's word was law. If she wished to hold Benedict North accountable for his actions as "Ben"—she must do it on her land.

"Why this?" Elliot asked. "For years I've heard of the dangers in the enclaves down in Channel City. What makes you motivated to stop this?"

Beneath her veil, the baroness smiled sadly. "I have been remiss, I suppose. For the longest time, the activities in the enclaves seemed to be something separate from me, from the society I presided over in the main part of the city. The Posts who lived there were not my Posts. They were not my problem. But every year there were more of them, and recently it's become clear to me that I have no right to take advantage of their fashions, technology, and even friendship if I abandon responsibility over the more unsavory elements of their situation. If the enclaves are my domain, then so are the illegal activities taking place there."

Elliot stiffened. Did the baroness know that her "friends" the Innovations were also engaging in illegal activities? "What will happen to him?" Elliot asked.

The baroness shrugged. "Very little, to be honest, Elliot. The tribunal has no punishment in place for a Luddite lord who mistreats someone from the lower caste. But if your father wishes, he might be able to use the scandal to leverage a challenge to his brother's will. After all, Benedict did abandon the estate for nearly a decade. If he truly wanted his inheritance, he could have claimed it years ago. Your father, for all appearances, has been running it since. His claim is likely to be a valid one, especially since the tribunal would be loath to hand an entire estate to a man who has been known to abuse the people in his care." She folded her hands. "I know that doesn't help your situation with the North workers much, but your father will drop the challenge to your grandfather's will once he sees how much easier the battle will be to win the North estate."

Elliot looked out the window. One step at a time. The trick with Benedict would be treading lightly. He'd written her once, asking both to visit her and for an answer to his proposal. Her first instinct had been to ignore his letter, but she feared raising his suspicions. And she certainly didn't want him visiting the Boatwright house. After a long consideration, she responded:

Dear Benedict,
Thank you for your letter. Rest assured, I am doing quite well
here, and my only concern is for the welfare of the North laborers.
I am sure you agree with me that it is important to remain
cautious and impartial for the time being, lest we raise my
father's anger.
Your cousin,
Elliot North
Chancellor Boatwright

The note satisfied the standard of truthfulness that Elliot's conscience required without betraying her real feelings toward its recipient.

Though she had been tempted to drag it through the floor of the Boatwright chicken house.

Now the baroness stood. "That's all the hope I can give you now, Miss Elliot."

"It's enough to go on." Elliot rose, too, and shook the

woman's hand. "Thank you, on behalf of myself and the workers on the North estate. And Andromeda, too. She may not admit it, but she'll relish any punishment Benedict gets."

"She'd prefer to see him dead, I think," the baroness observed. "Perhaps instead of forcing him before the tribunal, I should just release him into the most dangerous neighborhood in Channel City with an ounce of gold jingling in his pocket."

Elliot's eyes widened, but there was no indication that the older woman was joking.

"At any rate," the baroness went on, "I'd do anything for the Innovations, or any of their friends."

"They've made that much money through your investments?" Elliot asked.

The baroness chuckled. "No, dear. They saved my sight." She lifted the edge of her veil, and for the first time Elliot saw her faceted, ERV-enhanced eyes. The baroness pressed her finger to her lips and departed, leaving Elliot to sit in stunned silence brought about by the sight of an abomination on a Luddite face. She'd assumed she was the only Luddite to know of the Cloud Fleet's secrets, but of course that couldn't be true. They had other friends—of longer standing than Elliot, and probably closer, too. They had to have allies elsewhere. And given the permissiveness she'd seen among the southern Luddites these past few days, given her own temptation when it came to her grandfather's illness and her recent conclusions about how her fellow lords would react to news of her wheat, it shouldn't surprise her that somebody had taken that step. The baroness said the Innovations had *saved* her sight. Would she have been blind without their interventions? Had Felicia used a therapy on Baroness Channel that had failed on Sophia?

And, most of all, how soon would it be until the protocols crumbled to dust?

She was still considering this when Kai found her several minutes later. Though she thought she'd see more of him now that they were living under the same roof, Kai spent most of his time down by the shipyard. From all reports, very soon they'd be finished, and she supposed his mechanical expertise was in high demand. Elliot remembered a time, long ago, when she'd imagined Kai working in the Boatwright shipyard permanently. What an asset he would have been to the estate.

And yet, if he'd stayed, would he have ever developed beyond the limitations set by the Luddites? Would he have invented the sun-carts, or the massive sun-ship that was slowly being assembled down by the docks?

As much as Elliot hated to admit it, the answer was no.

"I've been to see Ro," said Kai. "And yes, I met your father on the border as I left. He wanted to make sure I wasn't smuggling her over."

"How is she?" Elliot asked, shaking free of her shock.

"Sad," he said. "I did my best to explain why you had to leave her the other day, and why you couldn't come to see her anymore. I don't know if she understood."

Elliot pushed out of her chair and began to pace the room. "I can't leave her there."

Kai studied her nervous movements as if debating his next words. "That's not all, Elliot. Your father has moved her out of her cottage. She's in the women's barracks."

Elliot grimaced and covered her face with her hands. She sucked in several deep breaths, then lowered her arms and stared at the compass on the wall.

Hold on, Ro. I'll be coming for you soon.

"We can't let her stay there."

"Can't we?" asked Kai. "She's eighteen. All the other girls her age have already been moved to the women's barracks. I love Ro as much as you do, but there are other Reduced girls there, and they're fine."

"They aren't fine in the birthing house," Elliot said. "I've seen it and I don't want Ro there."

She felt his hands on her arms, and he gently turned her to face him. "Elliot," he said softly. "It's all right. It isn't a torture chamber." Even without the benefit of enhancements, she was sure she noticed every twitch of Kai's muscles, every tiny jerk of his head, every beat of his heart. His skin on hers felt warm enough to burn. "My mother, Ro's mother, their deaths were not your fault. They weren't your mother's fault, either. And keeping Ro alone won't protect her from everything."

She spun away from him. "Don't tell me how things work on the North estate."

"I'm not. I'm telling you how they work in our world. I want that to change, not just for Ro. For everyone."

Elliot was quiet for a moment. She looked at the compass, out the window, anywhere but at Kai.

"If you decide for her that she will always be alone—never have a family of her own—how is that any better?"

Elliot swallowed thickly as tears of shame burned her eyes. He was right, there, too. Ro would make an excellent mother. She was kind and playful and full of joy. She could teach her children—Reduced or maybe even Post—to laugh and dance and grow flowers.

"I suppose," she said ruefully, still looking away, "that's all I'm good for. A Luddite imposing limits on the people under my care."

"That's not true," he replied. "And it's not what I think, either."

She turned and gazed into his superhuman eyes.

"I want you to know . . . ," he said, his words halting, careful. "I probably should have told you this some time ago, but . . . I understand now. I understand why you stayed."

Her breath caught in her throat.

"For a long time, I tried to tell myself otherwise. That when you said . . ." He hesitated again. "When you said you were a Luddite and I was not, it was that you—" He bit his lip.

Her letter. The letter she'd sent because she hadn't the courage to tell him to his face that she wouldn't be going with him. She hadn't the strength to try, because she was too fearful that she'd never be able to see it through.

"I tried to believe you thought you were better than me."

She opened her mouth to speak, but he held up his hand.

"It was easier, I guess."

Easier. Like writing him a letter instead of risking going near him when she knew she'd never let him walk away alone. How much had they both suffered doing things they thought were easier?

"But I do understand. I see you doing it again now, doing whatever you can to protect the people on your lands. And . . . I'm proud of you, Elliot."

She choked back a sob, though she wasn't sure she could hide it from his enhanced ears. She didn't want his pride. She wanted something much greater and far more elemental. Something foolish to even think of right now, when her friends were suffering on the North estate and she had no idea how to get them back. When Kai was building a ship so he could leave these islands for good. When Olivia Grove lay injured at the estate next door, waiting for a visit from the captain she loved.

She'd been wrong. Maybe talking four years ago would have made Kai understand—but it wouldn't have made it *easier.*

There was the sound of wheels crunching on the gravel outside, and Elliot turned her head to see Horatio and Olivia pulling up in a new sun-cart. It gleamed red and gold against the bare winter browns, and Elliot drew away from Kai in surprise. So he'd made Olivia a sun-cart in her favorite colors.

Perhaps he hadn't been spending *all* his time in the shipyard.

She turned her back on Kai and brushed tears from her eyes as Horatio helped his sister down from the cart and up the front steps of the porch.

"Here for your music lesson?" Elliot called to them as brightly as she could manage. Olivia came every day like clockwork to sing with Donovan. Felicia called it music therapy, and it was true that the girl's diction was much clearer when she sang. Horatio believed the benefits were more emotional than physical. "There's something magical about Donovan's playing," he'd told Elliot a few days earlier, and Elliot hadn't had the heart to tell him that he was very nearly right.

"Yes," said Olivia. She lowered her chin and sneaked a glance at Kai that was probably meant to be coy, but came across as shy and even reluctant. "Will you come to listen, Mal'kai?"

"No," he said curtly. "I have work on the ship. Perhaps some other time."

The girl nodded and Horatio scowled his disappointment in Kai's direction. Kai shook Horatio's hand, kissed Olivia's, sent one last, perplexing look in Elliot's direction and departed.

"I don't know what we'll do when they leave, Elliot," said Horatio. "Olivia will be bereft. Her daily visits are the only thing that keeps her happy."

Elliot knew just how she felt.

"Where's Donovan?" Olivia asked. "It's time for the music."

Forty-one

TATIANA WAS LIGHTING THE sconces in the star cavern when Elliot arrived, more than a week later. She'd thought it prudent to wait until her father had grown tired of spending his days patrolling the border between their estates. In the past week, Benedict had left for the Channel, and Felicia had received word from the baroness that things were proceeding according to plan. Elliot had been relieved by the news, but it wasn't enough. Kai had been right. This wasn't merely about Ro, or even Dee or Jef. This was about every person on the estate, including the ones in her family, who would be in trouble if the baron's edicts were maintained.

The winter chill lingered down here, and Elliot wrapped her shawl more tightly around herself. In the flare of the matches, Elliot could see that her sister wore long, fingerless gloves and a thick scarf.

"It was very dangerous of you to come here," Tatiana said when she saw her. "I could tell Father."

"You could," Elliot replied. "But I don't think you will."

Tatiana moved to another set of sconces.

"I've heard you've been spending a lot of time down here. More than you did even when we were growing up."

Tatiana shrugged. "I'm paying homage to our dead ancestors." Her voice was clipped, but there was a slight waver at the end that gave her away. Tatiana was frightened.

Mags had sent word that Tatiana spent hours in the sanctuary every day, lighting candles and saying prayers for the soul of the Boatwright. Her father's decision rested uneasily on her. Tatiana possessed many faults, but callousness toward the Luddite traditions her ancestors held sacred was not one of them.

It was Elliot's only chance. "His spirit would be more at peace if he was sent out to sea."

"Your obstinance has made that impossible."

Elliot shook her head. "I have never forbidden anyone from coming onto the Boatwright estate. It's our father who won't cross the border, not even to lay our grandfather to rest in the manner of his ancestors."

She saw Tatiana swallow hard. Her eyes looked glassy in the candlelight. "Is that what you're here to do? Order me to relinquish Grandfather's body?"

"I'm here to talk to my sister about doing what we both know is right for him."

For a moment, Tatiana was silent. "It was over the line," she said at last. "Our workers belong here. But Grandfather does not." She sat down in a nearby alcove. Above her, the insect stars glowed dimly. "But if he goes, Father will be so upset."

"And then what?" Elliot asked.

"Then *he'll be upset!*" Tatiana repeated angrily. "That must not seem like much to you, but I don't like disappointing him." She looked away. "I'm enough of a disappointment already."

Elliot drew closer. "What do you mean?"

"I failed to get the Boatwright estate for him. I failed to win Benedict's hand. We'll be left with nothing when Benedict gets back from Channel City and takes over the estate."

Elliot couldn't help but smile at this. "Benedict won't take over the estate, Tatiana. Even now, he's being detained by Baroness Channel for crimes committed in Channel City."

"What?" Tatiana exclaimed, and the syllable echoed around the cavern, inciting the stars.

"You heard me. He'll appear before the tribunal. He may have his land stripped from him. At the very least, it puts you and Father in a good position to take back the estate for good."

Tatiana's expression was suspicious. "How do you know about this?"

"From Baroness Channel," said Elliot. She spread her arms. "What inducement would I have to lie? Like you said, it's not my estate."

"What kind of crimes?" Tatiana asked. "If it's like before, he won't get any punishment from the tribunal."

Elliot wasn't so sure of that. Baroness Channel was on the tribunal, his activities had taken place in her city, and she had a strong incentive to come away with a decision that

376

would keep the Cloud Fleet happy. This might be one time that the corruption of the Luddites would work in the Posts' favor. And there was something more, too. Something none of the Luddites—except, perhaps, Benedict himself—had taken into consideration.

"He won't get any cooperation from the North Posts if he tries to take over here, either," said Elliot. "Whatever else he is, Benedict is no fool. He will know he'd be facing a full-scale revolt if he returns here. And he doesn't want the North estate enough to risk it."

Tatiana considered all this. "So it's mine?"

Elliot gave a curt nod. "If you want it."

"Of course I want it!" Tatiana stood and swept away. "It's our ancestral land."

Her sister's possessive tone made Elliot anxious. "It's a *farm*, Tatiana. First and foremost, it's a farm. And you, my dear sister, are not a farmer."

Tatiana whirled around, and her face was contorted into an angry mask by the shadowy light. "You can't have this, too, Elliot. I won't be left with nothing."

"And what will you do with it?" Elliot's voice remained calm. She prayed that her sister wouldn't make everyone miserable out of spite. "How will you manage a farm?"

"I'll get help. I'll hire . . ." Tatiana bit her lip. "It's none of your business."

"What if it was?"

Tatiana's eyes narrowed. "What do you mean?"

"What do you want, Tatiana?" Elliot asked. "Do you want to stay here, on this farm, for the rest of your life?

Do you want to milk cows and count hay bales and tend to the Reduced women in the birthing house? You'll have to, you know. You won't have me here to do it for you anymore. Or do you want to live in Channel City and ride horses and get new dresses and be beautiful?" Beautiful and useless, Elliot almost wanted to add, but it would hardly help her argument.

"I'm not giving you the estate," her sister scoffed.

"I don't want you to *give* it to me," said Elliot. She'd thought this through very carefully. "I want you to rent it to me. Just like we rented the Boatwright estate to the Fleet. Rent it to me, and go live in Channel City. Let me do with this place what I want. In return, I'll give you enough money to keep yourself and Father in high fashion down in Channel City. He'll still be Baron North, and you can be baroness, when your time comes."

"Father will never agree to that!"

"That's why I'm not talking to Father," Elliot replied. Her father was angry, vengeful, vindictive. He'd hurt his own workers just to show them he had power. He'd keep an estate he didn't want, an estate he couldn't manage, just to punish Elliot.

Tatiana's desires were different. Elliot was hoping that they could align.

Two days later, she got the answer she needed when Tatiana showed up on Elliot's front lawn driving a cart that contained the wrapped remains of Elliot Boatwright.

"Come, Elliot," she said solemnly. "It's time to put our grandfather out to sea."

ELLIOT WOULDN'T PRETEND IT was the memorial her grandfather deserved, and yet as she and Tatiana stood alone in the mist on the shore, watching the glowing pyre tugged out to sea by a rowboat filled with Reduced, she found she preferred it to any of the pomp that would have accompanied the Luddite-attended event a week earlier. Here, at least, she didn't have to worry about strangers staring at her, reading worlds of meaning into every fallen tear and questioning whether she was a worthy heiress to her grandfather's legacy.

When the rowers were far enough out, they unhooked the ropes connecting the floating pyre to the boat and pushed it away. Soon, it would be picked up by the current and swept out into the deep, returning her grandfather's body to the sea and the air and Boatwright ancestors of millennia past.

The sisters stood in silence, watching the fire recede into the mist-swept waters. The only sound was their breath and the waves and the soft dip and creak of the Reduced's oars as they rowed back to shore.

"Chancellor Boatwright," Tatiana said softly, almost to herself.

Elliot looked at her. Was she speaking of their grandfather?

"It suits you," she went on. "I can't say why. But it would not have suited me." She gave a halfhearted shrug. "Though I often doubt Baroness North will, either, for all the time I've spent imagining it. I find it difficult to picture it on any woman aside from Mother."

Elliot remained silent, unsure of how to respond to such an admission. The rowers neared the shore as the mist began to burn away.

"I am eager to go to Channel City," Tatiana said now. "I know it will be a vast change, but I suppose I should accustom myself to change all over these days. Even here in the North. The Posts grow more powerful everywhere. Do you suppose Captain Wentforth will wait to marry Olivia until he returns from his voyage?"

Elliot turned to Tatiana, but there was no malice in her sister's expression. "I—I don't know."

"I can't imagine Horatio will allow him to take her with him. Not when she's still recovering. Do you see her much?"

"Every day." Olivia never missed a music lesson.

Tatiana nodded. "I have not visited as often as I should. She seems so odd ever since her accident. So dull. She only wants to talk about music anymore." She sighed. "I guess it's just as well a Post will have her. She might have trouble finding a husband otherwise."

Elliot found it impossible to imagine Kai as a consolation prize, and she wondered if Tatiana would still devote so much attention to other people's marriages if she had any other understanding of power. To her, you were born a Luddite lord or you married one. But Elliot was a lord now, and she still considered it less of an achievement than coaxing seeds into fields of wheat that would feed a hundred families, than building ships from scratch or searching for new lands, or even a cure to the Reduction itself.

The Reduced finished securing the rowboat on the beach and they turned to trek back up the steep path that cut through the cliff. Elliot raised her eyes to the land above them, and saw a figure standing at the top, his superhuman eyes shadowed by the diffused, misty light, the ends of his blue velvet jacket blowing behind him in the wind.

Her steps faltered. Was Kai's hearing so unnaturally good that he'd been able to make out Tatiana's words, even from so far away? As she watched, he gave her a stiff bow, and when they reached the top of the path, it was Tatiana who spoke first.

"Captain Wentforth," she said, and there was only a trace of mockery in her tone. "Have you heard that my father and I are leaving the North estate?"

"I had not."

"We're leaving it in the hopefully capable hands of my sister," she said. "And we'll be living from now on down in Channel City."

He turned to Elliot. "Is this true?"

She nodded. "I'm to take over management of both estates, beginning at once." She expected him to look happy, but his face remained grave.

"Yes," said Tatiana. "*Both* estates. And we shall see if she's up to the task."

Kai was silent for a long moment, and then took a deep breath, smoothing his frown into something that almost, but not quite, resembled a smile. "I'm sure she is."

Forty-two

DEE GAVE BIRTH TO her baby on the first day of spring. Since her father and sister had packed up and left, Elliot had transformed one entire wing of the North house into chambers for pregnant women, new mothers, and babies—both Reduced and Post. News of her father's departure had spread quickly through the enclaves, and many of the old North Posts had returned to the estate, starting with Thom. Elliot was glad that he was there to witness the birth of his daughter. Felicia had attended the delivery, which was a relief to Elliot. Felicia was training some of the North healers to improve the quality of medical care on the estate, and had brought her students along to demonstrate some techniques.

"We're naming her Li," said Dee, cradling her newborn in the bed that had once been Tatiana's. "After you."

"And me," Felicia said with a laugh.

Elliot squeezed Dee's free hand. "Thank you. I don't know what I'd do without you."

"You'd better figure it out," Dee said. "It'll be a few months before I can go back to work."

Planting season had begun in earnest, and Elliot had bravely—or foolishly—decided to expand her experiment this year. Over half the wheat fields on both estates had been devoted to her special strain. If it performed as expected, it would cut down tremendously on the amount of work the laborers would be forced to do, and if it didn't, she still had planted enough conventional grain that they would be able to feed themselves this winter.

As she drove with Felicia back to the Boatwright house, Elliot stared out over the plowed fields of her vast home. This is what she'd wanted for four years—the North estate, happy and prosperous. The Boatwright estate, returned to its former glory. The laborers well taken care of, the Posts rewarded for their work with freedom and autonomy.

The only downside of having all these extra Posts on the estate was that she found herself with more free time than she'd ever had before. Indeed, if she wasn't cautious, she might find herself with as little to do as the laziest Luddite lord. Between the relatively low maintenance of her special strain of wheat and the dozens of workers who'd flooded back to the estate—most with more experience in farming, labor management, and animal husbandry than Elliot ever had—her duties had suddenly become remarkably light. The irony that if her father had treated his servants better, he might have enjoyed the same opulent lifestyle without renting out his estate was not lost on Elliot.

She wondered if it would ever become clear to the

baron. For Tatiana, she had somewhat higher hope.

Even her new projects for the Posts had become self-sustaining once they'd begun. The schoolroom she'd decided to set up for Post children was being handily managed by an adult daughter of Gill and Mags who had been making her living as a governess in a Luddite household down in the enclaves. Felicia had helped her find a trained healer from among her friends in Channel City who was now helping to bring the nurses on the estate up to speed. And Admiral Innovation had already alerted her to friends of his who'd be interested in renting the shipyard for the summer season. Elliot was happy to delegate these projects to people who had more experience than she did in these matters. She was glad she'd turned her lands into a place the Posts found safer than the enclaves, and where they had more autonomy and opportunity than most estates, but she was practically drowning in leisure.

It was dangerous. Somehow she'd weaned herself from rereading Kai's old letters, but now she found herself poring over her grandfather's old books—tales of daring explorers, of brilliant scientists, and, worst of all, lifelong loves. It was silly. It was pointless. But there it was.

She and Kai were friendly enough now. He spoke to her from time to time about her plans for the estate, about Dee's progress, and occasionally she saw him in the garden with Ro. But though Ro always waved her over, Elliot made sure to keep a polite distance. It was safer for her to wish him well, but stay away. Soon enough, he'd be gone from the estate. That would make it easier. She hoped.

They would be friends. That was good. It could even be world changing. She was the owner of a shipyard, and he built ships. That was enough friendship to survive on, and she had the added satisfaction of knowing that, in some small way, they were fulfilling the dreams they'd once spoken of in their letters. Kai would leave. He'd see the stars. And Elliot would remain, and work the farm, and silence any voice in her heart that screamed for more.

The lawn of the Boatwright house had been scarred into ruts by the tracks of the sun-carts, and Elliot maneuvered their ride over the bumps. Perhaps she'd get a sun-cart of her own, and maybe she'd pave a bit of this lawn to make a driveway for the machine. Once the Cloud Fleet left, she planned to move back into the Boatwright house, but for now she avoided it along with the shipyard and Kai.

"There you are!" Andromeda shouted, appearing at the door. She stomped down the porch steps, her face pink with anger. Elliot didn't think she'd ever seen a Fleet Post stomp. She didn't realize it was possible, given the enhancements. Kai appeared behind her, eyes wide. He waved his hands in warning at the two occupants in the cart.

"I know what you're doing, Malakai," Andromeda growled. She glared at Felicia. "You have to come inside right this minute and talk some sense into my brother."

"Why?" Felicia asked. She climbed out of the cart and shook out her skirts.

"Because he claims he's not coming with us. He says he wants to stay here. On the *estate*." Andromeda's voice dripped with derision. "I have not fought for us all these years for him to abandon us for some stupid Luddite." She turned to Elliot. "Hello, Chancellor. Just so you know, you aren't the stupid Luddite this time."

"Ann!" Felicia cried.

Andromeda rolled her eyes. "Please, can we just stop pretending now? Can we just drop all this scraping and pretense and all of it? Can we just get on the boat and leave? Donovan will change his mind once we're out to sea, I know it. Can't we just tie him up and throw him on board and not let him loose till we're out of sight of this godforsaken island once and for all?"

"Yes," said Elliot, nodding her head. "You can. You should. It's what I would do, if I were you."

All three Posts turned to her and blinked in astonishment.

She pointed at Kai. "It's what I told him to do four years ago. Run away. Get out. You can. You have no one who depends upon you for survival, and indeed, all our survival may depend upon you. So your God-given duty is actually to go."

And then Andromeda cracked the first real smile Elliot had ever seen from her. "Perhaps I should have *you* make this argument to my brother."

For his part, Kai had said nothing, but there was a strange look in his strange eyes.

"Very well," said Felicia. "Lead me to him. Maybe he makes a good point."

Andromeda groaned and the whole party headed inside, where they were greeted in the parlor by Horatio at the door, Olivia in the chaise longue, her legs covered in blankets, and Donovan in the chair beside her, tuning his fiddle. He looked up at his sister and frowned.

"Hello, everyone," Horatio offered awkwardly.

"Hello," said Felicia. "I am told I'm here—despite the fact that I got fewer than three hours of sleep last night after delivering a baby—to intervene in a family squabble?"

"It's more than a family squabble," Andromeda said. "He's endangering the mission if he stays behind."

Donovan's expression toward Andromeda was now one of pure hostility. "I can't believe you did that."

Andromeda crossed her arms over her chest. "Go ahead, Don. Tell her. Tell her what you told me."

Donovan shook his head in disappointment. "You're being cruel."

"No, you're being cruel. To all of us. This woman has given everything to you, and this is how you repay her?"

"Can we have this conversation somewhere else?" Donovan suggested.

Horatio cleared his throat and addressed Elliot and Kai. "Should we, er, leave them to this?"

Elliot was appalled. Why was Andromeda dragging them all into this? If Donovan planned to quit the Cloud Fleet, why bring Felicia to talk him out of it, rather than the admiral? She looked to Kai for clarification. But he was standing as close to the door as possible, and seemed to be searching for escape routes himself.

But then Felicia spoke. "No, Andromeda. Donovan is right. You're being cruel. This was an ambush, and frankly,

I'm surprised." She turned to Donovan, and her voice grew tight. "You may do as you like, son. I'm going to bed."

Olivia raised her good arm off the cushions. "Mrs. Innovation. Please. You have been so good to me. I owe you so much, and it would kill me to think I have hurt you . . ."

All at once, Elliot understood. *Some stupid Luddite.* All those weeks of daily music lessons. Donovan didn't want to go on their latest expedition. He wanted to stay on the estate. The Grove estate. *With Olivia.*

She looked to Kai again, to find he had retreated even more into the shadows of the foyer. She wondered how long he'd known that Olivia had transferred her affections to Donovan. Was that why he'd been refusing to attend her music lessons? She wondered if he was hurt, if he hated Olivia now, the way he'd hated Elliot for so long.

And of course it would hurt Felicia to discover that her daughter's great love had moved on. The Innovations both still mourned Sophia, and she knew they took pride in the fact that Donovan seemed to, too.

Felicia gave a deep sigh and addressed Donovan. "You are a young man. You loved my daughter. My daughter is dead. How foolish it would be of me to expect you to never love again. Above all else, I want you to have the happiness I couldn't give to Sophia."

Andromeda stamped her foot. "That's it? You're just going to let him go like that? Felicia, help me!"

Felicia shook her head sadly. "Andromeda, he is not indentured to me. He owes me nothing. You of all people should understand that." She turned to leave and

Andromeda rushed after her.

Kai put out his arm to block her path. "Let her go, Andromeda. Don't you think you hurt her enough? She didn't need to find out now. She didn't need to find out this way."

"I can't lose him!" the older girl sobbed, low enough that even Elliot, who was closest, could hardly hear her. "I can't leave him to *them*."

Kai gave her a pitying look. "They aren't all bad."

"You *would* say that, Malakai. You've loved one all your life." She shoved past him and out of the room. He shook his head, and then his eyes met Elliot's.

The world stopped spinning. She'd heard. He knew she'd heard. Every atom in the universe seemed to coalesce into a point in the space between them.

I don't want to talk about Olivia right now.

Somewhere, Horatio was calling to her, asking her something about apples. Or maybe aphids.

This is all a nightmare.

Elliot only had eyes for Kai. They could stand here forever, it seemed. Not moving, not blinking, not *breathing* if that's what it took to plant this moment into reality. She didn't care that Olivia and Donovan were holding tight to each other for comfort, that Andromeda had run off to cry, that Horatio was chattering about plants as if he could somehow bring the level of discourse in the room back to the mundane, that the sun was shining or the seeds were sprouting or that the ship lay in the harbor waiting for Kai to sail away on it.

There are things I need to make you understand.

Kai had never loved Olivia Grove. He'd loved Elliot—*he'd loved her*—all his life.

"And I'm worried," Horatio was saying, "that if they spread, we might lose as much as half the crop . . . Elliot?" He brought down a meaty hand in front of her eyes. "Did you hear me? Have you seen any on your seedlings this spring?"

The estates. Right. The estates, and the people she was still responsible for. The people she would always be responsible for, whether Kai loved her or not.

They stared at each other and then, at last, Kai closed his eyes and nodded his head, just once.

The estates would always win.

ON THE DAY OF the launch, Elliot stayed out in the fields all day. If she saw no one, then no one could talk her into attending. No one could force her to watch Kai sail away from her. Everyone else was going: Horatio, Olivia, and Donovan; all the North, Boatwright, and Grove Posts; and dozens more Posts who'd shown up in the last few days from Channel City with sun-carts and tents, prepared to camp out and celebrate the launch. Even her father and Tatiana were going, to keep up appearances. Dee had promised Elliot she'd take Ro to the launch. She'd called Elliot a fool, but hadn't argued.

Baroness Channel had come too, and had extended an invitation to Elliot to spend the summer at her estate in Channel City. Elliot was seriously considering accepting. She was bored stiff these days, and once the Cloud Fleet was gone, she'd be in dire need of the kind of distractions a vacation in a city—her first ever—might provide.

When the sun finally dipped close to the horizon, she figured she should go inside. If she could see the sky, she'd know the precise minute he left her lands. But if she went to the house, she risked running into Dee, who was still staying in the nursery with baby Li. She'd risk losing all her nerve. So instead she stopped by the North barn, under pretense that she should make sure the dairymaids were keeping to their schedule. It was no longer her responsibility—not strictly, but old habits died hard.

All old habits. As she passed over the threshold, she almost laughed. At last, she'd gotten her wish. If she wanted to, she'd never have to set foot in this barn again, and she'd be freed from the tyranny of that knothole. But, as always, she looked anyway, and stopped dead.

Tucked inside lay a tiny white paper glider.

Now

Dear Elliot,

I can wait in silence no longer, but I'm afraid I'm already too late.
I am trapped between agony and hope—believing I have no right
to speak, but knowing more how much I'd regret it if I did not. Tell
me I'm not wrong. Tell me that, this time, you will accept my offer.
Because I'm making it again. I want you with me, Elliot. It's all
I have ever wanted. I offer you everything I have—my world, my
ship, my self—perhaps they will be enough to replace what I know
you would be giving up if you came with me.

Come with me.

I know what you owe the estates. I know how many
depend on you, and I know I've no right to want you for my own.
Come with me, Elliot, and I promise I'll bring you home in time
for harvest. I'll be happy to shorten my mission if I know I'll
spend every day of it with you by my side.

I have loved no one but you for these four years. For all my
years. I have been cruel to you. I have been unfair to you. But I
have not been inconstant. I was so angry because I loved you
so much. I want to believe that you still feel something for me,
too, that I am mistaken in fearing you don't, the way everyone—

including you—was mistaken thinking that Olivia Grove ever meant anything to me. You can't imagine the relief I felt when I learned she'd come to care for Donovan—and I couldn't tell anyone. I didn't deserve to.

I was foolish, and I know now that I paid attention to her because it bothered you, but it was the wrong thing to do—I toyed with her, and when she was hurt, I felt responsible for her injuries, and then, later, responsible for being the person that she and everyone else seemed to think I was. I wore that responsibility like a badge, but it wasn't my true self.

I believe, though it may be false, that you feel the same. You have fought so hard for your land, for the people on it, that you have forgotten a time when you ever wanted to be anything but a Luddite lord. But I remember a girl who stood on the cliffs with me, who studied star charts and who dreamed of ships. Regardless of anything else, I want you to know that she still lives. Even if you never set foot off this estate again, you are the bravest girl I've ever known. If you ever trusted me, trust me in this.

But I hope for more. Come with me, Elliot. I have wanted to ask you for weeks, but I have waited, out of fear and doubt and the belief that it's nothing but my own selfishness that wants you with me. I wrestled with this, and chance after chance passed me by. I can't afford to lose this one.

Please accept. This time, please accept.

And please believe that no matter what, I am, ever,
Your
Kai

Forty-three

THE DARK SERENITY OF the barn had always soothed her, even when Elliot had been at her worst, but the effects of this letter were too much to bear. No lowing cows, no smell of hay, no soft strokes of Nero's tail across her ankles would give Elliot tranquillity as she scanned the words over and over. Kai's familiar pen strokes hadn't changed with age, and they formed words that wrapped around her heart like a vine and held tight.

There was no date on the letter. She had no idea if he'd written it four minutes ago or four days. All this time, she'd been waiting for word from him—and here it was. How long had he been waiting for an answer from her? He knew how often she went in the barn, he'd seen how she always looked for his letters. Had he assumed she'd been ignoring him?

But one thought soon crowded out all the others:

Yes.

They were about to launch. She had to get word to him that she accepted. She had to tell the Posts she was going much farther away than Channel City. She had to take her leave of Ro—*Ro*. If she hurried back to the house, she might still catch her and Dee.

Elliot ran from the barn to the North house. Ro was already waiting patiently by the door for her ride.

"El!" Ro cried happily when she saw Elliot. But then her face turned grim. "El . . . Kai . . ." She frowned and pushed away. "Go."

"Yes," said Elliot. "Kai's leaving. And this time, so are we. Pack your favorite seeds, Ro, and don't forget your scarf."

Ro looked at her in confusion.

"I said pack!" Elliot shouted and twirled around. "We're going on a picnic, just like we used to. But this one will last forever!"

Ro's eyes were wide, and she made the sign for *tomorrow*.

"Yes!" Elliot grabbed the girl's hands and spun her around in a circle. "For all of our tomorrows!"

Or at least until harvest, as Kai had promised.

It took minutes to pack Ro's meager belongings, and then she grabbed the girl's hand and half dragged her back to Elliot's room to pack a bag for herself.

Elliot was soaring higher than any paper glider had ever dared. Kai wanted her, and this time she was going to go.

At the door to the house, she saw Dee pulling up in the Boatwright estate's new sun-cart, a parting gift from Felicia.

"Elliot, have you changed your mind?"

Elliot shoved her hair behind her ears and beckoned to Ro. "Have I!"

Elliot lobbed her bag into the cart, then climbed in behind it. Ro did the same.

"What's that for?" Dee asked in suspicion.

Elliot only laughed. "You need to stop by the Boatwright house." Dee didn't move. "Drive!"

Dee did not drive. "Elliot, have you gone mad? What's in the bag?"

The future. She giggled. "Drive, Dee, or I might burst."

"What's going on?" Dee asked again as soon as they were on the road. She drove slowly, carefully compared to the Posts, and the headlamps of the cart illuminated the rocky road before them.

"I'm leaving," Elliot sang. "Think you can manage without me?"

"To Channel City with the Baroness? Good. You deserve a bit of a break."

"No. I'm leaving on the ship. Tonight."

"What?" Dee blurted. "Elliot, you've just planted your wheat. And you promised Tatiana and your father that you'd take care of their estate."

"I *have* taken care of the estate," said Elliot. "Look at it!" She spread her arms wide. As far as the eye could see, shoots burst through the well-tilled soil. They'd have a record harvest. More Posts were coming to the estate every month, happy to work and eager to take part in either the farming or the shipbuilding ventures on the land. "You don't need me to run the estate, Dee. You know what to do. Be fair to the workers. Water the crops. We'll be back in time for the harvest."

"And if the boat sinks?"

"And if the sun explodes?" Elliot countered.

They arrived at the Boatwright house. It was dark and empty as everyone had already headed toward the docks to see the launch. Elliot rushed inside. She didn't have Kai's night vision, but it didn't take her long to find what she was looking for. She yanked the compass off the wall and sprinted back to the sun-cart.

"This is about Kai, isn't it?" Dee cried when she saw the compass. "Elliot, wait a moment. Let's think this through. Can you really leave?"

"Yes, I can," she replied. "This time I can. I've thought about it. Everything is running so smoothly now. If I stay, I'll die. I'd just watch the plants grow and hate myself. I was raised to work, not to be an idle Luddite lord. And that's what I've been, ever since all the Posts have come back. Think about it, Dee. How much time have I spent cuddling your baby? How much time have I spent sitting in the house reading books and playing with Ro's flower pots? Some of the Luddites go to resorts in the south and spend all summer swimming around in thermal pools. You yourself said I should visit the city. We're not needed. *I'm* not needed. The shipyard has been rented for the season, and Donovan told me he'd help oversee it, so I'm not needed there. And Tatiana won't care what's happening on the North farm as long as she and Father get their money. I'm going to do this. I have to, Dee. I have to take this chance."

The older woman furrowed her brow but didn't disagree. "And Kai, he knows?"

"He asked."

But Dee still looked skeptical. "Elliot, I know how you feel about him, but don't be hasty. It's not a pleasure cruise they're on. They're all going to be working hard. You're a farmer," Dee said. "What will you do on a Fleet ship?"

"Anything I want to!" Elliot threw her arms wide, feeling the wind slapping against her skin as they drove toward the beach. For once, she believed it. She could smell the sea in the air, but more than that, she could smell the scent of the grass as it awoke from its winter slumber. She could hear the sound of crickets as they sang to the emerging stars. It was springtime on the North Island. It was springtime for the world.

Ro squealed with delight and copied her.

"I'm not a farmer, Dee," Elliot went on. "I tried to be, for the estate, but you're a much better farmer than me. I made the wheat, but you're the one growing it."

Dee was silent for a moment, considering this. "Well, that's true."

"And Donovan Phoenix is a better shipbuilder than me. And Horatio Grove can help you get a better deal at the market. If you can name one thing I'd be better at doing than someone else here, I'd like to hear it."

"You give us hope, Elliot," she said. "Because of you, I believed that the North estate was a place worth saving. Because of what you've done here, I believe that the world will change, that my children can grow up to be whatever they want."

Elliot dropped her arms and looked at her friend. "Oh, Dee. . . ."

"But," the Post continued, and smiled. "I suppose that's a mission accomplished. So let's get you to that ship."

They started down the path to the bay. There, on the beach, sat the buildings of the shipyard, little more than shadows against the pale sand. The sun-lamps burned down on Fleet workers bustling around the docks, loading crates and sun-carts and golden-finned machines Elliot had no name for on board the ship. It was massive—bigger than any vessel Elliot had ever seen. It floated gently by the dock that jutted out into the sea, illuminated from prow to stern by sun-lamps. Giant sun-sails lay furled against its masts.

"Ooh," said Ro, but they all three were thinking it.

As they descended the slope toward the beach, Elliot could make out the name of the ship, painted on the side in glittering gold: *Argos.* She caught her breath. The sun-cart's tires crunched in the shells along the path to the shore, and the workers looked up as they passed. Finally, they drew up to the end of the docks. Elliot jumped out of her seat before Dee had the chance to fully stop and scanned the area. Where was he? Where was he?

Just then, he emerged from one of the entrance ramps, saw her, and froze. That's all it took—a single look—and he knew.

Elliot smiled at him.

He smiled at her.

And then they were running. Her shoes smacked hard

against the boards of the dock, which swayed a bit beneath her feet but didn't slow her down. And Kai's strides were long and sure, buoyed by his enhancements but more by something else entirely.

They met. They touched. And then she was in his arms, again and at last.

"You got my letter," he whispered in her ear.

She nodded. "I always have." She looked into his eyes. "This morning, I thought I was dead. I thought I was dead every morning since you went away."

"Are you sure?" he asked. "This time, with everything you're giving up?"

"I'm not giving up anything," Elliot said. "The estate will be fine. Horatio and Olivia and Donovan and Dee and Gill and all the rest will make sure of that. And we'll be back for harvest, like you said."

"Yes," Kai said, in a breath filled with relief and joy. "For you, I'll do anything."

Elliot leaned back, still holding tight to Kai's hands. She never wanted to let go. "The world has changed, Kai. We've changed it, these four years. Imagine what we might do in four more."

Ro had caught up to them by this point. She was dragging both of their bags. The rest of the Cloud Fleet had come to the deck of the ship to see what all the commotion was about. They looked down at Elliot, Kai, and Ro. Elliot shaded her face from the sun and waved at them.

"One more!" Kai called.

Elliot tugged on his arm. "Two. We're bringing Ro."

He broke into a huge grin. "Yes we are!" He threw the strap of her bag over his shoulder and led her up the ramp to one of the loading entrances.

Felicia met them there. "Greetings!" she called gaily, as Kai presented them. He stood behind Elliot and interlaced his right hand with hers. "It's Ro, right, dear?"

Ro nodded.

Felicia smiled. "Well, *Argos* is a Post-Reduction ship. We all have Post-Reduction names."

"Tomorrow," Elliot said, signing for Ro's benefit. "Her name is Tomorrow." It couldn't be anything else.

Ro beamed at her and went aboard.

Kai lifted their joined hands to his mouth and kissed Elliot's knuckles, as she'd done to him so long ago. Elliot burned so bright, she reckoned she could power the ship all on her own.

The interior of the *Argos* was dim, filled with unfamiliar machines and curious instruments. Elliot's heart raced, and her breath grew short, but then she felt Kai's hand, tight and secure around hers. This was *his* ship. It was extraordinary.

In the cabins, she found her bag and withdrew her grandfather's compass. As always, the wheel spun and spun, but for once, Elliot knew exactly where she was headed.

Kai chuckled when he saw it. "I suppose it's fitting," he said, "that we bring along something from the old world, as we sail off into the new."

"Tell me," Elliot said. "How are you going to find your way?"

He reached for her. "I'll show you."

They climbed on the deck again. The night had arisen around them, the stars winking into life like the ones in the roof of the cavern sanctuary, but a thousand times more brilliant. Kai held firm to her with one hand, and pointed up with the other. "I can see them, Elliot. I can see them all. In the night, in the day, through clouds and storms and the setting sun."

She stared at him in wonder. This was his miracle, and he was sharing it with her. "Thank you," she said, "for coming back for me."

"Elliot." He bent his head close to hers, and looked deep into her eyes. His gaze was no longer strange to her. He was just her Kai, the man he'd been born to become. "No matter where I went, I always knew my way back to you. *You* are my compass star."

And he was hers.

Acknowledgments

THEY NEED TO MAKE some kind of medal for editors who go above and beyond the call of duty. Kristin Rens, you are a goddess of patience. Were it not for a constancy rivaling Elliot North's and your passionate belief in this story, I would have gone mad four letter-rearrangements ago. Thanks also to Sara Sargent, who possesses a name worthy of a captain of the Cloud Fleet. I will always cherish your declaration about what you'd do if Kai and Elliot didn't work it out. I am also grateful to the entire team at Balzer + Bray: Alessandra Balzer, Donna Bray, Emilie Polster, Caroline Sun, Amy Ryan, Joel Tippie, Jon Howard, and Margery Tippie.

I am in debt to my agent, Deidre Knight, for convincing me that I could write this book and helping me dig for the perfect title. Special thanks go to first readers Justine Larbalestier (who called from the other side of the world), Jacki Smith, and Mari Mancusi; Erica Ridley for her brilliant brainstorming advice and Lavinia Kent for her historical romance know-how. And to Carrie Ryan, who offered countless hours of encouragement, brainstorming, critique, admonishment, comfort, and last will and testament wording assistance . . . what do you want? A kidney? A crate of champagne? My firstborn? (Just kidding about that last one—don't look so scared!)

And to my husband, who got all excited at the thought of me finally writing sci-fi (and less so when I clarified that it would be *Jane Austen* sci-fi), I hope I haven't scandalized you with the absence of tech. (I'll make it up to you next time.) I will never forget our brainstorming session of "but what *caused* the apocalypse?"

I'm so lucky to have real-world friends who'll listen to me blather on about the imaginary ones in my books: Elizabeth, Glenn, Chris, Megan, Adam, Maria, Ernie, Eva, Dana, and Shannon; and a family kind enough not to laugh when I explained my premise (Luke, Brian, Ten) and willing to watch *Persuasion* on TV with me. (Mom and Dad—I promise, guys, good parents next time!) Thanks to Rio for being the best brainstorming-hike partner a girl could ask for, and to Eleanor for so often coming along for the ride. (I'm sorry for accidentally calling you Elliot those times.)

Thanks also to my readers who have been so excited about this story during its long, long gestation. I hope it was worth the wait.

Most of all: thank you, Jane Austen. Thank you for making me fall off the couch at sixteen as I thrilled to Mr. Darcy's first, horrible proposal; for making me blush if Mr. Knightley so much as took Emma's hand; and for making me cry *every single time* I read Captain Wentworth's letter to

Anne. Thank you for creating these characters and these situations, for giving generations of mothers and daughters endless topics of conversation, for writing strong women and true love and happy endings. Thank you for giving me the bones of this story, and forgive me for the changes I've made to its DNA.

Forget everything you ever knew about unicorns . . .

Don't miss Diana Peterfreund's killer unicorn books

www.epicreads.com